Sailing by Orion's Star

The Constellation Trilogy, Volume 1

Katie Crabb

Published by Kathleen Crabb, 2022.

SAILING BY ORION'S STAR

First edition. April 26, 2022.

Copyright © 2022 Katie Crabb.

ISBN: 979-8-9855638-1-8

Written by Katie Crabb.

To B and Spencer, for everything.

Chapter 1

Kingston Harbor, Jamaica. December 1695.

Nicholas Jerome has not uttered a prayer since he was twelve years old. Not one.

He doesn't pray when he's in his hammock at night, inches away from the next sailor. He doesn't pray when storms transform the sea into a mythic monster frothing at the mouth, when thunder rattles the whole ship and his soul along with it, Davy Jones whispering promises of death in his ear.

Never.

God doesn't care about him.

No one cares about him.

He gazes up at Orion shining silver against the black sky, Poseidon's son bleeding starlight onto the shores of Kingston Harbor.

Tonight, he breaks his vow. Tonight, for the first time in a decade, he prays. Not to God, but to the stars themselves. They're more use to him than God, anyway.

Perhaps it's a wish more than a prayer.

Childish.

Foolish.

But it's all he has.

The stars keep his secrets.

"Tell me what to do," he whispers to nothing and no one but the silent sentinels above him. "*Please*."

He checks his pocket watch. The glass on the front is cracked down the middle, the old thing almost as useless as the father who gave it to him.

How long has it been since the convict laborer and the slave escaped him while he was on guard duty? How long since they knocked him to the deck and disappeared into the unforgiving night? An hour, at least. Surely. He lowers the pocket watch toward the puddle of moonlight at his feet, reading the time.

Not even. Three-quarters.

His eyes flick toward the East India Company ship *Agincourt*, which sits anchored in the harbor, freshly arrived from a short voyage. He suspects he won't be able to call the ship home for much longer. As much a home as it ever was, anyway.

A line of naval officers and East India Company sailors run past him in hot pursuit of the fugitives. He's been relegated to waiting outside the tavern for his commanding officer, who currently stands in conference with the head of the Kingston naval fleet. He wants to be out searching. Then he can fix his mistake. Maybe. Kingston is only so big—they must be somewhere. Unless they've made for the mountains or Spanish Town or the wilder interior?

No. No. It hasn't been long enough.

They might still find them.

The fury in his captain's voice floods out beneath the door, so Jerome looks out at the ocean for solace, the dark water brimming with infinite mystery, but the sea only reminds him of the convict who just slipped through his grasp.

Danso.

Ajani Danso, and that rage in his eyes. Rage and ... pity? A flash of gentleness buried beneath. One that Jerome didn't understand.

The name sears his memory, and he swears he'll never forget it, not until he makes this right. He remembers the gunshot the slave fired into the air, distracting him from striking Danso down. She could have aimed for him and left him dead on the deck.

And yet, she didn't.

He can't recall her name, but he'll never forget that gunshot. The memory of her mercy crawls up from his fingertips to his elbows, leaving gooseflesh behind.

He's alive because a convict and a slave decided to spare him.

Why?

He shakes his head as the conversation on the other side of the door grows louder and more urgent. The breeze catches his hair, pulling a black strand loose from the ribbon keeping it back at the base of his neck. He tucks the stray piece behind his ear, knowing he must look as presentable as possible. Even at this hour, sailors' laughter spills out from the open windows of the newly built taverns around him, drawing Jerome's attention away from the water. A deep, midnight darkness envelopes Kingston, an infant city replacing Port Royal as the major hub of trade in Jamaica after an earthquake devastated that notorious town. The skeletal body of a pirate hangs in a cage where the docks begin, a wooden sign attached to the front.

Pyrates Beware.

Port Royal was once infamous for its leniency toward pirates—Kingston is far less forgiving. A wanted flyer for Henry Avery lays near Jerome's feet, a muddy boot print smeared across the bottom.

Wanted For Pyracy. The Notorious Henry Avery.

The door of the tavern bangs open, and one of the *Agincourt's* officers gestures Jerome inside, pointedly avoiding his eyes. The admiral walks past without a word, the naval medals on his coat glimmering in the starlight. Jerome's hands are clammy; nerves and the thick, hot air coat his palms with a thin layer of sweat. His career might be over, and what will he do then? Sailing is what he knows. Sailing is what he loves. Sailing is all he has.

Without it, there's nothing.

But he is not a coward. He is *not* a coward. He takes a deep breath, and the sharp, salty air calms him a fraction. Then, he steps inside.

"God damn you, Jerome!" Captain Langley's shout echoes through the tavern, all the other officers falling silent.

Jerome walks toward his commanding officer. "Sir, I—"

Captain Langley's hand flies through the air, slapping Jerome hard in the face.

His cheek burns with the sting, but he mustn't reach up. It's weak. He's been hit before. Worse than hit. A caning when he was thirteen at the hands of a merchant captain that left scars on his back and legs, and certainly a slap or two after he first joined the East India Company at sixteen.

Probably others he's forgotten. He's never been flogged, but that's likely about to change.

The point is, he's used to it.

"Explain." A cold, hard mercilessness drips into Captain Langley's voice. "Now."

"You have my endless apologies, sir." Jerome folds his hands behind his back, standing absolutely straight as a sliver of irritation slips into his tone. "I am still to blame, but Carver and Adams were drunk and of no help, which is something I feel you should know. When Danso and the slave came up behind me, I had no assistance."

Captain Langley rolls his eyes. "None of your excuses. Do you recognize the gravity of this situation, Jerome? Not just a convict laborer, but a slave, cargo already bought and paid for. I give you one task and you can't even manage that, can you? That'll be ten lashes, whether we find them or not. Five more if we don't."

Jerome swallows, mortified. He is a good sailor and a hard worker, but he cannot say those things. He cannot argue because he must obey his captain and he must not interrupt. Things will only turn worse if he does.

"Whatever you think is right, sir."

The door comes open again, interrupting Captain Langley's next diatribe.

"Captain." The messenger moves a few steps back from the pair of them, likely not wanting the stink of Jerome's failure on him. "Lieutenant James from the naval fleet said he went 'round to the Delacroix house, and the captain is out at sea as we thought, but Mrs. Delacroix answered the door and said she hasn't seen Danso or the slave."

Captain Langley pauses, an idea gleaming in his eyes. "Delacroix," he whispers. "Now there's something."

Delacroix. Jerome knows the name, of course. Michel Delacroix is the most powerful captain in the East India fleet sent to Jamaica no more than three years previous. He's also the son-in-law of Jamaica's governor, which makes him nigh untouchable. Jerome's seen him near the harbor with his young son, though he doesn't know the boy's name. The two were playing with wooden swords at the time, and Jerome noticed Captain Delacroix's graceful movements, a fine swordsman even with just a toy.

"Yes, I'm going to request you be sent to Delacroix's crew." Captain Langley draws Jerome out of his reverie. "He likes rehabilitating failures, so I've heard, and if you make another error, you won't just have to answer to him. You'll have to answer to Governor Travers himself." He smirks, looking over at his first lieutenant in amusement before focusing back on Jerome. "I should have known better than to take on someone with a past I know very little about. Your mother was French, wasn't she? So you're only half English. No wonder you're insufferable. Delacroix is more unbearable than most Frenchmen, so maybe you should have been on the *Steorra* from the start."

"My parents weren't anyone important, sir," Jerome responds, panic fluttering in his chest. No one can suspect his past. Not a single piece of it, or he's ruined. Even more ruined than he is now. "I'm no one important."

"You're damn right you're no one." Captain Langley jabs his forefinger into Jerome's chest, his breath reeking of liquor. "And you never will be."

Jerome supposes he's right about that.

"*Dismissed,*" Captain Langley sneers. "Be on deck at dawn and we'll see to your punishment."

Jerome nods. "Yes, sir."

He steps outside, willing himself calm. He will not cry. He will not be afraid. He will not be angry. All of that is useless to him. He closes his eyes, and all he can see is Danso looking at him for a split second before disappearing into the night, a multitude of emotions passing across the convict's face in the space of a breath. Rage. Pity. Sorrow. Fear.

A spark of rebellion.

All he can hear is the slave's cry of anguish after he took her one remaining possession mere hours before she escaped: a small locket, just a glint of silver in the shadows of the hold.

Slaves are not permitted personal property.

The truth, no matter how unjust.

I will not give this to you. I'm not hurting anyone by having it.

He took it anyway, and she spit in his face.

Jerome glances up at Orion once more, his eyes caught on the belt. He read a battered copy of *The Odyssey* as a cabin boy on a merchant ship, the volume abandoned by one of the officers. Facing long days at sea, he read it

over and over again, passing the time with long-ago stories of a brave Greek
hero fighting monsters.

*And then I glimpsed Orion, the huge hunter/gripping his club, studded
with bronze, unbreakable/with wild beasts he had overpowered in life/on
lonely mountainsides, now brought to bay/on fields of asphodel.*

Stories are slippery things. Malleable. Changeable. Both immortal and
easily lost. Jerome marvels at the idea that an ancient epic poem somehow
made it onto paper for a young sailor boy to read centuries later. He had
liked reading about Odysseus, finding comfort in the story of a man trying
to reach his home. Truthfully, he's jealous, because he hasn't possessed a
true home for a very long time. Not since his father dragged them away
from his mother's family, leaving those early, warm memories behind. He
reaches into his pocket, pulling out a brown leather bracelet made for a
child. It's the only memento he carries of a childhood he keeps hidden from
the world.

A childhood rife with piracy.

Of desperate, poverty-stricken parents.

Of the father who escaped from jail, but never returned. Of the mother
he lost one day in a market, and never saw again.

She's the only person he's ever loved, his father included.

Maybe something happened to her.

Maybe she just left him.

Either way, he's alone.

It's better like that.

He contemplates the bracelet in the starlight before his eyes trail down
toward his olive skin, not taken for much more than a sailor's tan. His white
father's features lighten his complexion, but his curtain of black hair comes
straight from his mother. Some people glance at him twice. Some don't.
That's the case with most of his mother's people, moving through the world
growing used to second looks, all of it depending on whether you pass beneath notice or not.

He's never entirely safe.

His mother gave him the bracelet long ago as a reminder of his heritage,
but despite her pride in it, he's never found anything but judgment. He un-

folds it, hearing his father spit the same word etched on the inside of this long-ago birthday gift, love turned to ash in his mouth.

Romani.

Interlude I: Escaping the Hunter—A Tale of Orion, A Promise, and Things Revealed by the Stars

Earlier that day aboard the Agincourt, near Kingston, Jamaica. December 1695.

Ajani Danso wants to run away, but that's the trouble with being at sea—you can't. The water makes you a prisoner.

Sometimes he considers going over the side and swimming for shore. He considers risking his life to be free. That risk would be better than his current fate, leased as a convict laborer to one ship after the other for the past seven years, and three more years to go. A vague plan to escape once they make port forms in his mind as he ventures to the hold. Ordered to scrub it clean now that their cargo has been dropped, he suspects the sailors just wanted him out of the way. The only trouble is, the enslaved woman they picked up in Saint-Domingue is still down there. He won't have time to himself if she decides she wants to talk.

The sound of crying pours into the silence when he reaches the hold, and voices, too. One male. One female. The crying doesn't surprise him because crying is part of the background of his life, a permanent stain intertwined into the fabric of it all. He doesn't want to think about the woman he hears crying now, because if he thinks, then he has to *care,* and caring is a dangerous, exhausting thing.

"No!"

The sharp, desperate word pierces the air as Danso climbs down, finding Jerome, the young East India sailor in charge of himself and the other convict laborer aboard, standing in front of the slave. Or just him, now, Danso supposes—Hawkins died of scurvy a few weeks ago.

"Slaves are not permitted personal property," Jerome says, every word firm and crisp like he meant them to be so. Like he thinks before he says a single one.

"I will not give this to you." The woman keeps a tight hold of what appears to be a silver locket, a burst of fire in her eyes. "I'm not hurting anyone by having it."

"It is against protocol. Captain Langley sent me down here to take it, and I will obey his order. I'm sorry."

"No you aren't."

The woman steps back, and Jerome's hand darts out, closing firmly over her wrist. He tugs on the chain and snatches the locket away, the woman simultaneously spitting in his face. It's a rash choice, but to her credit, it does make Jerome let go. She's breathing hard, and even if there's the tiniest hint of fear in her eyes, she doesn't stand down. Danso can't say he doesn't admire that. He puts his mop and bucket down, securing the worn-out piece of cloth keeping his long locs tied back.

Jerome wipes his cheek with his sleeve, his eyes narrowing. "How *dare* you!"

The lad's barely more than twenty, Danso suspects, and the woman perhaps three years older. Despite his youth and the angular frame he's still filling out, Jerome's height and broad shoulders make him look intimidating.

Danso knows he'll only get in trouble if he says anything, and since he hasn't been noticed yet, he stays quiet. He studies the woman, and she does, he thinks, look a bit like the sister he hasn't seen since he was arrested. Umber-brown skin. Short curls. Small frame. Eyes that pop with life. His sister might be dead. Or she could be alive and stuck in some hell. He has no way of knowing.

"This locket holds a piece of my daughter's hair," the woman says. "A daughter that was taken from me. Surely you can understand that? Surely you had a mother yourself?"

"Sir." Danso comes further inside the hold, his heart reacting before his head says otherwise. The word *sir* sounds strange on his tongue when Jerome's a decade or more his junior. "They're looking for you on deck."

Jerome spins on his heel. "What?"

"They're looking for you on deck." Danso repeats the lie. He doesn't know why he's doing it, exactly, only that the sound of this woman's desperation made his chest twinge.

Jerome looks away from him and back at the woman, his fingers closing over the locket.

"*Please*," the woman begs him.

It doesn't do any good.

Jerome turns to go, slamming the hatch closed louder than necessary. The woman sits back down with her head in her hands, and when she looks up again, tears are rolling down her cheeks.

"That man is Romani, at least partly," she says. "You would think he might understand. There are Romani slaves, too."

"Romani?" Danso asks. "How do you know?"

"I heard him use a curse word under his breath when he was unloading and they brought me on. He didn't even seem to realize he said it, but I recognized it. There were two Romani slaves I knew on the sugar plantation, and they used the same word. I thought he might be different, but he's just as bad as the rest of them."

"He passes for being one of them, or at least can make the attempt." Danso lifts his mop, aiming to do the cleaning he came for. "It's better than being one of us."

The woman considers him. "They weren't looking for him on deck, were they?"

Danso shakes his head, and the woman grins.

"I'm Abeni. What's your name?"

"Danso," he replies gruffly, drawn toward the light in her eyes despite himself. "Ajani Danso. People usually call me Danso. They just brought you on a few days ago when we docked in Saint-Domingue. Where did you come from?"

He puts his mop inside the bucket of soapy water, the rivulets running toward the stacks of empty crates surrounding Abeni, as if she might just be the same as cargo they're transporting. To the people up above them, she is.

"My family comes from the Jamaican Maroons, so I was free until ...." She stops, swallowing back against an obvious wave of emotion. "I wasn't born into slavery. I ended up on this ship because I was sold to a family in Kingston to work in the house."

"Better than a sugar plantation." Danso remembers his father's stories of his enslaved boyhood, and he won't soon be forgetting them. He can't. Especially not here in the West Indies.

"Maybe." She studies him as she wipes her tears. "But further away from my daughter. Her father had me framed as a runaway slave when he decided he'd had enough of me, you see. Which was right after I birthed the child he didn't want. I was eighteen, and I've been on that plantation since. Eventually, Flora was sold off somewhere else, to a family called the Merciers. She was barely four. That was a little over a year ago."

"Well," Danso grumbles, bothered by how much this woman looks like his sister. "I'm sorry."

Why is she telling him this?

She runs a hand over her short black curls. "What about you? How did you end up here?"

"Why?"

"We're here, aren't we? Might as well talk. No one else on this ship except East India officers, and I don't think they want to talk to us."

"I'm a convict. I'm not sure you want to talk to me."

She laughs, and he senses that it was once a merry rather than a melancholy sound. Maybe in another life, it might be merry again. "I'm not worried."

He stops his mopping. "What if I'm a murderer?"

"They wouldn't have a murderer doing convict labor on a ship. You'd be dead. Besides, you don't look it. Just tell me."

"I stole food when I was twenty-five, about seven years ago. My mother was Carib. My father was an escaped slave from Senegambia. Both died before I was eighteen, so that left me in charge. My older sister has five children, so you can imagine how hard it is to feed that many mouths, even with their father and me working while she took care of them."

"I can." She speaks softly, and the kindness wounds him. "Where are you from?"

"Barbados," he answers, bewildered by this woman but unable to tear himself away. No one here *wants* to talk to him. No one but her.

"I kept that locket as a reminder that I'd do whatever it took to get back to my daughter," she informs him, a glint of defiance in her eyes. "And now that bastard took it."

Danso remembers leaving his small home in Saint Michael's Town, drawn back by the cry of his one-year-old nephew who slept nearby. The child—who his sister said looked like him—reached his hand out, grasping Danso's finger. At first it was all he could think about: that final moment when he quietly promised the child he wouldn't go hungry anymore. He's banished it since, unable to think upon it for long without summoning unwelcome, overpowering emotions. He hasn't cried since his first few nights in jail, and he doesn't plan on starting now.

Jahni Franklin, he said when his nephew was born. *That's a mouthful for a baby.*

He's going to do things, his sister said in reply that night, hope in her eyes despite their circumstances. *He's going to be smart.*

"Do you miss them?" Abeni asks, breaking through this rare reverie. "Your family?"

His stomach aches at the question. "It doesn't do me any good to miss them."

Abeni frowns. "It's human nature to miss people we love."

He looks at her again, words coming out of his mouth before he realizes what he's doing. "I miss them," he mutters.

Abeni's about to ask him something else when Jerome's voice cuts into their conversation from above, and Danso knows he has to go or there will be hell to pay.

"I'm ..." Danso stumbles. "I'm sorry he took your locket."

He grabs his mop and his bucket. Jerome is there the moment Danso comes on deck, seizing him by the sleeve.

"They were *not* calling me up from the deck," Jerome whispers harshly. "You were distracting me from the slave."

"Her name is—"

"I don't care what her name is," Jerome snaps, like hearing the name might hurt him. Like he can't *bear* to hear it.

"You *should*," Danso insists. He's more protective of Abeni than he would have predicted twenty minutes ago.

Jerome's eyes go round, making him look as young as he is. The sun strikes against the black hair swept entirely out of his face and tied back tightly. It's those eyes, Danso decides, gray and gleaming with something he recognizes as loneliness, even if Jerome might not, and he is definitely running from something. Perhaps from being Romani, if Abeni is right.

"You didn't call the captain when Abeni spit on you and wouldn't give you the locket." Danso keeps his voice low, confused at his own interest. "Why?"

Jerome doesn't answer, his eyes darting away.

"You were afraid he'd think you incompetent," Danso says, the pieces coming together as he speaks, and there's an unexpected twinge of sympathy in his chest.

Jerome stares ahead of him, his fists clenched and his jaw set. "You don't know me."

"You don't like the way he runs his ship," Danso presses. "You're frustrated he doesn't recognize your talent. I've been around ships my whole life. Worked at the docks before I was arrested. You're a good sailor. You don't seem to shirk your duties like some of the others. And you're damn good with that sword. I saw you sparring with one of the men."

"He is my captain, and I will obey him. Back to your work."

Jerome moves away, but Danso feels his gaze lingering as if suspecting the vague escape plans in his head. Something about it spurs him forward.

If he can escape when they reach Kingston, he swears he will.

It's late when they make port, nearing midnight. The sailing master's calculations were off, and the wind wasn't on their side, so they've arrived later than expected. Once they come into the harbor, Captain Langley leaves Jerome and three other men in charge of watching the ship until their remaining cargo—and Abeni—are unloaded in the morning.

Captain Langley turns to go, giving Jerome a final warning. "Captain Delacroix of the *Steorra* is meant to be in port in three days' time, and asked to come examine the ship on his father-in-law Governor Travers' behalf. I don't need him talking down to me again, so I don't want any trouble. Do you hear me? Keep an eye on the convict."

"Yes, sir," Jerome says, his Bristol accent laced with echoes of France.

Delacroix. Danso knows that name, powerful as it and *Travers* are for bringing East India to the West a few years ago. Adams and Carver pull out their hidden bottle of rum almost as soon as the captain departs, and though Jerome protests adamantly, they continue drinking anyhow.

"The captain left us to watch Danso and the slave," Jerome insists. "You shouldn't be drinking that much rum. You've already had your ration of it for the day."

"Oh, calm down, Jerome." Carver rolls his eyes. "This is why no one likes you, because you're always ruining the fun."

Jerome tries again, huffing when he's met with nothing but resistance, and he walks away, striding across the deck toward the helm. He gazes at the sea of stars above him, the tiniest hint of a smile on his face. Danso makes to sit down so he can look at the stars awhile himself, but Jerome catches sight of him first.

"What are you doing?" he asks, the ire in his voice dampened by his youth and awkward demeanor.

"Nothing."

"Go below to the cargo hold then. I want you and the slave woman in the same place for now. Sleep there."

"Yes, sir." Danso keeps his anger at bay. He doesn't want to make Jerome suspicious.

He makes his way down to the hold, passing Erickson, who looks slight and easy to knock out. With Adams and Carver quickly falling prey to inebriation, Jerome remains the most obvious threat.

Abeni glances up when he comes inside. "You're back. You don't usually sleep here."

"Jerome told me to." Danso's eyes catch on a loose piece of rope on one of the empty crates, broken from being tossed around by the rough waters over the past few days. "Most of the crew left for a tavern, probably for the chance of some decent food, and Captain Langley left Jerome and three others to watch the ship until we unload. Mostly to watch me, I expect."

She surveys him, squinting. "What are you planning?"

"Nothing."

"What are you *planning*?"

"*Nothing.*"

"You're going to try and escape," she whispers, cognizant of Erickson just outside.

"I—" Danso starts, irritated that Jerome and Abeni both seemed to guess his motives. He's not used to people paying attention to him since he was arrested, let alone reading his movements.

"You are. I'm coming with you."

"I ... no." Danso pushes down the impulse of kindness telling him to let her come with him. "Managing myself is enough. I can't be worried about someone else."

"Worried?" Abeni quirks an eyebrow.

Danso clears his throat. "You will be in my way."

"I could make it difficult for you," Abeni says after a pause. "I could shout, alert the guards."

"You wouldn't."

"I might."

She wouldn't, probably, but that's not the point. He can't take her. He can't risk it. Except, who is he if he leaves her behind?

He sighs, half regretting his choice already. "Fine. But you have to do as I say."

Abeni crosses her arms over her chest. "Fine. Have you ever thought I might be a help as opposed to a hindrance?"

"I am not used to having help since I was arrested," Danso says. "Or making friends, of any sort."

Abeni smirks. "Friends?"

"We'll see."

"What's your strategy then?"

"Two of the men are already drunk. Erickson is small, I can—"

"Kill him?"

"No!" Danso exclaims in a whisper. "Why is that the first thing on your mind?"

"I don't *want* to kill him," Abeni insists with a shrug. "I would rather just knock him out, but if we have to, we have to. I'm not letting him kill us, is what I'm saying."

"Remind me not to cross you."

"That leaves Jerome as the biggest obstacle," Abeni says. "Do you think you can overtake him?"

"I think so. Particularly if we have the element of surprise. He's one. We're two."

Abeni reaches for the locket she no longer possesses, one hand falling down limply at her side before clenching into a fist. "Let's go. There's no reason to wait."

"They'll be after us almost immediately," Danso warns. "You know that, I hope? This is risky."

"I know." Abeni looks back up at him. "But I have nothing left to lose. If I don't get out of here I'll never see my Flora again."

Danso meets her eyes, feeling a strange desire to protect her. Though, he's not entirely certain she *needs* protection.

"Did you see if they left the gangway down?" Abeni gets up, wiping her hands on her worn-out skirt.

Danso pauses. "I didn't. Jumping might be a shallow hit, even in this deep harbor."

"If you'll handle Jerome, I'll make sure the gangway is down."

"Thank you." Danso fights a smile, almost impressed.

Almost.

They come up out of the hold, and Erickson's there immediately. As soon as the other man's arm shoots out Danso takes hold, twisting it and knocking the sailor's head against the wood. Erickson falls to the floor, groaning before he passes out entirely, but it won't last long. Danso starts up the stairs, stopping when he notices Abeni isn't behind him.

"What are you doing?" he asks, watching as she picks up Erickson's pistol.

"Just trust me. Go."

Danso complies, and the two of them pause when they come above, taking in the situation on deck. The two other sailors, in a decision Danso finds lacking intelligence, are up in the crow's nest with their bottle of rum. Jerome alone remains, standing at the wheel halfway across the deck with his back to them.

"To the gangway," Danso says. "I'll handle him."

Abeni creeps across the deck without a sound, a feat only achievable by someone so slight. Danso hesitates, knowing his own step will not be as soft and vying to make it as quiet as possible. He's almost to the wheel when one of his feet lands on a particularly creaky board. Jerome turns around, but he can't take in the situation fast enough. Danso's fist connects with Jerome's stomach, and such is Danso's own strength that the other man almost hits the deck. There's a small clatter and then a glint of silver visible on the dark wood, something fallen from Jerome's pocket.

Abeni's locket.

"How dare you!" Jerome exclaims once he catches his breath, his hand going to his sword. "Stand down immediately."

Danso finds himself at the point of Jerome's cutlass in payment for his distracted glance at the locket, his chest tightening with grief and anger.

A gunshot explodes into the air.

Orion shines bright above Jerome, dripping silver onto his black hair. The world freezes around Danso as everything screeches to a halt, his entire existence spinning on the fragile edge of this moment.

The sound startles Jerome for just the split-second Danso needs. Danso swings his leg and knocks Jerome's feet out from under him, sending him crashing to the deck. He scrabbles for the locket with the tips of his fingers, meeting Jerome's eyes for one fleeting lifetime. He could kill this man right now, it would be easier if he did, but something stops him, something important that he cannot name, and he runs like hell instead. Abeni's waiting for him at the gangway, the tang of gunpowder sharp in the air as both of them sprint down the dock and dash into the darkness, running and running and running for a solid ten minutes before darting behind a building so they're out of sight.

"You fired the gun." Danso almost smiles, not quite daring.

"Just into the air." Abeni breathes hard, and she *does* smile. "Couldn't let him stab you."

Danso doesn't answer, opening his hand and revealing the locket.

Abeni's eyes widen, her grateful, glistening tears looking a little silver in the starlight. "My locket. Thank you. Thank you so much, Danso."

They run into the night, the sound of the ship's bell sounding the alarm off in the distance.

A beni's lungs burn, but they can't stop running.

She doesn't know Kingston well, but she does know Jamaica. She knows the mountains where she grew up in her tucked-away Maroon community. She knows Spanish Town, where she eventually went looking for more of the world. If only they can get there—surely she'll find people she knows if the community still exists, but if something happened ....

"Here." Danso interrupts her musings, his hand grasping her arm and pulling her into a hidden grove of palm trees forming a circle in the sand. The trees obscure them from view just as a line of sailors run by, shouting something Abeni can't make out.

"They called in the Navy?" she asks, trying to catch her breath. "Surely they have better things to do?"

Danso bites his nails, nearly making them bleed. "Not in the middle of the night, when a convict and a slave are missing."

Abeni shuts her eyes and thinks of Flora. It gives her a sense of certainty, stokes the fire in her belly, and gives direction to her determination. She has somewhere to go, now. They're going to get out of here. They *have* to get out of here. She has to get to her little girl. They start running again, going up the hill toward a big yellow house. They find refuge in a well-kept garden by the side door as yet another line of officers runs by.

"We're going to get out of here," she whispers in Danso's ear. "We will."

"You don't know that." He doesn't look back, his eyes too busy searching for East India and naval officers, fear slicing into his tone as if he's afraid to trust in anything good happening to him. "You—"

The rest of his response is cut off when the door opens, a woman's voice floating toward them.

"Is someone out there?"

A white woman who must be something like thirty or so steps out into the garden. Abeni studies her under the starlight. The woman had clearly been preparing for bed, already out of her gown and her petticoats and her stays. She's dressed in a nightshift and a green damask banyan, her long fair hair done in a loose plait. The bushes rustle when Danso tenses, no doubt preparing to run again, and the woman turns, narrowing her eyes in confusion.

This is it. They'll be caught for certain now when this woman lets out an inevitable scream. Only, the sound Abeni expects doesn't come, and the woman looks at them both before focusing on Abeni. She doesn't say anything at first, her hand curling over the doorknob. When she opens her mouth, Abeni expects a *get out* at best. She gets something rather the opposite.

"Come inside."

"So you can call the guards?" Danso scoffs. "I don't think so."

"Just come inside," the woman insists, furrowing her eyebrows. "They'll be back this way again. I can promise you that."

Apprehension floods Abeni's veins but she goes anyway, both because there's quite literally nowhere else *to* go, and because there's something in the woman's eyes, something Abeni's not sure she has a name for.

"Abeni—" Danso tries, but Abeni spins on her heel.

"What choice do we have? Come in or get caught. We already took the risk."

Danso relents, but it's clear he believes her too trusting. Maybe he thinks they should just keep running, but they need to think, or they'll just run into a pack of those sailors. The mysterious woman leads them inside, locking the door behind her and ushering them to a back parlor, drawing all the drapes shut.

"What are you doing?" Abeni asks, turning to the woman. "How can we trust you?"

"I heard that a convict and an enslaved woman escaped at the docks," the woman answers. "My maid came in with the news right after it happened."

"And that's reason enough?" Abeni presses. "For a woman like you?"

"Do I need a reason?"

"A woman like you?" Danso echoes. "Yes." He points up to the crest on the wall, emblazoned with the family name.

Delacroix.

And a second.

Travers.

"I know both of those names." Danso steps toward the woman, whose green eyes flit back and forth, but she still doesn't scream like Abeni expected. She still doesn't send them away. "Michel Delacroix is an East India captain, and you must be his wife. Travers is the royal governor of Jamaica, so you must be his daughter. My captain spoke disparagingly of your husband." He doesn't move forward again, but he does stand up straighter, looking even taller than before. The woman steps back, and there's a flare of irritation in the pit of Abeni's stomach.

"He's not going to hurt you," she snaps. Even if Danso is trying to make use of his height, she knows he won't hurt this woman, even if she barely knows him. He's just afraid this woman will betray them, and Abeni can't blame him. "He's a convict because he stole to feed his family. Not for something horrid."

"I'm sorry." The woman shakes her head, and she does seem sincere. "I've never done anything like this before. I'm figuring it out as I go along."

She meets Danso's eyes in apology. Abeni nods, meaning for her to continue.

"Did you mean Captain Langley?" the woman asks, directing her question to Danso.

Danso's expression softens a fraction. "I did."

"I thought so. He and my husband don't often agree," she says, admitting to Danso's speculations about her identity. "I'm not surprised you heard him talking."

"Where is your husband?" Danso asks.

"At sea. For another three days if the schedule holds, and accompanied by my young son. He certainly won't be bursting in tonight. My husband's valet is with him on the ship, and the only other people here are our cook, our housekeeper, my maid Molly, and our driver James, who sleeps in the rooms above the stables. They've all gone to bed. Besides that, they would keep my secrets. If I'm wrong, I'll deal with that later."

Abeni reaches for the locket, which is safe around her neck again. "It still doesn't answer the question of why."

The woman's eyes hold a dagger's glint in the dark. "I simply wanted to help. I understand if you don't trust me. You don't have any reason to. But I have never agreed with the slave trade or convict leasing, even if I largely have to keep it to myself. I'm Astra."

A tiny fragment of tension leaves Abeni's shoulders at the informal introduction, her heart still racing. "Abeni."

Danso looks down at the floor as if he can't quite parse what's going on, speaking more softly than earlier. "Ajani Danso."

Abeni's eyes travel toward the same spot where Danso saw the family crests on the wall, a portrait hanging front and center over a fireplace. There's a woman who is clearly Astra, a fair-haired man, and a little blond boy in the center, looking like he wants to smile but was told not to for the sake of the pose.

"I—" Astra starts, but a pounding knock at the door interrupts them.

Danso jumps, fear hitting Abeni like a lightning strike. Oh *no*. Astra hasn't had time to warn anyone, so what ....

"Stay here," Astra says, retrieving a candle from a table in the corner. "Get on the floor, just in case. I'll be back."

She goes after that, her nightdress fluttering behind her.

"She could very easily turn us in," Danso whispers as he gets down on the floor.

Abeni shakes her head. "She could. But I don't think she will."

The front door opens with a great, resounding creak in the quiet, followed by the sound of a man's voice.

"Mrs. Delacroix, I'm Lieutenant James of the Royal Navy. My apologies for disturbing you at such an hour, but I saw your candles still lit in the window, and I wanted to check and see if you'd laid eyes on the convict and the slave woman who escaped this evening from the *Agincourt*. And if you were all right."

"I haven't, Lieutenant James," Astra replies, and Abeni admires the steadiness of the lie. "Though I heard word of the escape from my maid. I will alert you if I see anything strange."

"Thank you, madam," the man says, clearly not suspecting her. "There's no chance anyone could have come in another door? I see you have a garden."

"That door remains locked at night when my husband is away." Astra remains cool under pressure, her tone even and without anxiety. "Is this why all the officers like yourself are about? I saw them out my window with East India sailors."

"It is. And if you see or hear anything, alert us as best you can. I wouldn't want the scoundrels harming you."

"I certainly will. Thank you."

"I appreciate it. Please give Captain Delacroix my regards when he arrives home, ma'am."

"I shall. Goodnight."

There's a murmured *goodnight* from the officer, and the door closes again. Astra pauses like she's waiting to make sure he's gone for good before she crosses the hall back toward the parlor.

"That should keep them away from here for a while," she says when she comes inside, gesturing at them to get up. "You can stay here tonight, and I'll try and get you passage out tomorrow. If you'd like to go you may, but I wouldn't recommend it."

"Passage for a convict and a slave?" Danso asks, but Abeni notes just how much his tone has changed now that Astra sent the sailor away.

Astra smirks, a strange thing on the face of such a woman. "Being the wife of a prominent captain gives one insight into the various ships that come in and out of Kingston. There's a merchant captain I know that smuggles slaves out when he can be convinced, and helps them get to a man called Ebele, who apparently finds slaves passage back to their homelands if he can, or otherwise finds them places to live. Or takes them onto his crew."

"That man who mutinied on a slaver and took it over himself?" Danso asks with a pinch of awe, and the same feeling spreads into Abeni's chest. She's heard stories about Ebele before. "He's just a legend, surely?"

Astra fiddles with a piece of her hair, twirling it around her finger. "He's quite real. Most pirates don't last very long, but he has. And Captain Barlow knows his whereabouts, somehow."

"The wife of an East India captain is telling us she'll help us seek out a pirate?" Danso asks, and Abeni can't blame him there. It's odd, to say the least.

Astra looks down at the floor, still toying with the end of her plait. "You showed up outside my door, and I'm taking it as a sign. I can't send you back where you came from."

Her meaning hangs heavy in the air, and Abeni knows the potential outcomes. Death, at worst. The lash, for certain. There are a few others she can think of.

Abeni can't help but ask the question most plaguing her one more time. "Why are you risking this?"

Astra's eyes catch on the brand on Abeni's arm. "I have always known material comfort. I have not been a convict or been enslaved or experienced that suffering. I do not know what that is like, and I never will." Her voice goes softer here, and Abeni hangs onto the words, to the story buried within them. "I have always hoped I might ease the cruelty of the world where I can, even if I lack the power of a man. My cage is gilded, that is certainly true. But it is still a cage."

It's an answer and it isn't, all at once, like opening a book that you can't turn past the first page.

Astra shows them to a room at the end of the upstairs hall. White curtains encircle two beds with light blue coverlets—soft to the touch—sitting atop the mattresses. A vase of hibiscus sits on a table between the beds, and Abeni recognizes the flowers from the garden where they hid earlier. Astra bids them goodnight, looking like a ghost in the moonlight.

Danso falls asleep almost immediately, as if he hasn't slept in years—he probably *hasn't* slept well in years. Abeni knows she hasn't. Even in sleep he stays tense, like he might spring up in defense of himself at a moment's notice. Abeni sinks into the mattress, thinking she's never been so comfortable, or at the same time felt so out of place in a room. She lays in bed for a half-hour. Exhaustion sinks into her bones, but still, she can't sleep. A creak in the floor alerts her to someone passing by in the hallway, and she climbs quietly out of bed, drawn toward the first room at the top of the stairs. Hopefully none of the servants catch her. She peers around the edge of the doorway, watching Astra strike a match and light a candle, the sound sharp in the quiet. The flame creates a solitary pool of orange in the dark, and Astra sits on the edge of the bed, holding a corner of the sunny yellow comforter in her hands. This must be her son's room—the little boy from the portrait downstairs who hid a smile. Abeni steps into the room on a rush of emotion she can't really name, and Astra jumps, closing what looks like a miniature with the hand that isn't holding the coverlet. Abeni swears she saw a tiny portrait of a woman before the gold enclosure snapped shut, but she isn't sure.

"I'm sorry," Abeni murmurs. "I didn't mean to disturb you."

"It's all right." Astra grasps the blanket tighter, as if it might summon her little boy to her here and now. "If I were you, I wouldn't be sleeping either."

"Was that your son? In the portrait downstairs?" Abeni asks.

Astra nods, and there's a new light in her eyes. "René. He's five and gone for two weeks on a very short voyage with his father, and I'll see him soon." Her fingers trail over the edge of the bedclothes. "But still, I miss him. Silly, I suppose."

Abeni shakes her head. "It's not silly." She stops, swallowing back a wave of grief. "When I still had Flora—that's my daughter—it felt like I missed her even when she was just sleeping. I've been separated from her. When that happened, I thought I might die. I've never cried so hard."

The confession rings in the room. A confession of loss. A confession of heartbreak and a *one day maybe* that might come to pass. Abeni had no idea this was the person she might confess it to.

Astra wipes her eyes, the green irises darker in the shadowy room. "I can't imagine being ripped from my child. I'm so sorry. How did this happen? You don't have to answer if you'd rather not."

That old ache comes to life in Abeni's stomach, but she wants to share the truth. "I don't mind. I grew up in a Maroon community here in Jamaica.

My grandparents were captured by slavers in Eko, near the Bight of Benin, and they escaped when England took Jamaica from Spain. I fell in love with a white man in town, eventually. Alistair. Things ended badly when Flora was about two months old. He framed me as an escaped slave—another woman with an infant had escaped not long before. I was separated from Flora when she was barely four, and someone came to the sugar plantation in Saint-Domingue where her father had sent us. They took her. That was a year ago."

Astra releases the coverlet, grasping Abeni's hand. Her skin is warm to the touch, even though Abeni thought it might be cold. "I hope you find your Flora again. I suspect your determination will lead you to her."

"Thank you so much for helping us."

Astra slides the miniature into the pocket of her banyan. "I'm glad I was able to. It wouldn't have been possible if my husband were home."

Abeni thinks of the downstairs portrait again, and the kind-faced but stern-looking man who must be Michel Delacroix. She shared something, so perhaps Astra will, too. "Do you like your husband?"

"He is kind to me. We are happy most of the time, even if we do not agree on everything. We love each other in our own way."

Another *almost* answer, but Abeni senses the *almost* is no small thing for Astra.

"I'm sorry for everything you're going through," Astra says with a softness that makes something twinge deep in Abeni's chest. "You and Danso both."

This time, Abeni covers Astra's hand. "Thank you again."

Astra lets her smile reach her eyes, looking alive in the dark as melancholy and hope rest together between them. "You're welcome. We should sleep. We'll have to be up early. Wait for me to come to you, in the morning."

Abeni bids Astra goodnight and goes back to her bed, returning to find Danso still asleep and curled up tight. She ghosts a hand over his shoulder before sliding under the sheets, and she's too tired to dream.

Maybe one day she won't be.

Astra wakes them before sunrise, pressing money into their hands with a whispered *you'll need this*, before leading them out of the house. Danso still can't believe any of this is happening, but he has to trust it, or he's dead for certain. He's not sure when he last did anything more than survive, but he knows he wants that, at the least.

Night hangs in the air as they go, the sun still sleeping below the horizon and dew clinging to the grass beneath their feet. A cool breeze wraps around them, a rare thing in Jamaica aside from the early mornings. They make most of their journey in silence, the streets empty at this time of day, though they duck behind buildings and trees a few times at the sight of a soldier. As they approach the docks, a ship called *Carina* appears through the dissipating fog, lending everything the strange, mysterious air of the beginning of a sailor's tale. Astra catches the eye of the young man near the gangway, who seems to understand what she wants the moment he lays eyes on Abeni and Danso, gesturing at them to board. They follow the sailor down the slippery steps, and he knocks at the door to the captain's cabin. A voice calls out his assent to enter, and the man Danso assumes is the Captain Barlow Astra mentioned earlier looks up, surprise flashing across his face at finding his man accompanied.

"Mrs. Delacroix. I did not expect to see ... a woman of your station on my humble ship."

"I'm seeking passage out for my friends," Astra says, one hand curling over her opposite elbow. "I was hoping you'd be the right choice. I'd heard you were an early riser and thought you might be here since you were in port."

Captain Barlow gazes at her and she gazes back, green eyes meeting brown with equal determination.

"Your husband isn't home?" Captain Barlow's eyes dart from Astra to Abeni to Danso then back again. He scratches at the sideburns running down into his beard, a few gray strands peeking out through the brown.

"No. He won't be home for another three days, at the earliest."

Captain Barlow surveys Danso and Abeni. Danso wants to look away. He's so used to looking away, but he stares this man straight in the eye, because he needs help, even if he hates admitting it.

Astra stares Barlow down. "Well?"

The captain raises his eyebrows. "I think your *friends* are the escaped slave and the convict that ran from the *Agincourt* when it made port last night. Word travels fast. Seemed like every navy man and East India officer in Kingston was out looking for them."

Astra blushes despite all her poise, and Danso's heart slams against his chest. If he can get out of here, maybe he can get back to Barbados and see his family. Maybe he can start over. Maybe .... He stops, not letting himself hope any further. It won't do him any good. But that hope burns against his skin, and maybe it came alive the moment he stepped inside that cargo hold to help Abeni. Maybe there's nothing he can do about it now.

"They just need passage out of Kingston," Astra presses. "I was told about a man named Ebele who helps enslaved people, and that you sometimes smuggle the ones you help escape to him."

Captain Barlow sighs. The tiniest hint of sunlight peeks out over the horizon, a touch of gold spilling in through the window of the cabin. Danso's heart pounds. If Barlow doesn't say yes, they'll be forced back out into Kingston harbor, and with the sun swiftly rising they'll surely be caught.

"Ebele is elusive," Barlow says, "but when I can, yes, I do."

"My husband knows all the ships that come in and out of Kingston," Astra answers, almost in challenge. "The East India Company knows there are rogue merchants who do what you do. They just can't put their finger on which one of you it is. Arthur Seymour told me about the rumors of Ebele. He also suspected the man funneling slaves to him was you, but he liked what you were doing, so he kept that secret from everyone but me, because he knew I would agree with it too. He never told my husband and swore he wouldn't, which is no small matter. This woman has been separated from her daughter because of the trade, and this man is hardly better off, convicted for the offense of stealing food for his family."

Captain Barlow studies them all again in turn, a tiny smile sliding onto his lips. "All right. But stay below, you two. They'll be looking for you, still. I have to go tend to some things on deck before we're able to set sail with the morning tide."

Captain Barlow gestures at his sailor to follow him, leaving the three of them alone. Sweet relief floods through Danso's veins, so much so that it makes his hands shake.

"Thank you." Abeni clasps Astra's hand, so easy with her emotions that Danso's jealous. "Thank you so much, Astra."

Astra clasps Abeni's hand in return, smiling back. Then, she looks at Danso. There's a spark of something in his chest. Something he can't name. Something like fate or magic or a wisp of the future he can't grasp onto, and a promise comes tumbling out of his mouth. The first promise he's made since he told his baby nephew he wouldn't go hungry. When those irons locked around his wrists in the dead of night just because he was starving, because *children* were starving, he swore he would never promise anything again.

"One day," Danso says in a hoarse voice, deep emotion strangling his words. He feels just a sliver of his old self again, and maybe someone new. "If you find yourself needing help, we will do whatever we can in return for what you've done for us today. I promise that now."

"Yes." Abeni nods, and she's crying a little. "Yes."

"You are kind despite everything." Astra's own voice trembles just enough to hear, and she grasps Danso's hand. "And thank you for that." She takes Abeni's hand too, whispering with feeling. "I hope you both find what you're looking for out there. And I think you might do well if you stayed together. Everyone needs a friend, don't they?"

Danso hesitantly touches Abeni's shoulder before drawing away, and Astra smiles at them one last time before going out the door and up the stairs, the scent of fresh flowers trailing behind her.

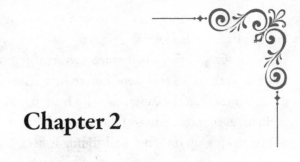

Chapter 2

The Caribbean Sea near Kingston, Jamaica. February 1696.

S tars explode across the heavens as the *Steorra* sails out from under the clouds, its flag whipping in the wind and the smell of saltwater sharp in the air.

Jerome's gaze lingers on the North Star, the ocean resting beneath the ship like dark blue glass. The stars rise and fall each night without fail, no matter the movement or chaos of mankind in the world beneath their glow. He breaks his contemplation of Polaris and moves to Orion next, the famed constellation vibrant in the winter sky. *The hunter.* Jerome thinks of the old legend about Orion walking on the waves. A benefit of being Poseidon's son, he supposes. The full moon glows above them, the additional light of the lanterns making their ship a bright orb in the dark. A stack of empty crates rests nearby, black lettering stamped across the top.

EIC.

The sound of laughter draws Jerome's attention. Captain Michel Delacroix stands near the helm with his first lieutenant and sailing master, Arthur Seymour, one hand resting on his friend's arm. The captain is tall, broad-shouldered, and has a pale, narrow face, his golden blonde hair swept back into a black ribbon with nary a strand out of place, his blue eyes filled with mirth as he listens to Lieutenant Seymour. The latter man stands about an inch shorter and a touch less pale, strands of sun-kissed auburn twisting their way through more tousled brown hair, his friendly eyes dark with flecks of amber.

Jerome's thoughts break off when something, or rather someone, runs into the backs of his knees.

"Oh, sorry, sir," a small voice says, and Jerome turns around, finding Captain Delacroix's son René before him. The boy's wavy blond curls—a shade lighter than the captain's—slip from the ribbon he's used to tie them back, his eyes apologetic and the same color blue as his father's. René looks down, picking up one foot and sliding it back and forth across the wood. He's tall for his age but with an unexpected waifish quality, like a stiff breeze might blow him away, and his skin is more alabaster than one might expect, given how much time he must spend in the sun.

"Be careful running across the deck," Jerome says, gruff. "It's slippery. Should you not be in bed?"

"We're going home tomorrow, so Papa is letting me stay up longer," the boy answers. René is allowed out on short voyages and knows the ship like it's his own home, even if he's only five. Soon to turn six, apparently. A May birthday.

Jerome surveys the child, noticing the two wooden toy swords in his hands. "I'm sure you'll enjoy that."

"How old are you?" René asks, gazing at Jerome with a strange intensity, as if he knows some kind of secret Jerome doesn't. As if he's deciding something.

"I ... one and twenty." Jerome's eyes flit upward as some of the men congregate on the other side of the main deck and gather around Prescott, the ship's boatswain, who's telling a tale. Or as sailors often call it, spinning a yarn.

"But you used to be assigned to another ship?"

The child's question draws his gaze back.

Jerome hesitates. He doesn't like talking about the transfer from the *Agincourt*, especially since there's been no sign of Danso or Abeni since that night. He reaches one hand toward his back, the wounds from his flogging only recently healed, though not quite all the way—fifteen lashes, while not the most severe, is no small matter.

"Two people who shouldn't have escaped on my watch unfortunately did so." Jerome doesn't elaborate. "So I was sent to your father's crew. He kindly took me on."

"It wasn't your fault." René offers a shy smile, and one corner of Jerome's mouth tugs upward. "Papa said so when he was telling me about you joining the crew. I don't think he likes your old captain. I'm sure you'll like it here better, anyway."

"Your father is excellent at his job. I have been here but a short time, and I already respect him a great deal."

The boy nods, his smile losing some of the shyness. Despite himself, Jerome finds he's charmed. Other people don't usually interest him, let alone children, and he suspects René's fascination with him won't last.

"I saw you looking at Orion." René glances up at the constellation, his eyes catching on first Rigel, then Betelgeuse, two of the brightest stars in the sky. "Papa was telling me one of the stars ... the ...." He frowns, looking annoyed at himself for not remembering. "It started with an S."

Jerome points upward toward the star in question. "Saiph?"

"Yes!" René exclaims. "Papa was telling me that one means *sword of the giant*. I liked that."

René continues peering at him, and Jerome's turning on his heel to walk away when the boy speaks again.

"Will you play swords with me, sir?" René asks in a barely audible but utterly earnest whisper.

Jerome turns back around, and René's still there, holding out the second wooden sword to him. He wants to say no. He wants to tell the child to go to bed. But he remembers sitting alone as a boy, playing with toys made from bits of wood that did nothing to quell his loneliness over the lack of any permanent playmate. Often not allowed to sail with his father, Jerome and his mother waited on one island or another, jumping from port to port. He always disliked his father, but how he feels about his mother is something else entirely. Her face appears in his head more clearly than it has in a long time, her curtain of black hair so like his own brushing against her smile. He shakes his head, focusing back on the boy in front of him.

He hesitates, but René looks so eager, his eyes bright with hope.

"All right."

René hands him the sword, and Jerome feels ridiculous at how small it is in his hand.

A moment later, René crosses it erratically with his own. "En garde, pirate! You will not defeat me."

"Why do I have to be the pirate?" Jerome asks, more petulant than he likes.

"Because I claimed being the navy captain first," René replies, matter-of-fact, though he said no such thing aloud. "It's the rules."

"Oh. Well, I didn't know. I'll try to remember."

René stops, studying him and growing as serious as a five-year-old might. "I'll tell you what. Since you're new, I'll be the pirate this time. I'm good at it, I think. But only if you agree to do it next time."

Next time?

Jerome bows in agreement, fighting another unexpected smile.

René's grin transforms his face, washing away the loneliness and sending cheer cascading throughout. Jerome taps the side of the boy's sword with his own and René taps back harder, mimicking a forward lunge he must have seen his father use. There's something like fate or maybe even a story in the clattering of the wooden swords, a wave splashing up against the ship as they play. They continue for a few minutes, moving across the deck until they're both standing in a puddle of moonlight near the main-mast. Captain Delacroix makes his way toward them then, and Jerome lowers the toy sword, feeling foolish. He doesn't want the captain thinking he's shirking his duties. At this, René finds his advantage.

"You're dead!" René pokes Jerome in the chest with the dull wooden point. "Felled by a pirate's sword!"

Jerome doesn't move, and René tilts his head expectantly. Captain Delacroix mimics his son as he reaches them, a half-smile on his face. The captain looks more casual than usual, missing his hat and with his cravat undone against the sticky night air. The gold on the front of his navy-blue coat shines, caught in the moonlight.

Jerome pauses before placing one hand over his heart. "A fatal wound!" He drops his sword to the deck, the hilt clacking against his boot.

René considers, then frowns. "That's not how you do it!" he says, serious even as his eyes brighten with glee. "You should fall next time. Or pretend you're bleeding."

Captain Delacroix musses René's hair so that it falls completely out of its ribbon. "Well, it seems you've been taught one must die dramatically."

"One must always die dramatically," Lieutenant Seymour adds as he approaches, pressing the captain's shoulder before squatting down on the deck so he's level with René.

Captain Delacroix's flawless reputation throughout the West Indies precedes him, no matter how much Captain Langley might have disliked him. He's the second son of a vastly wealthy French vicomte, so Jerome had heard, and married into an English family of the nobility who've long owned ships in the Company. His father-in-law is not just the governor of Jamaica, but a baron, as well. The men on the *Steorra* seem more content than most merchant sailors, and Jerome's noted that Captain Delacroix runs his ship more effectively than Captain Langley ever managed.

"Is that a letter from your son?" René asks, pointing at the papers in Lieutenant Seymour's hands. "In Saint-Domingue?"

"It is." Lieutenant Seymour touches the end of René's nose, drawing out a smile. "He and his mother are well."

"I hope I can meet Frantz one day, and Miss Chantal too," René says.

There's something sad in Lieutenant Seymour's eyes. Jerome isn't privy to the details of the sailing master's family situation other than the rumors he's heard about him fathering a son with a free African woman from Saint-Domingue.

"I'm certain you will, dear boy. I miss Frantz and Chantal both a great deal and can't wait for them to meet you." Lieutenant Seymour grins. "I also see you are becoming quite the swordsman."

"Oh." René blushes. "Thank you, Uncle Arthur."

"You'll be as talented as your father one day. Don't you think, Michel?" Lieutenant Seymour asks, smiling at his friend.

"Better than me I think." Captain Delacroix winks at his son. "Did you thank Jerome for playing with you, René?"

René turns back to Jerome, shy again. "Thank you, sir. You're pretty good with swords, you know."

"A bit of practice goes a long way." Jerome clears his throat, awkward now that Captain Delacroix has stumbled upon their childish game. At five and thirty the captain looks astonishingly young, a verve for life clear in his eyes.

"Jerome is a fine swordsman. I saw it for myself when he challenged those bandits at the docks in Kingston last month. They didn't stand a chance against him." Captain Delacroix clasps Jerome's shoulder with warmth, his French accent landing elegantly on the English words.

Jerome freezes, tensing at the touch.

God damn you, Jerome! He hears Captain Langley shout, the memory making his cheek sting.

He failed, that night. But it did bring him here.

"All right, Jerome?" Captain Delacroix asks, concern in his voice that Jerome can't quite parse.

Jerome shakes his head, mentally clearing the smoke of the past. "Yes, sir. Simply tired."

"Could you teach me about swords?" René asks in turn, the wooden sword still in hand as he stands up on his tiptoes, tugging at Jerome's coat.

"I thought you wanted me to do the very same." Captain Delacroix throws on a mock pained expression. "I see where your loyalties lie, son."

"I never said I didn't want you to." René smirks at his father, his posh English accent tinged with a touch of Paris, caught between his parents.

The captain laughs and Jerome does too, something about the captain and his son drawing it out of him.

"So, you should like two teachers then?" Captain Delacroix asks.

René nods, looking between the two of them with eagerness. There's a pause, and Jerome doesn't know what he's agreeing to, exactly, what he's promising, but he answers, anyway.

"With your permission, sir," he says, "it would be my pleasure."

Captain Delacroix smiles. "Permission granted."

René jumps into the air with an excited shout, seizing Lieutenant Seymour's hand and dashing off down the deck with him in tow to tell some of the other men. Lieutenant Seymour winks at Jerome, and Captain Delacroix watches them go, looking fond.

"René has taken to you," Captain Delacroix says.

"Oh." Jerome feels oddly pleased. "No. I'm sure that's easily done."

"René is quite shy actually." Captain Delacroix gazes up at the clear sky above them, his eyes lingering on the stars. "There are not many children his age in Kingston at all, let alone any who are appropriate playmates, and I know he is lonely. He's talkative with adults he knows well, but less so with new people. The way he behaved with you was different. I like seeing him so happy."

"He is a charming child," Jerome says, surprised at himself.

Across the deck, René's chattering to Prescott while Lieutenant Seymour stands by, placing his son's letter lovingly back in his pocket.

Captain Delacroix gestures Jerome over to stand by the rail and away from the rest of the present crew. "You are wondering about Arthur's family situation."

"Oh." Jerome repeats, tearing his eyes away from the lieutenant and following the captain. "It's not my place to ask, sir."

"It's all right. I know people gossip. So does Arthur, so I'm sure you've already heard something," Captain Delacroix says. "But he has a son on Saint-Domingue, as you heard. Frantz, and his mother Chantal Mensah, whose parents were from the Gold Coast. Arthur visits them as often as he can. Frantz is just six months younger than René. Exceedingly smart child."

There is not, Jerome notes, as much disapproval in the captain's tone as he expected, but a sort of wistfulness and worry. There are definitely pieces of the story Captain Delacroix isn't sharing, though Jerome can tell that Lieutenant Seymour loves the mother and the child, just from the ache in his voice when he said their names. Jerome doesn't really wonder at them being apart. Marrying someone of a different race isn't illegal in England even if it's taboo in the upper classes, but the West Indies are something else. Some colonies have no laws against it, but others do. On Antigua, people are fined—or flogged, depending on their race— for breaking those rules. Needless to say, Jerome can imagine the reaction of Lieutenant Seymour's family, even if he doesn't know them. He's heard the name Seymour before, and they're well-to-do in London. Ship owners, he thinks, merchants who have climbed their way up the social ladder.

"You've known the lieutenant a long time?" Jerome asks, thinking that a safer question than any further rumination on the lieutenant's family situation.

"Since we were boys." Captain Delacroix confirms what others on the crew told Jerome when he joined. "We ended up at the same boarding school in France since Arthur has family there on his mother's side. With my elder brother Rémy to inherit my father's title, and Arthur's brother the family business, I convinced him into this job with me. He thought it would be quite the adventure. My brother often tries to tempt me back to Paris because he curses the heat whenever he visits Jamaica. That, and my apparent love of the English."

"Lieutenant Seymour is a talented navigator. Hard to find."

"He is." Captain Delacroix glances over at Jerome, looking intrigued. "I am glad you were sent to us. Whatever the qualms of Captain Langley, I find you a talented sailor. Dedicated. Prescott has been most impressed with your work."

"Thank you, sir."

The captain pulls a pocket-watch from his coat, flicking it open and looking at the time. Jerome reads over the inscription on the back: *fair winds and following seas.*

"A gift from Arthur on the occasion of René's birth," Captain Delacroix tells him, checking on René's progress coming back to them from across the deck before quirking one eyebrow at Jerome. "I'm afraid René may force you to borrow him now and again if you've agreed to teach him about swordplay."

Jerome laughs, astonished at his own ease. "That's all right, sir."

"Astra will be pleased to hear it I think," Captain Delacroix says, referencing his wife, who Jerome's only seen from a far distance in Kingston. He studies Jerome. "How long have you been sailing? You were in the East Indies for a while, I imagine. Captain Langley used to be."

"Since I was twelve, sir," Jerome answers. "And yes, I grew up in this area after coming over from Bristol, but I was in the East for a while when I joined the Company. My father was a sailor himself, from England. My mother grew up in France."

"A longtime sailor then, and with some French in you too." Captain Delacroix nods in appreciation. "I first went out on my Uncle Victor's ship when I was eighteen. My father's youngest brother. Taught me a lot of what I know. Felt like home."

René runs back up to them, and Captain Delacroix catches the boy in his arms, a grin sliding across his face as he places his son on his hip, both of them laughing.

Jerome marvels at the sight. It feels important, no matter how commonplace it might be.

"Papa!" René points up to the sky toward Gemini, sitting comfortably in his father's grasp. "I can see those stars you were telling me about. Castor and ... and ..." he pauses, searching for the word.

"Pollux," Captain Delacroix finishes, smiling over at Jerome. "Do you remember the story?"

"Yes, I think so. The men the stars were named after helped stop a storm. They had fire?"

"They did indeed." Captain Delacroix holds René closer with one arm, indicating the two stars in question with his free hand. "They were on a voyage with the Greek hero Jason—a demigod, so the son of a god and a human— searching for a mystical golden fleece. Jerome, do you know the story, lad?"

Jerome nods, letting himself smile too. "I do. They were brothers. Flames appeared around their heads and abated the storm. Now sailors pray to them during bad weather."

"Wow." René's eyes widen in awe. He looks up at the two stars and then back at Jerome, that shy grin on his face once more. "You didn't tell me they were brothers, Papa."

"I guess I forgot to mention it, didn't I? But I've got to get you to bed, mon etoile," Captain Delacroix says. *My star*, Jerome translates in his head. "Goodnight, Jerome. Get some rest. I know you've kept late watch these past few evenings."

"Yes, sir," Jerome agrees.

René waves at him in farewell, resting his forehead against Captain Delacroix's neck.

Jerome raises his own hand, waving back.

Interlude II: The Ballad of Captain Ebele

St. Michael's Town, Barbados. January 1696.

———— ⬦ ————

"Ebele's ship is here." Captain Barlow sounds like he's smoked one too many cigars in his time. "Help us dock if you would, Danso? Then we can go speak to him. He meets with people about a mile from the harbor in a secluded spot where there are fewer prying eyes."

Danso lowers his voice. "He's a pirate. How does he dock here without notice?"

"Some pirates keep a store of flags on board." Barlow jabs his thumb at his own ensign, the red and white cross of St. George—the usual for English merchants. "For different situations. They also have ways of making themselves look like regular merchant ships." He pauses, straightening his shoulders. "Ebele and his ilk do good work. I used to be a buccaneer, you know. For England. But these pirates, pirates like Ebele, they don't help one country by going after another. They're doing something more than what we did. Something better. That's why I'm willing to help."

Danso nods, going to assist some of the men with securing the sails. Abeni emerges from below with some of the smaller boxes of textiles, helping unload the ship so they don't look suspicious. Captain Barlow is still a merchant, and upholding that reputation is even more important in light of his illegal activities. Danso doesn't blame him for looking so tired, the purple bags under his eyes more pronounced. Word spread of patrol ships out searching for the missing convict and slave, but they avoided questions, thankfully. To his credit, Captain Barlow kept them on, hiding them below until the danger passed.

Danso finishes his work, breathing in and looking out at the island where he grew up, the island where he was arrested, and the island where he said goodbye to his family. He has no idea if they're even here anymore.

"Captain Barlow?" he asks as the captain passes back by. "I understand it's a risk, but I grew up in St. Michael's Town, and I wanted to see if perhaps my family was still here."

"You can't stay here even if they are. If they keep looking for you this will be the first place they'll search."

"I know. But I really need to go and see."

Captain Barlow frowns, grumbly but compassionate. "Make it quick. Meet me when you're done, but if you get caught, I'm afraid it goes beyond the realm of my assistance."

Danso nods, noticing Abeni watching them from across the deck. She follows him when he makes toward the gangway, and he's frustrated that only part of him finds her company unwelcome.

"Where are you going?" she asks. "To look for your family?"

He keeps walking, his growing fondness for her jabbing at him. "Yes. But you should stay here. It's safer."

"You're just as much in danger as me if you're caught." She keeps up with his long stride, though she has to take several speedier steps to accomplish it because of his height. "Let me come. No, I *am* coming."

Danso looks over at her. Warmth glistens in her dark brown eyes, alight as they always are with a hope he can't help but be jealous of. Over the past few weeks he has begrudgingly come to enjoy her friendship, and now that he's no longer a convict he finds he also enjoys sailing far more than he realized. The sea speaks to a part of his soul he didn't even think existed anymore, as if slowly healing the wounds life left behind. Sailing is difficult work and hardly glamorous, but he feels at home anyway.

"I don't need you to come with me."

Abeni sighs, long-suffering. "I didn't say you needed me. You've made it clear you don't need anyone. You'll find you're wrong about that one day. But I thought you might like the company anyway."

Danso sighs too, more dramatically than necessary. "Fine."

"You like me more than you let on."

Abeni grins, and Danso tries and fails to avoid smiling back. He's so afraid of his bad luck splattering on anyone else. He's so afraid of getting close to anyone again because what if they leave? What if they die? What if ... so many things. Guilt seeps into his bones, because he almost left Abeni behind to her fate. If he had, he wouldn't be standing here right now, and he's grateful.

He just wishes he could let himself say so.

He thinks of that promise he made to Astra Delacroix, and God, what was he thinking? He'll never be able to help a woman like her.

"Lord," he mutters, allowing himself to keep the half-smile. "I won't like you if you keep teasing me."

They walk in silence across the harbor, Danso's footsteps tracing the path home from memory. Some of the small huts he remembers are no longer there, many of the familiar palm trees splintered and broken in half. His family lives near the docks, or they once did.

"Was there a hurricane here?" Abeni's eyes flit over the smashed trees and obviously missing homes.

"I don't know." Danso feels uneasy. He didn't get much news once he was leased out. No news, really. The feeling of unease intensifies when he goes to the spot where his family's home should be.

There's nothing here.

There are pieces of splintered wood, palm fronds, and evidence a house *once* stood here, but nothing else. There used to be other small houses here as well, the residents making up a portion of what was left of the Carib people across the West Indies, all intermarried with escaped slaves or white escapees of various persecutions in Europe. His sister's husband Henry was from a white family escaping religious oppression—his parents were Anabaptists, and came over to the West Indies a year before he was born. Joliette and Henry were not married according to English law, but they were in the eyes of their community. Everyone found a home in their tiny circle on the island, taking refuge in the acceptance and the semblance of safety with one another. It was similar to the Maroon community in the mountains of Jamaica that Abeni belonged to, only smaller and less isolated, with more varied members. The people in his community were the only freemen Danso knew of here—the rest of the people who looked like him worked in the sugar fields on the interior of the island. Barbados is the origin point of the harsh slave code in force throughout the English West Indies, and Danso remembers his father shivering with terrible memory every time they saw a slave with a brand, or lash marks, or their nose slit, all punishments for angering their wealthy masters.

When he looks around at his old home, there's nothing left.

He looks around for any signs of their humble farming area. The practice of farming yucca and yams—in a particular way that doesn't tire out the soil— is one of the only things passed from previous generations on the Carib side of his family, the rest of it destroyed as so many of his mother's ancestors were. Danso knows how to tend the soil on this island, and he missed it when he went searching for work at the docks repairing ships to bring in more money. A bad storm destroyed their little crop one year, and that was the year he had to steal. He knows what bad weather can do.

"It's ...." He stumbles over his words as a torrent of unwelcome emotion crashes over him.

Maybe they left. Maybe they've gone somewhere else. He searches around him, desperate for any sign of life, any answer at all, but the trees and the sky and the ocean beyond offer him nothing.

"Are you looking for the family that lived here?" a woman asks.

"Yes." Danso turns toward her, vaguely recognizing her as a neighbor from nearby. "My sister Joliette Danso and her husband Henry Franklin."

"I'm afraid they're gone. Have been for a little less than a year now. You used to live here too, didn't you? But I haven't seen you in years."

"Gone?" Danso asks, ignoring her question. "What do you mean? Where did they go?" His heart races in his chest, and he suspects just from her expression and the sick sense of foreboding that he already knows the answer.

"Two of the children died before the hurricane," she says, and Danso's stomach sinks lower and lower. "Then it came, and I'm afraid to say the rest of the family perished when the house caved in. The youngest boy survived."

"Jahni," Danso whispers, anger swooping through him, hot and irrationally directed at the woman in front of him. "What happened to him?"

"The family was in some debt," the woman replies, not without sympathy, "to one of the shop owners in the market. He took the boy as an indentured servant to pay it off, but the shop is gone now, like so much else around here. Some kind of ship captain bought the debt, a slaver I think, but I don't know who. Everyone else who lived here scattered, after that. I wish I knew more."

"You have to know who!" Danso shouts. "I need a name."

"Danso," Abeni says, keeping calm, though her voice shakes. "It's not this woman's fault. Let's go, all right?"

She places her hand on his arm, and despite the fury and grief still pulsing through him he responds, giving into her plea. They walk for a few minutes and Danso pulls his arm away, the tears in his eyes making good on their threat. They spill down his cheeks, shards of sobs making their way out of his mouth, and he cannot stop. He thinks of his sister's smile. Her husband's laughter. His nephew grasping his finger.

The only one to survive.

He sees the hunger in his family's faces as clearly as if someone painted a portrait. He remembers the ache it caused in the center of his chest, and how he grew determined to erase it so that they'd never be hungry again. He remembers Astra Delacroix's sad smile, the secrets in her eyes mixed with desperation to find them a way out. Why was she so kind? What drove her to it? Why is Abeni so eager to befriend him? Why did Captain Barlow agree to help them? He cannot make sense of these acts of kindness that seem like blazing lights in the darkness shrouding his life.

"Danso." Abeni grows even softer now, and he's not sure he can bear her sympathy.

He leans against a palm tree, unable to catch a deep breath. His entire body throbs. Grief bursts out of him. The grief he buried long ago. The grief he can't hold back anymore, and now, it's worse.

"I'm so sorry," she says, and even in his distress he hears the sincerity in her words. She refrains from touching him again and stands back, giving him space. "I'm so sorry, my friend."

My friend.

Danso breathes in, controlling his tears, but he can't look over at her. She is too kind and she saved his life and it *hurts*. He wants to know how she can be so compassionate after everything that has happened to her, because this is what life is, this loss, and he let himself hope when he sailed off on Barlow's ship. Why did he let himself hope or believe or *promise* anything?

"We can find Jahni," Abeni adds, and there's such fire and life in her voice. "Just like we can find my Flora."

"You have an idea where she might be. I have no idea where Jahni is, just a shred of nothing about a ship captain buying his debt. He could be anywhere. He could be dead."

"He's not."

"You don't know that."

"I don't," she says, and Danso realizes that she's crying too. "But I will hope until proven otherwise, just like I do with Flora. I can't do anything else. We can help each other if we try. Neither of us has anyone except these children we're looking for, and we've been put together by coincidence or some deity or fate or whatever you'd like to call it. And I'd rather not do this alone. Please don't make me do this alone."

He wipes his eyes again, turning from the tree and looking at her, unable to resist the glimmer of faith in her eyes. Despite the ache pounding through him, he smiles, and Abeni smiles back, and that *is* something, isn't it? He opens his mouth to respond when someone comes up behind them, both of them jumping in alarm.

"Pardon," the approaching man says. "I didn't mean to frighten you."

Danso tenses, studying the stranger. No uniform. No move to pull out a weapon. He has dark brown skin a shade or two deeper even than Danso's own, wearing a simple russet-colored coat and a tan sash with a single sword tucked into it, the leather sheath cracked from use. A tri-corner hat rests atop long locs tied back with a black ribbon.

"Are you the two who were sailing with Captain Barlow?" the man asks. "He told me you'd gone this way."

"Yes," Danso answers. "That's us."

"I'm Captain Ebele." The man reaches out his hand, shaking each of theirs. "I'm pleased to meet both of you."

Danso eyes him skeptically, but he's drawn in nevertheless, because this is a legend standing in front of him. Sailors talk about this man like he might be a ghost. "You have quite the mysterious reputation."

"I've found it's best that way." Ebele's smile stays genuine. "Captain Barlow told me about the two of you and your situations. I'd like to help."

"Why?" Danso asks. He's full of wonder, like he might be a child again listening to his father tell stories around a fire. He's scared to be that child. Scared to trust.

Ebele's story stuck with him from the moment he heard it. It made him believe in a man he'd never met, and on those dark nights aboard the *Agincourt*, sometimes, he would tell himself the tale of the slave who took over the slave ship. When did he first hear it? From a sailor's mouth, no doubt. Stories were sewn into the fabric of his life growing up. Stories about his father's people—the Mandinka in Senegambia. Old Carib legends that his mother passed down. So many of those stories are lost. The stories from before slavery and genocide took over. The stories that, when he was younger, he swore he would never forget. He held onto hope by his fingernails by remembering them, but that hope shattered when he was arrested.

"I was enslaved, once," Ebele says, "separated from my mother at an auction when I was small and kept in the trade until my fellows and I found a way to freedom." He doesn't elaborate, looking at Abeni with empathy in his eyes. "Somewhat like you and your daughter. Where is she?"

"Saint-Domingue," Abeni answers. "At least, she was. With people called the Merciers."

"Normally I take runaways where they'd like to go or find them passage there," Ebele tells them. "I have done the round to West Africa twice myself. But as it happens, I have a few positions open on my crew. If you're willing."

"To be pirates?" Danso questions.

"A far more democratic way of life than those who hunt us would lead you to believe." An unexpected roguish grin appears on Ebele's face, making him look younger than the graying hair at his temples implies. "You don't find merchant or naval captains voting for their leaders, let alone letting people like us sail as equals."

"You accept women on your crew?" Abeni puts a hand on her hip. "Don't most sailors call that bad luck?"

Ebele laughs, and the sound warms Danso, chasing away some of the terrible, pounding grief in his chest even as his broken heart threatens to leave a bruise behind. "Most sailors are too superstitious for their own good. I think differently."

Abeni nods, looking impressed. "My first priority is finding my daughter."

"I can help you. My crew is experienced in these matters. It's what we've dedicated ourselves to."

"What do you say, Danso?" Abeni asks.

Her eagerness is apparent, and Danso knows that he cares about her even if that terrifies him. He owes her this for helping get him off the *Agincourt*, for almost leaving her behind. He gazes back in the direction of where his family's house once stood, anguish flooding him with every beat of his heart. He looks forward again, swearing he will take his lost family with him as he goes. "All right. I'm already an escaped convict. I suppose it can't hurt to try my hand at being a pirate."

They start making their way back toward the harbor as night falls. Abeni walks ahead on the shoreline, lighter on her feet than Danso's seen since they met, the hem of her skirt skimming the water. He and Ebele walk together, the sunset bathing them in a brilliant orange-red glow. Ebele points out his ship in the distance. The *Misericorde*, it's called—a former sixth-rate naval frigate with twenty-two guns refitted for merchant service.

"You lost your family." Ebele's voice is as soft as the twilight around them, and Danso hears the loss in it. "I heard a bit of your conversation as I approached. I'm so sorry."

"All but one. My nephew. Most were killed in a hurricane, so I learned." Danso's surprised at the things spilling out of his mouth without restraint. "I was arrested for stealing food to feed them. I always worried they might be gone, but I hoped not."

"We can find your nephew. I have contacts. Ways to find people."

"Abeni thinks I can find him, too." Danso looks over at the older man, envying him his faith and wishing he could share the same. "You sound quite similar to one another."

"I cannot promise." Ebele meets his gaze, a breathtaking kindness in his face, but Danso senses the anger living beneath the surface somewhere, turned into something new for the purpose of helping others. "I wouldn't do you that disservice. But I will do everything in my power to help you find him."

"Why?" Danso asks, barely remaining steady. "Why do you want to help me? Abeni? There are so many people out there."

"Yes," Ebele says, and there's a thread of melancholy running through his words. "But the two of you are here right now in front of me. I cannot change the world all at once, but I can change things for you. I can set up a life in opposition to the way things are here in the West Indies, which is a rebellion in itself, you know. And then perhaps you might change things for someone else one day. Maybe the world will follow after."

Tears fill Danso's eyes again. They're quiet this time, different from the sobs that wracked him earlier and may well wrack him again when he's alone. Ebele doesn't embarrass him by speaking, clasping his shoulder instead and reminding Danso of the father who died when he was a child.

Danso looks up at the horizon, the sun sinking down as red bleeds into the space where the sky meets the water. He's devastated, and his heart might burst from the confusing mix of feelings welling up within him, grief foremost among them, but for the first time in years he also feels real hope, and maybe, just maybe, he'll let it grow.

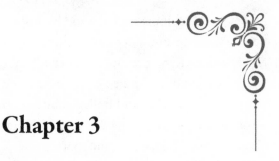

Chapter 3

Kingston, Jamaica. December 1696.

Almost a year to the day since he joined Captain Delacroix's crew, Jerome finds himself with a supper invitation. Their routes usually involve transporting goods—largely sugar as of late—from Jamaica and other islands in the West Indies up to the port cities of the American colonies, and sometimes down around New Spain depending on the state of affairs with Spain itself. Although their journeys are frequent, they are not as lengthy as those many sailors experience, so they're home often, and recently returned from a voyage to New York.

He never expected an invitation from the most prominent family in Jamaica, no matter his recent bouts of playing with the captain's son. A captain has never respected him like this before, let alone invited him into his inner circle when he is, at present, only a boatswain's mate.

Sir, Jerome said upon hearing the request. *I am honored you would invite me to your table.*

I would have done it before now if there'd been the time, Captain Delacroix answered. *The society in Kingston leaves something to be desired since it's still settling. Arthur will be there, and my father-in-law, who I don't believe you've met. And my wife as well, who looks forward to making your acquaintance.*

Jerome didn't dare argue, didn't dare say *are you certain, sir,* so he stood in front of his wardrobe for a quarter of an hour, deciding if there was anything appropriate for him to wear. He settled on a pair of his best navy-blue breeches with the matching coat and waistcoat, looking longingly at his beloved East India uniform and his boots laid out near the bed. Perhaps he might invest in a finer suit if there are more invitations in the future. Maybe some brighter color or a touch of embroidery, loathe as he is to draw attention to himself. There's no time for more thought on the matter, so he puts on his stockings and pulls his buckle shoes out from under the bed, thinking they need a shine. He knots his cravat, laying his sketchpad atop his neatly made bedclothes and sparing a nearly done drawing of the *Steorra* a glance before he goes. He has spent time drawing the buildings and ships and the sky around him since he was a child, finding it soothes his anxious mind.

He sets out on the walk from the boarding house toward the Delacroix home, reaching his destination after about twenty minutes and waving to the carriage driver, James, who he's met a few times in passing. Kingston is still new and growing, so much of it taken up by sugar plantations and smaller buildings where sailors live while in port, that seeing a home like this up-close makes Jerome stop in his tracks. Built in the new Georgian style and finished with a pleasing shade of yellow paint, its grandeur stands out from the rest of this yet-untamed place haunted by the wild ghosts of old buccaneers. Taking a long look at the structure in front of him, it's clear to Jerome that this is no longer the Jamaica that called Henry Morgan lieutenant governor.

He's greeted at the door by Mrs. Hudson—the housekeeper—and René himself, pulled inside immediately by the latter, surprised at the strong tug of a child's hand. He barely has a chance to glance at the portrait visible through a crack in the door of what looks like a small parlor, spotting a sliver of René's almost smiling face. Captain Delacroix's Irish valet Peter waves at him, busy carrying up one of the captain's coats. Jerome takes hold of the gleaming mahogany rail as he starts up the stairs, René's fingers gripping his tightly.

"René," Jerome chastises. "I'm certain that I ought to introduce myself to your mother before you have me gallivanting about her house. This isn't proper."

"Papa went to find her just before you came in," René answers, unconcerned and still dragging Jerome along. "Besides, Grandfather hasn't arrived yet, so there's one less person to mind."

Jerome hardly has time to wonder about the pinch of anxiety he hears at the mention of Governor Travers, who lives in the nearby capital of Spanish Town—though he spends half his time in Kingston, apparently—before they arrive at the top of the stairs.

"Here!" René exclaims once they reach the chosen door, and he pushes it open with his foot. This must be the boy's bedchamber.

You will mark up the wood, Jerome wants to say, but suspects it will not do any good. René goes through, and Jerome follows. Sunlight floods in from the bay window on the other side of the room, a pile of books and an unfolded map resting on the seat. Two paintings of the ocean hang in gilt frames next to a four-poster bed with a sunny yellow coverlet.

Jerome quirks an eyebrow, resting one hand on the light blue wall. "Your love of the ocean is well represented, I see."

"Yes." René looks out the window, the sea peeking out from behind the buildings. "I want to be a captain when I'm grown up."

"You would take over your father's position?"

René grows serious. "Well, I would like to be a captain in the navy, but Grandfather says that's not appropriate, as I am to inherit his title, and his land in England. I'm not sure what that has to do with anything."

"Oh." Jerome folds his hands behind his back, clearing his throat.

"Papa says I can take over his position, one day," René adds, rambling in the way only children can. "He and Grandfather argue over it sometimes, because Grandfather owns ships but doesn't captain them, and he says I should do the same. I don't see why Papa could be a captain and I could not. Grandfather says I'll have to go back to England one day. I'm not sure I'd like that very much. My other grandfather was a vicomte in France, you know, and now my Uncle Remy is, since my grandfather died. He's been here once since we came, to visit, and he brought my Aunt Sophie, Papa's sister, too, and they always tell wonderful stories."

René furrows his brow and Jerome stays careful, not wishing to overstep in this new, fragile situation. He can make no missteps if he wishes to keep Captain Delacroix's esteem. "I'm certain everything will work out."

René studies Jerome in that particular way of his, the smile on his face bright and eager once more as he changes the subject. "Have you ever fought pirates?"

"Once." Old panic rises in Jerome's chest, but the boy can't know about his past or his parents. "On my other captain's ship, the *Agincourt*."

"Did you win?"

"We defeated them, yes."

Jerome wonders if perhaps he ought to amend some of his statements for the boy. He doesn't really know how to talk to children and finds he can only talk to them as he does adults. René doesn't seem to mind.

"What happened to them?"

"Oh." Jerome halts, unsure how to approach this. "Well. They were executed for their crimes. It is the punishment in most cases."

"Oh," René echoes, his face darkening. "I didn't know that."

"They break the law," Jerome explains. "And steal from innocent people."

"I heard about"—René pauses, searching for the name—"Henry Morgan? And Tortuga? That was a pirate island, wasn't it?"

"It was, until a few years ago," Jerome says. "Though it was a buccaneer island, to be specific. Some of them had the support of the English government to attack enemy ships. Privateers, if you've heard the word. Some ... did not. Those are more like the true pirates you're thinking of."

He does not tell the child that he once set foot there with his parents when he was no more than ten, his father a member of a buccaneer crew of the latter kind.

"Wow." A note of admiration rings in René's voice. "Papa's been talking about Henry Avery showing up in Nassau? I think. And that the governor there was ... well, I heard Papa say *he's a damned fool*, to my mother. But then Avery disappeared! Papa said they're looking for him and that some of his men are in jail."

There's another note of interest, and while Jerome suspects it is merely a child fascinated by stories, he cannot let it go. The men René's referring to were put on trial in London, and they're worse than on trial now. They're dead.

"Henry Avery *is* a pirate," Jerome says, sharper than he means. "He does not deserve your attention. He caused quite a bit of trouble for East India, you know. And Governor Trott in Nassau is not the most honorable man."

"And did you know that there are"—René searches for the word, not really registering the reprimand—"Maroo ... I can't remember how to say it."

"Maroons," Jerome finishes.

"Yes!" René nods with such enthusiasm that he nearly topples over. "In the Blue Mountains? Some of the sailors were telling me about them. They seemed to think they were scary, but I didn't know why. They said they were escaped slaves a long time ago, and I thought that sounded interesting."

Jerome quirks one eyebrow, surprised. "Aren't you well-informed then?"

They're interrupted by a firm knock on the door, turning to find the woman who must be Astra Delacroix filling the frame, a gentle smile on her lips as she looks at her son. She wears a gown of light green that matches her eyes, her pale blonde hair arranged in the sort of intricate up-do Jerome sees other society women wear. She looks rather like a doll, but there's an intelligent gleam in her eyes, mixed with what Jerome supposes he might call mischief.

"You must be Mr. Jerome," she says. "I'm Astra Delacroix. I'm pleased to finally make your acquaintance."

"Mrs. Delacroix." Jerome's cheeks warm as he strides back toward the door. "My apologies for not introducing myself first."

"Quite all right." She holds up a hand, looking fond. "I know my son sometimes does not give one a choice."

"Mama," René mumbles behind them.

"I have heard a great deal about you over the past handful of months," Astra continues, her tone polite but guarded. "All good things, I assure you. My husband is impressed with your work."

"Thank you, madam." Jerome bows. "I am pleased to meet you."

"And I you." She shares a genuine smile with him, and he suspects this is no small matter. "René has told me how you play with him sometimes when he is aboard Michel's ship. He even said that he wouldn't mind you tutoring him in swordsmanship when the time is right."

"*Mama*," René repeats, blowing a piece of hair out of his eyes.

"No need to be shy, my darling." Mrs. Delacroix warms when she speaks to her son. She cranes her neck, looking around Jerome and smiling at René, who goes over to give her a hug.

There's the sound of more footsteps coming down the hall, and Captain Delacroix appears, a wide smile on his face. "There all of you are. I should have known René would wish to show you his room, Jerome."

"Quite," Jerome responds, and much to his surprise René elbows him lightly in the side, smiling quickly before looking away. Despite himself, Jerome smiles back.

"Shall we head downstairs?" Captain Delacroix reaches for his wife's hand, pressing a kiss to it before letting go. "I believe I heard a knock on the door, and I'm famished."

"As you always are, Michel," Mrs. Delacroix answers.

She shares another inch of her smile with her husband. It is not, Jerome thinks, the smile of a woman desperately in love, though it does contain real affection. As the captain looks back at his wife, Jerome sees something rather different: a grown man looking like an enraptured schoolboy. Governor Travers was an acquaintance of Captain Delacroix's father, apparently, and arranged the match. Jerome doesn't know more.

"Let us go down," Mrs. Delacroix continues. "Pauline's made a roast that smells divine. Enough to please even my father, I'm sure."

René hangs back a moment. His parents go ahead of them, and he pulls on Jerome's hand once more.

"Did your parents love each other?" he asks, studying his mother and father as they go out the door.

Jerome clenches his free hand at his side. Images play in his mind. Hazy ones from when he was very small. His mother and father sitting side-by-side, their fingers intertwined. Voices come next. Their voices, cutting and desperate and screaming about money. One day his father was arrested for piracy, and there were rumors that he escaped from jail.

He never came back to them.

René keeps peering, so Jerome's forced to answer.

"I believe so."

"My parents laugh together a lot," René offers with the unchecked honesty of a child. "But I remember them doing it more when I was smaller. My grandfather never seems to laugh."

As if on cue, Mrs. Delacroix's genuine laughter comes floating up from the direction of the staircase, followed by Captain Delacroix's deeper chuckle.

"René!" Mrs. Delacroix calls out, the amusement and love in her voice restoring the light in René's eyes.

"Come on!" He gestures Jerome forward. "You don't want to miss Pauline's cooking!"

Jerome pauses, affection burgeoning in his heart, along with a shot of fear. He cannot care for this little boy, not in a way that matters, and yet he already does. He is fond of Captain Delacroix, too. He is comfortable on the *Steorra*, and he cannot allow himself that, can he? No.

René tugs on his hand again, pulling him down the stairs, Captain and Mrs. Delacroix just ahead of them. A snippet of conversation floats up from the entrance hall, along with the sound of Lieutenant Seymour talking to the man who must be Governor Travers.

"I don't believe we have any issues with our crew, sir," Lieutenant Seymour's saying. "I'm certain Michel would not object to you taking a walk about the ship and meeting more of them. But I would be pleased to vouch for every man."

"Yes, well," Governor Travers replies, giving a sharp sniff, "don't be lenient on them. Some sailors develop bad discipline if you're too soft. Surely you know that, with your family being ship owners themselves." The governor pauses, and there's marked distaste when he speaks again. "But then, I suppose your older brother took on most of the responsibility, so perhaps you don't know how to keep a crew in line." There's another pause, and Mrs. Delacroix stops abruptly on the stairs, her posture tensing. Captain Delacroix stops beside her, looking perplexed even as his eyebrows knit together and he leans forward, hanging on to whatever the governor might say next.

"Michel and Astra told me that you are considering moving your son here when he's a little older?" Governor Travers continues. "For what purpose, might I ask?"

There's a thick, heavy silence before Lieutenant Seymour responds.

"For his education, my lord." Lieutenant Seymour bites out the address. "He's near to a genius. I can give him better access to tutors here in Kingston, and his mother is eager for him to learn about sailing from me, as well. I also think he and René might make fast friends."

Jerome twitches. He hadn't realized the tension between Governor Travers and Lieutenant Seymour existed to such a level, or even that it was a point of issue at all.

"Will his mother move here?" The disapproval drips off Governor Travers' words. Whether it's about Frantz's mother or the idea of him being friends with René he dislikes, Jerome isn't sure. Perhaps both.

René's whisper cuts into the quiet. "Why are we standing here?"

Jerome glances at Captain and Mrs. Delacroix, who seem to come out of their frozen state when their son speaks.

"No." Lieutenant Seymour sounds uncomfortable now, and grief-stricken. "Chantal will stay on Saint-Domingue, but we will take turns visiting if this comes to pass."

He doesn't add anything else. Jerome doesn't know the exact details, but some stipulation from Lieutenant Seymour's family prevents him from living with his son's mother, and marriage between them is disallowed by law in many English colonies, though not in the French colony of Saint-Domingue, where Chantal lives.

Captain Delacroix shakes his head, and the four of them continue their journey down the stairs.

"I've heard tell of a new abolition group in Saint-Domingue," Governor Travers says. "You've attended such a meeting, haven't you, Lieutenant? Michel keeps no slaves in this house, and his servants aren't even indentured. Can you imagine? No doubt my daughter's influence. She's always held misguided opinions. Apparently, her opinions and yours have influenced him. Neither of you may possess a choice about transporting slaves, soon enough. Plenty of Company ships already do, in the East Indies. The Company keeps slaves in those pepper factories in Benkulen, as well as on St. Helena."

Captain Delacroix frowns deeply as they reach the landing and walk into the entrance hall, Mrs. Delacroix sighing in what sounds like irritation.

If Jerome had possessed any questions on how Astra Delacroix felt about slavery, he doesn't now.

Dai, Jerome asked his mother once when they saw slave ships in Bristol harbor, a place well-known for its part in the trade. *Did those people do something bad to end up slaves?*

No, darling, his mother whispered back. *Some people think it's all right to own other people. It isn't.*

English only here, Nicholas, his father chided. *We can't have anyone suspecting. They're already looking at your mother twice.*

His father was always like that. Embarrassed that he married a Romani woman. Jerome passes for white—usually—where his mother never could, but even so, if people found out he was Romani, he would not be considered such. The skin tones of his mother's people vary, but their treatment does not. Jerome doesn't like the slave trade, but if he protests, his own secret might come spilling out.

Lieutenant Seymour and Governor Travers are standing a good two feet away from one another when Jerome finally catches sight of them, both of them frowning. Jerome's not sure he has seen Lieutenant Seymour narrow his eyes at anyone in such a way, jolly as he normally is.

The governor wears a powder-white wig, half-moon spectacles resting midway down his nose, and a suit in sea green with intricate gold brocade on the coat and waistcoat.

"Uncle Arthur!" René exclaims, dashing past his parents and letting go of Jerome's hand, interrupting whatever Lieutenant Seymour's response to the governor's last comment might have been. "I'm glad you're here. Is that another letter from your son?" he asks as the lieutenant slides the letter in his hand back into his coat pocket.

Lieutenant Seymour opens his mouth, thwarted when Governor Travers' stern voice slashes through the air.

"René. You came downstairs without even greeting me. Is that any way to treat your grandfather?" The governor's sharp tone wounds his grandson's enthusiasm, and René alters his course, going over to him instead. "And it is *Lieutenant Seymour.* Mind your manners."

"He has called me *uncle* since he could talk, sir. I'm his godfather," Lieutenant Seymour protests, but Governor Travers waves his hand, cutting him off.

Lieutenant Seymour shakes his head, and Captain Delacroix gives him a tight smile in apology. The lieutenant returns it, stepping forward and pressing a kiss to Mrs. Delacroix's hand in greeting. She smiles as well, and brightly, so they must be fond of each other.

"I'm sorry, Grandfather," René replies, his shoulders sagging immediately. He hugs the governor, a little glint of hope in his eyes as he pulls back.

"Good lad." A strange, obligatory smile stretches across Governor Travers' face. He reaches for René's waistcoat and jerks the boy forward, closing an undone button and smoothing his grandson's hair. "You are a sight, René. You know how I feel about that."

Governor Travers puts a hand on René's shoulder as he focuses on Jerome, and the boy's vibrancy sags under the weight. Jerome knows it was the governor's idea to bring a fleet of ships to the West Indies, given that the Company primarily operates in the East. He had to get a dispensation from Parliament and the King to do it, which gave the Company the ability to operate a small fleet in the West Indies and the North American colonies. It took quite a bit of work, Jerome heard—something about the charter had to be amended—but plenty are eager for the Company to take in the profits of the flourishing sugar trade. An influential member of East India's Court of Directors, there were rumors that Lord Travers wouldn't take the governorship unless Parliament agreed to his wishes, and Jamaica was in need of a change in leadership.

"You must be Nicholas Jerome." Governor Travers steps past Lieutenant Seymour, and Jerome's startled that he didn't wait for Captain Delacroix to do the introductions. "I have heard excellent things about you from Michel." He nods at his son-in-law. "I'll be taking a walk about the *Steorra* before you head out for your next voyage."

Jerome bows in greeting. "An honor to meet you, Governor Travers. It is a pleasure to work under your son-in-law, sir. I am indebted to his good word of me."

"*Sometimes* Michel has excellent instincts about people." Governor Travers stops for just a moment too long, and Jerome doesn't dare glance over at Lieutenant Seymour. "You are quite young and doing so well after that unfortunate incident on your previous ship. The convict who escaped with the slave woman was never found, was he? Someone must have hidden them, I assume, or they couldn't have gotten away. Wretched scoundrels."

Embarrassment prickles in Jerome's chest, and he notices Mrs. Delacroix rolling her eyes at the word *scoundrels*, or perhaps at the situation entirely. She is a strange one, and Jerome thinks he doesn't want to know what it might be like to cross her.

"No, your lordship." Jerome clears his throat, looking back at the governor. "Unfortunately, they were never found. To my great regret."

"Devious people, and whoever helped them too," Governor Travers replies. "But you have worked hard to overcome your mistake, and that is admirable."

Something about those words make Jerome think of his mother, and how she sang to him in soft, velvet whispers on nights when bad dreams haunted him, especially after his father disappeared. It's the kindest thing he remembers from his childhood, those songs his mother sang in the dialect of the Romani language used by the family she left behind. He shakes his head, pushing it away and cutting off any remembrance that might come next.

"Thank you, sir."

"You are an excellent addition to East India." Governor Travers glances at Lieutenant Seymour in his peripheral. "Someone who doesn't cause any trouble."

Lieutenant Seymour scowls outright, and Captain Delacroix cuts into the conversation, subverting any argument.

"Let's go into the dining room, shall we?" the captain says, clasping Lieutenant Seymour's shoulder briefly. "Everything smells wonderful."

Captain Delacroix hangs back as the others file into the dining room, taking Jerome's wrist to stop him for a moment. Jerome tenses. Has he done something wrong?

"Arthur and my father-in-law aren't terribly fond of one another," Captain Delacroix tells him in a low voice. "I apologize for any awkwardness. But I am pleased you accepted my invitation. I know René was, too." He pauses, a chuckle on his breath. "I can tell Astra likes you, and she doesn't like just anyone, you see."

"No need to apologize, sir." Jerome laughs a little too, struck once again by that foreign sensation of belonging. The longer he stays on the *Steorra*, the more he feels it, no matter how afraid that vulnerability makes him. "I was honored by the invitation, and Mrs. Delacroix is very charming." He tries and fails at fighting a smile. "René has been persistent about wanting to show me the house and his room, as well."

Captain Delacroix grins. "Yes, he has. Come, let's go join the others."

Jerome follows, even as fear and affection battle for dominance in his heart.

Caring about people is dangerous. Caring about people means attachment, but now he *is* getting attached, and as Captain Delacroix presses his shoulder with warmth, he fears he might not have a choice in the matter. He's lived in Kingston for a while now, but for the first time, that word resounds in his head, the one he wouldn't let himself think of before. It's a fragile wisp of a thing, and the last time he dared think it he was too young to really understand what it meant.

Home.

Interlude III: Honor Among Thieves (On Democracy and the Pirate Code)

The Caribbean Sea. May 1696.

"**D**anso." Abeni takes him by the shoulder, a rare note of fear in her tone. "You've only had a few months of training with that thing." She indicates the cutlass in Danso's hand. "And now you're going to jump right into a fight? Knowing about sailing isn't the same as knowing about swords."

"They need my help today," Danso insists. "And I know it's no small thing to be on the boarding party."

"Ajani." She tries his first name, looking for a different result. That was his father's name too, and when Danso hears it, he just hears his mother whispering it as his father lay dying. So he prefers his surname, all things considered. His father took it in honor of another man from Senegambia who helped him escape the plantation. "We said we were in this together."

"We are." He clears his throat, his heart racing as they grow closer to the *Columbus*, the slaver they've tracked for two weeks. They heard of the ship's whereabouts from a sympathetic customs officer in Nassau—a place becoming known for its lenience as far as piracy is concerned—and they've been tailing it for hours. "Don't tell me you wouldn't be running straight into battle with me with that dirk Robins has been teaching you with if Ebele would let you."

"Help me convince him to let me go over the side." Abeni's hand slides down, taking Danso's wrist. "Let me help."

"No," Danso says, firm. "You ... *we* haven't found your daughter yet, and you shouldn't risk it. You've helped me a great deal already. You got me out of Kingston. Just let me do this."

"Danso." Abeni puts a hand on her hip, looking irritated. "If this is about you thinking that I'm a woman and can't do this, then think again."

Danso shakes his head, and he almost *almost* smiles. "It's not. I learned not to underestimate you that first night. But Flora is waiting for you, and Ebele's right when he says you need some more training to learn how to defeat people bigger than you with speed. I know you can do it, Abeni, but please don't risk yourself right now. Ebele said this captain has been known to trade with small-time slave runners like the Merciers, so he might have information. I don't want you to miss this opportunity."

Abeni grins at him, a glimmer of faith in her eyes. Faith in him. He's not sure what to make of that.

"Don't you dare die out there." She grasps his hand, her touch warm, and it anchors him to the here and now, allowing him, just for a moment, to forget his anxiety. "I forbid it. Do you hear me?"

"I hear you," Danso says, more sincere and more earnest than he's heard himself sound in years. "I'll be back. Next time you can come with me. I know you'll be a master with that dirk before we know it."

"Is that a promise?"

Her words wound him. He's not sure he can make himself promise anything at all. He promised his family and his baby nephew, then ended up leaving them to death and debt and servitude. He promised Astra Delacroix something, and who knows if he can really follow through if she ends up needing him to? He's not sure how long he can keep Abeni from a battle. Not long, probably, and it wouldn't be fair to her fighting spirit to be chained down by his anxiety.

"I'm certain it will happen," he answers, evading any sort of vow. "Go back below now, please?"

She does as he asks, glancing back once more as the *Columbus* answers the *Misericorde's* warning shot with their own. The men hoist the black flag, the sight of it letting the other crew know they are no fellow merchant ship.

"Prepare to board!"

The order goes up from Captain Ebele himself, and Danso breathes in deep, closing his eyes. He's never seen battle before. No Spanish privateer, let alone pirates, ever tried taking the *Agincourt* while he sailed with them, though he heard stories of them encountering the latter a month before he was sent aboard. It was the only time he heard Captain Langley commend Jerome, saying something about his skill with a sword.

He looks up as the black flag takes its final place, a skeleton sewn into the fabric by careful sailors used to mending rips and tears. He supposes if he does this, there won't be any turning back, but then, where would he go, besides?

"Fire in the hole!"

The cannons explode on the port side, and the *Misericorde* is the first to fire a broadside, the swing guns set to repel boarders.

He follows the other men into the longboats so they can crawl up the side of the slaver, taking a grappling hook in hand and throwing it as he sees the other men do, the metal biting into the rail of the *Columbus*. He knows it's an honor to be chosen for the boarding party, especially with how new he is, so he swears he'll do his best to earn the trust the crew has given him. Pistol fire pops into the air, crackling sharply against the boom of the cannons. The clanging of cutlasses rings in his ears, somehow louder than all the rest. No one engages him, and he makes his way in the direction of the hold. He goes below, throwing the hatch open. Even without explicit direction, he knows their objective.

Find the slaves.

A stale stench hits him as soon as he climbs down, even if half the slaves are gone. Ten people sit chained before him—five men and five women in route to a plantation somewhere in the Leeward Islands. They look up at him, frightened and defiant all at once, because it's not unheard of for free black men desperate for work to sail on slavers. He doesn't have it within himself to contemplate the tragedy of that, right now. It's rarer in these parts away from the western coast of Africa, but he has seen a few.

"I'm not here to hurt you," Danso says, realizing now that he doesn't have anything to break the chains. He doesn't know how many of the slaves, if any at all, speak English. At least one relaxes, an older man who has like-

ly been enslaved for a while, or at least long enough to understand. Some
of the men on the crew speak various languages: Igbo, Akan—including
Twi—Yoruba, and Wolof, among others. He speaks some Fula, himself, as
well as the Kalinago language of his mother's people. Hopefully, some form
of communication or translation can be cobbled together. Ebele seems to
handle it well enough, and Abeni has helped, lately, with any Yoruba slaves
they pick up.

"Right behind you, Danso," says Coburn, the *Misericorde's* friendly
Scottish quartermaster. "We're here to help you all." He looks at Danso,
resting one gnarled hand atop his. "Go stand lookout right above, if you
would?"

Danso nods, climbing the slick, narrow stairs up onto the deck. It's
clear Ebele's men are winning the fight, but the crew of the *Columbus* hasn't
given up just yet. A man comes swinging at him right as he comes above,
Ebele's voice a memory whispered in Danso's ear.

Half the battle's in the speed of the draw.

Danso unsheathes his cutlass, swinging it around in a curve until it
strikes the sailor's with a loud clang, the sheer force of his blow knocking
the other man to the deck. His skills aren't refined yet, but this is a start.
The metal crashes together just as the cannon fire dies off, and the *Columbus* strikes her colors, signaling surrender.

"How many men were injured?" Ebele asks.

Robins bends over the ship's books as Ebele and Danso look
on, writing things down with ink splattered in his hair and a small cut still
bleeding on his freckled hand. He's a former convict like Danso, forced onto a shady merchant crew upon his release for lack of any other options. He
was chased off a few months later when the captain discovered him caught
up in a romance with another sailor, threatening to have both of them arrested and executed under the Buggery Act. Collins is Robins' partner, and
a damn good card player. Ebele took both of them on after encountering
them in port, and they've been aboard ever since. Robins was the first per-

son Danso spoke to at length once he joined Ebele's crew, their shared experiences making him easier to talk with.

"Just one in any serious manner. They surrendered quick. No surprise, since we outgunned them." Robins' Irish accent is thick, one hand fiddling with a ginger curl fallen loose from the worn-out ribbon at the base of his neck. "So, minimal injury payments. And no one dead. Their crew wasn't much to contend with. Mr. Coburn thinks we'll make the papers again. If they're willing to admit we exist, anyhow. Sailors will tell the story if they don't."

Ebele chuckles, holding the slaver captain's ship log, the name *Mercier* written on a page somewhere in the middle. It's another step on their path to finding Flora, who was no longer on Saint-Domingue when they went there. "Coburn likes to tell stories, though he's right in this instance. And how many people did we rescue in total?"

"Ten," Robins responds, "so we'll need to pay for their necessities until we can get them passage where they'd like to go. But the coin and the sugar we took to trade will be enough to do that and give all the men a small amount each. The bastards must have picked up the sugar when they dropped the rest of those poor souls before we could get to them, but we can do a bit better than break even this time. That contact we have on Nevis will buy from us, and we need to go to St. Kitts anyway, to look for the little miss."

"Thank you." Ebele clasps Robins' shoulder with a smile.

"If you keep letting me teach Abeni how to use a dirk, she may just insist on taking part in the next fight," Robins says, not hiding his grin. "Don't you think, Danso?"

"She absolutely will, if my conversation with her this morning is any indication." Danso raises one eyebrow. "She's getting quite good with it, thanks to you."

"And you with your cutlass," Robins points out. "For being new to swordsmanship, you have a lot to boast about. Graceful for such a strong man, too. I saw you knock that gent to the deck."

Ebele bids Robins farewell, then beckons Danso to follow. They go back above, observing the men clearing up after the battle, Toriano the boatswain going around with the ship's carpenter Laurent to examine the damage. Another sailor follows behind with a crutch beneath his arm, his prosthetic leg scraping against the deck. Danso was astonished to hear that pirates keep on their injured comrades, not only compensating them for the injury, but giving them less strenuous work and making sure they get equal shares of the haul. It's a thousand times more generous than any merchant or naval ship Danso has ever heard of.

"That slaver won't come after us?" Danso asks. He's uncomfortable watching other men work while he observes, but he doesn't argue, sensing Ebele wishes to teach him about the process. Why him in particular Danso's not sure, other than he's a fresher recruit.

Ebele shakes his head. "Not likely. They'll want to make port and nurse their losses, I expect. And explain it all to their insurers about how they lost their *cargo*."

"They treat silk and sugar with more care than people," Danso mutters. "It's enough to make a man mad for how they twist themselves into believing it's moral."

"The commerce of human beings is lucrative," Ebele responds darkly. "Free labor leaves them more money. It also leaves them awake at night fearing a rebellion." He turns, tapping one finger against his lips as he studies Danso. "Our network of contacts is paying off—we found that slaver fast. I was thinking I might train Abeni in cultivating those relationships. Helping get intelligence, and the like."

Danso tilts his head, pondering the idea. "I think she'd like doing that."

They continue their walk, heading in the direction of the quarter deck. Danso shoots a grin at Abeni, who listens intently to Asante the sailing master as he gives her a lesson on something to do with the measurement of their speed.

"Do many pirates free enslaved people?" Danso asks.

"There's some history to the practice, yes, and plenty other than me do so. It started with some bands of Jewish pirates last century. We can also sell the sugar made by slave labor and use the money to pay the men and keep up the ship, rather than letting it go into the deep pockets of powerful men, since it has to go somewhere," Ebele tells him. "There are of course some pirates who participate in the trade for the money, though I select not to associate with them, where I can avoid it. Some pirates deserve the credit they get, but some men's stars rise too high. Henry Avery was a good man when it came to inspiring and taking care of poor, mistreated sailors, which I thank him for. He was less moral when it came to enslaved people."

"What happens when pirates do free them?"

"Many end up pirates themselves, given most regular crews wouldn't treat them as equals. I try my best to get them passage wherever they might like to go if I can manage it. Some aren't interested in this life, and I can't blame them. They want peace, rather than a fight."

Danso nods. "I was spared the horrors of being enslaved. I was lucky, considering some of my mother's people were, by the Spanish. My own father was."

"I don't know that I'd call being an English convict laborer lucky, lad." Ebele rests his arms on the railing and looks out at the horizon. "That's a form of slavery in itself."

"Yes. But at least my ...." The word *family* dies on Danso's lips, and he grasps the railing tightly. The wound runs too deep to even say the word aloud, and pain slices at him when he thinks of his nephew, possibly alive and out in a world so wide Danso doesn't even know how to search for him. "You were separated from your mother," he continues, and Ebele, bless him, doesn't push. "And Abeni from her daughter. In the cruelest way possible."

Ebele gazes out at the sea, a far-away look in his eyes. He grasps Danso's forearm in comfort, studying him a moment before turning away again and fingering the necklace he wears. It's not elaborate—a simple string of red wooden beads—but the emotional worth is clear.

"You never found her, did you?" Danso asks. "Your mother, I mean."

"I didn't need to." Ebele stares out at the horizon, grief dripping into his voice like a slow leak. "I watched men kill her at the same auction where they took me because she fought back against our separation. They shot her then and there."

Something deep and dark and heavy drops to the bottom of Danso's stomach. "I'm so sorry," he whispers, horrified by the images the story evokes. "That's awful, Captain Ebele."

Ebele remains soft as he speaks, as if he doesn't quite trust himself to stay steady. "I know what it's like to lose family. To be truthful, I saw myself in you that day when I found you and Abeni in Barbados."

"You did?" Danso's intrigued now, touched and almost anxious at the idea that a man like this finds kinship with *him*. People whisper stories about Ebele across the West Indies and the western coast of Africa and the coastal cities in North America, some in fear and some in respect and awe. A legend, either way. Danso can't imagine anyone ever talking about him like that. He's not sure what he'd do if they did.

"I did," Ebele echoes. "You were so angry, but you were more resilient than you knew, full of more love and compassion than you understood, and I remembered being that way, too. I still am, sometimes. But I found a place to channel that feeling. And I found a new family. They don't share my blood, but they matter to me as if they did. I'd like that for you. You, and Abeni."

Danso looks back again at Abeni, watching her study the hourglass in the sailing master's hands, sand running from top to bottom. He has lost one sister, but perhaps, with closer inspection, gained another.

"Thank you." Danso's voice trembles, full of grief and inspiration and loss and hope, all mingled together. "I believe I'd like that too."

Chapter 4

Kingston, Jamaica. November 1697.

———— ⬥⬥⬥ ————

"**Y**ou should all come to Spanish Town for a few days next week," René's grandfather says, taking a long sip of his tea. "Your next voyage isn't for another fortnight, is it, Michel?"

René and his family are gathered in the drawing room after supper, and he finds himself bored by the conversation. His mother is next to him on the settee, her hands folded so tightly her knuckles pop white, with his father and grandfather in chairs across from them. He sits back further so his grandfather might pay him less mind, his legs not quite long enough for his feet to reach the floor. A collection of old sea legends and pirate folktales rests in his lap, and he fingers the edges of the pages, the small movement calming him. Prescott, his father's boatswain, wrote the stories down for him a few months ago, binding the loose pages together with string.

"Yes," his father answers, "we've a large shipment of sugar to take to some of the mainland colonies. Charles Town again, and perhaps New York. Maybe Boston. We'll be taking some from here and picking up more in Barbados, as well."

Governor Travers lays down his teacup, a thin, stretched, and out-of-place smile on his face. "You said you were eager to move Jerome up in the ranks?"

Michel nods. "I've got my eye on making him second lieutenant. Jerome's young and there might be some arguments about seniority, but he's the hardest working man I've got, aside from Arthur and Prescott. He's done the best work of any boatswain's mate I've ever had."

A look of disgust passes across his grandfather's face at the mention of Uncle Arthur, so René shifts a little closer to his mother.

"I heard some rumblings that some of your sailors were asking for a pay raise?" Governor Travers asks a second, probing question. "Is that true?"

Michel nods again, looking hesitant. "I told them the rates are set in London by the Board of Trade, but that I'd write and see what I could do. I don't hold out much hope."

Governor Travers scoffs. "They should be grateful you're even bothering to ask for them. They're paid a wage, and if the officers aren't complaining, they shouldn't be either. And what's this you've said about Seymour bringing his son here to live? That's actually happening, is it?"

"Oh," Michel says, biting his lip. "Well, yes, Arthur is bringing Frantz here in a few months. I think he and René might make fast friends."

René's eager for a friend his own age, and he likes hearing stories about Frantz from Uncle Arthur. He doesn't like the look on his grandfather's face, the look that says he might say *no*. Governor Travers stays quiet, for once, and that makes René even more unsettled. The conversation fades into the background as he flips through the pages of the homemade book, landing on the story about a Jewish pirate called Moses Cohen Henriques, who helped capture a Spanish treasure fleet, and established a pirate island off the coast of Brazil. His imagination runs wild, illustrating the words on the page with the images in his head. He's asked Uncle Arthur to add a few of the more frightening myths to the book, famous as he is for his ghost stories aboard the *Steorra*. There's one of Prescott's recent additions in the back, about a Captain Ebele that René hasn't read yet. He thinks he's heard the name before.

A harsh voice smacks into the air, drawing him away from the safe harbor of the pages in his hands.

"René!" his grandfather shouts. "What are you doing?"

"Reading, Grandfather." René jumps, confused at the sudden severity.

"And are you *supposed* to be reading while we're all sitting together?" His grandfather raises both eyebrows. "Answer me now."

"Sir," Michel tries, placating, "it's all right. I don't mind him reading while we discuss things he's not interested in."

"I do mind," Governor Travers snaps, and fear pricks René's skin when even his father flinches. "No one told him it was all right for him to read right now." He turns back toward René, stabbing the air with his forefinger. "You are not to misbehave, René, or do anything without permission. You don't want to be a bad child, do you?"

René shakes his head, shrinking back against the settee. "No, Grandfather."

"Father." René's mother sits up straight, her eyes flashing. "He's seven and may read when we're talking rather than being bored. I won't abide you talking to my son like this."

René tugs on the red ribbon holding his hair back, a gift from Jerome on his last birthday.

Perhaps this will keep that wild hair of yours back when we spar? Jerome said with gruff but brotherly affection. *Lieutenant Seymour suggested it when I wasn't sure what to get you. He said the red suited.*

René twists the silky ends between his fingers, pulling it partway loose.

"Oh you won't, will you?" Governor Travers grows harsher, but Astra doesn't blink. "When you're teaching him bad manners? I expect better from my heir." René tenses when his grandfather rises from his chair and steps over toward them. "What is this you're reading? It doesn't look like a proper book to me."

"It's just a book of old sea legends." René's fingers curl tight over the pages, protective of the stories held within. "Mr. Prescott on Papa's crew made it for me, and Uncle Arthur and the men added others."

His grandfather pulls the loosely bound book from René's hands, flipping through the pages. "Henry Avery? And even that Ebele wretch, who is still out there thieving? These are pirate tales."

"Not all of them," René protests. "There are stories about mermaids and ghost ships and things too. Mr. Prescott just wrote down the stories some of Papa's sailors tell."

Governor Travers looks back at Michel. "You let your men write down this pirate nonsense and give it to your son?"

"It's harmless," Michel says, still in that placating tone. "They're just stories, and even the true ones about pirates are half made-up. Sailors tell tall tales, Andrew."

"It is inappropriate," Governor Travers stresses.

"Father, stop." Astra puts an arm around René's shoulders, pulling him flush against her side. "You're upsetting him."

"Oh, am I?" Governor Travers tosses the book to the floor, hard, the strings that serve as binding coming loose as pages spill across the hardwood.

"That's *mine*," René objects, not thinking about the consequences. "You can't just throw it on the floor like that."

He curls in toward his mother when his grandfather raises a hand, those cold blue eyes narrowing.

Is his grandfather going to ....

"Father!" Astra shouts the word, and Governor Travers lowers his hand, clenching it into a fist at his side instead.

Tears of shock prick René's eyes, a few slipping loose even if the last thing he wants is to cry in front of his grandfather. He only gets shouted at when he does.

"I think that's quite enough," his father says, standing up from his chair. "You and I should have some brandy, sir, and let Astra and René go upstairs."

Governor Travers assents by his silence. Michel helps René up as Astra picks up the pages, glaring at her father.

"Why don't you go upstairs and let your mother read to you a while?" his father suggests, whispering in René's ear and wiping away the stray tears. "I'll be up after a bit. I'll get Mrs. Hudson to bring some more tea."

"Coffee?" René asks, hopeful. His favorite drink is hard to get in Jamaica, and they usually have to wait for shipments from Europe or the Ottoman Empire. His father told him that they're starting to grow it here in the Caribbean, which will make it easier to obtain.

"Too late at night, mon etoile. But some tea will do."

René nods, letting his father kiss the top of his head before going toward the stairs with his mother, though he stops halfway up when his grandfather speaks again.

"A good caning sets children straight, you know," Governor Travers says, and René stiffens. He's seen other children get caned, and sailors too.

"You should think of it. Boys need a firm hand, and I think with René that will be especially true. He's already rebellious. Astra's influence, no—"

"Sir." His father cuts his grandfather off, and René admires the bravery. "I am not a proponent of that method of discipline. Not with my sailors unless I have to, and certainly not with my son. He's very young."

His mother ushers René up the stairs and into her bedchamber, shutting the door behind them and cutting off whatever his grandfather might say.

"I'm sure Prescott will sew this back up for you, darling." Astra rifles through her armoire, a piece of paper with faded writing falling out of one of the drawers in her search. "I might have some embroidery thread in here that will do."

"It's all right." René hoists himself up onto the edge of her bed. "We can look at it." His eyes land on the piece of paper. It looks like an old letter, worn and creased from someone reading it too many times, a legible signature scrawled across the bottom.

Imogen.

"Mama?" he asks, drawing her out of her distracted search. "Who is Imogen?"

His mother jolts, spying the old letter laying on the floor.

"Oh," she says, and René thinks her voice sounds higher than normal. She touches the familiar gold bracelet she's worn since he can first remember noticing. "She was one of my dear friends in London, growing up."

"Like Papa and Uncle Arthur?"

"We met when we were young like them, yes." Astra picks up the letter, placing it with care back in the drawer before coming over to join him on the bed. "So a bit like that. Her mother was a friend of my mother's, your grandmother."

René nods solemnly, thinking of the paintings he's seen of his grandmother, who died when his mother was fifteen. "Did Imogen give you that bracelet?" he asks, and his mother smiles, her cheeks pink. "You touched it when I asked."

"My, but you are perceptive." She puts an arm around his shoulders, kissing the side of his head. "But yes, she did. Just before I married your father. René?"

"Hmmm?" René responds, looking at the pages again, which are all out of order now, but if he works on this, then maybe he won't cry. He won't think about that raised hand. He won't think about his grandfather telling his father to cane him.

"It's not right for your grandfather to speak to you that way. And if he ever does it when I'm not there, I want you to tell me, all right?"

René nods, but there's still a question lingering on the edge of his mind, one that makes him want to cry again.

"Mama?"

"Yes, my love?"

René blinks, and tears well in his eyes.

Astra keeps hold of him, her hand running up and down his arm. "René, darling, what's the matter?"

René sniffs, staying still as his mother wipes his eyes with a handkerchief she pulls out of her pocket. "Am I bad? Grandfather's always saying I am. I don't want you or Papa to think so. I try to be good. I promise I do."

Astra holds him tighter, drawing her handkerchief away. "You are not bad. You're a sweet, smart little boy who I love more than anything in this world. Your grandfather is unkind sometimes, and you don't need to listen to a word he says." She pauses, trying a smile at him, and it does make him feel better. "What do you say we put these pages back in order, and not think about him, all right?"

René agrees, and the two of them set to the project of putting his beloved book back together.

"Prescott didn't happen to put any stories about Grace O'Malley in here, did he?" his mother asks.

René shakes his head. "Grace O'Malley?"

"She was quite the fearsome pirate. Irish."

René tilts his head, fascinated, this interesting news diverting his thoughts away from his worry over the events downstairs. "A girl was a pirate? Is that allowed?"

His mother laughs, a light in her eyes he wishes he saw more often. "I suppose she made it so, didn't she? I think you'll find women can do quite a lot, even if we aren't usually doing the same thing as the men. Although sometimes we'd like to."

René leans against her, looking at the pages. "I think you could do anything you like, Mama. Could you put in a story about Grace O'Malley? I'm sure Prescott wouldn't mind you adding one."

His mother agrees, and a half-hour hence there's a knock at the door. His father comes in, carrying a tray with the mentioned tea from Mrs. Hudson.

Michel lays the tea tray down. "I thought I'd just bring it myself and let Mrs. Hudson go to bed."

"Is Grandfather gone?" René asks, his earlier anxiety returning, and he twists his fingers in his lap.

"He is," his father answers, handing them each a cup of tea with a strained smile. "Well, he's retired to his guest chamber for the evening, in any case. He has to leave early to return to Spanish Town, so we won't be seeing him at breakfast."

There's a pause, and René wonders if his parents are thinking what he's thinking.

"Was Grandfather going to hit me?" he whispers. He's seen other boys getting hit in the street by men bigger than them. Sometimes those men are their fathers.

Michel squeezes René's shoulder. "I think your grandfather has a temper, sometimes, but it shouldn't be taken out on you, René. I want that to be clear."

It is not, René notices, a *no*.

"He needs to learn to control his temper, and quickly." Frustration cuts into Astra's tone. "Thank you for cooling him down, Michel."

His parents share a swift kiss, and it makes René happy to see them smile.

"Mama was telling me about Grace O'Malley, Papa," René tells his father. "She was an Irish pirate. And a girl!"

Michel laughs, sharing a fond look with Astra. "Yes, I gathered that from the name. I've heard of her before. Arthur likes to tell the story to the men sometimes, but with the pirates flooding into the Indian Ocean lately, I think perhaps we shouldn't encourage them." Michel looks over again at Astra, quirking one eyebrow in amusement. "Being a bad influence on our boy, are you, mon amour?"

Astra winks at René, and laughter bubbles up in his chest at his mother's mischief. "Always, mon cher," she responds, chuckling as she pats Michel's cheek.

Michel assists with fixing the pages, and René settles in-between his parents. His father smells of the lemon cologne he always wears, mixed with just a hint of the sea, the scent familiar and comforting. All of them take turns reading aloud until sleep steals René away, thoughts of pirates and mermaids and ghost ships overtaking the image of his grandfather's raised hand.

Interlude IV: Mischief, Guile, and a Rather Fortuitous Card Game

Basseterre, Saint Kitts. July 1696.

The captain's log Ebele snatched from the *Columbus* leads them to Saint Kitts. The pages revealed that the *Columbus* picked up slaves from a Martin Mercier, the very same man who appeared on the sugar plantation in Saint-Domingue one day and "bought" Flora, claiming she was old enough to be separated from her mother. The memory still burns Abeni to this day. She's not sure if Alistair had anything to do with it years after he framed her, but she suspects he might have. The man she used to love appears like a hazy memory in her mind, the wounds from his betrayal still festering. On the day that changed everything, she was going to meet him with a baby Flora in tow.

Two slave catchers greeted her instead.

They accused her of escaping from a plantation outside Spanish Town—she'd seen flyers for a missing slave with a baby weeks before. It didn't matter that she had no brand, or any other sign of ownership. It didn't matter that they didn't take her back to said plantation. It didn't matter that she cried out Alistair's name when she caught sight of him as they loaded her onto a ship bound for Saint-Domingue.

Abeni never suspected a man with his smile capable of the things he perpetrated, but she was so young, and she believed the lies that smile told. Even when she was happiest with Alistair, something tugged at the back of her mind, telling her *you are not enough, something isn't right*, but she ignored it in the face of his *I love you*. She has sworn off any kind of romance for a while, unless she finds a woman who is so inclined, as she did with her friend Ife in her Maroon community. Ife was, in fact, her first kiss. Finding such a woman, however, is a difficult thing on a ship full of men. Thankfully, none of them have tried to pursue her, and she doesn't intend to pursue them, even if she thinks one or two of them handsome.

Night cloaks the harbor around her, the full moon spilling light onto the dark water just beyond. She looks back at the *Misericorde*, tucked away on the far side of the bay and flying an English flag. Hiding in plain sight, as it turns out, is a good piece of advice. She crumples the page Ebele ripped from the *Columbus'* log, the stamp of the customs officer who collected their dock fees covering the corner of the page in bright red ink.

Henry Miller, Basseterre Bay Harbor.

Ebele thinks the customs officer might have seen the Merciers in the process of his work, or at least heard of them. If so, they can find out whether the Merciers are still here in Saint Kitts or if they've gone somewhere else. Abeni volunteered to go looking for this customs officer herself. Ebele agreed, thinking her more likely than any of them to get information because women often go unnoticed, or at least people suspect them less. Coburn and Robins have seen this man before when docking here, and pointed her toward the tavern he usually frequents, along with the people he frequents it with. Old buccaneers, apparently, Mathurin Desmarestz and the like. She's heard the name, but the buccaneers are a dying breed—proper piracy is the growing order of the day.

"I can do this." She slides her fingers beneath the arm of her coat to touch her freshly inked tattoo: a depiction of Olokun, an ancient Yoruba sea deity. "I can."

She removes her yellow bandanna, tying it around her neck instead, and runs her hand over her curls, grown longer on the top of her head in recent months, but still kept short and off her neck. The harbor town bustles around her. Dockworkers talking with each other. People headed toward the taverns for a bite of supper. Merchants calling out from their shop doorways to make one last sale for the day. In all of that, no one really notices her.

Danso hugged her before she left. A first, she thinks, and no small matter for him. He keeps those walls up around himself, and she understands, even if her walls are different and less thick. Still, she sees them breaking down. She likes to think she's helping with that.

Be careful, he said. *Please be careful.*

I'll be all right, she assured him when she pulled back, her hands curling around his forearms. *I promise.*

He flinched at the word *promise* but smiled anyway, reaching back and tightening the black ribbon around his long locs, looking sheepish.

The *Misericorde's* crew, Danso, and Ebele remind Abeni of her early days, of the few memories she has of her parents before they died, and the more vivid memories of her Maroon community tucked away from the colonists outside their door. She hopes that raising Flora on the *Misericorde* will make Flora feel as free as she did when she was young, before it all changed.

She makes her way toward Christopher's Tavern—the place Coburn and Robins mentioned— which is no doubt named after Saint Kitts' more formal name, Saint Christopher Island. She feels for the dirk on her belt, covered by the man's coat she wears over her white shirt, tucked into a long green skirt. She knows the dangers of being a woman, and even more so a woman who looks like her, late at night in a harbor tavern. She steps inside, a wall of noise greeting her. Good. The more people in here, the less she's likely to be remembered. She goes toward the bar and orders a glass of beer, putting a coin down in payment. The bar maid looks at her curiously but doesn't comment. Abeni supposes there aren't many women who frequent this tavern, if any at all. She knows the trouble she might get into, so she has to do this right. She has to be careful. The good news is, in a place like this, at this time of night, people are less likely to report anything suspicious like they do in the light of day. It's easy to forget she escaped enslavement when she's on the *Misericorde*, at least sometimes. She's free aboard that ship in a way she can't be on any island.

She searches the room once she has her beer, spotting a group of men playing cards at a large table in the corner, several of them dressed in the extravagant coats and hats that are a mark of buccaneers and proper pirate captains alike. One of the other men is dressed more plainly, and she wonders if he's the customs officer she's looking for. She'll only find out if she tries something.

She strides across the room, injecting more confidence into her step than she feels. She clears her throat as she reaches the table, gesturing toward the one remaining empty chair. "Would you gents mind if I played?"

They all look up at her at the same time, with varied expressions of surprise.

"I won't cheat," she says as the silence endures, taking a sip of her beer.

"Women don't usually play with us," the plainly dressed man comments. "Not sure the gambling would be to your tastes."

"Ah, come on Miller"—one of the buccaneers puts a hand on his compatriot's shoulder—"let her play. What will it hurt?"

Miller. She was right.

"We're playing Faro." Miller quirks his eyebrows, and she isn't sure if it's a challenge. "You know it?"

Abeni folds her hands on the table when she sits down, leaning forward. She's played before with some of the *Misericorde's* crew, though without gambling because the ship's articles forbid it. "I've played."

"A gambling woman!" one of the other buccaneers howls, pleased. "Color me surprised if she doesn't take all our money."

Abeni eyes the board laid out on the table, the suit of spades pasted to it in numerical order. She pulls the money she brought with her from her pocket, given out of the ship's common fund. She places her coins to bet, and the game begins.

"What brings you to Saint Kitts?" One of the buccaneers asks the question, the gold rings on his fingers glittering in the candlelight.

Abeni takes a long swig of her beer before answering, keeping focused on her cards. "I'm hoping I can find someone."

"Intriguing!" one of the other buccaneers chimes in. "Looking for a lost love?"

Abeni does look over at him now, Miller's eyes on her. "I think you're looking for a story. But no."

He tips his hat at her. "A sailor's prerogative, ma'am. If not love, then what?"

"Revenge!" one of his crewmates shouts, as Miller draws another card in his role as dealer. Or in the case of Faro, the banker. "Revenge is a good reason."

Abeni shakes her head. "Not revenge. Just a conversation."

The men all laugh at this, the sound loud even in the already raucous tavern, pleased that they've drawn out a secret even if they haven't at all. It keeps them interested in her without being *too* interested, and that's what she wants. The game continues even as the mood in the room grows more unruly, the sound of glass breaking nearby making a sharp *ting* in Abeni's ear. They make their way through the deck of cards, and then it comes time to make their last go. Abeni bets on aces, and the whole table gives a roar of approval when Miller turns over an ace of hearts from the shoe.

She slides the coins she won toward her, putting them into her coat pocket. "Thanks for letting me play gents, but I've got to be going."

"Another round!" one of the buccaneers crows.

She smiles, the weak smell of cheap scotch coming off all of them in waves.

"I'm afraid not. Enjoy your night, gentlemen."

She gets up from her chair, walking back across the tavern toward the bar again and standing in the one spot near the door that isn't packed with people. She waits a few minutes, watching Miller bid goodbye to his now very drunk buccaneer friends. He makes for the exit, but she beats him to it, stepping outside just seconds before he does and blocking him from going any further. Before he can say anything, she pulls the coins she just won out of her pocket and grabs his hand, placing them in his open palm as the tavern door closes behind them.

He doesn't look entirely surprised, but he doesn't give in just yet.

"You just won this, so I'm not sure exactly what you're doing."

"I'm looking to learn what I can about a family by the name of Mercier, and if you can tell me, I'm glad to pay you for the trouble. Have you heard of them?"

A roguish smile slides onto his face. "A lot of people come in and out of this harbor. Can't remember them all."

She pulls another coin out of her pocket and puts it in his hand. "They did a deal with a slaver called the *Columbus*, who made port here."

Miller narrows his eyes, though in intrigue and not in anger. "How do you know that?"

Abeni takes a step back so she's not as close, but she thinks he might be impressed by her rather than about to summon the law. "I just do."

She won't say *please*. She won't say *I'm looking for someone*, because she won't give her desperation to a man she isn't sure she can trust with it.

Miller's fingers close over the coins. "Mercier used to run slaves across the Caribbean in a beaten-up sloop. Small-time stuff. Some that were brought from Africa, most that were picked up here by other illegal runners like him. So I saw him around, argued with him over not paying his fees, but it didn't work out for him because he kept getting in trouble. I haven't seen him in a few months. Word had it he went to Guadeloupe to try and start a small sugar plantation."

"That's all you know?"

"That's all I know," he echoes, with something like admiration. "You must really want that information if you're willing to give me money for it. Clever, playing cards first. You'd make a good spy."

Abeni doesn't say anything else, because a thousand secrets might come spilling out if she does.

I'm a runaway slave.

I'm a pirate.

And sometimes, I'm afraid.

She only nods before she turns to go, one hand remaining near her dirk.

Finally, something. Finally, a lead.

Miller's voice cuts into the air.

"Tell Captain Ebele if he wants another contact on Saint Kitts, he might have one in me."

Abeni jolts, spinning around on one heel. She only hopes this won't get Ebele caught. "What?"

"I heard rumors that he had a woman on his crew." Miller sounds more like a young sailor enraptured by a new tale than a grizzled customs officer. "I figured no one but a woman who found her way onto a pirate crew would have enough bravado to come up to our table."

There's no point in lying, and she suspects it might make him respect her less, but she doesn't quite move her hand from where it rests. "But why would you want to help a pirate?"

Miller looks out at the harbor beyond them, the ships casting shadows on the water and looking like ghosts in the night. "I've been working these docks for a decade. I see the wealthy ship owners and captains get coins in their pockets while I scrape by. While their sailors scrape by. I think Ebele and pirates like him might just have a point. I assume you already know my name, so you can just tell him I said that."

Abeni removes her hand from the hidden dirk handle, daring to smile. "I will. And thank you, Mr. Miller."

He tips his hat at her and walks into the night, keeping half the coins and giving the rest back. He doesn't ask her name. He doesn't ask who she's looking for, and she's thankful for that. As soon as he's out of sight, she runs. She runs and runs and *runs* toward the *Misericorde*, a hysterical joy filling her up to the brim.

There's a lead. A real lead.

She's going to find Flora. She swears it.

She rushes past the crew members on deck when she reaches the ship, spotting Danso first and throwing her arms around him.

"What's going on?" he asks, looking bewildered even as he shares her smile. "What happened?"

"I found a lead on Flora." She takes Danso's hands, pressing them tightly. "We need to go to Guadeloupe."

Chapter 5

Kingston, Jamaica. June 1698.

René is impatient.

He sits at the dining room table, his feet grazing the wood floors beneath. He sighs and rests his chin on his hands, eyes flitting upward to where both the Delacroix and Travers coats of arms hang above the mantle. The grandfather clock ticks in the nearby entrance hall with a resounding echo, finally chiming the hour.

How long is this going to *take*?

"Something the matter, René?" Jerome asks, looking up from his place gazing out the window, his hands clasped behind his back.

"Where is everyone?"

Jerome turns toward him. "Your mother is at Mrs. Taylor's for tea and your father has gone to meet with Lieutenant Seymour and his son to bring them here."

"I know *where* they are."

Jerome raises his eyebrows. "Then why did you ask?"

"I meant what is taking them so long?" René says. "They've been gone ages."

"They have been gone a half-hour at most," Jerome points out, sitting down at the table now. "Or has turning eight affected your sense of time passing?"

"Well, it *feels* like ages," René mutters.

"Is there a reason you're so anxious for their arrival?"

René looks up, his cheeks burning. He isn't sure why he's embarrassed, only that he is.

"I just thought ..." he begins, trying to form the words he means. "Frantz and I are the same age, and I've played with other children, but they either move away or are older or younger than me or Papa deems them inappropriate and—"

"You thought he could be your friend?" Jerome asks, and there's something in his eyes René doesn't fully understand.

He knows how lonely he gets sometimes, and he wonders if Jerome does, too. He remembers Jerome from the first night they played together, a young face holding gray eyes that looked older than his twenty-one years. Other sailors seem afraid of Jerome and his sternness, but René can't imagine being so. Jerome is tall, but for a long time, René remembers worrying that Jerome didn't weigh as much as he should. He asked his father about it once, receiving the reply that Jerome might not have had as much food growing up as René does, and it takes time to correct these things. Jerome is more filled out now, his broad shoulders looking less bony, and René feels satisfied. He wants to look out for Jerome because until Jerome came aboard the *Steorra*, it didn't seem like anyone was.

René nods in response to Jerome's question, sitting up and folding his hands on top of the table.

"I'm sure they'll be here soon, and I don't see any reason why Lieutenant Seymour's son wouldn't like you." A smirk creeps across Jerome's face, and he quirks one eyebrow. "Perhaps then you will no longer need me to play the pirate in your sword games."

René jolts, a protest on his lips as he grasps at the arm of Jerome's coat. "No!" he exclaims, drawn from his anxiety. "I want you to play with me. You still will, won't you? I can even be the pirate, sometimes. I think I might be good at it. You're always so stiff, like you're uncomfortable when you play the pirate."

"Yes," Jerome says, patting René's arm awkwardly. "I'll still play with you. I was only teasing. Critiquing my acting skills now, I see?"

The door opens then, interrupting whatever René might have said next.

"René," his father calls out. "Come here, won't you?"

René vacates his chair, his hands sweaty as he straightens his green coat and goes into the entrance hall. Uncle Arthur's wide smile holds unquenched joy as he gazes at the boy standing next to him. A smaller, nervous smile flashes on the boy's face as he pushes his spectacles up the bridge of his nose with one finger. He has a head of short, thick black curls, and lighter, cool brown skin that brings out the darker shade of his eyes, which contain hints of amber like his father's.

This must be Frantz.

"René Delacroix." Uncle Arthur keeps hold of his son's hand, and Frantz looks back at his father with an intrigued, deep fondness. "This is my son, Frantz Seymour. Frantz, this is René, my godson I've told you so much about."

Frantz waves, his accent a unique mix of English, French, and perhaps an African country René does not know specifically. "Hello. I've been interested to meet you."

"Hello." René sticks his hand out as he's seen his father do, hoping Frantz will shake it in return.

Frantz considers, then smiles again and puts his own hand out.

"Nice to meet you," René says, swaying back and forth on his feet after he lets go.

"You too," Frantz answers. "My father's been telling me about you on the way here. And in his letters and his visits."

"He's told me about you, too," René replies. "I've been hoping you might come to live here."

"I started teaching Frantz how to read charts, as well as how to use the dividers and compass, on our journey from Saint-Domingue." Uncle Arthur keeps Frantz's hand as he crouches down between the two of them, taking one of René's as well. "You two share a love of the sea, just like Michel and I."

René looks up at his father, who stands a few feet back next to Jerome, smiling and nodding in encouragement.

"Would you like to see René's room, Frantz?" Michel asks. "I think you might find some books and maps in there to your liking."

Frantz nods so enthusiastically that it looks as if he'll topple over, so René takes his hand, leading him up the stairs. They reach the landing and

Frantz looks around, wide-eyed, trailing behind even as René still loosely clasps his fingers.

"Your room is so big!" Frantz exclaims as they step inside, adjusting his spectacles again, eyes catching on a large map spread out across the window seat. "A map!"

"Yes! I was looking at it and thinking of all the islands and places I'd like to visit." René gestures at Frantz, indicating he should sit next to him as they place the map over their laps. Drawings of sea creatures adorn the edges, a kraken most prominent of all.

"Papa knows so much about navigation and the stars." Frantz sounds proud, and René doesn't blame him. He loves Uncle Arthur very much. "I can't wait to learn more from him. Have you ever been off this island?"

"We came here from England when I was three, but I don't really remember much." René's finger traces the distance from the British Isles to Jamaica. "And sometimes I go on voyages with Papa and your father and Jerome. I've seen the Bahamas before, but we never seem to go back there now. And I've seen Barbados and some of the Leeward Islands. I'd like to see New York and Carolina and Boston one day."

"I just came from Saint-Domingue." Frantz points at the island. "It's the first time I've ever been away. My mother's been a few different places, but not in a long time."

Frantz's eyes fall onto the map, and René gazes at him, feeling a strange and near-immediate sense of comfort with the other boy. He knows that lots of people with Frantz's skin color are enslaved, though when he questions the adults about it he never gets a straight answer on why. All he knows is that his mother and Uncle Arthur don't like the idea. His father doesn't seem to, either, but he's less talkative about it. They don't have any Black slaves in their house, only white servants. His grandfather does have slaves, and René has seen him shout and slap them. He has heard him say his slaves should be so lucky, working in a house and not out in the sweltering sugar fields. René doesn't understand how any of that is fair, or kind. Frantz looks up again, smiling at him and breaking through his reverie.

"Are you going to stay here for a while?" René asks.

"I think so." Frantz folds his hands over the top of the map. "Papa mentioned tutors and sharing yours. It's why my mother wanted me to come live with him, for now, and so I could learn about sailing. It's hard for my parents to live together. Papa's family has rules or ... something like that. Something about money. Mama's set to visit in two months, she and Papa said."

"You miss her?" René asks, hearing the ache in Frantz's voice.

Frantz nods, pulling a stack of envelopes out of his pocket. "She wrote me a few letters to get started until I could get here and write her. She's so smart, my mother! She taught me French since so many people speak it in Saint-Domingue. Her parents were from the Gold Coast in Africa and couldn't read or write in English, so she learned from someone on the island. She taught herself sums and things, which is helpful for running the business she does, out of our house, but she never had things like tutors." Frantz pauses, looking up at René again as if he isn't sure if it's safe to say what he wants. "She wanted me to have that chance."

"I would miss my mother too," René says. "You will have to meet her! I know French. Or, well, I know a good bit of French, anyway. Papa has a house in Paris, but I only went there when I was little, so I don't remember very much. My Uncle Remy comes to visit us here sometimes. He's a *vicomte* in France, which I think is the same as a viscount, in England."

"Your grandfather here is a baron, isn't he?" Frantz asks. "Papa was telling me. Does that mean you will be a baron, one day?"

"Yes." René wrinkles his nose at the prospect. "I suppose it does. I'd like to be a captain of a ship, though. My grandfather says when I'm older I'll have to go back to England. I have an older second cousin named Thomas living there now who would probably like being a baron better, but he doesn't have any children to inherit."

"Being a captain sounds better than being a baron," Frantz agrees. "Do you like sailing with your father? Papa says I will go with them sometimes, like you do. I'm excited for that."

"Yes!" René exclaims. "My favorite thing is to sit on the ship when the sun comes up and watch it spread colors across the water. It makes it look like the sky is on fire."

"Mine is the sunset." Frantz looks out the window as the dying rays of afternoon sunlight filter through, striking the center of the map and landing on New Providence Island, near Nassau Town. "I like the way it slowly sets behind the trees back home, and then leaves room for the stars."

A contented silence ebbs into the moment, and both boys look from the map to the ocean beyond, just barely visible on the horizon from this house on the highest hill in Kingston.

"Do you like stories?" René asks.

Frantz nods with such enthusiasm that he nearly upsets the map, his kind eyes lighting up. "Papa tells good ones, especially scary ones."

René grins, getting up and putting the map away before going over to his nightstand and retrieving his storybook, which is now bound up with thicker string and kept inside an old leather diary cover that had its pages removed. He brings it over, flipping through and landing on the one about Grace O'Malley his mother added in her near-perfect script.

"My mother added this one," René says, "about a girl pirate from a long time ago. I didn't know girls could be until I read this. Do you want me to read aloud? I try to do voices when I can."

Frantz scoots closer, the book laying over both their laps as the map had. "Yes! We can take turns, if you like." He seems shy when he looks up, but there's a shared excitement between them. "I have some stories my mother told me that I could put in."

René nods, his smile stretching so wide it makes his face ache. He starts reading one story and then Frantz another, about pirates and mermaids and things that are true and some that can't possibly be, but he loves them, anyway. They don't stop until their fathers call them down for supper and the sun's long gone from the sky, replaced by bright, glittering stars.

Interlude V: The Curious Kindness of Pirates (Part the First)

Saint-Pierre, Martinique. January 1697.

A beni breathes in deep.

The ramshackle Mercier home stands mere feet away, and with it her own miracle.

Flora is *here.* Alive. Within her grasp.

After Saint Kitts they went to Guadeloupe, and it took patience and time to sort out that the Merciers were gone from the island. Finally, they got word from some old neighbors that Martinique was the place to go next. Now they've arrived, after taking weeks to locate the Merciers in the bustling port town of Saint-Pierre, and after days of scoping out the place in order that they might choose the best time to approach. Gooseflesh runs up and down Abeni's arms despite the heat, but Danso's hand rests on her shoulder, steadying her.

What if she doesn't remember me? she asked that morning.

She will, Danso assured her. *I know she will.*

"All right," Ebele whispers, like he's afraid someone might be watching them among the trees. "Let's go."

They walk quickly but quietly toward the house, looking behind them for any signs of the Merciers returning. They've been coming to case the Mercier home for a week, trying to determine when they might be gone—between five and seven in the evening, as it turns out. Ebele does the work of unlocking the door with a knife, pushing it open easily once they hear the tell-tale click.

The floorboards creak under the weight of footsteps.

A sharp, tiny gasp pierces the air from around the corner.

And then, a broom-wielding little girl steps in front of them.

Flora. It *is* Flora. Abeni only saw her for a brief moment while they watched the house, but now ....

It takes everything in her not to cry. Everything.

Flora is *so* thin, her curls falling in half-matted tangles down her back because the Merciers don't know how to brush them and decidedly don't care. Black dirt is stuck beneath her fingernails. The fear in her little girl's eyes cuts Abeni to the quick, and she takes another breath, stepping forward as Ebele and Danso follow her lead.

"We're not here to hurt you." Abeni kneels down to Flora's level, gentle and easing her into the situation. "We're here to take you away from these people. Do you remember me, darling?"

Flora slowly lowers the broom, putting it down and leaning it against the wall. She analyzes Abeni from a foot or two away, tilting her head as if she remembers but cannot quite place her mother's face. She steps forward, fingering one of Abeni's curls with a heart-wrenching hesitation, her body tensing out of instinct before reaching up for the locket next. Abeni remembers her playing with it as a baby, laughing while she made it twirl around. Flora's eyes go to Abeni's face, a spark of familiarity in them.

"Mama?" Flora's words are a whispered, broken prayer that threatens to break Abeni's heart. Or maybe her heart was already broken, and she's just been working to put it back together.

Abeni's power of speech fails her. She wraps her arms around Flora, hugging her close. Flora freezes, and though she doesn't return the embrace, her little hands clutch at Abeni's shirt, holding on tight. The world could crumble right now, and Abeni wouldn't care. Nothing matters except that Flora is here. Nothing. She will tell her daughter every day that she never left her on purpose. That she never would, and she never will.

"Abeni, we should go," Danso prompts, gentle, but urgent.

"We need to get you out of here, my love." Abeni searches her daughter's face, her daughter who still looks afraid, and Abeni could kill whoever put that fear in her eyes. She very well might. "Is there anything here you want to take with you?"

Flora nods, padding over to retrieve what looks like a tattered rag doll and slipping it into the pocket of her apron. Just as she reaches Abeni again the door opens, banging back against the wall. Flora jumps, crying out in fear.

"Intruders!" Mercier shouts. "I thought so." He surveys the room, his wife standing behind him. "Just what the devil do you think you're doing in my house?"

"We're here to take young Flora with us," Ebele says without preamble, and Danso's hand goes to the hilt of his cutlass. "Allow us that, and we'll leave without any trouble."

"That child is our property," Mrs. Mercier answers, shoving in beside her husband, her fair skin red with sunburn.

"She is my daughter." A storm rises up in Abeni's chest, rage crackling around her as she stands up and shields Flora, who hides behind her legs. "And she is no one's property."

"You can't come in here and take her away just like that!" Mercier insists. "We bought her."

"*Oh.*" Ebele steps forward so he's nose-to-nose with the other man. "I think you'll find we can."

Abeni's never feared Ebele, but as his voice lowers, danger lingering within it, she sees why someone might. He doesn't openly engage with naval ships or East India where he can help it—not yet—but she has seen him frighten some of the captains of slave and merchant ships they've overtaken with a burning glance or a sharp word, when he needs to. He is so often the kindly older man that it still surprises her when she sees him do it. Danso has the same ability even if he doesn't realize it, and it makes him well-liked among the other men on the crew.

"You'll pay us for her, or we'll alert the authorities," Mercier says.

"And alert them to your illegal activities, running slaves without the proper contracts and digging into their profits?" Ebele smiles, and this is somehow even more disconcerting because it lays bare his rage, the rage they all have, burning burning *burning* beneath the kindness. "No, you won't."

"You're pirates, aren't you?" Mrs. Mercier shouts. "I think they'll be more interested in that than in us. You're that Captain Ebele fellow. I've seen flyers."

"We're not paying you for a little girl you participated in enslaving." Danso speaks up, his voice a deep, thunderous rumble. "So if you don't mind, we'll be going."

"I do mind." Mercier's eyes narrow and he pulls out a pistol from under his coat, pointing it at Danso. "I think you'll find I mind a great deal, in fact."

Abeni pushes Flora fully behind her. It seems all a blur, but Abeni thinks that's Mrs. Mercier lunging for Ebele, who shoves her to the ground. Hesitant to use his sword unless pressed, he pulls it out like lightning now, pointing it at her to keep her down. In almost the same moment Danso grabs the end of Mercier's pistol, pointing it at the ceiling. Mercier pulls the trigger and Flora gasps at the bang, the bullet lodging in the ceiling above them. Not much of a match for Danso's strength, Mercier loses his grip on the gun, and Danso tosses it across the room before seizing Mercier's collar and shoving him against the wall.

"As Captain Ebele said"—a slow fury scorches Danso's words, but he doesn't shout—"we'll be going now with the child." He lets go of Mercier's coat with a glare.

"We don't want to hurt you," Ebele adds. Abeni thinks the glint in Danso's eyes indicates he might feel differently, but he holds himself in check. "Just let us go with the girl and we'll be no more trouble to you."

Ebele's disdain for the couple is evident in the way he clenches his jaw, but their priority is Flora. They need to get out and away from the island before the Merciers report them or before anyone else realizes just whose ship is sitting near the harbor. Finally, Mrs. Mercier relents, holding up her hands, and Ebele surveys her for weapons before removing his foot from her chest.

"Abeni." Ebele gestures to her. "You go out first with Flora. We'll be right there."

Abeni obliges, but Mrs. Mercier calls out after her, stopping her progress.

"Your daughter is a weak, worthless brat! Could barely manage anything I asked."

Abeni's mind goes blank, dark with rage and nothing else. She whips around, pulling out the dirk on her belt without thinking. She doesn't point it at the woman, but the weapon in her hands is enough of a threat.

"Look at this violence!" Mrs. Mercier crows.

"You have beaten and enslaved my six-year-old daughter." Wrath surges into Abeni's voice like a flood, flowing into the crevices of every word. "Don't talk to me about violence. *She* is not the one who is worthless. If you don't back up right now, I swear I'll kill you myself."

She's never killed anyone before, or even threatened it, but she knows that if anyone touches her daughter again, they won't live to tell the tale. Silence reigns as she turns on her heel, putting Flora in front of her and walking outside. Flora doesn't look back, holding tight to Abeni's hand and the crumbling rag doll.

"You're really going to take me away from here?" Flora asks once they're a few feet away from the door. "You're not going to send me back?"

"Oh, darling." Abeni blinks away tears, and she's shaking and Flora is shaking, but it will be fine. She will make it better and she will give her daughter whatever she needs to heal those broken places and fill them with light. "No. That will not happen."

"How did you get here? I remembered your voice, even if I was small when they took me away. I remembered how kind it was. I didn't know if you'd ever come back."

"I would never leave you on purpose, my darling. I've been trying to find you ever since."

She puts her arms out to Flora, but doesn't want to push her to accept. Flora considers for a long minute before she lets Abeni pick her up from the ground, both of them clinging to each other.

"My love. My sweet girl," Abeni murmurs close in Flora's ear. "I love you. I loved you every moment we were apart."

The Merciers' cries of protest pierce the air in time with Ebele and Danso coming outside to join them. Flora jerks and Abeni holds her closer, one hand resting upon the tattered curls.

"They won't hurt you. I promise you they will never hurt you again."

Abeni runs a hand down her daughter's back, feeling the marks of freshly healed wounds beneath the thin dress, the skin raised like Flora had been struck with a tree branch.

"I'll find you! Mark my words!" Mercier shouts. "I'll get my property back, you scoundrels!"

Abeni winces at the word *property*, wishing she could erase the memory from Flora's mind. It takes every ounce of her self-control to stop from turning back and giving the couple another verbal lashing, but that's not the point of today. The point of today is already accomplished, whatever might come next.

"Of all the people to call someone else a scoundrel," Ebele says, his eyes flashing. "Let's go. We need to get back to the ship."

He leads the way, sparing a kind smile for Flora before setting off, and Danso stays behind so they're protected from both sides. After a few minutes, Flora turns back around to Danso from her place in Abeni's arms, her eyes wide with curiosity.

"Are you ...." She hesitates, fearful but drawn in. "Are you my Papa? I don't remember him."

Danso halts in his tracks, then seemingly remembers the urgency of their departure and keeps walking. If it wasn't such a serious moment, Abeni might have laughed at his flabbergasted expression. It's caught somewhere between a smile and a frown, a grown man stumped by a simple question from a child. There was something softer about Danso while they spied on the Merciers, something gentler when he saw the little girl emerge from the house. Abeni wonders if finding Flora has made him think of his nephews and nieces who died, and especially of Jahni, lost somewhere in the wilds of the West Indies. She silently vows that she'll do whatever she can to help him find the boy. With her daughter back, Abeni believes all things are possible, even if the world says no in the face of her optimism.

"No, little one," Danso says, unsure. "But I'm glad to have helped you out of there. I'm Ajani Danso, your mother's friend."

Flora considers him, a shy, tiny little smile breaking out on her face.

"I think you would be a good Papa," she declares. "You fought Mr. Mercier to save me. It seems like something someone who would be a good Papa would do."

"I'm not sure—"

Abeni silences Danso with a shake of her head, hiding her own grin.

"—that doll is sufficient," Danso finishes, following Abeni's lead. "We should find you a new one."

Flora buries her face in her mother's neck, shy after her burst of interest. Abeni winks at the still-bewildered Danso, shifting her daughter on her hip and carrying her to the safety of Ebele's ship.

Chapter 6

The Caribbean Sea aboard the Steorra. July 1699.

———⚬⚭⚬———

Jerome's taking his turn at the wheel when bright, childish voices interrupt his thoughts. René and Frantz appear, René's ever-growing homemade book of sea tales in his hands.

"Can Frantz and I sit here and read aloud while you steer?" René asks. "We won't bother you."

"Oh," Jerome says. "Certainly. Go ahead."

"Papa and Uncle Michel were talking about something to do with Spain and France, and a war over a dead, or perhaps almost dead, king in Spain, and it wasn't very interesting," Frantz replies in that blunt way of his Jerome's getting used to. "So we thought we might come here instead."

"Is there something you'd prefer to hear, Jerome?" René asks as he and Frantz settle down on the deck a few feet away. "I know you don't really like the pirate stories."

Jerome considers. "How about that one with the Flying Dutchman? You like that one."

"That one's only good at night," René points out. "Besides, Uncle Arthur tells that one best, and it frightens the daylights out of Papa, so we need to wait until dark. I'd read the one about Scylla and Charybdis since you like *The Odyssey*, but Papa told me not to read that aloud on deck anymore because it spooks some of the men into thinking we might run into a whirlpool or a monster because we said the names aloud, and if Odysseus can't defeat them both then how can we?" René pauses, flipping through the pages. "What about the one with the selkies? I think that should suit us all. And then the one about the first mermaid, maybe."

Jerome nods. "Quite fine with me."

He gazes at the boys as they read, half-listening even as his own thoughts overcome the words of the story. René and Frantz look so different side by side. The light makes René's fair hair gleam, his pale complexion leaning toward red under the intense sun. Frantz's light brown skin turns darker under the rays, the tips of his short black curls burnished auburn. While it's obvious Frantz takes after his mother—who Jerome's seen once in port—those amber-brown eyes are Lieutenant Seymour's. Jerome wonders if society will allow a friendship such as this to flourish beyond childhood. The rules say no, but their souls, if there are such things, say yes. Jerome finds he's unsure what to do with that. He considers the fact that he can pass as white—most of the time—and that Frantz certainly cannot, and how that affects the way they're allowed to move in the world. On the other hand, Frantz also has educational opportunities and money that Jerome never did, because of Lieutenant Seymour's wealth and status.

The boys read for three-quarters of an hour, looking expectant when Jerome hands the wheel off to another crewmember.

"If you're done with your work"—René's slow and pointed with his words, clearly hoping he might get what he wishes—"could we spar?"

"If your father doesn't require me for anything more at present, then yes." Jerome was recently promoted to second lieutenant, and although Captain Delacroix encourages and approves of the swordplay with René, he doesn't want to shirk his duties. "Go ask him for me, if you would, and get the swords from his cabin if he says yes."

René must have easily gained approval from his father, because he reappears alongside Frantz a few minutes later with the wooden swords in hand, both boys discarding their coats on the deck. Given the heat, Jerome finds himself jealous.

"Hand me your coat," René says, apparently reading his mind. "I can put it over here with ours."

Jerome pauses, remembering the shouts ringing through the front door as he approached the Delacroix household a few weeks ago, Governor Travers' blocking the doorway.

You will keep your coat on, boy! You will not be out in public looking like a common, undressed worker.

Jerome hesitates. "Your grandfather doesn't like it when you're without your coat."

"My grandfather is at home in Spanish Town," René argues, the dormant embers of rebellion coming to life in his eyes, and something about it unnerves Jerome. "And Papa didn't say anything. It's fine."

Jerome slides his coat off and hands it to René, who lays it carefully on top of his and Frantz's much smaller ones. Jerome rolls up his sleeves, feeling a bit like a lad again. He could never take off his coat like this in port, but on ships, things are different.

Frantz settles near them on the deck, the spare third sword sitting next to him. He holds one of his father's charts in his hands, a letter resting atop. René hands Jerome one sword, *N. Jerome* written in messy, childish scrawl near the handle.

"I'll be the pirate this time," René informs him, taking the sword with his own name, and Jerome jolts at the sudden change of pace. He doesn't remember René offering that of his own accord since the first night they played.

"Pardon?"

"I said we would take turns." René places one foot in front of the other, prepared to lunge forward. "I was reading a Henry Avery story in my book earlier. I want to try it out."

Jerome's still bewildered, an odd, anxious feeling he can't quite understand settling in his chest, but he accepts. "So you did. All right."

The breeze blows hard off the ocean, and René's lengthening hair slips out of its ribbon.

"Hold on." René puts the sword down, attempting to re-tie his hair and keep the toy from sliding down the deck at the same time, one foot holding it in place.

"Here, use this!" Frantz exclaims, pulling a red kerchief out of his pocket and handing it over. "Tie it like a bandana. Pirates are always wearing bandanas in drawings. And some in real life, from what I've seen."

"You've seen *pirates*?" René asks, intrigued at this piece of information.

"They were on Saint-Domingue sometimes," Frantz says, looking at Jerome. "You've seen pirates, Jerome. Did they wear bandanas?"

Jerome quirks an eyebrow. "I confess that I don't pay much attention to the fashion sense of thieves."

"There!" René draws their attention back, the red bandana crossing his forehead and tied in a small knot at the back, waves of fair hair sticking out beneath.

"Red suits you, lad!" Lieutenant Seymour calls out from across the main deck where he stands with Captain Delacroix, both of them pouring over some newspapers. "I've always said so. Doesn't it, Michel?"

Captain Delacroix turns, smirking. "It does. That's quite a look, my boy."

René smiles, shy as he holds his sword out.

"Beware, pirate." Jerome crosses his sword over René's. Wooden swords or not, René's talent for swordsmanship is obvious even at his young age, something that hasn't gone unnoticed by anyone.

"Are you sure you don't want to join us, Frantz?" René grins, whacking Jerome's sword again.

"I'm fine," Frantz replies, smiling at them before turning back to the chart, his eyes narrowed in thought. "I've got this letter from my mother to read, and this chart I want to look at. After all, if you're busy fighting, someone has to be able to point the ship in the right direction, don't they? So I should learn."

"Yes! Though I like learning navigation, too." René looks back at Jerome. "Come on, you can hit harder than that."

"I will hit as hard as I see fit, René."

They continue back and forth across the deck for several minutes, the sounds of their swords echoing against the mast and into the sea breeze, the sun shining down on them in warm pools of golden light. René slips abruptly on something Jerome doesn't see, landing on the deck with a thud as the sword falls out of his hand and slides away.

"René!" Jerome calls out, Frantz running up behind him in concern. "Are you all right?"

"Fine," René says, but he doesn't get up. "There's a loose board there. Stay in character!"

"René," Jerome insists. "You're hurt. Your father will have my head if I ignore such a thing."

René waves him off. "I'm not, I swear. Come on. We can't stop the game in the middle! Someone has to win. You wouldn't let a real pirate go just because he slipped, would you?"

Jerome hesitates, looking over at Frantz and hoping perhaps he'll argue. It seems that in their focus the other men didn't hear René fall. They're still bent over their newspaper, frowning and speaking in whispers Jerome cannot quite make out. Frantz only nods in agreement, and Jerome releases a long-suffering sigh, turning back to René.

"The victory is mine, scoundrel." Jerome puts the dull edge of the toy sword against the collar of René's shirt. "Now surrender."

"I will never surrender to the English Navy," René says, "or to the East India Company. I'll die first."

Jerome pulls his sword back. "I am not going to pretend to kill you, René."

"It's a *game*, Jerome." René huffs. "You let me pretend to kill you all the time."

"Yes, well." Jerome clears his throat, a strange, unnamed emotion filling his chest. "That's enough for now, I think."

René looks as if he's about to argue when the voices of Lieutenant Seymour and Captain Delacroix drift over in their direction.

"This new pirate Danso, or at least the one you think is Danso," Lieutenant Seymour says, his whisper caught in the wind. "He's the one who attacked that merchantman the *Rose-Marie* last month. To hear some sailors tell it, the ship started sinking during the fight because the captain didn't tend to her, and Danso took those sailors to shore somewhere safe despite the fact that he won and could have easily left them to die."

"Arthur," Captain Delacroix chides, a lecture on his breath. "You cannot tell me you somehow admire a pirate? He robbed them, even if he didn't mercilessly leave them to die."

Lieutenant Seymour ignores the reprimand. "You're saying it's that Danso fellow who slipped away on Jerome's watch?"

Jerome freezes, aware of René's and Frantz's eyes on him, every muscle in his body tensing up.

"It is not a stretch for a convict laborer to turn into a pirate," Captain Delacroix says. "And he has a Black woman with him. The Danso who escaped that ship also escaped with an enslaved woman who was being transported. There are rumors they're sailing the ship that Ebele fellow took over in a mutiny a few years back."

"The enslaved man who took over the slaver," Lieutenant Seymour half mutters. "He was a mysterious chap. He must have passed on. How do you know it's Danso, aside from your theories? The papers just call him Robin Hood."

"Pirates find themselves with allies across the ports of the New World," Captain Delacroix answers. "People say Ebele, Avery, and other rogues could get information on where to trade, how to avoid various navies, and where to find merchant ships from people willing to give it. Apparently, Danso let his real name slip to one of his contacts who was in it more for the coin than the ideals, I suppose. So that man told someone else, and so on. The description matches what Jerome's told me: African, with perhaps some Carib in him. And again, the woman, who I think is the quartermaster, if you can believe it."

"You have to give them some credit, my friend," Lieutenant Seymour says, audible admiration in his tone. "Pirates can run quite an operation. Apparently, they vote for their leadership, too, taking some lead from the old buccaneers. Not everyone looks out for their crew like you do, Michel. Too many captains don't, in the merchant service or the Navy. Equalizing the power structure doesn't sound so bad."

"There are rumors that Danso gives some of the money he steals to the poor around the islands. That he leaves it at doorsteps like Robin Hood. Hence the name, I suppose." Captain Delacroix scoffs, not paying mind to Lieutenant Seymour's admiring tone. "What nonsense. Pirates are far too selfish to give away anything, and even if the stories *are* true it's not their money to give, regardless. For all we know, Danso might have killed Ebele and took his place that way. Perhaps that new piracy act they passed last year will help put a stop to a true resurgence. More pirates are the last thing we need, if the war over the Spanish succession does come to pass."

Jerome's hands clench into fists at his sides. He *knew* this would come back for him. He *knew* this would ruin him, and now at five and twenty, all his fears ring true. The man and woman he let escape are *pirates*. He hoped they would just disappear. It would certainly be smarter. He steps forward, a small hand tugging at the sleeve of his coat before he can escape below deck.

"Are you all right, Jerome?" René looks up at him with wide eyes, but Jerome can't quite control his anxiety.

"Yes," he snaps. "I'm fine, René."

René lets go, flinching at the sharp tone.

"I'm sorry," Jerome says, realizing himself and softening his voice. "It's nothing to do with you. I only ... I need a moment."

René nods, not asking any further questions, though he does grasp Frantz's hand. Jerome puts his coat back on and goes below deck to the mess, devoid of any of the crew. He puts a trembling hand in his pocket, feeling for the old leather bracelet still resting there, and he can't quite get a deep breath as he examines the piece of jewelry made for small, childish wrists. The piece of jewelry that is the only thing he has left of the one person he is sure loved him.

Do not be ashamed of your heritage, his mother said one night when a privateer crew booted his father off a ship for that exact reason, marking their family's final descent into the world of piracy. *What they're doing is not right.* His mother told him never to feel shame even as his father soured on her, even as Thomas grew angry and impatient at the looks she earned them. His mother left her family—unheard of in Romani circles—because his father wanted to go back to England, but she only got shouted at when she mentioned that sacrifice. Maybe that's when Jerome started hating half of himself, when he saw the look of disdain in his father's eyes, or when he heard him say *your mother's family are damned thieves and wanderers.* Ironic, from a man who eventually became a pirate. He holds blurry, kind memories of his mother's large extended family from his very early years, before they left France for his father's native Bristol, and then later for the West Indies. He wishes he could change the wild stories people tell, nasty stories like the ones about Romani people kidnapping children that couldn't be further from the truth. But he can't.

He runs his thumb over the word *Romani* etched into the leather, remembering his mother and fortifying himself against her memory. She was the only thing that made him feel safe growing up, and sometimes he still misses her, but he has to remind himself that she left him, too. Just like his father. He doesn't *know* what happened that day in the market, but when he went to meet her she wasn't there and didn't come back for the entire two days he waited. The door next to him swings open and he jumps, dropping the bracelet on the floor. He reaches out to pick it up, but Captain Delacroix steps inside first, retrieving it instead.

"Sir, please."

Captain Delacroix's gaze falls on the word *Romani*.

Frustrated tears wet Jerome's eyes and he swipes at them. He can't cry it won't *do*.

"Sir—" he says again, but Captain Delacroix holds up a hand, bidding him silent.

"You are of Romani descent." It's phrased as a statement, but it holds a question.

Jerome can't lie when directly asked. Not to Captain Delacroix.

"Yes, sir." He folds his hands behind his back and stands up straight. Unfortunately, it doesn't quell the sick feeling in his stomach. Captain Delacroix is going to dismiss him. He's sure of it. He can't believe he was fool enough to believe this could last. That he could belong. He dared think the word *home*, and this is what he gets for believing that. "My mother. Her family did try and settle in France, and she was raised there, so when I told you she was French I didn't feel like it was a lie, but I apologize. She gave me that bracelet when I was a child. It is the only thing I kept from the past."

"Your father?"

"He was a gadjo. He was English," Jerome explains at Captain Delacroix's perplexed look when he says the word for someone who isn't Romani. "My mother married him when she found out she was with child. She didn't want to leave her family, but he had us go to Bristol for a few years and then here to the West Indies, eventually, so she had to." He doesn't mention that after that, his mother never looked entirely happy again.

"You think that because of this I would no longer trust you?" Captain Delacroix asks, and he doesn't sound angry, somehow.

"The Roma are not well accepted," Jerome says, phrasing it diplomatically and damning his heart to hell. "I kept it from you because I am used to keeping it from everyone, if they don't suspect something."

Captain Delacroix rests a comforting hand on Jerome's shoulder, but his gaze is as intense as his son's, and Jerome cannot do anything but look back.

There's a pause, and Captain Delacroix asks another question.

"Were they pirates? Your parents?"

"Eventually," Jerome admits, his face hot with shame. "My father started out on buccaneer crews, but he went rogue when one of them kicked him off. He was arrested for it. Escaped jail, somehow. We didn't see him again."

"You are one of my most trusted men, Nicholas," Captain Delacroix continues, and Jerome doesn't miss the use of his first name. "I hope for the success of your future. You have absolutely proven yourself independent of any attachment to piracy, or the like."

Jerome's not sure if *or the like* means the inevitable transient lifestyle of his mother's people due to prejudice, but Captain Delacroix doesn't elaborate. Jerome doesn't quite know what to say, so he doesn't say anything.

Captain Delacroix's voice turns sad, and when Jerome looks up he sees affection in the captain's eyes. Affection for him. "What happened to your mother? You never really said."

Jerome shakes his head. "I don't know. I was separated from her one day in a market. I don't know what happened, and I never found her."

"Nicholas," Captain Delacroix repeats, gentle and reassuring. "I assure you that your place on this crew remains secure. You needn't worry—your secret is safe with me. However, it would be best if we don't let my father-in-law know the truth." Captain Delacroix tenses, as if fearing his father-in-law might appear. "He won't take kindly to the matter. But you may trust me. I promise. Kingston and this ship can be your home, should you wish it."

For a moment Jerome cannot respond, the world trembling beneath his feet.

Home.

He runs a hand over the sword sheath on his belt, a gift from the Delacroix family for his twenty-fourth birthday that was selected by René, who handed it to him that day with a shy but infectious grin.

I told Mama and Papa I wanted to put our family crest on it, René said. *Since you didn't seem to have one, I wanted to share ours. But they said it might make you uncomfortable. I hope you like it anyway.*

An excellent choice, Jerome said, touching the dark brown leather, his initials etched into the top. *I like it very much.*

"Jerome?" Captain Delacroix questions, the memory fading away.

"I just ...." He hates how inarticulate he is today. "Why are you so invested in me, sir?"

"When I met you"—Captain Delacroix is as careful with his words as he has always been with Jerome's wounded heart, even if Jerome never asked it of him—"I saw a young man with a great deal of potential. And I wanted to give that potential a chance. I saw an officer." He pauses, meeting Jerome's eyes again. "And even more than that, I saw a young man looking for a place to belong, and I felt the place might have been on my ship. And possibly as my friend. I have found both to be true." He clears his throat, folding his hands behind his back, but he still doesn't look away. "I've also seen you become like a brother to my son. That means a great deal to me."

"Thank you, sir." Jerome breathes in, regaining control of himself. "You do not blame me for Danso and the slave woman's escape? Even if they have become these troublesome pirates?"

Captain Delacroix shakes his head. "I do not believe that it has any bearing on your ability. Far more seasoned men than you have had similar, if not much larger, escapes happen on their watch. If they were so desperate to escape they would have found a way, no matter who was watching. And if they become enough of a nuisance, we will help catch them ourselves, should that help clear your mind of the matter. The Company has long hunted pirates in the Indian Ocean. I'm sure the same could apply here, were it necessary. In fact, there have been some rumblings about doing patrols around the islands, in the future, should the Navy request our help. We'll see."

There's a moment of quiet, and Captain Delacroix hands the bracelet over. Jerome puts it back in his pocket without sparing a glance.

"Would you care to go back up on deck?" Captain Delacroix doesn't comment on the bracelet. "René and Frantz were a bit worried about you. But if you need a moment?"

Jerome closes his eyes, an emotion he cannot recognize filling him up. No one has worried for him in a long time. Here is his chance to be a part of something, accepted, even, in a way he never really was on his other ships.

Here's his chance to be part of a family.

Maybe those stars he prayed to did hear him, that night.

"I'm fine. We were in the middle of a game when I overheard the news of Danso, and René was insisting on his own dramatic death."

A fond smile breaks out across Captain Delacroix's face. "He finally agreed to be the pirate, did he?"

"Volunteered, as it happens. I won't tell him, but I think he makes a far better pirate than I do."

Captain Delacroix chuckles, and they go up the steps onto the deck. The captain's swept away by Lieutenant Seymour for preparations for the officers' supper on the gun deck that evening, a tradition on the final night of any voyage. René and Frantz greet Jerome, looking worried.

"Are you all right?" René asks, moving up and down on the balls of his feet.

"Quite fine," Jerome assures him. "How about you and Frantz read some more of your book to me until supper?"

René nods, not pressing him. Frantz suggests the story of the Vodou loa Agwé he added to the book himself— Agwé is the patron of sailors—taking a turn reading aloud as René looks on with intrigue. Another hour passes, the sun beginning its descent below the horizon. The boys' voices faded into the background a good fifteen minutes ago, and Jerome glances down, realizing they've both fallen asleep on the deck, the men's work shanty serving as their lullaby. *Haul on the Bowline*, if his ears don't deceive.

"Boys," he says. "Boys. Wake up."

No response.

"René. Frantz."

Still nothing.

Jerome turns at the sound of footsteps coming toward him.

"They're lost to the dream world for a while," Lieutenant Seymour says, approaching them. "Michel got caught up with a dispute between a couple of our younger lads in the general sleeping quarters, but said you could put René in the cabin if he'd fallen asleep."

"Yes, sir."

Lieutenant Seymour picks a sun-soaked Frantz up off the deck, wrapping his arms securely around the boy. A piece of paper nearly falls out of Frantz's pocket—a letter from his mother, Jerome assumes. Lieutenant Seymour pushes it carefully back in, his fingers running over the beads of the necklace Frantz has worn since the day he arrived, and his own matching bracelet visible when his coat sleeve slides up. Something else from Frantz's mother, Jerome knows for certain. Chantal. He saw her from afar on her last visit to Kingston when she met Lieutenant Seymour and Frantz in the harbor. Lieutenant Seymour kissed her in view of everyone, earning a few less-than-friendly gazes from passerby. Frantz glared at the gawkers in response until his mother drew him to her, holding him tight.

Jerome reaches down, hooking his arms under René's legs and back and hauling him upward with more force than needed, forgetting how light the child is compared to himself. Even still, he remains asleep. He remembers the boys enlisting his help to build a sandcastle a few months after Frantz's arrival. They fell asleep abruptly then, too, caught under Morpheus' spell, deep and sudden, the sort of sleep Jerome can't replicate as an adult. He carried René home from the beach that day, delivering him into the arms of his mother as twilight fell.

"I will see you in about a half-hour," Lieutenant Seymour says, turning away toward his own quarters.

Jerome looks toward the horizon, the sun bleeding red and orange and gold across the blue sky as it sinks further and further beneath the water.

He makes his way toward Captain Delacroix's cabin, shifting René's weight so he can open the unlocked door. René moves, his eyes cracking open just slightly.

"Jerome?"

"I'm just putting you in bed." Jerome adopts the soothing tone he's heard from Mrs. Delacroix, certain his own deep voice is far less efficient than hers. "You fell asleep on deck, but we're nearly there."

René nods, exhaustion claiming him again as he closes his eyes, one hand reaching up and grasping Jerome's collar. Jerome moves the bedclothes back, laying René down and removing his shoes before tucking him in, fair hair spilling across the pillow beneath the sweaty red bandana. His eyes linger on the boy's sleeping face, a soft, warm feeling taking root in his chest. A younger brother was one of his greatest wishes growing up, and this feels like something close. He looks down as he leaves the cabin to change for supper, finding two blond hairs mixed in with his own black ones, resting together against the navy blue of his coat.

Interlude VI: The Origin of Captain Ajani Danso, the Pyrate Robin Hood

The Caribbean Sea aboard the Misericorde. November 1698.

"**M**ama!" Flora exclaims, running across the deck and leaping into Abeni's arms. Abeni catches her, delighting in her daughter's laughter. Flora's long, thick black curls cascade down her back, the edges finally even again.

"Careful running across the deck, please," Abeni says. "What are you so excited about, darling?"

"Papa Danso is teaching me how to swordfight!"

"Pardon?" Abeni tilts her head and glances at Danso, who looks sheepish.

"I asked one of the carpenter's mates to carve some wooden swords and I thought ...." He trails off. "I thought it might make a fun game for Flora while we're out at sea."

Abeni pretends to frown, her eyes narrowing playfully. "Ah, well in that case. I was worried you were teaching her how to use a cutlass."

"What?" Danso objects, his Barbadian accent thicker in protest. "I would never—" He stops, raising his eyebrows. "You're teasing me again. What have I said about teasing me?"

A grin plays at Abeni's lips. "That I should do it as often as possible."

"Why do I tolerate you?" A chuckle erases Danso's attempted scowl, and the laughter spreads to Flora.

"I don't have time to give you the list."

"Are you arguing?" Flora asks, bouncing up and down on the balls of her feet.

"No, little one." Danso laughs again, touching a finger to the edge of Flora's nose. Abeni marvels once again at just how much he's coming into himself. Slowly, but surely, all the same. "We're teasing."

"Oh!" Flora turns back to her mother, eager. "Can we show you what Papa Danso taught me?"

Abeni nods as Flora takes the second wooden sword from Danso's hand. Nearly since the day they rescued her Flora latched onto Danso, always calling him 'Papa Danso' and sometimes just 'Papa.' No one corrects her, including Danso himself. He asked her once if she minded, and Abeni assured him she didn't. She doesn't have to share a bed with Danso for him to be like a father to her little girl, or for him to be important to her, for that matter.

We're family now, aren't we? she asked him not long ago.

Yes, Danso said after a moment, testing the idea. *I do suppose we are.*

This certainly isn't the life she predicted, living on a pirate ship with her daughter calling the man she sees as a brother 'Papa', but she's happy. Happier than she ever remembers being in her tumultuous life. Free. They're still looking for Danso's nephew, Jahni, searching for information anywhere they can get it from Ebele's network of contacts, from the newspapers at slave auctions, or from the word of a sailor. Still, they haven't found anything. Abeni had at least known the name of the people who had her daughter. She's determined, nevertheless.

"En garde!" Flora shouts, clearly having just learned the phrase. "You scoundrel naval officer!"

Abeni's laugh bounces into the air, and she loses her breath with amusement at the flustered look on Danso's face.

"Wait." He pulls back with a quizzical expression. "I didn't agree to be the naval officer."

"*I'm* the pirate," Flora says, matter-of-fact. "So, you have to be the naval officer."

Danso winks at Abeni. "As you wish, my lady." He bows and Flora giggles, smacking her sword against Danso's with as much force as she can muster.

They continue until the sound of coughing comes up from the direction of the captain's cabin, and Danso stops, his face falling.

"What's the matter?" Flora looks between them. "Is Captain Ebele still sick?"

"He's not feeling well, no," Abeni says. "Say, Papa Danso and I have some duties we need to tend to. How about you go over to Asante?" She gestures to the sailing master, who stands at the wheel. "I know you like looking at his maps, and he doesn't look busy."

Flora nods with such enthusiasm that she nearly topples over, kissing Abeni's cheek when it's offered and dashing across the deck.

"Don't run!" Abeni calls out. Not that Flora will hear her. She turns back to Danso with a sigh, speaking in almost a whisper. "We make port in three days?"

"According to the calculations," Danso answers, "though the wind isn't cooperating as much as I wish it was."

"He's no better?"

"I relieved Robins last night and sat with him for hours," Danso replies, his eyes mired in sorrow. "Ebele coughed so much he barely slept, and when he did sleep I feared he wouldn't wake up. I think he caught something when we were in Jamaica speaking to that customs officer in St. James' Parish. He was looking for clues about Jahni, and now he's ill. I feel like it's my fault."

Because they don't have the name of the ship captain who bought Jahni's debt from the shopkeeper in Barbados, Ebele's idea was to look for slaver captains who might be known for dealing in children, thinking that a captain like that might be the sort to take on a child as an indentured servant, not to mention how easily he could pass him off as a slave if he wanted to. Indentured servants sign contracts for a certain number of years, often in exchange for passage to the New World and sometimes other debts, but Jahni would not be the first victim of a broken one, especially since he isn't white. If someone landbound bought the debt it would still be difficult to find out who, but a ship captain makes it an even more insurmountable task. Ships go everywhere.

"Danso," Abeni says, "one has nothing to do with the other. Him falling ill isn't your fault. He just wanted to help like he always does. You didn't make him. Mullins says he doesn't think it's consumption?" she continues, referencing the *Misericorde's* surgeon.

"He doesn't think so. But I don't think he's certain what it is, either. Ebele claims he's simply growing old, but he's trying to make it easier on the rest of us. There's a doctor in Tortuga Mullins knows, and we can make port there without too much fuss."

Abeni nods, her response cut off when one of the men approaches, informing them that the captain wishes to see them. They go into the cabin, finding Ebele lying in bed with the quartermaster, Mr. Coburn, at his side. Ebele looks frail and feverish, the bags under his eyes pronounced.

"I have discussed things with Coburn," Ebele says without preamble as soon as they sit down. "And I will be transferring the captaincy to him for the time being, until I call the vote in a few days and the new captain accepts and settles in."

"Captain," Danso protests, already grief-stricken. "You're not going to call for the vote already, surely?"

"I'm not long for this world, lad." Ebele lays a hand on Danso's knee in comfort. "I want to make sure things are tended to before I go."

"The men will vote for you, won't they Mr. Coburn?" Abeni asks, confused by the smile on the quartermaster's face.

"I'm taking myself out of the running." Coburn looks over at Ebele with fondness, a strand of melancholy running through. "I've enough money to retire from the life, and it's not my face on those wanted posters. I've got a widowed sister in the Virginia colony who could use my help with her children."

Danso glances at Ebele in question. "Who will the vote be between?"

"I've spoken casually to the others," Coburn says, "and haven't heard anyone speak of wishing to replace the captain. They did imply they'd vote for you if you were to put yourself in the running, Danso."

"But I haven't been on this ship nearly as long as so many others," Danso argues, panic flaring in his eyes. "It seems unfair, and I'm not sure I'm qualified for the post."

"The men will ultimately decide who replaces me." A cough mars Ebele's words, smearing them with sickness. "But this conversation is about whether or not you want to put yourself in the running. If no one runs against you then we shall simply call a yes or no vote. As to your qualifications, you showed bravery and skill in a fight very soon after you joined and haven't let up since, which earns respect, and there can be no arguments as to your sailing qualifications, which you had before you even joined the crew. There are a lot of older men on this ship, and I think we'll all agree we'd like to see someone younger take on the mantle. Someone who will expand upon what we already do and has the time to accomplish that. This life is a rough one. It takes its toll, even when you aren't so old."

Danso hesitates, indulging in his common habit of biting his nails. Abeni thinks he would make an excellent captain, but he ultimately has to decide that for himself.

Danso stops biting, settling for picking at his nails instead. Sunlight filters in through the window, lending his form a soft, golden sheen. "If that's what you wish, then I will."

"I want to know if it is what you wish," Ebele insists. He coughs again, breathing in deep when it relents, an unsettling, wheezy rattle growing in his chest.

Danso pauses, contemplating the question, probably because not many people have asked him what *he* wanted. Abeni knows the fears he has. Fear of losing this fragile happiness they've gained. Fear of civilization breaking down their door. She understands it entirely. She only hopes it won't drive his decision.

"Yes," he finally says, and there's something like stars in his eyes, a new light bursting to life. "It would be my honor."

Ebele makes an appearance on deck once they make port in Tortuga and gather for the vote, the whites of his eyes red from lack of sleep. No one's put forth their name in competition with Danso, so it's come down to a simple majority vote. Abeni isn't sure what will happen if Danso doesn't get enough votes, but the thrill of the ability to choose not only leaders, but objectives, doesn't escape her.

There is no king here. No queen. No emperor. Just them.

Mr. Coburn drew up pieces of paper for each crew member to mark *yes* or *no* for Danso, keeping the individual votes a secret and making it simpler for some of the men who are barely literate or not at all. Abeni squeezes Danso's shoulder when he tenses beside her. Flora looks on, reveling in the excitement.

"Well," Mr. Coburn says with a telling smile at Danso, "with only five votes against, it seems you have an overwhelming majority, Danso. Congratulations."

A loud cheer erupts from the men, and they surround Danso, patting him on the back and teasing him good-naturedly. Robins leads the pack of them, his red hair blown about by the breeze, and he catches Abeni looking, giving a dramatic wink. His less rambunctious partner Collins stands at his side, one hand in Robins' and the other clapping Danso on the shoulder.

"Is Papa Danso the new captain now?" Flora asks, tugging on Abeni's sleeve.

"He is." Abeni picks her daughter up, lifting her so she can see the commotion properly. "I think he'll be excellent."

"I think he'll make the best captain," Flora declares. She turns her gaze away from the jolly crowd, contemplating her mother. "Does that mean you'll get to take Mr. Coburn's place?"

Abeni laughs, kissing her daughter on the side of the head and eliciting a stream of giggles. "I don't know about that just yet. We'll have to vote on it once Mr. Coburn leaves."

Flora grows thoughtful. "I'd like it if you were."

"Thank you very much, darling," Abeni says, and Flora hugs her neck.

The crew's grown fond of her, but Abeni wonders if they'd accept a woman in charge of them, or if they'd come to her with their problems as they do Mr. Coburn, creating that vital bond of trust between crew and quartermaster. For the first time, she gives the idea real thought. The sun sets beyond them as the merry chatter continues, grief waiting in the wings. Stars appear in the sky, blurry and without their full power in the freshly fallen night. Abeni's attention goes back to Ebele as he beckons Danso over, and Danso jerks his head, indicating Abeni and Flora should join them. Ebele pats Flora's cheek before pressing Abeni's hand, his skin holding a chill even in the permanent heat of the Caribbean.

"If I can be proud of anything," Ebele says, looking around at the three of them, "I can be proud of helping bring you all together. And I hope you find the fourth you're looking for. Part of me senses you'll find more than that." He focuses on Danso, his breathing labored even from this small effort. "Congratulations, my lad." Ebele puts both hands on Danso's shoulders, and Danso's posture shifts as if taking on the metaphorical burden Ebele passes him. "I am most certain you will lead this crew well and honor the spirit of equality we strive for on this ship. Keep looking for that nephew of yours. Use my contacts to help you. I know you'll do me proud."

"I will try." Danso holds a reverence in his voice, the kind of sacred sound one might reserve for a deity, and though Ebele might not be a god, he is a hero. Danso sheds the man he was the night Abeni met him, turning into some combination of old and new: the man he was, the man he is, and the man he hopes to be all rolled into one. "I swear to you."

In this moment, Abeni's sure that one day people will tell stories about Danso the way they do about Ebele. She wonders if she'll be a part of the tales too, a Maroon woman's name whispered with awe and admiration as much as the heroes in legend.

Mr. Coburn brings out a box, removing the top and revealing a brand-new green coat for Danso, who slides it on at Ebele's request.

"Green, like that old English folktale Coburn's told me about," Ebele whispers. "Robin Hood. I think it's fitting. Stealing from the rich to give to the poor."

"Thank you, Captain." Tears well in Danso's eyes as he grasps Ebele's hand. "It is."

When they're alone for a small, fraction of a moment among everything, Danso grasps Abeni's shoulder, five words spilling from his lips.

"Tell me I won't fail."

"Never, Danso," Abeni whispers back, fervent in her faith in him. "I promise you won't fail."

A few days later, Ebele breathes his last, and they wrap his body in sailcloth before putting him to rest in the sea.

Abeni returns to her quarters afterward, finding a deep brown coat with golden embroidery on the sleeves laying on her hammock, similar to Ebele's own. A single piece of paper lies on top, a few words written in shaky black ink.

Put your name in for quartermaster.

And then, two more.

Maid Marian.

Chapter 7

Kingston, Jamaica. October 1699.

"Father, that's enough."

René's mother swipes her hand through the air, anger curled around her every word—the kind that might burn you. Unfortunately, René thinks, his grandfather doesn't seem afraid.

"René's tutor tells me he missed a question on his mathematics examination." Governor Travers' words, innocuous as they are, are nothing less than knives. René looks between his mother and grandfather, sweat dampening the underarms of his shirt and coat both. He and Frantz finished with the tutor they now share not twenty minutes before, met by his grandfather at the end of their lessons. The governor dropped in unexpectedly from Spanish Town, making demands of Mr. Edwards until the poor man looked like he might vomit.

"Mr. Edwards says he is doing very well," Astra argues, speaking overloud in the parlor where they usually take their lessons. "Missing a single question is scarcely something to concern yourself over. Besides that, if you come in here interrogating the poor man half the time we won't *have* a tutor, and we were looking to add a second. This isn't London. There isn't an endless supply of qualified academics."

"You do not dictate what I will and will not be concerned over, Astra," Governor Travers says, stepping forward. Astra flinches but holds her ground, staring him down. The governor's gaze moves, landing on Frantz with malice. "Ever since he's been taking lessons with this boy, René's grown distracted. I won't have it."

"Grandfather—" René tries, but his mother puts a hand on his chest, keeping him back.

"Actually, Mr. Edwards says he's done even better since Frantz's arrival," Astra points out. "They work splendidly together."

"I don't like my grandson spending this much time with an illegitimate mulatto child." Governor Travers's voice cracks through the air like a whip. "It is not proper, and I never should have allowed it."

Frantz clenches his fists and his jaw with a gleam of anger in his eyes, biting his lip against an argument. René's thoughts grow clouded, but he knows that the danger his friend faces here is greater than his own.

"Don't talk about Frantz like that." René moves closer to his grandfather and out of reach of his mother's hand. He's shaking and he wishes he wasn't, not in front of his grandfather, but he can't help it.

His grandfather narrows his eyes, glaring at René over the edge of his gold half-moon spectacles. "What did you say to me, René?"

"I said don't talk about him like that!" René shouts.

The world freezes when his grandfather's open hand comes flying toward him, connecting so hard with his cheek that he falls down. René's elbow smacks hard against the floor, pain shooting upward with a spasm of agony. His cheek stings and his elbow throbs and shock has sucked the breath from his chest. But he must stand up. He *must*. Terror rushes through him and he forces it back, getting to his feet. The injured cheek protests when he raises a hand to touch it. The terror fades into a strange buzzing sensation. Silence blankets the room. Thick. Stifling.

Until one voice breaks through.

"You *hit* him." Frantz steps toward the governor, and nausea sweeps through René, leaving him certain that *he* might vomit.

Astra recovers from her surprise, taking Frantz gently by the shoulders and preventing him from going forward.

Governor Travers stares at his hand, but any trace of remorse vanishes quickly as he scowls at Frantz's comment. "You will keep your mouth shut around me, boy." He glares at Frantz, then directs his attention toward his daughter. "Astra. Let's—"

Astra cuts her father off with a black look, and he falls silent—an unheard-of thing in René's estimation. She steps over to René, getting on her knees as carefully as she can in her gown before taking both of his hands in hers. René jolts instinctively at the touch, then grasps his mother's fingers. Having her near makes him feel less like the world is spinning.

"I think you should go, Father," Astra says. "Now."

Governor Travers puts his hat back on, anger staining his cheeks a mottled red. "This is not the end of this discussion."

He stalks toward the door of the parlor just as the front door opens, Uncle Arthur and Jerome coming in a moment later and looking perplexed. Arthur's eyes dart to René's red cheek, then back to Governor Travers.

"Just what exactly is going on here?" Uncle Arthur asks, his eyes narrowing.

"What's going on is that your idiot mulatto son is a predictably bad influence on my grandson!" Governor Travers shouts. "You—"

"That is enough." Uncle Arthur holds up a hand, cutting the governor off. "You will not speak that way about my son in front of him, or in front of me."

"I shall speak however I like," Governor Travers snaps. "How dare you?"

"Did you hit René?" Uncle Arthur asks, the tension in the room building to a breaking point, like the floor beneath their feet might snap in two.

Governor Travers narrows his eyes in turn. "It is none of your business if I did. I will discipline *my* grandson as I see fit. You don't get a say. I plan to be having more of one."

René glances over at Jerome, who stands stock still, his face expressionless and made of stone as he watches the scene in front of him. René almost reaches out before containing the impulse, fear rising like a monster in his chest. Does Jerome think he deserves to be hit? No. That can't be true. René changes his mind, tugging on Jerome's sleeve to get his attention. Jerome smiles quickly at him and pats his shoulder, mouthing a silent *it's all right* before drawing away again. Jerome has something in his hand, a notebook of some kind. René can't read everything, only the words *Robin Hood spotted near the Leeward Islands*, the rest trapped beneath Jerome's tight grasp.

"I am going to speak to Michel about this right now." Uncle Arthur leans forward, looking the governor directly in the eye, and René admires his courage. No one speaks to his grandfather like that, except his mother. Not even his father does.

"Do as you wish, but I would suggest you don't cross me, Lieutenant." Governor Travers jabs his finger in Arthur's direction. "Or you and your son will both regret it. You are far more trouble than you're worth, and I'll make sure Michel knows it. I can find someone to replace you as sailing master, I promise you that. And tell your son he'd best learn not to be smart with me."

"I'd like to see you try, Governor Travers." Uncle Arthur turns cutting and cold. He gestures to Frantz, pulling him to his side and wrapping a protective arm around him. "So long as I live, you will not threaten my son like this. Ever."

"Ohh," Governor Travers says, the sound making René shiver. "Don't challenge me, Lieutenant. One more wrong move from you, and I'll make sure you are out of Michel's inner circle permanently and back in London with your family. They're already quite embarrassed of you, aren't they? Then your brat will be away from my grandson and back in Saint-Domingue where he should be. At this juncture, you're lucky you're still standing here with your pride and your rank intact for speaking to me like this, and you will not do it again."

Governor Travers keeps his eyes trained on Frantz like a hunter watching his prey, and it scares René down to his bones. Uncle Arthur notices too, the first glimmer of fear appearing in his eyes. Every muscle in René's body tenses and tightens.

Uncle Arthur is never afraid.

"Sir," Uncle Arthur says, holding his position but evening out his tone. "Your family matters a great deal to me. I'm sure we can find some common ground and avoid these arguments."

Governor Travers holds up a hand, heading toward the door. "Stop. I've heard enough for today."

The governor slams the door behind him, leaving them dumbfounded. Uncle Arthur's gaze lingers on René's reddened cheek, and he squeezes Frantz's shoulder in comfort, still holding him close. René lets go of his mother's hands, pressure building behind his eyes. He dashes toward the front door. If he can just get out of here, if he can just get to the ocean, maybe he can breathe again.

"René!" his mother calls out, but he can't hear what else she says, opening the front door anyway and running down the drive, his grandfather's carriage kicking up dust just beyond. He does hear Uncle Arthur saying something to Jerome, something about letting Michel know, or asking him to wait in his office for him to pay a visit. René can't quite make it out. He jumps at the sound of footsteps behind him, a gentle hand grasping his sleeve.

"Woah, there," Uncle Arthur says. "Are you all right, René?"

"Yes." *No.* He wipes at his eyes, his voice a cut-through whisper falling to shredded pieces on the ground. "Just ... just please let me go."

Uncle Arthur complies, but René doesn't keep running, standing frozen and looking away from his godfather.

Uncle Arthur speaks again. "Your grandfather did hit you."

René's face grows hot, a sense of overpowering shame rushing through him.

"Could I take a look at your face?" Uncle Arthur asks, handling his words like fragile, breakable things, and the kindness in them makes René relent.

He turns and faces Uncle Arthur properly, tears spilling down his cheeks.

Uncle Arthur meets his eyes. "I would never hurt you. I hope you know that. Do you trust me?"

René hesitates, then nods. Uncle Arthur brushes his thumb against René's cheek, the touch gentle. The skin still stings, and René winces.

"It hurts?"

René nods once more but doesn't speak.

Uncle Arthur blinks away his own tears. "I don't think there will be bruising."

"I don't"—René bites his lip, trying to steady himself—"I can't make my grandfather happy about *anything*, and he gets angry over the smallest mistakes, and he won't listen. I feel like he hates me and I don't know why and—"

René's voice breaks, but his resistance bears no fruit, and he starts openly sobbing. Uncle Arthur envelopes him in a warm, snug embrace, running a hand up and down his back.

"You didn't do anything wrong. You didn't, René."

"Then why did he hit me?" René pulls back, his hands grasping the sleeves of Uncle Arthur's coat. "Why is he always telling me I'm doing something wrong? It makes me feel like I'm ... like I'm bad."

"I don't know, dear one. I don't claim to understand your grandfather, and I'm afraid his opinion of me is rather low. But you are not bad. I promise you."

"I try to be good, but nothing I do is right." René meets Uncle Arthur's eyes again, seeing nothing but love there. "I promise I try."

"You are a sweet, kind boy," Uncle Arthur assures him. "Don't let him make you think otherwise."

René wipes his eyes, embarrassed. "I hate that my grandfather doesn't like you, and that he says terrible things about Miss Chantal. And I don't like the way he treats Frantz. That was part of what we were fighting about today."

Uncle Arthur raises his eyebrows. "Do you mind my asking what happened?"

"He said Frantz was a bad influence." René lets go of Uncle Arthur's sleeve, clenching his hands into fists. "He said I shouldn't spend so much time with him, and I told him not to speak to Frantz that way, and that's when he hit me, because I shouted." He looks up, abrupt alarm striking him. "Will I not be allowed to see Frantz anymore?"

"Of course you will," Uncle Arthur says, firm, his hands resting on René's shoulders. "Never fear that. No matter what happens, that is not up for debate. Now, what do you say we go back inside? I'm sure your mother and Frantz are worried. I love you, my lad. You know that?"

"Yes. I love you too."

The wild, desperate desire to escape dies down inside René's chest, though it leaves behind a residue of fear and shame he can't quite rid himself of. He walks back inside, met with the fretful face of his mother.

"Darling, are you all right?" she asks, offering her hand out to him.

René takes it, his heartbeat finally slowing down, but the sense of humiliation he can't entirely parse out still won't go away. "I think so. Uncle Arthur helped."

His mother shares a smile with Uncle Arthur. "He tends to. Thank you, Arthur."

Another hand comes to rest on René's back, the touch familiar. Steady. Gentle.

"I'm sorry he hit you," Frantz says, his own eyes wet. "You don't deserve that."

"He shouldn't speak to you like that." René takes Frantz's hand tight in his own, hoping that he makes Frantz feel as safe as Frantz makes *him* feel.

Frantz shakes his head. "No, he shouldn't. But he shouldn't hit you, either."

Uncle Arthur puts a kiss on Frantz's curls, pride in his eyes. "Are you all right, my boy? René is right—Governor Travers should never speak to you that way."

"I'm all right, Papa," Frantz says, reassuring his father. "I know you wouldn't let him hurt me. But he shouldn't treat René like that. I couldn't let him."

Uncle Arthur smiles. "I was going to speak with Michel." He directs his words toward René's mother. "But I didn't see Jerome pass us."

"I sent him out the side door through my garden so he wouldn't disturb you, and he was going to alert Michel that you were coming," Astra answers. "We'll be all right here. Go. He listens to you."

"I'll be back as soon as I can," Uncle Arthur tells the two boys. "Don't you worry."

He grasps Astra's fingers and kisses her hand, a look passing between them that René's seen before. A worried look. He stumbled across them in the kitchen when he went down for some chocolates a few weeks ago, their voices filtering out beneath the door. He found them both with cups of tea, Uncle Arthur having brought over new seeds for the garden, but they dropped their conversation as soon as he stepped inside. They were talking about someone named Captain Barlow, a name René's heard before.

René watches his godfather go out the door, gratitude swelling up in his chest. Uncle Arthur's been a part of his life since he can remember, present in some of his first hazy memories of London, and he's never been anything but steady and brave and joyful. Seeing him so angry is something new, and it scares him.

"Oh my dears, I am so sorry," Astra says when Uncle Arthur leaves, leading them toward the dining room. "Let me get you a cold cloth all right, my love?" she asks René. "It will help with the stinging."

"Thank you, Mama." René sits down in one of the chairs and Frantz sits next to him, clasping his hand.

"I won't let him do that to you again," Frantz says, and his gentleness makes some of the tension in René's shoulders ease. "I swear, René."

"He'll hurt you worse." Anxiety pricks at every inch of René like stabbing needles. "I know he will."

His mother returns with a cool cloth, pressing it to René's face with a sad smile and leaving a kiss on his uninjured cheek. Mrs. Hudson brings a puzzle as a distraction, the pieces spilled out across the table when his father and Uncle Arthur arrive back at the house three-quarters of an hour later.

"Papa." Frantz gets up from his chair, walking over to his father and hugging him around the waist.

"Michel," Astra says. "You spoke to Arthur?"

"I did." Michel meets her eyes, squeezing her hand briefly before turning back to René.

René shrinks into his chair, his right hand curled around his left elbow.

What if his father thinks his grandfather was right?

What if his father thinks he's bad, too?

It makes his stomach hurt to think about it.

"Are you all right, my boy?" his father asks, squatting down in front of him.

René almost says no, tears threatening him again. He doesn't feel all right, but he also wants to show his father he can be brave. He blinks, shoving the impulse down and sitting up straighter. His father takes the hand grasping his elbow, pulling it back into his own.

"Yes," René says after a beat. "I think so."

"Does your cheek hurt?"

René shakes his head. "Not anymore. My elbow does, from hitting the floor."

His father pauses, looking worried and placing both hands on René's shoulders, instead. René flinches out of instinct, even if his grandfather is gone.

"I will not strike you, son." Michel grows even gentler now, and it does reassure René. "I promise. I will speak to your grandfather about doing so, as well as the way he spoke to Frantz that I know upset both of you."

René nods again, reaching out and hugging his father. Michel gathers him into his arms, pressing him close. René feels safe again. Safe with his father.

That is, until Michel speaks again.

"This is not your fault, my boy." Michel pulls away, running the back of his hand down René's cheek. "But you must try not to anger your grandfather, all right? I know it's hard."

His father sounds afraid. He sounds afraid like Uncle Arthur did earlier but deeper, and that frightens him.

Nausea creeps up from René's stomach. "Will I still be allowed to see Frantz? Please say I will."

"Yes of course," Michel whispers, his voice wavering just slightly. "That was never a question. It will never be a question."

René looks over at Frantz and catches his smile, some of the heaviness in his chest finally evaporating.

His father would never lie.

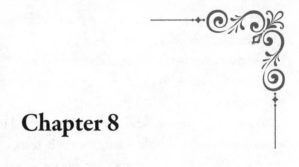

Chapter 8

Cap-Français, Saint-Domingue. June 1700.

Arthur spies Chantal on the beach as soon as he steps off the gang-plank, but Frantz gets to her first.

Frantz frees himself from Arthur's protective grasp, running as fast as he might down the dock, all thoughts clearly directed toward his mother. Arthur grins when the two crash into each other, Chantal picking up their gangly son and swinging him around in delight. Chantal's more beautiful than the last time he saw her, somehow, and he is as much a fool for her now as he was when they first met. He was here on East India business with Michel several years before he moved to Jamaica, and happened by her shop when he accidentally ripped a pair of breeches. He hasn't been the same since.

"Hello, my sweetheart," Chantal says. Her thick, curly braid hangs over one shoulder as she squats down to be at Frantz's level. She doesn't have so far to go now, for all that Frantz keeps growing taller. Arthur cannot believe how beautifully the sunlight kisses her golden-brown skin. "How are you? How is René?"

Less reserved around Chantal than anyone else—apart from René—Frantz rattles off several things at once, excited as he is to learn about anything and everything and impart the information to an eager audience. He says something about one of the navigation lessons Arthur has started giving him, and then something else about René's sword lessons with Jerome, and then something else about a story he heard in port, but as carefully as Arthur usually listens to his son, right now he can only gaze at two of the people he loves most in the world, wishing wishing *wishing* they could be like this always.

And as soon as his father is dead, they can.

A terrible thing to think, but true nonetheless. He only feels a pinch of guilt about it, given how unkind his father has been to him his whole life, caught up in his money and his reputation, and irritated with the son who seemed always in trouble. His mother is somewhat better, but not brave enough to stop his father, and it is his father's death that will give Arthur the inheritance that is currently keeping him apart from Chantal. The inheritance that will, even more than the money he's earned working, ensure Frantz's financial security. More of it will go to Arthur's older brother Matthew, who not long ago took over the family's lucrative shipping business, but Arthur will take what he can get. He wonders if he can last until then. He wonders if he can bear East India, and their practices.

"Papa?" Frantz asks with a laugh, part of him unearthed here in Saint-Domingue where he was born, that is not as present in Kingston. "What are you doing?"

"Apologies, dear one." Arthur echoes his son's laughter as he strides up to his family. There's a sticky feeling in the air, something apart from the humidity, like someone might be watching them. "I was rather lost in my thoughts." He stops in front of Chantal, whose eyes grow bright as Sirius in a late winter sky. "Hello, my love," he says, taking both her hands in his. That sticky feeling grows more prominent, though he doesn't turn to look just yet. "How are you?"

"Better now that you are here, as always." She runs the back of her hand down his cheek. One of her fingers is bandaged, as they so often are from the little needle pricks she gets from her work as a seamstress.

She is the gentlest person he knows, the kindest, and his heart beats faster as he catches her hand, pressing his lips to hers with enthusiasm out here in the harbor. There is nothing illegal about it in Saint-Domingue, unlike in many English colonies. Of course, that does not mean it is easy. Still, as Chantal returns the kiss with that steady warmth he knows so well, he cannot be bothered to care who sees—other people's judgment has never meant anything to him.

"Enough!" a voice calls out, and that odd sensation of a moment ago returns, interrupting his greeting with Chantal. "None of us need to see that display in broad daylight."

Arthur spins sharply on his heel, keeping Chantal's hand in his own and putting the other on Frantz's shoulder.

"Pardon, monsieur?" he asks, the thinnest veneer of politeness in his tone that will shatter any second.

"You heard me, Monsieur Seymour."

Arthur releases Chantal and Frantz, stepping in front of them and closer to the offended man. "You know me, do you?"

"I run slaves around the French Indies," the man says, jerking his thumb toward a ratty old slaver just down the harbor, the crucifix he wears swinging out from beneath his collar. It is against the *code noir*, after all, for anyone in a French colony to practice anything other than Roman Catholicism. "Anyone who makes port here knows you, with your wench and your bastard. It's a sin against God, isn't it? The rest of us don't need to see it, and we don't need your abolitionist nonsense, either. Men depend on the slave trade around these parts."

Arthur's face goes white-hot, and he clenches his fists, taking several deep breaths in a row as a small crowd of onlookers gathers nearby.

"I am not the one committing a sin here, monsieur." Arthur bites out the words, trying desperately to avoid hitting this man. The bastard deserves it, but Arthur fears trouble for Chantal if this escalates. Though, he would not be the first to get into a brawl on the beach. "I am not the one enslaving other people. *That* is depravity. And you will not speak to my family in such a way again. Am I understood?"

The man steps closer, several of his compatriots not far behind him. "You think you're so high and mighty but, you're just a hypocrite, working for East India. Go strum your harlot somewhere else."

Chantal says something, Arthur is certain she does, and Frantz too, but he can't hear any of it. He can't hear anything other than the ringing in his ears as he takes four long strides forward, cocking his arm back before socking the sailor directly in the nose so hard the man goes tumbling to the ground. Blood spills onto the sand, and it takes every ounce of Arthur's self-control not to strike the man again. An image of René appears in his head, an image of the governor's handprint red and mottled on his skin. This sailor is not an innocent boy, but still, Arthur will not hit a man when he's already down. He will not be like Andrew Travers.

Chaos follows.

Three of the slave ship men come for him, but oddly, he isn't alone. No, two of the onlookers, a sturdy-looking, dark-skinned man with long, tied-back locs, and a Black woman with a yellow bandanna are there too, the woman's hand on the man's arm as if warning him to be careful. Arthur's ribbon comes loose as he sends a well-aimed kick at the stomach of the fellow swinging toward him, something he learned as a young man while sailing on the ship of Michel's merchant uncle, who said he had a knack for a brawl. Michel didn't much like that, but Arthur was delighted. He swipes his hair out of his face while the man with locs takes down another sailor, and his woman companion a third. Someone shouts, and more men start coming down from the slaver—Arthur notes the name for later—but then there's an arm going lightly around his waist, ushering him away along with Chantal and Frantz.

"Where are we going?" Arthur asks, making sure Chantal and Frantz are in front of him, his boots kicking up sand as they go.

"Keep running," the man says, and he looks familiar. He looks ....

"If you get away fast enough they won't be able to pin you down, or it will get them in trouble too," the woman adds.

I'd like to see them try is what Arthur doesn't say. He doesn't like to use his clout as an officer on a powerful East India ship often, but he will in this case if he has to. He abruptly remembers the light bag of clothes he brought along, wondering if it was left on the sand, but Chantal has grabbed it. Arthur sweeps Frantz up into his arms, noting that his son is growing tired from the abrupt getaway. They leave the beach behind them, stopping near a grove of palm trees not a quarter mile from Chantal's house, where she also runs her business.

"Thank you." Arthur lets Frantz slide down, trying to catch his breath as he takes a good look at the man and woman in front of him. "I—"

"Stay safe," the man says, before Arthur can even finish his thought, and there's something in his gaze, like they might have met before, somehow, even if Arthur knows they haven't.

Then there's only the press of a hand to his shoulder and the pair are gone, the man's green coat blowing in the wind.

Wait ....

A green coat. Green like the Robin Hood legends of old. He hasn't heard tell of a garment color in the wild stories beginning to trickle through port cities across the New World about Robin Hood, but he's definitely heard about that particular pirate's woman quartermaster. He *knew* the man's face looked familiar. He saw it on a wanted flyer in Kingston, freshly put up in the center of town a few weeks ago. That was him. It must have been.

"We should get home," Chantal says, a nervous edge to her voice as she presses a kiss to Arthur's cheek. She takes Frantz's hand, but he doesn't move when she tugs gently upon it, staring off into the distance where the potential pirates disappeared.

"Frantz?" Arthur asks. "All right, my lad?"

"Was that ... were they ...." Awe slips into the spaces between Frantz's words, the awe that took root in Arthur's heart the very first time he heard about this Robin Hood fellow, no matter Michel's disapproval. "Was that Robin Hood and Maid Marian?"

"Robin Hood?" Chantal looks at Arthur in question.

"Some pirates who are starting to become quite famous," Arthur says in answer. "You know, son, I think they might have been." He picks Frantz up again as fascination pulses through his veins, and he might be a young lad again at the docks in Wapping, listening to the madcap stories of sailors. He should tell his son not to admire pirates, but he cannot summon the desire to do so. "But don't tell your Uncle Michel, all right? Promise me."

Frantz nods in earnest, but he tilts his head, and Arthur knows there's a question coming. "May I tell René? He can keep a secret."

Arthur can't help but grin, knowing he shouldn't be encouraging his godson to keep secrets from his father, but Michel feels half-lost to him, these days, and he knows how much René would love the story, collecting them as he does.

"Yes," he says, touching the end of Frantz's nose. "You may tell René."

"Why did you ask Frantz not to tell Michel?" Chantal inquires several hours later when they're alone in their small bedroom, a familiar Caribbean rain pattering on the tin rooftop. She picks up her brush from where she sits in front of the mahogany vanity Arthur bought her last year, starting in on her hair. "About the man and woman who helped us, I mean. That you think are pirates. Not that I'd be surprised. Pirates are always here, to the delight of the townspeople and to the chagrin of the governor and the planters."

"Here." Arthur stills Chantal's hand, his fingertips touching hers as he slides the brush out of her hand. "Let me. Start from the ends, right?"

A fond, featherlight smile slides across Chantal's lips, the smile she reserves for him.

"Michel, you will not be astonished to know, does not care for pirates," he says, brushing her hair gently in the way she taught him while he stayed with her in the final weeks of her pregnancy. The decision to go to her made his parents furious, and he nearly lost his position with East India for it, but he wouldn't give up that time for the world.

She quirks an eyebrow. "And you do like them." It isn't a question at all, and she does not sound surprised. "I see where Frantz gets his interest."

He meets Chantal's eyes in the mirror. "I like these pirates, at least. They free enslaved people. They steal from merchants who are cruel to their men, and leave some of the plunder at doorsteps across the West Indies. I can't say I *don't* approve somewhat. If I tell Michel what happened today he will tell Jerome, and as luck would have it, the pirate called Robin Hood is also a man called Danso, who, along with a woman, escaped from Jerome a few years ago. It was how he ended up on Michel's ship. And if I'm right, if they helped us ... I simply do not want to hear Michel's lecture about how I should have turned them in."

She hears the pain in his voice, he knows she does, but she doesn't speak to it just yet.

"You were very brave today, you know. But I don't care what wretches like that slaver captain say about me. I'd rather you not get hurt over it."

Arthur smirks as he lays the brush back on the vanity, leaving Chantal's hair down. "They didn't even get a swing in on me."

"Arthur."

He bends closer, wrapping one arm around her chest, and she takes his hand snugly in her own. "I care what they say about you and our boy," he whispers. "But I shall try and keep my temper, for your sake. Next time."

"Hmm," she replies, sounding thoroughly unconvinced. "You did look terribly dashing. I won't complain about that."

He kisses her, long and deep and ardent, and he wants to savor this. He wants to imprint every feeling he has for her in this one moment, because the moments are too far apart. She keeps his hand as they go to bed, sliding beneath the covers but not yet blowing out the candles. Their fingers intertwine as they lay side-by-side, and Arthur thinks that no lightning strike, nor God himself, could make him let go. Chantal tucks her head beneath his chin, and her body warm against his is a miracle. The events of earlier prickle deep in his chest, blossoming into a worry he cannot chase away. He wants safety, for his family. He wants safety, for himself, so that he does not have to look behind and wonder who might be watching, waiting, to harm all three of them for daring to break the rules.

"What's going on with Michel?" she asks, returning to her earlier line of questioning. The wind kicks up outside, sending an eerie whistle through the cracks in the window. Frantz will be knocking at their door before the night is out—Arthur's told him too many ghost stories for it to be otherwise. "There's something. I can tell. Other than not wanting to tell him about the pirates."

Arthur sighs. "He's just not himself. About anything, it seems. The Governor's doing, I have no doubt. And now this business with Travers hitting René, recently." He shakes his head. "Michel reprimands the governor, but it scarcely does any good. He has to be firmer. Do more. Something. René deserves to feel safe."

A beat passes, and Chantal scoots even closer as Arthur's arm slides around her waist.

"You can't make Michel's choices for him, you know," she tells him, still very kind. "He has to make them for himself. And you will protect René, should he need it. If things grow too terrible, perhaps you could convince Astra to bring René here while Michel sorts things out with Governor Travers. I know you would not like to fight with Michel in such a way, but you love René enough to do it, and I doubt Astra would find fault with the idea."

Arthur breathes in Chantal's scent, and she smells of fresh rainfall and the vegetable garden she keeps outside. He smiles again, thinking of Astra and her flower garden, both women feeling at home planting new life in the dirt. They liked each other when they met, and he hopes one day there will be time for them to grow that acquaintance. Astra has never been anything but a trustworthy friend, and they hold secrets between them, secrets of the small rebellions in Kingston that even Michel does not know, the truth of Captain Barlow's exploits foremost among them. The man in the green coat comes back to him again, and he recalls asking Astra once, shortly after the infamous escape of Danso and his woman companion in Kingston, if she had heard the rumors that Barlow helped them escape. She just smirked in that particular way of hers, the way that most people miss because they don't suspect intrigue from a woman like her, and said she had. Arthur, for one, thinks she might have helped the man and woman he saw today, and that secret he will take with him to his grave.

Chantal, however, is the only one who knows his secrets about Michel, about his feelings for other men, as equal within himself as his desire for women.

There was a kiss, in boarding school, a kiss that was an *almost*. Many memories from his earlier years have faded, but that one never has. He passed an exam he was convinced he would fail, and then, without giving it thought—something his father often accused him of—he kissed Michel on the mouth while alone in their shared room. And most astounding of all, after a split second's hesitation, Michel, prim, proper, perfect Michel, kissed him back. Arthur was gentle at first, and then it was Michel who deepened the kiss, eagerly letting Arthur explore. They fell onto the small boarding school bed with the clumsy passion of adolescents, Arthur's hands in Michel's soft hair, their clothes mussed, and they kissed until they couldn't breathe anymore. They fell asleep next to one another, Arthur's body aching to touch Michel anywhere, everywhere, but he would not push his friend. Not ever.

The next morning when he awoke, Michel turned from his place sitting on the side of the bed, his cheeks flushed red.

We mustn't, Michel began, his words heavy with shame, a shame that's followed him ever since. *I have to go to the library. I'll see you this evening.*

Arthur simply nodded, even as his heart cracked. Their friendship did not change, but they never spoke of it again, and Arthur dared not bring it up for fear of losing one of the most important people in his life, a friend he could not imagine being without. He still can't. There is no doubt Michel is in love with Astra, but Michel is like him. He's certain of it.

When he found Chantal, she set his heart on fire. He loved her and he loved her and he loved her, and he did not look back. She soothed the sharp pain beneath his ribs, the one that felt like the sound of Michel's name. He loves Michel and he always will, but as his dearest friend, that old, almost unbearable infatuation now just the distant hum of a song he once knew.

"I know." He slides his ankle between hers, the rhythm of her breaths matching his own. "I know I can't." He hesitates, unsure of how to bring this up to Chantal, unsure of how to speak to the brewing instinct he's felt lately, born from a place of fear that he does not like to admit aloud.

"I brought a will with me," he says, a righteous boom of thunder nearly drowning him out, "and the paperwork to enter into *placage* with you. I don't know the specifics of how that will work, given you live in a French colony and I in an English one. It is not the marriage I want, not yet, but I could quietly settle the money and property I do have on you and Frantz, should anything happen to me, without my father knowing. Even if he did find out, he only stipulated that I could not marry or live with you in order to keep my inheritance. He cannot argue the point on this. The law says I may do this and have a wife. Of course I will not, unless she is you."

"Arthur." Chantal pulls back, searching his face. "Why do you think something will happen to you?"

"I'm a sailor, my love," he says softly, the truth of that hovering between them and neither reaching out to touch it. "There is always a chance. I want the two of you to be safe, to have something if I am gone and my inheritance is lost. That's all I'm asking." He takes a deep breath, tears springing to his eyes. "I will marry you legally one day, Chantal, but you are my wife now. Please know that."

"I know." She puts herself flush against him, grasping onto the sleeve of his nightclothes. "I will agree to this if it eases your mind, and I do not object to any attempt at securing Frantz's future. Whatever we can do to manage that, I will do."

He does not say that if something should happen to both of them that Frantz's custody will pass to Michel, because he cannot bear to even speak aloud the idea of something happening to Chantal. They can discuss that piece tomorrow, though Michel and Astra are the only choice, should the worst happen, in order to keep Frantz out of his family's hands.

"You know," Chantal says, and she's reading his mind, as usual, "I saw a ship the other day with crates bearing the stamp of your family's company. We don't usually see English goods here. We might not for long, with talk of a war brewing, besides."

Arthur rolls his eyes. "Matthew expanding the empire, I assume. He wrote me a letter recently, and I have yet to respond. I'm sure it's driving him mad."

"What did he want?"

"God knows. I haven't even opened it. If I could simply replace Matthew with another chap like Michel's brother Remy, that would suit me just fine."

Chantal laughs, and they fall asleep not long after. Frantz comes in sometime during the night, when the storm reaches its peak and lightning casts a violent glow across their bedroom window, making himself comfortable between them beneath the covers. This, Arthur is certain, is something he could get used to, and it drives the remaining dark thoughts from his mind. He thinks of the man and woman who helped them, and the spark he saw in the man's eyes. That spark of rebellion. He remembers the old tales boys would tell when he was growing up in London, tales of a crusader turned thief in Nottingham, the stories of the green coat and the merry men so ubiquitous and treasured that they didn't even need to be written down to live on.

Robin Hood, indeed.

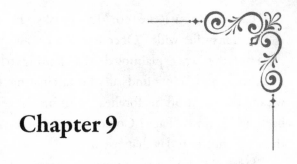

Chapter 9

Kingston, Jamaica. September 1700.

———◦◊◦———

"**Y**ou use the backstaff to measure the altitude of the sun, and you keep your back to it to see the shadow cast on the horizon vane," Frantz says, committing the information to memory. "And that measures the latitude and that's ...." He shuts his eyes, determined to get it right. "North and south? Of the equator?"

"Good show, Frantz!" Arthur leans over to point at something on the chart, his shadow covering the page as the sleeve of his dark green coat brushes the paper. "You can also use other celestial bodies like Polaris, also called the North Star."

"Polaris is one of the brightest stars!" Frantz exclaims, enthusiastic at the lesson. "Mama told me that."

"She and I used to look at the stars a great deal, when we first met," Arthur tells him, nostalgia thick in his voice. Frantz knows well the details of his father's family and the conditions they put down when he was born, and how it prevents his parents from living together. If they try, any and all money of theirs will be cut off. Connections. Everything. Frantz knows those things are important, but he hates it because he just wants all three of them together for more than a week or two at a time.

"Polaris is used for latitude largely because it stands almost motionless," his father continues. "Longitude, I'm afraid, is a bit more difficult to measure because of the movement of the earth. There's a method called the lunar-distance method we use now, though it's still being refined. I'll explain it to you next time we're at sea."

"Can you show René too?" Frantz asks. "He wants to learn more."

Arthur smiles wide. "Of course. René is always welcome."

His father was explaining dead reckoning to him before they moved on to latitude, and Frantz finds all of it fascinating. He blinks against the sun, wiping the sweat off his forehead with his sleeve and sliding his spectacles back up his nose. "Papa? Could we move into the shade of that tree over there? It's hotter today than usual."

"Splendid idea." Arthur picks up their books and papers, as well as the flintlock pistol he was using earlier to show Frantz how to shoot targets, before moving over to the tree. They settle down again, but the moment of silence gives Frantz a chance to start worrying.

His mother's ship is late.

She was meant to arrive five days ago. The passenger ship his father paid to bring her here hasn't arrived, and there has been no letter. Ships are late all the time, but as the days keep passing, his knowledge of the usual length of the journey from Saint-Domingue to Jamaica—depending on the wind and the current—spins around in his head, anxiety gnawing at him.

Akoma mu tɔfe, his mother said—my sweetheart, in Twi—when they were bidding her goodbye after their last visit to Saint-Domingue, one hand running through his dark curls. *Learn your lessons well, all right? I know you'll have even more interesting things to tell me when I come to Kingston. Tell René I'll be ready for more of his stories. I love you.*

If his parents lived together, he wouldn't need to worry about waiting on a ship. He hates the way worry clouds his mind, preventing him from thinking, and thinking is his best strength.

"Papa?" Frantz asks. "Are you worried about Mama?"

"I'm sure her ship will arrive soon." Arthur's voice goes just a touch higher than normal, betraying his anxiety. "But if it doesn't make port here in a few more days, you and I will go to Saint-Domingue and see if anything's happened. The ship may have met some unexpected repairs, or any number of things."

Frantz twists his fingers, not appeased. "What if she was in a shipwreck?"

"I haven't heard word of anything like that in the area yet." Arthur turns Frantz's face gently toward his. "Let's not allow our imaginations to run wild. What we invent is often worse than what happens."

Frantz nods, and the knot in his stomach loosens, but it doesn't entirely disappear.

She'll show up soon. She has to. She will. Five days is nothing.

"Can we walk?" Frantz asks. "I think René might be around here, somewhere."

"Of course." Arthur gets up, packing their things into a bag and slinging it over his shoulder, a piece of his brown hair falling loose from his ribbon, the sun streaking several strands auburn. "Is René out sparring with Jerome this morning?"

Frantz nods. "They fought a few days ago, but I think René isn't angry anymore."

"René angry at Jerome?" His father furrows his eyebrows. "Why?"

Frantz sighs. "René snuck out to the docks a few nights ago. Aunt Astra and Uncle Michel were out at a supper party, and his grandfather was staying at their house and René didn't feel like being around him anymore, so he went for a walk by the shore. Jerome found him and took him home, even though René said he was trying to avoid Governor Travers, but Jerome wouldn't listen. When René got home Governor Travers was there, and he slapped René hard on the bottom almost ten times for misbehaving. He called him a *monstrous boy*. René told his parents, but it was already over by then. I don't like it, Papa. Him hitting René like that."

"I'll have a talk with Michel. I'm afraid Governor Travers believes in punishments that are more common than they ought to be, but I know Michel does not, usually," Arthur assures him, irritation slicing into his tone, an irritation Frantz isn't sure he has heard directed at Uncle Michel before. "Was Jerome there? When Governor Travers did that?"

Frantz shakes his head. "No, René said his grandfather took him upstairs to Uncle Michel's study and sent Jerome away."

"Hmm," Arthur says, tapping his chin. "Perhaps René can stay with us tonight. That might cheer the both of you up."

"Yes, please," Frantz agrees.

He hates the way the governor treats René. He hates the way René's face falls whenever the governor walks into a room. Frantz doesn't like hating anyone, but he's certain he hates Governor Travers. He's also certain Governor Travers hates him, and his father, too.

He makes me feel like something's wrong with me, René confided to Frantz a few days ago. *Do you think there's something wrong with me?*

No, Frantz said emphatically. René is his best friend, and he can't stand to hear him sound that sad. *There's nothing wrong.*

"Ah, but look!" His father points down the beach once they've walked a bit, sunlight making the turquoise water glimmer. "There's René and Jerome now. They are sparring."

René and Jerome stand a few feet away with their new training foils, a knob attached to the bottom to prevent injury since René won't move to a real small sword for a few years. The swords cross over and over again with a sharp, metallic sound, and Jerome's saying something Frantz can't hear, but he sees René adjust his grip. Both of them move in a fluid way that almost looks like dancing, Jerome with more strength and René with more speed. They're practicing what looks like a parry and attack combination, and when René gets a hit in, Jerome's eyes brighten with pride.

"*Good,* René," Jerome says. "The timing was perfect but watch your distance, you were a little too close. Let's try the circular parry again."

The art of swordsmanship is like chess, Frantz remembers Jerome telling René not long ago. *You must be aware of not only what you're doing, but you must anticipate what your opponent might do. That is as crucial as your own choices.*

"Hello, you two!" Arthur calls out. "Care to take a break and join us on our walk?"

René grins when he spots them, the concentration receding from his face. He looks over at Jerome with a tiny trace of anxiety, the residue of their old argument still present. "May we, Jerome? Please?"

Jerome raises his eyebrows, not fooling any of them when he fights a smile. "Yes, we may. Though I didn't think anything could tear you away from sparring."

"My hand is tired. And besides, Frantz and Uncle Arthur are here! That is one thing that's more interesting than sparring."

Jerome does smile before looking up at Arthur, who winks at him. "Indeed."

"We were just going to walk a while," Arthur says. "Perhaps we can go toward Michel's office."

Frantz falls into step with René as his father and Jerome talk about something to do with the *Steorra*. René tucks his hand into the crook of Frantz's elbow after handing his foil to Jerome, listening intently about the earlier navigation lesson. A group of sailors stand not too far from the *Steorra* in the harbor when they pass by, at least two of them appearing injured and all of them in an argument with their captain over wages. Frantz has seen plenty of ill and bruised men come off the merchant and naval ships that sail into Kingston. His father's crew doesn't look like that, but sometimes he wonders if the way Uncle Michel and his father treat their sailors is less common. The sharp, salty scent of the ocean mixes in with the smell of dirty clothes as several crews embark from their ships, many of the sailors heading toward the nearby taverns. They keep walking, and Frantz asks René about his own lesson before they're both distracted by the crowd of people gathered around something. Another scent floods Frantz's nose. Something sour. Something that smells like the damp, sweat-soaked sheets from a bed after someone's been feverish. A voice rings out.

"Sold! To the highest bidder."

Frantz's stomach sinks, and he realizes what's happening before they even round the corner to find proof.

A slave auction.

He's seen them in Saint-Domingue, but he hasn't seen one in Kingston, nor one this large. He has seen enslaved people here of course, because you can't live in Jamaica and not see them every day, but this is different. Frantz catches René's eye, understanding passing across his friend's face as another *sold* pierces the air. Arthur spins on his heel, his hands coming down onto Frantz's shoulders. Jerome stops too, discomfort twisting his expression.

"Do you have your freedom papers?" his father asks. "Show them to me please, my boy."

Frantz tilts his head. "Papa, they aren't going to take me."

"I know." Arthur swallows back some of the alarm roaring in his eyes. "But just show them to me, all right?"

Frantz reaches into his coat pocket, pulling out the neatly folded papers he always carries.

"Good." His father speaks in a whisper. "Good. Let's just ... let's walk and ... I need to see something."

The boys and Jerome follow, but Frantz doesn't think he's ever seen his father look so afraid, at least not since the day he fought with Governor Travers over striking René.

And then, Frantz realizes.

His mother.

His father is worried she's been picked up by slave runners. That must be it. There are groups around the West Indies that kidnap free Africans and pass them off as slaves because it's easy to do. It's not nearly as common as bringing people from Africa, but it does happen now and again. Despite the thick, wet heat outside, a sudden chill runs up Frantz's spine and across his arms, a tight, squeezing pressure taking root in his chest. René's hand slips into his as they walk forward, following on Arthur's heels while Jerome brings up the rear.

The auction appears more clearly before them as they round the corner, and they find themselves at the edge of the large crowd. Frantz sucks in a breath as he looks at the slaves. Some stand on the auction block while others are gathered in a knot nearby, their hands tied in front of them. Despite their skin shining from the grease the slavers use, and despite the new clothes they're wearing, he cannot miss their ill, yellowed eyes, their posture steeped with exhaustion. A few of them look stronger than others, but none of them look healthy, even if the people purchasing them might fool themselves into thinking so. Someone buys an enslaved man from the block, and the wailing of one of the women mixes in with the crying of the child at her skirts. The man calls back in a language Frantz recognizes: the Twi dialect his mother taught him bits and pieces of, passed down from his Akan grandparents who once lived on the Gold Coast of Africa before they were plucked away. The man struggles against the guards holding him to the point where Frantz thinks he might slip loose, but he's silenced when someone strikes him, the *thwack* echoing into the air.

Run to the mountains, he wants to shout. *Run to the Maroons in the mountains.*

The Maroons are fierce, an even match for English soldiers.

"Jerome," Arthur says, "I need you to stay here with the boys for a moment, please. Do not move. Do not let Frantz out of your sight."

Jerome nods, paying strict attention. "I won't, sir."

Arthur speaks to Frantz once more. "Stay here, dear one. Do not leave René and Jerome for any reason, and hold your papers in your hands. I'll be right back."

"Yes, Papa." Frantz squeezes his father's hand in an attempt at reassurance, and it draws out an inch of a smile. "I won't move. I swear."

His father squeezes back before silently moving along the edge of the crowd until he can get a look at the slaves up for auction.

"He's looking for my mother," Frantz whispers into René's ear, his voice shaking. "He won't say it. But that's what he's doing."

René tightens his grip on Frantz's hand, and it's the only thing anchoring Frantz to the ground beneath his feet. It's the only thing stopping him from retching or crying out in dismay, which won't help those slaves.

What if his mother is ....

No. *No.* His father is only looking to make sure.

That has to be it. It has to be. Five days is nothing. Ships are late all the time.

But if something's happened to her, if she has been taken, he knows his father will find her. His father is brave—both of his parents are—and Frantz knows Arthur would do anything to find Chantal. Frantz touches the necklace of brown beads his mother gave him before he left Saint-Domingue, the smooth wood drawing out a memory.

These three in the middle are painted, his mother explained when she gifted it to him. *Blue, white, and sea green. The colors of Agwe. The patron loa of sailors and fishermen. Do you remember?*

Yes, Mama, Frantz answered. *I like those stories.*

Your grandparents used to say that he watched out for us when we started our life here on Saint-Domingue after their dying slave master freed them, his mother said. *And I know he'll look out for you on your journey to Jamaica. Keep this with you, and you'll always have me, too. Your Papa has a matching bracelet that I made him.*

Arthur returns to them after a few minutes, looking relieved, though he's still holding tension in his shoulders.

"Come on boys, lets ...." He trails off as he looks back into the crowd, and at first, Frantz doesn't see what he's looking at, not until he hears René's soft gasp. He follows his friend's gaze to a man standing near the block. A man buying a middle-aged female house slave.

Governor Travers.

Everyone in the crowd stands a few feet back out of deference, which keeps the line of sight between Governor Travers and their foursome clear. Governor Travers seems to sense he's being stared at, because he glances over after a few seconds, wrinkling his nose in distaste when he sees Frantz. He looks over the edge of his half-moon gold spectacles as the sun glints off the frames, locking eyes with his grandson. Jerome grasps René's wrist, and Frantz isn't sure if it's a comfort or a warning. René jumps at the lightning in his grandfather's eyes, and Frantz tugs him closer. Governor Travers turns his right hand palm up and arches his forefinger, beckoning René forward. Jerome lets go of René's wrist, and there's so much being said in something other than words, there's so much happening, that Frantz can barely think for all the blood pounding in his ears, the thoughts dashing through his brain so fast he can't make sense of them. He smells nervous sweat in the air, the scent clammy and bitter.

René shakes his head, and there's something other than fear in his eyes. Something angry. Something blindingly bright that Frantz is not sure he's seen before. Not exactly like this. It is not a happy brightness.

"You're not going with him, René," Arthur whispers, pressing René's shoulder. "We're leaving."

Arthur's hand slips into Frantz's free one, holding more firmly than normal. Governor Travers narrows his eyes and meets Arthur's gaze, the two men glaring at each other until people start to notice, a murmur of curiosity spreading through the crowd. The four of them leave the governor and the auction behind them, but Jerome looks back one last time, fear glimmering in his eyes. Frantz knows he can't ever *really* leave the auction behind, because auctions like this take place all over the ports of the New World, and the grandfather of his best friend, the most powerful man in Jamaica, was just taking part.

He listens for the sound of the governor's footsteps all the way home.

"**A**re you boys sure you're all right?" Arthur asks the question of both of them, his eyes dull with worry. Frantz doesn't like it.

"We're all right, Papa."

They're in Frantz's room, the two boys ready for sleep in their night-clothes and Arthur in just his breeches and shirt, coming to bid them good-night. Empty cups of tea sit on the bedside tables, prepared a half-hour ago by their housekeeper Mrs. Brooks. René is staying over, and Frantz is grateful, because he doesn't want to be alone. If René wasn't here, he'd probably sleep in his father's bed.

"I'll be just down the hall if you need me." Arthur presses a kiss to the top of René's head before putting his hands on Frantz's shoulders, the touch reassuring and gentle and exactly what Frantz needs. "I'm so sorry about to-day, Frantz. If you want to talk about it more, I'm here."

Frantz pulls one of his father's hands down, clasping his smaller fingers around Arthur's own. "I know, Papa."

Here in Kingston, he misses his mother and the small community of freedmen he knew in Saint-Domingue. In Saint-Domingue, he missed his father, longing for the opportunities and the friends he might make here in Jamaica. Sometimes, he fears he doesn't fit anywhere.

"You belong here with us. I promise you," Arthur says, like he might be capable of reading minds, a fierceness in his voice as he holds Frantz's fingers tight and puts a kiss on his forehead. "And I will keep you safe, dear one. Always."

Frantz hugs his father close, smelling the faint, apple-scented traces of his cologne as he leaves the room. Even in the early years when Arthur didn't yet live in the West Indies, Frantz knew his father loved him. Arthur visited when he could, sending letters and gifts constantly. When he moved to Jamaica and came to visit more often, Frantz was overjoyed. He misses his mother so much, but he also likes getting to live with his father. None of this is fair, because they should all be together. One day they will be. His father has sworn it, and he knows it.

Frantz pulls back his hunter-green bedclothes, and he and René slide under them into the soft, cream-colored sheets beneath. Only, when Frantz blows out his candle, René hesitates.

"What is it?" Frantz questions, and there's a glint in René's blue eyes, a glint that says he might be up to some mischief.

"I brought something with me." René reaches over toward the table on his side of the bed, grasping a box Frantz saw him pull out of his bag earlier, but didn't pay much attention to.

René removes the lid, taking out the familiar homemade book of old sea legends, added to over time. There's a new cover page in Aunt Astra's neat cursive.

This book belongs to René Delacroix, Future Captain.

That is their dream, sailing together, with René as the captain and Frantz as the navigator like their fathers before them. René puts the book aside, pulling out something else.

A newspaper article from the *Boston News-Letter.*

René gently blows the dust off the worn paper and lifts the candle, the glow illuminating the story on the front page.

Piracy on the Rise? Robin Hood and Maid Marian Terrorize Slavers and Merchants!

"I have a few of these in the box," René explains, looking a bit sheepish even as he whispers, clearly thinking that even mentioning this might be dangerous. "About other pirates too, but mostly about them. I've wondered about them ever since I found out they were the ones who escaped from Jerome. After you said they helped your parents when you were visiting your mother a few months ago, I wanted to know more. I thought maybe if I showed you these, you might feel better about what we saw today, and about your mother not being here yet." René lowers his voice still more. "I love the stories in my book, but these are real for certain, and maybe ... maybe the ones about Ebele and the other pirates were truer than I realized. The pirates have all sorts of people on their crews. People who look like you *and* me. So I've heard some sailors say, anyway, and they usually know. It seems so for Danso and his quartermaster. I don't know her name."

Frantz remembers one of the local ministers shouting sermons near the harbor while holding several newspapers containing pirate stories, and trying to dissuade any tempted sailors in Kingston.

The pirates are hellhounds! Sea monsters! God does not recognize their humanity and nor should you! Don't be tempted by them, lads. They've no manners and no religion, which created the problem in the first place.

Something comes to life inside Frantz's chest, something he can't even really name, but it's powerful, nonetheless. It rushes through his blood, and when he looks at René, the same feeling is reflected back at him in his friend's eyes.

"Thank you," Frantz whispers, because this has to be their secret and theirs alone, though his father seems to like the pirates too, at least a little. Perhaps more than he can say aloud.

"You're the best friend I could ask for," Frantz continues, moving closer to René until their sides are pressed together. He's picky about who to trust, but he loves René very much. "Read these newspaper stories to me? And then some of the pirate stories in the book? You do good voices."

René grins.

They read for an hour at least. René's voice floats into the darkness, brimming with excitement and a little bit of danger. The two of them flip through the pages, landing on a story about an old pirate stronghold in Madagascar, where the pirates made friends with the native people there. St. Mary's, it was called, according to the story one of the *Steorra's* sailors wrote down. That bleeds into another story a generation before, when bands of Jewish pirates robbed Spanish and Portuguese ships in retaliation for their cruelty against Jewish people in their countries. They read until they're forced to blow out the candle, Frantz's eyes falling shut and one thought resounding through his mind. If Robin Hood and his crew are freeing enslaved people, how are they the enemy?

Interlude VII: The Curious Kindness of Pirates (Part the Second)

The Atlantic Ocean off the coast of Carolina. April 1700.

Danso counts down the minutes, his heart pounding with a manic madman's energy.

Thirty minutes until they catch the slaver they're chasing.

Twenty-five.

Twenty.

Fifteen ten *five*.

He's spent much of the time since Ebele's death crossing names off two lists—names of slaver captains known for dealing in young lives, young bodies, young spirits they seek to break. One he got from an ally in Tortola, and the other for no small amount of coin from a contact in St. James Parish, far away from Kingston on the other side of Jamaica. Jahni is in indentured servitude, yes, but Danso doubts the slave ship captain who took him on would keep to the terms of any deal. So this is where he looks, in-between chasing down merchants to keep money in the men's pockets. This is where he searches for his nephew. His new moniker splatters across newspapers, and it makes him feel defiant. Brave in a new way.

Piracy on the Rise? Robin Hood and Maid Marian Terrorize Slavers and Merchants!

This particular target is Beckett, a man who specializes in transporting children ripped from their parents on the islands, and taking them to the mainland American colonies. Anger pierces Danso's soul at the sound of this name, for reasons he can and can't explain. He might be Robin Hood Full of Rage if he doesn't keep himself calm today. Something's happening, something's in the air, and the touch of Abeni's hand on his shoulder is a lightning strike.

"All right?" she asks, studying his face, and no doubt noticing his quickened breathing.

He nods, catching her glance, and there's so much in it. *I want him to be here. I want to hurt this man for hurting these children. I want my boy.* He doesn't have to say any of this, because Abeni knows. She always has, somehow, from the moment they met, seeing the soft parts of him, the truer parts of him, the farmer he was before even the ancestral land beneath his feet didn't belong to him anymore, and there was nothing, *nothing* but the sea.

"Flora is safe below?" he answers instead.

"She is." Abeni has one hand on the hilt of her dirk, a liquid bright eagerness in her eyes and a smirk playing at her lips. "Let's give this bastard a warning, shall we?"

Danso gives the order, and the *Misericorde* fires a single warning shot. The *Ruby* doesn't fire back, but there's no sign of struck colors, either.

"Interesting play," Abeni murmurs. "I suppose we'll see if he wants to fight. Perhaps he just wants to avoid our cannons and have it out on deck alone."

Normally, the quartermaster goes first in the boarding process if they are set to speak to the men about how their captain treats them rather than starting off with a fight, but this situation is an odd in-between. When the *Misericorde* comes astride the *Ruby*, grappling hooks biting into the wood of the rail, Abeni beckons Danso over with her as she has each time they've encountered a slave ship of this particular sort—three in total since they lost Ebele, and two more before he passed. There is no need to save the threat of the captain for last, and this is no merchant ship where he can be a gentleman and barter. No, they know what they're here for, and there is no need for games.

The soles of Danso's boots land hard on the deck of the slave ship, his green coat fluttering in the wind as Abeni steps up evenly beside him. He takes stock of the crew, which does not pose a terrible threat, other than their eagerness to do violence. Half of them seem drunk, a problem with crews like these, generally. Cuts and bruises spatter the skin of the vast majority of the men in front of him, men desperate for work and willing to throw their souls away to get it. They're sunburnt and too thin. They glare at Danso, trained by their captain to hate him, to see him as less than. Merchant sailors often join them, eager for better conditions. These men, he suspects, will not.

"We would prefer not to do battle with you," he says, tamping down his own anger and swearing he will remain Robin Hood unless this man gives him a reason to do otherwise. "We know you have enslaved people on this ship, so if you hand them over to us, I promise you we will do you no harm. Otherwise, we'll have to start firing, given you have not opted to surrender." His voice hangs in the air, and despite the gentleness of the threat, it is a threat, and several of the sailors step back.

The man who must be Captain Beckett scoffs. "You want me to give my slaves away so you can profit off them?"

"No," Abeni says, a snarl replacing her usual warmth. "So they might be free."

"You're that Robin Hood upstart I've seen in the papers." Captain Beckett narrows his eyes, his nostrils flaring wide. "And ah, *Maid Marian*, is it?"

"Correct," Danso answers. The words are a dare. A challenge.

He wants this man to know who's taking from him.

Tension hovers over them like a cloud, wringing all the water out of the air and leaving the back of Danso's throat dry. Merchant ships they rarely even have to tussle with, but slave ship captains are different. Cruel. More willing to go down just to prove something. He is not out for blood, but captains like these usually want to make him spill it, and then call him a monster for his trouble.

A boy hovers near the captain, a Black boy who can't be more than thirteen, and he's staring at Danso like he might be looking at some kind of hero from a long-lost legend. Danso doesn't have time to contemplate that, or why the lad is up here and not with the other slaves, because Captain Beckett fires his pistol directly at one of the crew. Thankfully, his aim leaves something to be desired.

Everything descends into chaos.

More of the *Misericorde's* crew throw over their grappling hooks at Danso's order, gunpowder tossing an acrid smell into the air. The ships are too tight together for anyone to use their cannons, but there's a fight breaking out on deck.

"Will you—" Danso begins, but Abeni's already nodding, knowing what he was about to ask as she beckons some of the men toward her.

She heads below to search for the slaves, leaving Danso to fight what appears to be the first mate, the captain keeping his distance for now as he shouts out orders to his men. Danso unsheathes his cutlass, the crash of the battle descending upon his ears as he takes the first swing. He's never felt the sword as any sort of extension of himself as he's heard some men say, though he's quite a good hand. His movements are less elegant than a classically trained student, perhaps, but more creative too, and he's willing to bend his skills to the situation. He parries the first mate's next attack before swinging his leg around and knocking the man's feet out from under him. His opponent groans and does not get back up, flinching as if expecting a fatal blow that Danso doesn't deliver. He will not, unless he must. He dashes over to Robins next, who has found himself up against two of the slaver's crew. Danso takes on one himself, earning a thankful grin from his friend in turn, and as unnatural as fighting of this kind feels to the man he once was and might still be, he cannot say the clang of the swords doesn't send a little thrill up his spine. Whatever happens today, he is making a difference here.

He's just stalking across the deck toward Captain Beckett when the still chained together slaves emerge from below, Abeni and the boy he noticed earlier at their heels. Abeni is speaking to the boy, her hand on his arm as she ushers him in front of her. The slaver crew, nearly overcome, barely notices this turn of events, the ring of swords and the pop of pistols echoing against the sky.

Captain Beckett, however, does notice.

His shout bursts through the air, violence dripping from his words in thick, nauseating drops. "You will not make off with my cargo!" He points his pistol directly at the last girl in the line, a girl not more than ten. "Or my servant boy. He has five years left on his contract. At *least*."

The words *servant boy* echo in Danso's head, hope seeping into his veins. He is here, he has searched across the Indies, and yet he cannot allow himself to .... He sheathes his sword, pulling out his pistol instead and aiming straight for Captain Beckett.

He doesn't pull the trigger.

Not yet.

"You are outgunned," he says. "Outmanned. And if we move away and fire on you the ship won't survive the damage. Save the lives of your men, and back down. There is no need for further bloodshed today."

A hush falls over the ship. Captain Beckett meets Danso's eyes, a hateful, coward's smirk distorting his face. Beckett's gun goes off, the sound puncturing the air with a loud *bang*. Several things happen at once, so fast Danso barely has time to think, but think he must.

The boy, the one Beckett called his servant, dives in front of the girl the captain aimed toward, the bullet grazing the side of his arm. There's blood. The boy collapses as Abeni kneels down next to him, taking advantage of the split-second lull and telling the nearby men to get the slaves onto the *Misericorde*. Captain Beckett yanks a pistol out of the hand of one of his men, aiming directly at the boy who is already perhaps passed out on the deck.

"He'll be dead before I let you take him," Beckett snarls, depriving Danso of a choice and forcing violence upon him.

Danso's heart leaps into his throat, but his hand is steady.

The sound of the gunshot explodes in his ears, louder, it seems, than it ever has been before. Captain Beckett falls when the bullet strikes his heart, his body landing on the deck with a heavy, sickening thud. Danso's men move in front of him immediately, ready to fend off any would-be attackers, except none come.

Enraged anguish sits deep in Danso's chest, but he cannot, and would not, take it back.

As soon as things are sorted, Danso sits with the boy, having him brought to the captain's cabin.

He does not speak of his suspicions to anyone, his suspicions, that maybe, possibly, this boy could be Jahni. He cannot, not even to Abeni, because there is every chance he's wrong, and he does not want to frighten the boy off or make him feel awkward simply by warrant of not being his long-lost thirteen-year-old nephew. Several hours pass, and the lad wakes up once or twice, his eyes fluttering open before he immediately falls back asleep. Flora sits a while with Danso, looking eager each time it appears as if the boy might wake up for good. It is not the wound so much that is causing the exhaustion, Danso suspects—the surgeon wrapped it and said it should heal well if tended to—but the ordeal of it all. Perhaps he is a fool. Perhaps this is not Jahni at all, and Jahni is far beyond his reach. Regardless, he feels fond of this young man, despite having never spoken to him. It took courage, after all, to do what he did saving that young girl. He studies the boy, thinking there is familiarity in his face, but maybe he is only desperate. Loose, long locs spill over broad shoulders, his skin a warm russet brown that is lighter than Danso's own, but darker than Flora's, and it does seem like he has a touch of Carib ancestry in him, but no. It might not be.

Finally, about five hours after they've left the *Ruby* behind, the boy wakes up, a small groan of pain escaping him, and even in his half-awake state he looks embarrassed at the vulnerability.

"Easy there," Danso says. "You should stay laying down. It was largely a flesh wound, but it needs time to heal, and I wouldn't recommend moving your arm too much or you'll start bleeding again. You also seem a good bit underfed, lad. We're going to try and help you with that."

"Why am I here?" the boy asks, wrapping his uninjured arm around himself when he sits up against Danso's advice, looking at him with intrigue and just a touch of trepidation. "What happened?"

"That captain shot you, I'm afraid. When you jumped in the way of that young girl we were trying to rescue. It was a graze, mostly, but still painful."

The boy nods, tilting his head. "Did you kill him? Captain Beckett, I mean."

Danso hesitates, and he shouldn't have any grief for the man he shot when even his own crew did not, but he does, anyway. "I'm afraid he left me with no choice. He was aiming to shoot you dead after you got in the way. I wish it were different."

"Are the others all right? Did you get them out?"

"We did. They're safely aboard. The slaver surrendered after the captain fell, and we let them on their way. There was no fight to be had, and I'd rather not put our guns against theirs, when ours are double."

"You didn't leave me behind." The boy stares at him, surprise in his voice.

Pain weaves its way across Danso's skin, pinching and pulling. Too many people, too many children, are hurting and alone across the islands and the mainland colonies, and he only wishes he could save them all. He could not save his nieces and nephews, his sister and her husband, but this, he can do. First Flora. Now this lad, Jahni or not. If he can help more, he swears he will.

"Of course not." Danso puts a tentative hand on the lad's chest, encouraging him to lay back down, but he jumps out of his skin at the touch.

"My apologies," Danso says softly, and once again he swears there is something in this boy's face, but he doesn't know how to ask the question. It's not as if Jahni could recognize him. "I didn't mean to startle you."

"Who are you?" the boy asks. "I mean to say, thank you for rescuing me, but I don't know anything about you, or where we might be going. I've only heard people call you Robin Hood. I heard stories in port, and the men on Beckett's ship talked."

The door opens, cutting off Danso's response, and Flora comes in, a smile lighting up her face.

"Oh, you're all right!" she exclaims, her long black curls bouncing as she clasps her hands together in delighted relief.

"Flora here has been helping me take care of you after my surgeon Mullins patched you up," Danso tells the boy. "I can attest she is rather excellent at the job."

"Oh," the boy echoes, his eyes widening as he turns toward Flora, who wears a white shirt with a ruffle down the middle, and men's breeches. "Thank you."

"Of course," she replies, and Danso warms at the easy kindness that has always been her trait. "How are you feeling?"

The boy's mouth opens and closes, and it takes him a moment to answer, like someone hasn't asked him how he is in a thousand years. "My shoulder smarts a bit. Thank you for asking."

Flora's smile widens, her light brown skin burnished darker by the sun. "I need to go tell Mama you're awake!"

She winks at the boy, kisses Danso on the cheek, and walks out of the room.

"Your daughter?" the boy questions.

Danso smiles, some of his anxiety ebbing as he glances at the closed door. "My adopted daughter. It's a bit of a complicated story. Her mother is my dearest friend and quartermaster, and we rescued Flora from slavery. Ever since she's referred to me as 'Papa Danso.'"

He says his real name without intent. Without preparation. If this boy is Jahni, he will know that name. If this is his nephew—and he probably isn't—he might be angry. He might feel abandoned. Perhaps it won't be the moment Danso's longed for at all.

But then ....

Then the boy is looking at him again, looking at him like he might be a hero, a legend, a myth. Danso's hands start shaking, both because he does not know how to carry such a thing, and because this boy seems to know the name Danso. Maybe it is nothing. Others with that surname have been dragged without consent from the shores of Senegambia, and Danso knows this because his own father, lacking a last name himself, took this one as his own.

"What did you say your name was?" The boy's question is a whisper. A hope. A prayer, even.

Danso swallows, willing himself steady. "Danso. My name is Ajani Danso."

The boy's eyes go wide again.

For a moment, Danso feels as if he might be existing outside himself.

"What's your name?" he asks. "Please tell me your name."

"Jahni," the boy responds. "Jahni Franklin. My mother—" His voice shatters, and he does not go on.

"Joliette," Danso finishes, very gently. He takes a deep breath, tears spilling down his cheeks when he blinks. "And your father, Henry."

"Yes." Tears fall from Jahni's eyes too, and he wipes them away. "Yes." It's him. Dear god, it's *him*.

"I went looking for you." Danso's words cut into the silence, wavering with so much feeling he can barely get them out, and cracked as they are, he only hopes he's making sense. "When I escaped with Abeni we went to Barbados, and I went looking for all of you. The neighbor, she said everyone had been lost. Except you."

"Yes," Jahni repeats. "The hurricane. My mother, she always swore you would come back. You were a myth more than a man, sometimes. She always used to say *Ajani is so gentle. I worry prison will make him hard. I pray every night it doesn't.* She talked about you all the time. She knew you would come back for us if you could."

Missing his sister and her family, his family, has been something Danso's only allowed himself in fits and starts. He never did, when he was doing convict labor, because he couldn't afford to be vulnerable. Abeni and Ebele taught him he could, but he still fears looking at his grief too long and too hard. Now, with his nephew here in front of him, all of those feelings rise to the surface. Danso reaches his hand out, hesitating a few inches away from Jahni's face and looking for permission. Jahni meets his eyes again in consent, and Danso brushes his thumb against the boy's cheek. There's a small, sharp intake of breath from Jahni, like no one has touched him like this since he lost his parents, but still, he doesn't say no.

"I looked for you after Barbados," Danso continues, drawing his hand away. "The neighbor, she said you were indentured, and that your debt was purchased by a ship captain, possibly a slaver. It was all I had to go on. There was so little that every trail I followed was for naught until we started looking for ships like Captain Beckett's. Even then, you were never there, on any ship I tried, because there's so many. My next thought was to try the round to Africa to see if I could find you on a ship taking the Middle Passage."

Danso studies his nephew, swearing he will give Jahni all the love he hasn't had since he lost his remaining family to one violent manifestation of Mother Nature's wrath. He made Flora safe. He can make Jahni safe, too. Jahni grasps Danso's sleeve, his fingers grabbing onto the green material for dear life. Danso's hand comes down, covering Jahni's with warmth.

He wants to hug Jahni, to pull the lad to him and never let go, but he will wait until Jahni is ready.

"Why did Captain Beckett buy your debt?" Danso asks, keeping hold of Jahni's hand. "We could never sort that out."

"Captain Beckett was looking for a servant, and he offered the shopkeeper money he couldn't refuse. I only worked in the shop for about six months before ending up on Captain Beckett's ship, so your instincts to look for men like him were right. I've heard stories about you." Jahni grins. "It sounds like you've been busy."

"A pirate named Ebele gave Abeni and me positions on his crew," Danso explains. "He's the one who taught me everything I know, and helped Abeni reunite with Flora several years ago, after they were both enslaved. Before he died the crew elected me as captain. I'm never sure I'm the right man. I'm often afraid, to tell you the truth. But I'm here. Your mother always believed in me. I wish I could have seen her again."

Jahni squeezes Danso's hand. "She wished that, too. Every day she wished it."

Silence falls between them and Jahni looks away, though he does not let go of Danso's sleeve, the green fabric bursting through his fingers like an evergreen new life.

"Oh, my boy," Danso whispers, and he's so *sorry* he couldn't save Jahni from everything he's been through. "You were my last memory of home. Before I left that night, you reached out and took hold of my finger from your crib. Everyone else was asleep, but you were there to bid me farewell."

There's a moment, a breath, and then Jahni releases his hand, grasping the lapels of Danso's coat instead, a quiet sob bursting out of him.

"My boy," Danso repeats, finally pulling Jahni close to him, and Jahni holds on tight, muffling his tears like he can't bear for anyone to hear, and that similarity makes Danso's chest ache. "I will never leave you again. I promise."

The word *promise* terrifies him much as it did that night he made such a vow to Astra Delacroix, but his world, unpredictable as it is, still rests steady beneath his own feet because he has made it so. He knows who he is now. Or at the very least he is sorting it out.

The door opens at that very moment, and Jahni pulls back. Flora comes in with Abeni, who looks back and forth between them, clearly noticing the atmosphere and the tear stains on both their faces.

"Is something the matter?" Abeni asks.

"Abeni, Flora." Danso turns toward them. "I'd like you both to meet my nephew. Jahni."

Both their eyes widen and Jahni *laughs*. The sound rushes like wine through Danso's veins, miraculous and marvelous and how is it possible that his nephew is *here*?

"Your *nephew*?" Abeni claps a hand to her mouth. "Oh my goodness. Oh my god."

Abeni, not having Danso's hesitation, throws her arms around Jahni immediately, enveloping him in an embrace.

"Mama," Flora reprimands. "Jahni's arm."

"Oh!" Abeni pulls back, realizing herself. "I'm so sorry. I only ... I feel as if I've known you for years. We looked for you."

"So my uncle was saying." Jahni clears his throat. "Thank you for that. And thank you for saving me now. I am so grateful."

"It was our pleasure." Abeni sits down on the arm of Danso's chair and takes Flora's hand. "I'm sure I speak for all of us when I say that you have a home here. Of course, you should confirm that with the captain."

She winks at Danso, who rolls his eyes with a fond laugh on his breath.

Flora shakes her head affectionately, sitting on the edge of Jahni's hammock. "Don't worry, you'll get used to their banter."

"Yes." Danso takes Jahni's hand again. "You absolutely have a home here. With us."

Home, Danso thinks, as Jahni smiles at Flora and Abeni, his blood family and the one he created finally joined together. *Home.*

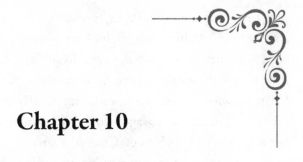

Chapter 10

Kingston, Jamaica. December 1700.

"Michel?"

Michel turns away from the window of his study. The sun vanished an hour ago, wispy clouds overtaking the night sky and half-covering the stars so that he can't make sense of any constellations. His decanter of brandy rests half-empty on his desk, he and Arthur both two glasses deep already.

"Hmm?"

"If I were ever to quit East India"—Arthur's slow with his words, as if thinking it might lessen the impact—"would you be furious with me?"

Michel jolts. "Pardon?"

"We already carry goods from the slave plantations because it is impossible not to, here," Arthurs says. "I can barely stand it, and soon they'll ask us to move slaves. You know they will. And that, I absolutely cannot do. I will not. East India transports them from Africa to Asia as it is. They won't deny themselves the profit here. Especially not now that the Royal African Company has lost their monopoly on the trade to the West Indies. They'll jump at the chance."

"I don't know that they will." Michel tries evading the question, though he suspects Arthur won't let him. "But even if they do, well, people say sugar is made with blood, and maybe they're right. But I don't know what we can do about it right now."

"I was naïve when we came here, thinking I could untangle merchant shipping from the slave trade. And there are illegal runners out there, snapping people up. Not that it's right when it's *legal* either, and Chantal could have been ...." Arthur trails off, looking away.

He returned only two days ago from Saint-Domingue for the second time in a few months, where he went with Frantz seeking answers as to Chantal's whereabouts. They went first in early September—Arthur had to take leave from their voyage—to see if Chantal was still at home, or why her ship didn't arrive. Except, Chantal wasn't home, and there were no clues as to why on this repeat journey. No broken windows. Nothing stolen. The only shred of anything was her front door standing open.

"Arthur." Michel steps over toward his desk and sits down, reaching across the space between them and clasping his friend's hand. "You can't."

Michel remembers the row Arthur had with his family over an intended marriage to Chantal, the threats to disown him and make sure he couldn't work as a sailor, both of which would affect the quality of life of a yet-unborn Frantz. Chantal is gainfully employed on Saint-Domingue with her seamstress work, but it cannot compare to the wealth Arthur has on hand. Michel can't forget the day when Arthur came into the house in London, half in tears already, threatening to quit and go live with Chantal on Saint-Domingue anyway, *damn his parents to hell*. Chantal finally talked him out of it in a letter, begging him not to give up his career, and even more, their child's opportunities, for her.

"I would bring Chantal here to live, so as not to separate René and Frantz, find some other means of employment on the island," Arthur protests. "If I can ever damned well *find* her. I don't know where else to look. I've sent out a hundred letters to anyone I can think of, and the passenger ship captain said she didn't show up to board. The magistrates here and in Saint-Domingue can't be bothered, because they think she just left on her own. I even found those bastard slavers who caused that ruckus when Frantz and I visited in June, but they swore up and down they had nothing to do with it, and I couldn't find any indication they were lying. There's no proof she's dead, and she would never just run away. She just wouldn't."

"You know you can't live together if you find her." Michel holds Arthur's hand tighter, wishing he did have an answer. He's met Chantal several times, and she doesn't seem the sort to just disappear without a word.

She loves Arthur and Frantz as far as he can tell, but maybe the stress was too much. He doesn't express that sentiment. "Your family will disown you and cut you off, and with no income from East India what will you do then? And don't say they won't know. Word will reach them in London eventually."

Arthur pulls his hand from Michel's, standing up so abruptly that he knocks his chair over. It hits the freshly-shined study floor with a loud, echoing *thwack*, yet the usual apology doesn't pass Arthur's lips. He runs a hand through his hair before turning back toward Michel, tears glistening silver in his eyes like little drops of starlight.

"I don't need to hear what I can't do, Michel!" he exclaims, in a wrecked, ruined voice, and the candles in the dim room only accentuate the purple smudges beneath his eyes, the alarming paleness of his skin. "I've some of the money I've earned put away. I own my house here. I would not be without means to quit."

"Your inheritance—" Michel tries, rising from his own chair.

"Damn my inheritance." Arthur sniffs, shaking his head. "Damn what I have sacrificed for it. My wife is *missing*."

The sob that comes next breaks Michel's heart for all that it is full-throated and not bitten-back. Arthur has never feared his own feelings, his own thoughts, and Michel has always envied him that. Arthur never feels ashamed of anything. Not his politics. Not his emotions. Nothing. A dangerous thing, to be sure, but enviable in some regards.

"Come here," Michel says softly, slipping his arms around Arthur and pulling him into a tight embrace. "Shhh, it's all right. It's all right."

Tears wet Michel's shirt as Arthur cries on his shoulder, and Michel lets him, for a moment, gathering what he might say next.

"You cannot quit right now, when Chantal is missing," he whispers. "I will give you whatever leave you need to look for her. And you cannot give up your inheritance so easily, not when you and Chantal have already sacrificed so much to make certain you would have it for Frantz. Chantal would not want you to make these kinds of choices without her. I know how worried you are. I know how much you love her."

He believes he is right about Chantal, but he also knows he does not want to bear Arthur leaving the Company, even if it doesn't mean him leav-

ing Kingston. He does not tell his friend, just now, about the Court of
Directors' and the Navy's interest in potentially sending them on patrols
around islands where pirates have been known to make port, hoping the
might of East India might scare them off and put a damper on their slowly
growing numbers. He suspects Arthur would not like it. Not like Jerome,
whose eyes lit up when he was let in on the news.

Arthur's fingers dig into the silk back of Michel's waistcoat, his voice
growing a little clearer. "I made the mistake of mentioning Chantal to my
brother in a letter, to make use of his contacts, and he only said he couldn't
help. Foolish of me. I need you, Michel. Frantz keeps having nightmares. I
can't sleep myself. I want to reassure my boy and I just ...."

"I am sorry, Arthur. I am. About Matthew's reaction, too."

Michel keeps hold of Arthur's elbows as his friend slides out of the embrace. He tucks a strand of auburn-brown hair behind Arthur's ear, and
something catches in his chest, something warm and old that he doesn't
like to name. It's not unusual that he feels warmth when he looks at Arthur,
and this is not more feeling, exactly, but different. It has more heat. This is
not the first time he's felt it, this particular sensation. His attraction toward
Astra has never been a question, as she is easily one of the most beautiful
women he's ever seen, and yet this has always .... It doesn't rise to the surface
often anymore, not with his marriage to Astra, Arthur's relationship with
Chantal, and the easy habits of their friendship. But there was a kiss, once,
in boarding school. A kiss that was no chaste thing. A kiss they haven't spoken of since. That is more his doing than Arthur's, no doubt.

It was a boyish moment, certainly not unheard of while surrounded
by only their own sex, and no terribly rare thing among sailors either. He's
suspected some of his own men over the years, but without substantial
proof—though for something rather more than a kiss—and isn't sure what
he'd do, besides. A few captains he knows let the matter go if the men show
enough discretion, not wanting to subject them to sodomy laws for something that is between them and God. Most captains do *not* leave it be, and
the result is either severe punishment or termination. It is illegal and im-
moral in any case, and sometimes men hang for it. None of this, however,
accounts for Michel's urge to kiss Arthur now. The urge that's brought him
shame ever since he first felt it.

"I worry, sometimes," Arthur says, sounding far away, "that I'm losing you to all of this. To the Company. To Governor Travers. That you're losing yourself. And I can't lose you right now, Michel. It's too much."

"You won't lose me," Michel promises. He cannot make himself answer the other part of the inquiry. "Sit and have some water. I think we should put the brandy away for now, before supper. It's—"

The front door bangs back against the wall without warning or notice, cutting him off. There's a voice too, the voice of his father-in-law early for his scheduled supper with them and shouting at René, who he must have found on his way in. A string of familiar sounds comes next, sounds that give rise to that familiar ache in Michel's heart, so deep and everlasting that its sharpness has faded.

A slap.

René crying, even as he tries his best not to.

Astra screaming at her father.

He rushes down the stairs with Arthur at his heels, and there's another familiar thing, a thing he's been seeing more of, lately.

That dangerous, rebellious glint in Arthur's eyes.

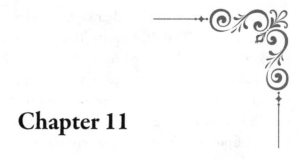

Chapter 11

The Caribbean Sea, aboard the Steorra. July 1701.

A ngry voices slice into the air as René stands outside his father's cabin. He raises his hand to knock on the door but pulls away at the last second, thinking he ought not interrupt. He's never heard them fight quite like this before.

"Trying to manage him, trying to anticipate his rage, won't work." Uncle Arthur's words are the first ones René makes out, surprised when they're punctuated by the slam of his godfather's hand smacking down on something. "Because one day the situation will spin out of your control, and nothing you can say will soothe his temper. René had welts on his back last week. I saw them when I took the boys swimming. And if you think René won't go up against the governor one day when he's had enough, you're fooling yourself. I don't want to see him hurt worse than he already has been."

Impatience cuts into his father's tone, directed at Uncle Arthur, of all people. "Astra and I stopped Andrew before it got very far. Do not suggest that I do not care to find a way to prevent this. I want to. You don't understand what dealing with him is like."

René touches his back in remembrance. His grandfather only got four hits in with the buckle of a shoulder belt on René's bare back before Michel and Astra burst in, stopping the punishment in its tracks. René can't even recall what he supposedly did to deserve the punishment, but it barely matters, anymore.

"I do understand," Uncle Arthur protests. He sighs, the floor creaking as he steps back toward the door, and René doesn't have time to make his exit without being seen. "I have to go see to Frantz. I told him I'd be back in a half-hour."

"Arthur, please. Let's just talk, all right?"

Arthur sounds tired when he speaks again. "Later. I don't want to fight with you. I want you to listen. But mark me, Michel, I don't care what the cost to myself, that man will not continue to treat my son or yours this way. Not while I live and breathe."

There's a pause in the room as if his father and Uncle Arthur might be staring each other down, and René's stomach aches afresh. This isn't the first time he's heard them arguing recently. There was another fight a few weeks ago, his father and Uncle Arthur's words echoing through the upstairs study, the two of them talking about the news about pirates who were arrested in the Indian Ocean by none other than an East India crew.

There were African pirates on that crew, Michel, Uncle Arthur said. *And they refused to even give them a jury trial because of it! They tried them under the slave code laws.*

They were spared the noose, Michel argued. *I'm not saying the lack of trial wasn't unjust, but at least they weren't executed without one.*

Uncle Arthur pulls open the door, his scowl morphing into concern as he shuts it behind him.

"René," he says, throwing on a smile that doesn't fool either of them. "All right, my boy?"

"Yes," René replies, unsure if he is or not. Probably not. "Should I not go into the cabin?"

Uncle Arthur looks back, his fingernails pressing into his palms. "How about you come see the sunset with Frantz and me instead? We can watch the stars come out."

René nods, following Uncle Arthur back above. His father appears a half-hour later, taking a shift at the wheel. Uncle Arthur watches him for a few minutes, frustration and worry twisting his expression before he looks away, staying well across the deck toward the forecastle. Silence reigns over the ship after nightfall, and René gets up from his place next to Frantz, drawn toward his father at the wheel. Michel looks more casual than usual, and René supposes it's because most of the men are keeping clear, sensing the tension between their captain and their navigator. Michel's coat hangs next to him, his sleeves rolled up against the humid evening and the top two buttons of his shirt undone, though it's still a pristine white beneath his waistcoat. His normally neat hair slips out of its ribbon as René's often does, and for some reason, this small thing gives René a feeling of kinship.

"Papa?"

His father turns, his hands still secure on the wheel. He smiles until the light reaches his eyes, which are a mirror reflection of René's own.

"René," he says, gesturing him forward. "I didn't even hear you approach. Learning to be a spy?"

"My step is lighter," René replies. "Jerome was teaching me some footwork when we were sparring earlier."

"I saw a bit of that. You get more adept by the day. It runs in our family."

"That's what Uncle Arthur says," René adds, relieved when his father doesn't grow angry. "He said you taught him most of what he knows, and he was hopeless."

The half-moon slashes into the dark night, clouds obscuring the stars and leaving the ship in the light of the lanterns. René can't make out any of the constellations, no matter how he tries.

A second, wider smile spreads across Michel's face. "Arthur gives me a bit too much credit and himself not enough. He is a better shot than a swordsman, but we each have our strengths, don't we?"

"Yes," René says. "He was teaching Frantz just before we left. He shot almost all the targets with the flintlock and showed us both how to load them properly."

"A true testament to his talent, given how pesky those things are with aim." Sadness weighs on his father's words, the heaviness settling in René's heart as silence wedges between them, a silence that once, not so long ago, was rare.

"I'm glad Frantz and I got to come with you this time," René says, and his father looks back over at him. "I'm always sorry to leave Mama on her own, but I missed sailing, and it means ...."

It means I am not around grandfather, is what he doesn't say.

Sir, his father said on the day the welts occurred. *I am his father. And I say no to this. I've told you that before.*

I am his grandfather, Governor Travers said while René sat shirtless, Astra practically shielding him with her body. *And he is my heir.*

Astra's voice vibrated with rage. *He is our son.*

Michel tilts his head, opening his mouth and closing it again as if he cannot form a response to the unspoken part of René's sentence.

"Come here," he finally says, positioning René in between him and the wheel. "Let me teach you how to steer. Would you like that?"

René nods, enthused. His father takes his hands, placing them on the wheel and then covering them with his own. A bubble of bittersweet nostalgia wells in René's chest and bursts, running down and leaving him overcome with a strange, sweet melancholy. A memory emerges in his head, a memory of his father pulling him up onto his hip and pointing at the multitude of stars, naming as many as he could. This is different, but René craves it still. He doesn't want to think about whether his father will protect him. He just wants his *father.*

"There are eight spokes on this wheel," Michel explains, his hands tightening over René's. "Sometimes there are more, sometimes less. But eight is standard. They all meet together at—"

"The nave. I remember."

"Very good," Michel says, and René can tell he's smiling. "And inside there's the axle."

"But steering in the dark like this, that's much more difficult, isn't it?"

"It can be. But you see these handles on the rim of the wheel here?"

René nods, and Michel takes one of his hands, moving it up toward the mentioned handle. "This one you feel with the extra grooves in it is called the king spoke. It helps me tell what position the rudder is in. When it points directly up, the rudder is dead straight."

"Do you think I'd be good at captaining a ship?" René asks. "Frantz always says I should be the captain and he should be the sailing master, though I like learning about navigation with him, too."

"A captain should have knowledge and skills concerning all parts of a ship and how it functions," Michel says. "But he should also have confidence in his men, learn to delegate duties so that he may oversee the ship as a whole."

A beat of silence rests between them again. For a moment, all René can hear is the sea, the water a deep navy blue in the night. His father takes a deep breath before running his thumb up and down René's hand with raw, breathtaking affection, and that small gesture is everything. It's the gesture of the father he knew when he was younger, and the father he wishes for now. The father who is slipping away.

"I think Frantz is right." His father pauses like he might be afraid, but he goes on anyway. "You would make an excellent captain."

"Like you."

Michel ruffles René's hair, both of them laughing. An old joy makes René light and happy even as it rests on a knife's edge, like anything might break it even if he wants to believe nothing could. Maybe these dark things will pass, and his grandfather won't win the day. He wonders if his father is thinking about the argument with Uncle Arthur, but he can't make himself ask because it frightens him, and right now he doesn't want to be afraid.

There is one question, one anxiety he will ask about, daring in light of his father's better mood. "I want to sail with Frantz more than anything in the world. I know you and Grandfather argue over whether I'll be allowed a captaincy or not, but I want to be like you. Not him."

His father stiffens, keeping hold of René's hands. "Let's see what the future brings, all right?"

A vague answer. Not an answer at all, really.

Or the answer René least wants to hear.

No.

"Papa—"

"René, *please.*" His father speaks sharply, like he's burdened by the protest. By René himself.

Like he's afraid.

René jolts, the moment snuffed out like a fragile, flickering candle.

"René," his father says again, softer, but the night's already broken into dark shards of glass on the deck.

"René!" Frantz calls out, cutting off whatever Michel might have said. "Papa is telling me about the Flying Dutchman. Come join us!"

René slides out of his father's grasp, ducking under Michel's arm. "Thank you for the lesson. I really do appreciate it. I'll be over with Uncle Arthur and Frantz."

Jerome approaches just as René goes, looking between father and son. René waves at him in greeting, looking back once he's a few strides away. Something about his father and Jerome standing there together strikes him, even if he can't say why.

"Michel, you asked me to read over that letter from Captain Evans about the attack on his ship ...." Jerome's words fade as René steps out of earshot, and he notices the use of first names between them. Before, Jerome never would have dared.

He sticks his hands in his coat pockets, his eyes running over the dark deck so he doesn't trip, though it's easier to maneuver in his sailing boots. Frantz's zeal and Uncle Arthur's smile greet him when he sits down, and his frown vanishes as some of the sailors gather around for a tale. Uncle Arthur's famous among the crew for his ghost stories, even if Michel chides him for encouraging the men's already outrageous superstition.

"The captain of the Flying Dutchman was determined to sail around the cape." Uncle Arthur's voice curls into the air, deep and smoky with an old legend that might just be real. René thinks it is, sometimes, when he's out here in the dark with nothing but water around him. It could be. The sea is haunted. He's certain of that. It is too ancient, and too many people have breathed their last out here for it to be otherwise. Sailors get their stories from somewhere.

Uncle Arthur leans forward, making eye contact with each and every man. "And now he finds himself the captain of the most notorious ghost ship on these seas, his sailors' bodies forty fathoms below in Davy Jones' locker. If you see it, they say, it may be an omen of bad things to come."

An unexpected hand on his shoulder makes René tense, but it's only his father sitting down next to him and coming to join the festivities, looking half-enraptured and maybe a little frightened as the tale goes on. Uncle Arthur stops briefly and gives Michel a tiny smile, some of the tension in the air dissipating.

Something about it makes René feel like he's caught between the pages of a story, what's behind and what's ahead spilling into one another as they sail homeward.

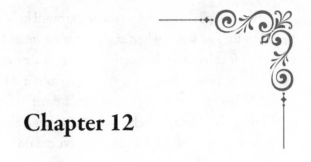

Chapter 12

The Caribbean Sea aboard the Steorra. December 1701.

"You lied to me, Michel." Boiling, bubbling rage courses through Arthur's voice, and Michel thinks he might melt under the heat. "You lied to me *directly*."

Thunder crashes outside as if in agreement with the accusation, and Michel knows they don't have much time until they need to go above and help with storm preparations.

"I did not lie to you," Michel insists. "I simply did not give you all the details."

"Unacceptable!" Arthur shouts, the words reverberating around the captain's cabin. "I am your second in command and you saw fit to keep the full details of the voyage from me? It's unsafe, and were the men to find out it would undermine their trust in us. You are a good captain, and you know better. I assume Jerome knows, which puts him in a bad position between the two commanding officers he directly reports to. It's unfair to him. You don't tell your second lieutenant something and not the first."

"I took no pleasure in it," Michel says, afraid the men might overhear them. "You wouldn't have come if you knew the lost cargo I mentioned were slaves, that we were looking for the pirate ship who might be responsible for taking them off an East India-affiliated vessel. If you must know, the Court of Directors is interested in us doing this more often. Patrolling for pirates. I've known for a while, but didn't know how to tell you with everything going on. There. I have nothing else to confess."

Arthur steps closer, rage crackling around him. "You led me on a voyage to search for lost slaves when at this very moment I am searching for Chantal, who I fear has been kidnapped into that very trade. When my son, who you claim to love, is not so far removed from it. His grandparents were enslaved. What are you going to tell him, hmm?"

"I do love Frantz." Michel swipes his hand through the air. "These are my orders, Arthur. What would you have me do?"

"Dammit, Michel!" Arthur shouts a second time, and the reprimand cuts Michel to the quick. "What pirates are we looking for? And don't you lie to me again."

"Danso, all right?" Michel bites out, half hating himself. "Robin Hood or whatever nonsense name he's called. And his quartermaster. They took the slaves, the report said. They dared to attack Captain Evans' ship because it was a smaller vessel, I suppose. Only contracted with East India as needed, rather than East India itself. Soon they'll go after East India ships directly. They're foolish enough, and pirates have done it before."

Arthur stares Michel down, and fury lights a wick behind those familiar amber-brown eyes, making them burn like Michel's never seen before. Lightning flashes in through the window, bathing the cabin momentarily in shocking white light.

"I have a secret too."

Arthur's whisper cuts through the volume of the storm outside, but the softness beneath his words is only grief, and there's something else, too. Something sharper. Something pleased. This is the Arthur Michel's witnessed with affection but never personally endured, the Arthur standing his ground with his arrogant parents, or dressing down a captain being cruel to his sailors in port, and, more recently, fighting righteously with Governor Travers.

The Arthur who is dangerous to the status quo.

"Danso and his quartermaster helped me," Arthur continues, "that day those slaver brutes went after Chantal and me in Saint-Domingue. I wasn't sure at first, but the more I see his face on those flyers, I know. I just didn't tell you because I knew you'd say I should have turned them in. I thought Jerome was acting strangely when we sailed out. He had that glint in his eyes he gets when Danso and his quartermaster come up in conversation. I should have known something was wrong."

For a moment that he does not possess, Michel cannot think, and yet, in that same moment, he is not surprised, at all.

"You are going to ruin your life!" he snaps, his words knives, *weapons*, directed at one of the people he loves most. "Sympathizing with pirates and pretending the world can be something it isn't? We have to live in the one that exists. This isn't a goddamned story, Arthur."

The fire in Arthur's eyes goes out, and he runs a hand over his face, shaking his head. The next words are gentle, and Michel doesn't know how to bear them. "I don't believe any of this is good for you, Michel. You hated the slave trade, and now here you are, searching for escaped slaves and lying to me about it! How do you suggest we explain where we went to René and Frantz? Though perhaps you don't care about that anymore. If Governor Travers had his say he would separate them and you know it. If you're so afraid of him that you're doing this, I don't know what you might do next."

"I promised the boys I would never allow that. You know I wouldn't."

"I don't know what you would do anymore," Arthur says, tears welling in his eyes. "You have power, you have wealth, but what will you have when that's destroyed your family? When it's destroyed *you*?"

Another crack of thunder explodes outside, the sea smacking against the side of the ship. It's not quite a gale, but there is a significant thunderstorm approaching. They're a day from Kingston according to the usual calculations, traversing the shipping lanes the pirates might be most likely to use, but the last dying dregs of a warm day clutch at them, and there's no bargaining with the weather to let them reach safe harbor first. Wind rattles the windows of the cabin, whistling through the cracks around the edges.

Arthur runs his hands through his hair, tangling it irrevocably and speaking into the silence between them. "When I took this job, I thought I would get to see the world with you. Maybe it started that way, but now we're just powerful agents of even more powerful men, taking land that isn't ours to take. I couldn't protect the woman I love, and God knows if I can protect Frantz, even if I love him more than I've ever loved anyone. Danso and his crew are out there changing the world. What are we doing, Michel?"

Michel shakes his head, looking out the window and up toward the sky, wishing he could find God out there, some star in answer to his prayer as twilight passes and evening takes hold, but there is nothing, *nothing* but the storm. He cannot even summon a response to this declaration, because Arthur knows what he would say.

Pirates are nothing to emulate.

Arthur swallows, then looks Michel directly in the eye. "I'm resigning from the Company when we arrive back in Kingston."

Michel stares, almost suffocating as his chest tightens. "What?"

"I am resigning," Arthur repeats, his voice cracking. "My family can damn themselves to hell if they choose to disown me for it."

No. This cannot be. It *cannot.*

"Arthur. You can't."

"I can, and I will. I listened to you. I gave it more time. I won't give it anymore."

"Arthur."

"Quit the Company with me." Arthur steps forward, grasping Michel's hand and tugging it close against his chest. Even in his anger, Michel can't pull away. Not from Arthur. "We can do it together like we've done so much else."

"It is not that easy." Michel gazes at the man who knows him better than anyone and who never fears challenging him, even in the face of his anger. "This job is important to me, Arthur, and my father-in-law would not hear of it. He's more powerful than either of us by a good stretch. Don't forget that."

"How could I? He reminds me of it every time I'm unfortunate enough to be in the same room." Arthur sounds bitter now, bitter and sad and strange. "He has threatened my position on this ship. He has threatened Frantz's safety and constantly belittles him, which I will not tolerate. He beats and berates René. He would stop your boy, who I love like my own, from becoming a captain—his dream since I can remember."

Michel hesitates. "I have lost that argument with Andrew, I'm afraid. He does not believe it proper for René to possess a title and sail a ship, and the title is inevitable. And while Frantz might find a sailor's job, the likelihood of anyone taking him as an officer is not as high as he deserves. You know that. I know the boys want to sail together, but it won't happen. I won't lie to them about it any longer. I won't create false hope or fantasy. They're too old for it now."

"Michel." Arthur hangs onto the name. "What aren't you telling me?"

Michel's heart races, the words bursting out of him before he's ready. "I'm telling you my father-in-law intimated that he would take more control of René's life if I did not come into his line of thinking. More time spent with him. Suggesting new tutors even though there is not an endless supply in Kingston. That sort of thing."

"You're his father, Michel. You have the final say," Arthur says.

"Please." Michel snorts, shaking his head. "I may have power, but my father-in-law has more."

Michel does not express his fears that the governor might try and take René from him flat-out, because he can't give those fears credence. Astra reassured him one night in the dark as they lay in bed together—a rarity, these days—that even if her father wanted to, he couldn't. That she, they, wouldn't let him. Michel knows, of course, that Andrew Travers can do whatever he likes. He brought East India to the West. He could take René, too. Flouting legalities are nothing to him. But Michel didn't want to think about that, so he thanked Astra, kissed her, and then lost himself in her arms. So much of his family life feels like it's slipping from his fingers, but he can at least tend to his wife well when she permits it. Though that too is growing less and less common.

Arthur's hand curls tighter around Michel's, tears sliding down his cheeks. "Andrew Travers is dangerous, Michel. If we quit, we can go. We can leave Jamaica, leave the West Indies altogether and get out from under his influence. Just me quitting won't do that, and I can't go without you. I can't separate the boys. I can't leave René here. I can't leave ...." The sentence dies in Arthur's throat, leaving little more than an unintelligible rasp that might be *you*.

Tears threaten Michel, and he chokes them back down. "Go where, Arthur?

"France. To your brother. Remy would greet us with open arms. You know he would," Arthur says, as another crash of thunder roars off in the distance, rain lashing the ship. "We could take Astra and the boys there, make them safe, and then I'll come back here to search for Chantal on my own and not give up until I find her or discover proof that I never can. We could do that. We could go when your father-in-law is traveling."

"Arthur—"

"Come with me."

Michel's about to respond, half-tempted by the offer, when Jerome calls to them from above, his tone laced through with unease and urgency.

"Captain Delacroix! Lieutenant Seymour!" he shouts. "The storm is coming on quicker than expected. We need you on deck."

When they follow Jerome out of the captain's cabin and onto the deck, Michel sees what he means. A slate gray sky has replaced the vague clouds from earlier, and the rain comes down in thick, unforgiving drops, hitting the wood with a hard, echoing sound. The stunning blue sea churns ominously, turning darker. Despite their fight, Michel knows he can count on Arthur, he knows they can work seamlessly together, and they do.

"Batten down the hatches and make sure the lines are secure or we'll be three sheets to the wind!" he orders, dashing up to the quarter deck as lightning rips the sky. "Trice the topsails, as well! Arthur, on the wheel, please."

For the next twenty minutes, there is only the storm. Michel gives orders. He runs to-and-fro across the quarterdeck. The wind roars in his ears, the rain coming down in sheets so dense he can scarcely see anymore. The weather is worse than he expected, and while the scuppers succeed in draining water from the deck and overboard, the gusts and visibility issues are the larger danger here. The storm hits abruptly like something from midsummer as opposed to late December, but the *Steorra* holds steady.

Until she doesn't.

Crack.

The noise is a dark omen, and Arthur's voice pierces through the wall of wind as he shouts at someone to take the wheel.

Crack.

Michel looks up, and oh dear *God*, the top of the foremast is cracking just below the topgallant sail, where the wood is more the victim of the wind and already in need of repairs.

Crack.

Someone runs toward him, strong hands shoving him out of the way.

Arthur. Of course it's Arthur.

Crack.

The top of the foremast breaks, and parts of the rigging and the wood come tumbling down, though the rest of the mast remains in place. Arthur is not yet fully clear. The *Steorra* gives a horrible, stomach-dropping creak, men scrambling down from tricing the sails below in case the rest of the mast gives way further, one man nearly falling overboard before his fellow catches him. The debris hits Arthur, and his head smacks hard onto the wood from the impact, Jerome pulling him out of the way before anything can fully pin him down. Blood from Arthur's head wound mixes with the rain, red rivulets running like tears across the deck.

The cries of anguish off in the distance come closer when Michel realizes they're his own, and he cannot tell the difference between those and Arthur's screams of pain echoing into the storm.

Footsteps pound up the stairs, a sharp, immediate tension shooting down Frantz's back. They sound like women's shoes as opposed to a man's boots, but the sound breaks into the quiet house with startling abruptness.

The person hesitates outside the door. For thirty seconds. A minute.

What's the matter?

There's a knock on the door, and he knows who it is by the sound.

Aunt Astra.

Anxiety contorts her face, and Frantz's heart starts racing when she looks at him first.

Something's wrong. Something is *wrong*.

"Frantz, darling, your father ...." Aunt Astra reaches for his hand, and her voice seems far away. "I'm afraid he's been badly injured. There was an accident during a storm, and one of the masts on the *Steorra* broke."

She grasps Frantz's hand tightly, but everything else falls away, his world screeching to a halt.

The front door opens.

He thinks René says his name, but he isn't sure.

He leaps off the bed, dashing down the stairs.

Uncle Michel's voice. Jerome's voice. Prescott's voice. He hears all of them.

He closes his eyes as he reaches the entrance hall, Aunt Astra and René following behind him.

Focus. Listen. What's happening?

He makes out *downstairs bedchamber* through the shrill, unending chorus of *oh no oh no oh no* in his head. Some of the sailors from the *Steorra* go down the hall, carrying a tall figure toward the bedchamber. His father. They're carrying his father.

He stops short in the doorway of the room, grasping the frame hard. The men lay his father out on the bed, gentle with his injuries. His father is a favorite with the whole crew, and there's no masking their concern. Uncle Michel thanks them and sends them off, leaving only himself and Jerome, each sailor pressing Frantz's shoulder as they go past. René joins him in the doorway, one hand on Frantz's back, and it's the only thing that feels real at all, right now. He looks at his father, every muscle in his body throbbing already. Arthur's hair is loose and spilled across the pillow, blood-streaked through from what looks like a wound at the back of his head. His ripped open shirt reveals another angry wound running diagonally across his chest, blood and bruising splattered across like a gruesome work of art. All the color's gone from his face. He's shivering and sweating and struggling for a deep breath. Arthur meets Frantz's eyes, the tiniest half-smile flickering on his lips.

"Frantz. Come here son, it's all right."

It's not all right. It's *not*.

Frantz moves forward, but everything feels slow as he climbs up on the bed. Uncle Michel says something about another doctor coming, another doctor who can help the *Steorra's* surgeon. René goes over to Uncle Michel, whispering something like *are you hurt?* But Frantz doesn't hear the answer.

"Papa, are you going to be all right?" Frantz whispers.

He isn't going to be all right. There is no way he will be all right, but he must be. He *must* be.

For a long, awful moment, his father doesn't answer. He brushes the back of his hand against Frantz's cheek, pain gleaming in his eyes as he tries another smile.

"Let's just wait for the other doctor to get here," his father says, but even those words don't come without a horrible, rasping cough.

The doctor arrives a few moments later with the *Steorra's* surgeon in tow, asking everyone save Michel to exit the room.

"No." Frantz shakes his head, wishing he could reason this away and he can't he can't he *can't*. "No, Papa, I can't go."

His father blinks back tears, pulling Frantz's hands toward him and pressing a shaky kiss to his knuckles.

"You can come right back in, dear one." Arthur presses Frantz's hands tight. "I promise."

Uncle Michel murmurs something about a fever, infection, potential blood poisoning, and a head wound to the doctors before shutting the door tight behind him. With a brief kiss to Frantz's curls, Astra goes toward the kitchen, off to retrieve wet cloths. Frantz slides against the wall until he hits the floor, scrunching the fabric of his breeches back and forth, the small movement keeping his breathing even. René sits next to him, their sides pressed together.

His father is ... his father ....

His father is going to die, isn't he? How can ... what will he do? His mother is missing, and his father keeps him safe. His father loves him. His father ....

Frantz puts his hand out, desperate for something to keep his thoughts from spinning. René takes it, his eyes wide with apprehension.

"I'm here, Frantz," René whispers. "I promise. I won't leave. Do you want anything?"

"Just stay with me, please," Frantz replies, keeping hold of René's hand. "I'm scared, René. What if ...."

He can't say *what if my father dies?* He can't.

Footsteps come toward them. Heavier ones than Aunt Astra's.

Jerome squats down, the movement oddly graceful even if he looks uncomfortable, his broad shoulders casting a shadow against the wall.

"Frantz." Jerome sniffs, and for the first time ever, Frantz thinks Jerome might cry.

Frantz's eyes flit toward Jerome's arm and the ripped sleeve covered in old, crusted blood, no doubt from getting caught on something in the storm. Sadness weaves its way through Jerome's voice, the usual gruffness gone.

"Frantz," Jerome repeats, pressing his shoulder in a genuine if awkward way. "Your father was struck pushing Captain Delacroix out of the way and saved his life. He's very brave. I know you're aware of that, but it bears repeating."

"Thank you," Frantz says.

His father had ... what? He doesn't have the presence of mind to ask questions, even if usually he can't ask enough. He just can't *think*.

His father saved René's, and now he might ... he might ....

Mrs. Hudson comes by, kissing both Frantz and René's cheeks before handing what looks like a mug of tea to Jerome, who thanks her.

"Drink some of this." Jerome holds out the cup, but Frantz doesn't think he can let go of René's hand to grasp it.

He shakes his head. "I feel sick. I can't."

"It will help calm you down a touch. Just a sip or two."

Frantz reluctantly releases René's hand, taking the mug with both of his own and swallowing down some of the tea. His stomach roils in protest. Jerome pats Frantz's shoulder, offering René a sad half-smile as he takes the mug back, keeping watch over both of them while the other adults are occupied. Astra comes back and goes into the room, cloths in hand. Frantz leans closer to the door that she left cracked open just enough for them to hear, but he can't make out what the doctor says, only that the tone sounds grave.

His father's voice breaks through, weak and cut through with pain. "Take care of him, Michel. Say that you will take care of him."

"I will, Arthur," Uncle Michel says, audibly holding back tears. "Frantz will be safe here."

"I know we fought before the storm," Arthur continues. "I just wanted us all to be happy. I wanted to keep Frantz and René safe. Please don't doubt what you mean to me."

Fighting? It doesn't surprise Frantz, exactly. His father and Uncle Michel have been arguing a lot more, lately, but still.

"I know," Uncle Michel answers. "And I could never doubt that. Don't worry."

"Please take care of him," his father says again, his voice breaking, and Frantz is sure he's breaking along with it. "Please say you won't separate the boys. They need each other. Don't let the governor hurt them."

Frantz takes René's hand again. He can't get a deep breath. He can't think.

"I won't. I promise you, Arthur."

"We'll take care of Frantz," Aunt Astra echoes, and she alone sounds steady. "I promise you that. We love you and we love him very much."

"I can't ...." Arthur breathes in, emitting a terrible sob that makes Frantz's guts twist in two. His father has *never* sounded like that before. "I can't send Chantal word because I haven't found her. You have to find her, Michel. Tell her I love her. That I never stopped searching for her. And you have to give Frantz that letter I wrote for Chantal. Please, Michel."

Oh God his father is dying he can't be *dying*.

Frantz holds René's hand tighter, perhaps too tight, but René doesn't complain. How will he find his mother now? Without his father it falls to him, and he swears he'll make it happen. The doctor tells Arthur to relax, and after a few more minutes the door opens, and they're called in again. Frantz goes straight to his father's bedside as the doctor and the ship's surgeon go into the hallway, giving them space.

"Papa?" Frantz asks. "Papa, what ...."

His father smiles, and Frantz curls up next to him, burying his head into Arthur's chest.

"I love you," Frantz mutters, his mind spinning so fast that he still can't think, and that scares him. "I love you, Papa."

"Uncle Michel and Aunt Astra are going to take care of you," his father says, tears sliding down his cheeks. "You will stay here with René. I love you too, my boy. I love you so much."

His father calls René over, and when Frantz looks up, René breaks away from Uncle Michel's embrace. Uncle Michel himself is white as a ghost, all color gone from his face like he might be dying too. Arthur pats the clear space on the bed and René climbs up, Frantz shifting as his father joins all of their hands.

"You two boys have a friendship worthy of the ages," Arthur tells them, his voice growing fainter with each passing moment. "And I want you to promise me you will take care of each other. Protect each other when you need it."

"We will." René sniffs, audibly fighting against the tears welling in his eyes. "I love you, Uncle Arthur. I promise I'll never let Frantz be alone."

"I—" Frantz pushes the words out, his heart hammering so hard he fears it might break through his chest. "I won't let René be alone, either. I promise."

Arthur kisses René's head, whispering *I love you too, lad*, before René climbs down from the bed, retreating into Astra's arms. Uncle Michel takes his place, pulling up a chair beside the bed and grasping Arthur's hand. Jerome stands by the door, his eyes wide as if he doesn't know how to process what's going on around him. Frantz curls against his father's side, making himself fit as Arthur toys idly with his curls. There's murmuring outside the door, but Frantz can't look up. All he can focus on is the sound of his father's breathing.

"I love you, Frantz," his father murmurs. "Look for me in the stars, my boy. I'll be there."

"I will, Papa." There's a broken, jagged sob somewhere off in the distance, and Frantz only realizes it's his own after a moment or two. It dies soon after, shock sucking away the rest of his tears and leaving only nausea and terror behind. "I love you."

"My boy," Arthur whispers. "My smart, dear boy."

Arthur jolts in pain, his grip on Michel's hand tightening.

"Michel." Arthur runs his thumb across Michel's knuckles. "I—"

"Shhh." Michel brushes away sweaty hair from Arthur's forehead. "It's all right. Don't talk too much."

Frantz curls in yet tighter against his father, shutting his eyes.

Then, they wait.

People come in and out. Mrs. Hudson with more cloths to wipe the sweat from Arthur's face. Molly with glasses of water that Michel has Arthur sip. Prescott with word from the crew about the state of the *Steorra*.

Arthur's rattling, wheezing breaths accompany their comings and goings like a horrifying symphony. Frantz only half hears it all.

It takes his father two hours to die.

"Michel," Arthur whispers, looking suddenly alarmed, his eyes bloodshot, Frantz tensing into a ball next to him. "The papers. You have to get them."

The papers. Frantz remembers some papers his father was signing one day with his mother the last time they saw her, papers he said Uncle Michel needed to sign too. Papers about him.

"My will, too, Michel, you have to get it. If you don't my family might try and take Frantz."

Frantz jumps, shocked out of his numb state by this comment. No one in his father's family has ever wanted him. Not his grandparents. Not his Uncle Matthew. No one. But clearly his father worries that might change when he ....

When he ....

Frantz still can't think the word.

"It's all right." Uncle Michel runs a hand down Frantz's cheek before turning back to Arthur, his tone soothing. "I know the papers are in your desk at home. I'll ask Mrs. Brooks for them."

"Chantal," Arthur mutters, his words half-coherent nonsense. "She ... I ... need. Michel, please find her, I can't ... I love her. You have to tell her I love her. Please tell her, Michel."

"Settle, my friend." Uncle Michel puts a hand on Arthur's burning cheek, taking a letter out of his coat pocket with his free hand and resting it on the bedside table. Frantz realizes that it must be his father's last letter to his mother. "I'll tell her. I've got the letter you wrote right here."

His father's fear makes something solidify in Frantz's chest. No matter how scared he is, he can't let his father *die* scared. He can't. He *won't*.

"Papa?" Frantz asks, sitting up a little, and it's this more than anything that draws Arthur back to himself. Frantz grasps his father's hand, looking him straight in the eyes. "I'll find her. I swear to you I'll find Mama. She'll be all right. I'll be all right. I'll be here with René."

"Frantz," Arthur says, so softly it's barely audible, but Frantz thinks he sounds a tad more at peace than he did a moment ago. "I love you. I love you. My brilliant boy. My miracle. You do look so like your mother. You do have my eyes though, don't you?"

A scream catches in Frantz's throat, but he doesn't let it out. "I love you, too." He swallows, taking a deep breath at the agony gleaming in his father's eyes. "It's okay, Papa. It's okay. I love you."

You can go, is what he hopes his father hears, because he can't quite say it.

A ghost of a smile crosses Arthur's face, and Frantz rests against his father's shoulder again, silence spreading like a slowly creeping fog across the room.

"Frantz," Arthur whispers. "My boy. My boy."

"Papa," Frantz murmurs, shutting his eyes again.

Then, nothing.

His father exhales one final breath before going still.

Frantz's entire body goes cold.

The shock doubles down against him with such force that he cannot even cry when he opens his eyes. He wishes he could cry.

His father is gone. His father his father his *father*.

For a moment, all he sees in his mind's eye is Arthur coming to visit Saint-Domingue for his sixth birthday. They met him at the harbor, the sun shining bright and without hesitance as Arthur leapt off the ship, running toward them at a full tilt. He laughed as he swept Frantz up in his arms before kissing Chantal deeply. He was so alive then.

His mother is *missing*. His father is *dead*.

If he knows anything, he knows he has to find his mother. He has to.

He can't extricate himself from his father's limp grasp, not yet, but he does look across the room at René, who sits on the settee with Aunt Astra. Jerome stands next to them, his hand going to René's shoulder. René meets Frantz's eyes, but before either of them can say anything, before either of them can move toward each other, a single noise shatters the silence like the sudden and unexpected sound of breaking glass.

Uncle Michel is crying. Sobbing.

Frantz isn't sure he's ever heard him cry before.

"Michel," Astra says, but Uncle Michel doesn't seem to hear, getting up from his chair in a daze.

Frantz sits up, watching Uncle Michel breathe in deep against his tears. Michel gazes at him and Frantz gazes back, struggling to understand the look in his new guardian's eyes. A thousand things pass across his face, things Frantz can't name, all of them wrapped in grief. Uncle Michel takes the letter off the bedside table, handing it to Frantz, but Frantz only reads the first line before he can't look anymore. Before he can't bear it.

My beloved Chantal.

Uncle Michel starts sobbing again, the sound sharp and awful and dissonant. He pulls Frantz tight against him, and Frantz doesn't know what to do but comply. He doesn't know what to do other than return the embrace, his fingers digging into Michel's coat, clinging onto something fragile.

It feels like the beginning of an end.

But unlike the stories he's read a thousand times with René, he doesn't know what that ending is.

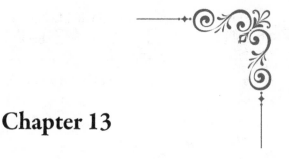

Chapter 13

Kingston, Jamaica. May 1702.

"They say Ebele started the mutiny when he saw the slaver captain beating a child." The sailor's voice brims with drama, mystery and myth overflowing the edge of a cup. "And that was enough for him."

René keeps his gaze on the small knot of sailors he and Frantz sit with at the docks, enraptured by the tale. René hasn't seen Frantz smile like this in months. Not since Uncle Arthur died.

Frantz grins at the sailors, running a thumb absentmindedly over the pocket-watch he inherited from his father, the back etched with stars. René knows his own father has a similar one, gifted to him by Uncle Arthur long ago. He looks off in the distance at the newly repaired *Steorra*, which has been renamed *Navigator* in Arthur's honor. He remembers the day they re-named it, because he remembers hearing his father cry the night before. He remembers Frantz running into his room with nightmares in his eyes, tears sliding down his cheeks. He remembers his father breaking the bottle of champagne against the mainmast—the tradition when renaming a ship—and how the men whispered when it took more than one try, though no one dared say *that's bad luck* aloud.

Red used to be the thing, Uncle Arthur said once. *And they'd pour the rest into the ocean to appease Poseidon.*

He shakes the memories away, turning back toward the sailors. Listening to them makes him forget, for a while, that someone he loved so much is dead.

These men are pirates in disguise. He's sure of it. They're known for masking themselves as merchants if they aren't well known enough to be recognized. Another merchant crew mills nearby, half the men looking as if they're listening in, including the captain. Barlow, René knows he's called. He heard his mother and Uncle Arthur talking about him before. Further down the way, there's a boy he's seen before playing cards with the sons of some ship captains.

"How did he do it?" Excitement buoys Frantz's words, drawing René back to the story.

"Apparently, Ebele charged at the slaver captain and was about to be flogged for his trouble," one of the other sailors adds, "and all the slaves from below rose up and overpowered the crew."

René leans forward, thinking of the newspaper clippings he has hidden under a floorboard beneath his bed, clippings about Ebele and Danso in particular. "And what happened *then*?"

"The slaver captain died in the struggle, but Ebele took control of the ship and had his fellow slaves drop the rest of the crew off at some island in the dead of night. Tortuga, maybe." The third sailor winks at René and Frantz. "The new crew voted him captain, and he's been a legend ever since. No one ever caught him. No one knows for certain what happened to him either, but that Robin Hood the Merciful fellow and his lady quartermaster Maid Marian sail the ship now. We all—" The sailor stops himself, letting the unsaid words hang in the air. "Well. They're legends, too. They say even the Navy doesn't like to chase them. Not yet. We heard one story lately, where they stole a captain's wine and left the rest because he was good to his men. Interesting, isn't it?"

Robin Hood the Merciful. That second part is new. René likes it.

"I heard that Danso wears a green coat," Frantz adds, but he does not divulge *how* he knows to these men. "A bright one."

"A detail we'll have to add to our tale," one of the sailors replies with a contagious grin. "I—"

A sharp voice cuts through the air, disrupting the story. René turns around, but he already knows who it is.

"Boys!" Jerome calls out, and the men they were talking with scatter while Barlow's crew looks on with unease. "You aren't supposed to be at the harbor without supervision."

René scowls, irritated at the reprimand. Jerome always seems to be reprimanding him, these days. "You're first lieutenant now, I'd think you'd be too important to nag us."

Jerome raises his eyebrows. "That's quite enough. Who were you talking to? You shouldn't talk to men you don't know."

"Some sailors," René answers, vague. "I saw their papers showing they paid their dock fees, so don't go thinking they're suspicious. They were just telling us stories."

A lie. He's gotten good at lying, lately. If those men were pirates, he doesn't want them caught, because he knows what the punishment for piracy is. There were gallows set up in nearby Port Royal when they visited a few weeks ago, the empty nooses blowing in the breeze and waiting for their victims to come at dawn. All things considered, he'd rather not see Gallows Point again.

"What do you think will happen?" Frantz gets up from the ground, resting one hand on his hip. "We're around your crew all the time."

"Yes, *our* crew," Jerome says, sliding his slightly tattered notebook into his pocket. He's kept it for ages, and René has surmised that it contains information on Robin Hood and Maid Marian's movements that Jerome learns from sailors in port. "Officers on other ships are one thing, but common deckhands could be a bad influence, and besides that, you don't always know who you're speaking with." Jerome's gaze goes to the crew they've been talking to off in the distance, no doubt noticing they're of more varied origin than the usual crews coming in and out of Kingston.

René frowns, challenging him. "Weren't you a common deckhand once?"

It's not exactly kind, but he's too irritated to care.

"I'm taking you home," Jerome says firmly. "No arguments."

René rolls his eyes but follows anyway, Frantz walking beside him.

"Your father said that court sword he had commissioned for you is almost done, René," Jerome tells them, breaking into their silent march. "You and I can begin lessons with it soon. Something to look forward to."

A flicker of interest stirs in René's chest. Whatever Jerome's bossiness, he does enjoy their sword lessons, and he knows Jerome does too. At least he hopes so. "Oh. Yes. I'm looking forward to it."

Frantz stops in his tracks, and René looks around, searching for the source of his friend's surprise. There's a group of naval officers walking by, boxing in two bedraggled, combative men.

"What's that?" René asks, furrowing his eyebrows.

"A press gang, I believe," Jerome answers. "They conscript men into naval service as needed."

Frantz scrunches his nose. "Without asking?"

Jerome glances at him, his expression impassive. "It's necessary. We're at war, you know."

René does know because it's always in the papers and there have been some skirmishes nearby, but he doesn't understand the alliances or why England is worried about a Spanish king, or why France is involved. It doesn't seem fair to force people to fight over it, in any case. They spend the rest of the walk exchanging a few words here and there, and when they reach the house, someone's waiting for them just inside the front door.

His grandfather.

René steps inside the entrance hall, his shoes squeaking on the wood when he stops. No. Not today *please* not today. He hasn't had any time to prepare himself.

"What are you doing here?" He speaks before he thinks, regretting his tone instantaneously.

Governor Travers frowns, narrowing his eyes. "Certainly not tolerating that sort of address from my grandson. Where were you?" His eyes flit over to Frantz with a flash of disgust before darting toward Jerome in question. "Lieutenant?"

Jerome swallows, his eyes roving back and forth between René and the governor. "We were just returning from the docks, Governor Travers. I was escorting them home."

"Hmmm," Governor Travers says, disbelieving and unimpressed. "You mean you were pulling them away from speaking to sailors without permission again. There is no need to protect my grandson. He doesn't deserve it."

The air in the entrance hall grows thick with anxiety as René's grandfather seizes him by the collar, shoving him in the direction of the wide staircase several feet away. Out of the corner of his eye, he sees Jerome reach his hand out before pulling away again, frozen in place.

"You know you are not meant to be in the harbor talking to God knows who without supervision!" His grandfather is cold, cutting, and without mercy, his small gold spectacles sliding down to the edge of his nose. At first glance the governor is not particularly imposing, but anger transforms him into a nightmare wearing an expensive waistcoat. "Talking to scoundrels, no doubt. Besides that, you knew you were supposed to have tea with me this afternoon when you were done with your tutors, and yet where were you when I arrived?"

René breathes in deep, clenching and unclenching his fist.

Calm. Calm. *Calm.*

"I was talking to some sailors," René replies, shaking already, but his emotions won't do him any good here. His grandfather seems in rare form today, eager for a fight with his favorite victim. "I wanted some air after we finished our lessons. I'd forgotten about the tea, sir."

The first slap comes before René readies himself, the *thwack* ringing through the room. He doesn't fall, but he raises his hand to his cheek, biting his lip against an angry remark. Usually, the worst happens when his father is at sea, and René finds himself dreading the longer voyages when he and Frantz can't come along. They're allowed less and less on any voyage, these days, and he doesn't know why. At least at sea, he doesn't fear the front door opening, waiting for the man who is both his and Frantz's terror to step through. His mother does her best to protect them, but his grandfather doesn't listen to her.

"You do not talk back to me, boy!" his grandfather shouts, seizing René by the collar again, pulling him closer and then shoving him away. René does fall this time, hitting the floor hard. He looks up at his grandfather, the blood rushing into his face as the elbow he caught himself with throbs from the impact.

"And your clothes are frightful, too," Governor Travers growls. He pulls René up from the floor by the front of his shirt, grasping the material tight between his fingers. "Your cravat is never tied, and you always look a sight.

You will not continue to be an embarrassment to me, René. Your mother is too soft on you, and sometimes I think if not for my guidance your father would follow suit. You are my heir, and you will not behave this way. Do you hear me?"

"Stop!" Frantz exclaims, drawing Governor Travers' attention, and René's stomach drops at the look on his grandfather's face. Jerome grabs the back of Frantz's coat, half dragging him over into the corner of the entrance hall near the front door, putting space in between the two of them and the governor. Frantz struggles against Jerome's grasp, and Jerome whispers something in Frantz's ear that René can't hear.

Contempt runs into the crevices of his grandfather's voice. "You'd best tell that friend of yours never to speak to me unless spoken to."

René glances behind him, searching for help, but Jerome's occupied keeping Frantz back, a fear in his face René's not sure he's seen before.

"Jerome, please, tell him we weren't doing anything wrong!" René begs.

Jerome doesn't answer, and René meets Frantz's eyes once more before the governor yanks on his collar, forcing his gaze back.

"Jerome can't help you," his grandfather says. "Nor should he."

René loses his patience, panic swelling in his chest until it buzzes so fiercely he can't catch a deep breath. Nausea rushes through him, his heart beating with a strange, arrhythmic pitter-patter.

"I just forgot, Grandfather." René hates pleading, but he wants this to end. "I made a mistake. I wasn't trying to upset you. I'm sorry."

His grandfather pauses, and for a brief, precious moment, René thinks it might be over.

He's wrong.

"We are going upstairs to discuss this in your father's study, young man," his grandfather says, and René knows what that means. It means getting hit with a paddle or a hand or a belt because his parents aren't home to say no. He refuses to move, and he regrets it immediately. His grandfather keeps hold of his collar, using it as an anchor when he grabs René's forearm, his fingers pressing hard into the bare skin beneath the rolled-up shirtsleeve. René gasps, biting his lip to stifle the sound. He tries tugging away, but the governor only holds tighter.

"You will obey me, René," his grandfather hisses, squeezing yet harder, his whole hand encircling René's skinny forearm.

"Grandfather, please let go." René's eyes fill with hot tears, and he swears he won't let them fall. He can't. That's the rule he set for himself: never cry in front of his grandfather.

"Say yes, sir, I will obey you."

René's bones tremble beneath the unrelenting grip. It's the same arm that hit the floor earlier, and the pain radiates from his elbow and down, growing fiercer the longer his grandfather holds on. He tugs away once more to no avail, and he can't look back at Jerome and Frantz, he can't do anything but stare at his grandfather, the whole world melting away in the sheer terror enveloping every inch of him. He hates being afraid.

One day, he swears he will be fearless.

The tears he tried holding back spill out, and his grandfather smirks.

"Yes, sir." René pushes the words out through clenched teeth.

His grandfather doesn't let go. "Yes, sir, *what*?"

René shuts his eyes. "Yes, sir, I will obey you."

Finally, his grandfather releases him.

A sob bursts past René's lips even though he knows better, his arm on fire with pain.

"None of that," his grandfather chides. "You're twelve years old and I won't stand for this weakness, René. Stop it right now."

"I *hate* you." A wave of fury crashes over René, making him numb to the fear. "I hate you for hating me."

His cheek stings in anticipation before his grandfather's hand even makes contact. The second slap echoes through the room, followed by absolute, utter silence.

"Do not miss tea with me again." His grandfather leans forward, grasping René's chin hard and forcing his gaze. "Go upstairs. Be sure I will speak to your father."

The governor stalks toward the door, sparing a nod for Jerome before shooting Frantz a withering glare.

"Out of my way, brat." The governor shoves past so he hits Frantz's shoulder before slamming the door shut behind him.

René goes toward the stairs and sits down, the red marks of a handprint seared onto his skin. He stares at an empty spot on the floor, wiping his eyes. Frantz is saying something to Jerome, but René's ears only ring, and he can't make out the words. A moment later Frantz comes over, sitting down next to him. René tenses when Frantz's hand comes gently to rest on his back, reminding himself that this is someone he can trust without question.

"Are you all right?" Frantz asks.

"It hurts," René admits. He presses his fingers to the skin, wincing at the tenderness. Jerome approaches next, stopping at the edge of the staircase.

"You didn't stop him," René whispers, dumbfounded. "You saw the whole thing. You dragged me back here. I asked you to tell him I hadn't done anything wrong. Why wouldn't you help me?"

"It is not my place."

"Not your place?" René questions, his voice wavering. "You're a part of this family, aren't you? Why would you let him do that to me? You were right there!"

Jerome's tone softens, but the determined glint in his eyes does not, and he jolts at being called *family* as if the words burn him. René's anger at Jerome builds and builds and builds until heat floods his chest. He's been annoyed at Jerome, but he never thought Jerome would betray him like this. He knows Jerome might earn his grandfather's ire if he interferes too much, but he didn't even try.

Maybe he picked the wrong heroes. His father. Jerome. Why won't they help him?

"I cannot interfere with your grandfather's discipline," Jerome replies, and René only glares at him. "Let me see your arm."

René pulls away before Jerome can touch him. "No. Don't touch me."

"I am not going to strike you, René," Jerome says, oddly gentle. "You know that."

René looks away, and he can barely think, nausea growing in the pit of his stomach. Jerome reaches toward him again and Frantz shoves his hand away, making Jerome's eyes widen.

"If you obey him, he won't hurt you," Jerome whispers, and René jumps at how vulnerable he sounds. "I don't wish to see you in pain, René. If you stop disobeying him, he'll stop hitting you."

"No he won't!" René explodes, and he doesn't care if it makes Jerome angry. "You're just afraid of him like my father is. Too afraid to protect me."

"I am *trying* to protect you," Jerome responds, swallowing back some kind of verbal retaliation at the mention of his fear. "You need to stop testing your grandfather's temper."

René gets up, and something cracks inside him, even if it doesn't fully shatter. "If all you're going to do is blame me, then please just leave me alone, Jerome."

"René," Jerome growls.

"He said no," Frantz adds. "Come on," he says to René, "let's go upstairs."

They go, leaving Jerome flabbergasted behind them, but he doesn't follow. Michel's valet Peter runs into them in the hallway outside Frantz's room, furrowing his brow when he sees René's arm.

"Everything all right, lads?" he asks, his Irish accent thick even after many years in Jamaica. "I heard shouting."

"Just my grandfather." René meets Peter's eyes, earning a sad smile in return. The servants are never anything but kind to them, and sometimes let them hide in their wing of the house when his grandfather is in a bad temper.

"Do you need me to go fetch your father?"

"No," René answers quickly, and Peter looks unconvinced. "But do you know where my mother is? I didn't see her after we finished our lessons with Mr. Edwards and Mr. Daniels this morning."

"She went to have tea with Mrs. Taylor just down the way, so Molly told me," Peter replies, referencing Astra's maid. "She's set to be home right around now. Should I send a note over in case she's late? James could take it."

"No," René repeats. "Just, if you see her, let her know where we are?"

"Certainly," Peter gives them a small smile as he goes, and René suspects he might go search for Michel anyway.

They go into Frantz's room, and René sits down in one of the chairs near the window, holding his arm as the muscles throb in protest. He studies Frantz's bed, spying a few letters laid across the covers, *My darling Arthur* written across the top of the paper. Frantz has recently been going through some of his father's things, and these must be letters Chantal wrote to Arthur. Frantz catches him looking, going over and taking the letters in his hands, stacking them carefully on top of one another with the utmost care.

"I found these in one of my father's boxes," Frantz says softly. "He kept so many, and it helps me to read them. To know how much my parents loved each other."

Frantz wipes his eyes and sniffs, trying to pretend he isn't crying, but he doesn't need to.

"We'll get your mother back," René whispers, and he wishes they could get Uncle Arthur back, too. "We will."

"I think sometimes of our last visit, and my parents talking about how some of my Uncle Matthew's goods were being shipped to Saint-Domingue, and also how he wouldn't help my father when my mother went missing, and I wonder if ...." Frantz bites his lip. "I don't know if I want that to be a clue just because he's a bastard, or if it really is one." He settles down on the arm of the chair, peering at René. "He really hurt you this time, didn't he?"

"I didn't know he could grasp my arm so tightly." René glances down at the slowly purpling skin, and Frantz does too.

A sob crawls its way up René's throat, his eyes stinging. Frantz gets up, pulling another chair over and taking René's hands in his own, their foreheads resting together.

"It's all right, René. I promise you don't deserve a single thing that happened. You don't. No matter what that horrible old man says."

René holds Frantz's hands tighter. Frantz had a nightmare last week, a nightmare about losing him, because he's already lost too much. "You shouldn't be worrying about me. I know you miss your father and you're worried about your mother, and I don't want to add to it."

Frantz clicks his tongue in annoyance. "I'm here for you like you're here for me. We promised."

René nods and shuts his eyes, listening.

"I think those men down at the harbor were pirates." Frantz lowers his voice even more, those words a secret just for the two of them. "Maybe one day we can leave here, if things get worse. Maybe we can find a crew like that and sail together like we've talked about."

A shaky smile forms on René's face, hope pooling like warm, golden sunlight in his chest and chasing some of the nauseating panic away. "What if we joined the crew they were talking about? I wouldn't mind being one of Robin Hood's men. We have been reading those stories about him and his quartermaster."

The sheer idea of that fantasy makes René's heart slow down. He's not sure if they can run away. He's not sure if they should. He's not sure if the pirates are as good as the stories say, but right now the idea of sailing away with Frantz sounds much better than being here.

Frantz smiles too, even if it's a little sad. "Maybe so. I wonder sometimes if ... well if my mother's still alive, if they could help me find her. If she's been sold into the trade, Robin Hood, or Danso, or whatever we like to call him, goes after slavers. I know she wouldn't just run off. Something happened to her, and I would know if she was dead. I just would."

There's a soft knock at the door. René's mother comes in, one hand grasping the skirts of her cream-colored gown, which is patterned with tiny flowers. She is one of the few lights left in Kingston, and the sight of her eases some of René's anxiety.

"Jerome told me something happened, then went to retrieve your father." Astra dashes over to them, looking worried. "Peter told me you were here, and Mrs. Hudson said she saw my father storming out on her way up the drive and she was worried." Her eyes fall to René's arm. A red handprint burns the skin, small dots of purple popping up. "Did your *grandfather* do this, René?"

"Yes," René answers. "I'm sorry."

"No." She raises her hand to swipe it through the air in emphasis, lowering it when René flinches. "You shouldn't be sorry. He should be. What else happened?"

"He slapped me," René admits, reluctant to cause his mother worry. "And then shoved me to the floor. Then slapped me again."

His mother kisses the side of his head, turning toward Frantz for a moment. "Are you all right, Frantz, dear?"

"I'm fine," he assures her, and she smiles at him, squeezing his hand. "But I'm concerned about René's arm."

Astra meets René's eyes, and with his silent permission slides his sleeve further up, gently touching his arm. René grimaces and she draws back, pursing her lips.

"Let's go get some cold cloths, all right?" She places a hand on the back of René's neck, toying with the fine curls resting there. She lets go of Frantz's hand, putting an arm around his waist instead, and they sit huddled together in their fragile, momentary safety.

A few minutes later, the three of them sit at the small table in the kitchen instead, the wood warm beneath their feet. René winces again as his mother wraps a cold cloth around his arm, wanting to be brave for her. They're only alone for twenty minutes before the door swings open and René jumps, fearing his grandfather's return. He releases a breath of relief when he sees it's just his father, but the tension in his shoulders doesn't dissipate.

Michel focuses on the cloth wrapped around René's arm. "I ran into Jerome on my way home, and he said I should come quickly. He looked upset. What happened?"

"What do you think happened?" Astra asks, immediately confrontational. "My father happened. He struck René in the face. He pushed him to the floor. Then he seized his arm so hard it's bruising."

She undoes the cloth carefully to show him, the red fingerprint marks still holding onto René's skin as if Governor Travers' grip remains even in his absence. His father reaches toward the injury, but René recoils.

"Please, Papa," he whispers. "Don't touch it."

Michel draws his hand back, looking apologetic before turning to Frantz.

"Are you all right, Frantz?"

Frantz nods. "He shoved me, but he really hurt René, Uncle Michel. Worse than I've seen before."

Michel runs a hand over his face, but he uses the same tone that Jerome did, the one that says *why can't you just behave, René*. "I'm sorry boys, truly. He must have decided to come into Kingston early for the ball we're hosting, but I hadn't expected him." He pauses again. "We need to send for a doctor to look at your arm, René."

René shakes his head, panic rising in his chest again. "I don't want one."

"You need one, son." Michel looks at Astra, worry marring his expression as he squats down in front of René. "We also need one who will be discreet if we tell him the truth."

"Is that all you're concerned about?" Astra asks, fury punching hard into her tone with every word. "People finding out?"

"We don't need your father angrier than he already is, Astra," Michel snaps.

René jolts, surprised at the tone. His father rarely speaks to this mother that way.

"Son," Michel says, putting a hand on René's knee, "I will talk to your grandfather."

René shakes his head. "You always do, and he never listens."

René meets his father's eyes, remembering the man who carried him around the deck of the *Navigator*, showing him the stars. He misses that, and he just wants his father back. He's heard his father say *I'll talk to your grandfather* countless times, but what good does it do, other than calming things down for a week or two? It scares René that perhaps his father values the governor's approval over his or Frantz's safety. This isn't the father he looked up to as a little boy. Where did he go?

"Jerome didn't stop him." René speaks again in the face of his father's silence. "Why didn't he stop him?"

"Jerome could face consequences for interfering with someone of your grandfather's station," Michel explains, and René looks away, his eyes going to the floor. "Severe ones. Your grandfather would not tolerate it, even if I stepped in."

"May I just go upstairs with Frantz, please?" René cuts in, that familiar sense of shame and anger mixing together in the pit of his stomach. "And wait for the doctor there?"

"Yes," his mother says before his father can even open his mouth. "Go wait there, keep the cold cloth on, and I'll be up in a moment. Your father"—she narrows her eyes at Michel, and there's a fight brewing between them, that's for certain—"will go for the doctor himself."

René doesn't even glance at his father, sparing a smile for his mother before leaving with Frantz. The sound of raised voices follows them out, Michel's French accent even more pronounced in his irritation. They walk without thought to René's room, and make for the window seat where they can see the ocean, shadows cast across by the sunset. René upsets the cloth when he sits down, and Frantz picks it up, placing it back on René's arm.

"I don't know if you want me touching it?"

René waves away the concern. "I don't mind. I just didn't want my father touching it."

Frantz nods, gingerly wrapping the cloth back around and holding it there. René's eyes trail from his arm and out the window toward the sea. One day, they might have to leave here. Before they're of age. Before either of them can get any money. One day, there might be no choice. He hopes he's wrong. For now, he'll believe in Frantz. He'll believe in those pirate stories and his mother and all the light he can summon into his soul. And despite the raging chorus of his grandfather's voice in his head, he swears he'll believe in himself.

He has to try.

"We'll get there, René," Frantz says. "We'll sail out there together one day. Away from here. You've said that to me before, and now I'm telling you. We'll do it."

"Yes." René engraves that dream on his heart, permanent and irreversible. "We will. Thank you." He squeezes Frantz's fingers. "Want to read aloud?"

Frantz nods, retrieving *Don Quixote* off the bedside table and leaning shoulder to shoulder with René.

A thought occurs to René just before Frantz starts reading. "What did Jerome say to you? When he was keeping you back?"

Frantz frowns, tapping his lips with one finger. "He said if I went after your grandfather that I'd end up hurt even worse than you. He sounded strange when he said it. But don't worry about that now. Let's just read."

René heeds his friend's advice, listening to Frantz's voice float into the air, and even if just for a little while, he feels safe.

Interlude VIII: The Naming of Robin Hood the Merciful

The Atlantic Ocean off the Coast of Massachusetts. February 1702.

Danso spots the English flag as soon as he looks through the spyglass, the cross of St. George stark against the white background.

"Asante says we'll have them in three-quarters of an hour," Abeni whispers in his ear as she comes up beside him. "They're bulkier and we've got the weather gauge."

"Is Flora safe in my cabin?" Danso asks, lowering his spyglass. He reaches instinctively for his cutlass, his eyes still trained on the ship in front of them. The *Spica*, no doubt named after one of the stars in the constellation Virgo. "And Jahni?"

"They both are," Abeni answers, pressing Danso's shoulder. "Robins and Collins are in there with them. Jahni argued a bit, said he was old enough to at least tend to some things if there's a fight."

Danso shakes his head, laughing a little. "We agreed on sixteen, so he has a year to go. If it were up to me it would be never, but I know that's not fair."

"Believe me," Abeni says, "I know the feeling."

Danso sat with Ebele on the deck of this very ship night after night as his mentor taught him about the stars, telling him about the legends behind them and the ones sailors were most fond of, the sky dark and infinite above them. In those days, he worried he had damned his nephew, his whole family, by getting caught stealing that fateful day, and that Jahni, the only one left, would never have a chance. But Jahni is here, now, learning about sailing and holding on to a new life.

When this ship was still a slaver, the captain pulled me out from the hold and had me work in the cabin as a personal servant, Ebele told Danso one such evening. *I was never sure why. Perhaps because I was quiet, he thought me dumb. Perhaps he took it as a sign I wouldn't rebel. What he didn't know was that I listened as he talked with his sailing master, because I learned English when I was brought here as a boy with my mother. I learned about navigation without them ever realizing. And then I sparked the mutiny against them. The stars don't just belong to men like them, Danso. They belong to us all.*

Danso never looked at the stars when he was young in Barbados. He was always looking at the ground, at his work, at his empty plate—constantly weighed down by trying to survive one day to the next, especially when he had to leave his farming behind to work at the docks for more money. But things are different now.

Abeni fingers the dirk Robins taught her to use, and Danso almost laughs at the memory of once worrying how she might fare in a fight.

After Ebele passed on, they continued his work of going after slavers, but at the men's urging they've started going after even larger merchant ships. Their main targets are captains known for treating their sailors badly—something other pirate crews often do. Catching those puts enough money in their pockets to let them chase slavers and still take good care of the ship and the crew. They even leave money on doorsteps throughout the West Indies, when they can.

He calls the men to their stations as they grow closer and closer to the *Spica*. He never imagined calling himself a sailor until he joined Ebele's crew, even if he'd been one through his forced servitude under East India. He certainly never imagined being a pirate, let alone a captain, but he won't walk away from this new family, from this crew who have given him their trust. From Ebele's legacy.

You failed your family, that dark voice in the back of his head whispers. *They died. All but Jahni. And look what happened to him.*

It's not your fault, Abeni would say. *You shouldn't have to work to the bone just to survive and have it still not be enough.*

He breathes in, thinking of the nights aboard the *Misericorde* when the men sing shanties, the sound echoing up toward the expanse of the sky, merry and wild and free. That sound drowns out the nasty voices in his head more often now. Jahni's been a balm for that too, a reminder that not everything was lost that day. Jahni and his quiet, determined love. Flora, and her joy. Abeni, and her undying friendship. It's just that sometimes he can't quite make the voices vanish, caught between who he was, who he is, and who he might become.

"Raise the black!" he calls out. "Make sure they know who they've got coming."

They'd been flying English colors—their usual habit to avoid suspicion—and the men haul them down, replacing it with their own: a more ominous black flag with a full white skeleton stitched across. Danso's been collecting various countries' flags, which lets them operate without suspicion until they're ready to attack. The black flag is a recognizable symbol for all who lay eyes upon it. A sign that pirates look death in the face and say *I am not afraid,* because what do any of them have to lose? They are more alive putting their minds to this than they would be otherwise, chained to whatever yoke each of them was faced with before they joined. Raise the flag too early, and the ship might make a run for it. Raise it too late, and they might be more eager to fight.

The minutes pass and they come in range of the *Spica,* but the captain doesn't strike colors.

"Fire a warning shot across when we're in range!" Danso orders. "Then wait."

A cannonball whizzes across the stern of the *Spica* five minutes later, smashing into the rail.

Danso waits.

He breathes in deep, steadying his racing heart. He doesn't want to fight, but he will.

The *Spica* strikes her colors.

"Boarding party prepare!" Abeni calls out. As quartermaster, it's her job to lead the first men across when a captain surrenders. "With me when we come astride her."

They come up next to the *Spica* a few minutes later, and Danso waits while Abeni goes across with fifteen of the men.

It makes Danso smile to see their crew trust Abeni. There were a few grumbles from men who voted no when she put her name in for quarter-master against a gent called Perkins, but they died away when she showed her care toward the crew and her new competence in battle, as well as her willingness to disagree with Danso when she thinks him wrong.

The *Spica's* captain approaches Abeni, looking entirely shocked at see-ing a woman standing before him. The other sailors seem unsure and a bit frightened when Abeni directs her attention toward them.

"I am here to ask how this man treats you," she says, sparing one glance for the captain. "Captain Baker, isn't it?"

Some of the men nod but don't answer just yet, and Danso has no doubt they might wonder if this is a trick.

"It's not a trick." Abeni gives the men a very slight smile as if reading Danso's mind. "I'm asking for an honest answer."

One man steps forward, twisting his hat in his hands. He's an older sailor by the looks of him, thinner than he ought to be with gnarly, sun-weathered skin. "Captain Baker treats us nice, ma'am. He's a kinder sort than other merchant captains I've sailed under. Feeds us better than most. Makes sure we get our wages. I think the other men here would agree."

There's a general murmur of assent that Danso takes as his cue. He strides across the gangway and steps onto the deck of the *Spica*, unsurprised when Captain Baker cocks his pistol and aims it in his direction. Some of the sailors respond in kind, but Danso merely puts a hand on his own pis-tol rather than drawing the weapon out just yet. He prefers his cutlass, all things considered.

"Kindly lower your weapon, sir," Danso says. "I will not attack a man who has struck colors just as a naval officer will not fire under a flag of truce."

Captain Baker holds his pistol straight out before lowering it, though not all the way.

"I've heard rumors about you from other captains. From the king's sol-diers. There was one where your crew attacked a ship, the *Rose Marie*, and there was a fight because the captain wouldn't give up his goods. The merchant ship was destroyed, and people say—"

Danso remains steady. "What do they say, Captain Baker?"

"That every sailor aboard died when the ship started sinking. But I've heard some sailors and people in port say ... well *they* say you took the remaining men to an occupied island and set them free. They also say you rescue children from slavery. I admit to admiring that."

Danso nods. "You should listen to the sailors. That captain was known for beating his men. Some until they died. They reported that he deprived them of their wages and sometimes of sufficient food. He was also sailing a ship that was highly damaged, which is why it sank when he started fighting. But we did take the rest of the men somewhere safe."

Captain Baker lowers his pistol all the way, studying Danso with curiosity, something softening in his expression, even if he still looks afraid. "I wish no harm to my men. Take what you will. You'll find tobacco and sugar in the hold, along with several cases of wine."

Abeni comes over to Danso at this, leaning close.

"Take the wine," Danso whispers. "We can sell that to Miller on St. Kitts. Leave the rest."

St. Kitts is where they're able to sell a fair portion of their stolen goods, their relationship with Henry Miller the customs officer paying dividends, especially when he told them of an ammunitions supplier on the more isolated island of Tortola who was willing to sell to pirates. Smaller planters across the West Indies, especially ones friendly with the old buccaneers, are sympathetic to their cause, and furious about being forced out by wealthier planters with bigger plots of land. This is especially true of those men farming indigo or cotton or cocoa. Sugar is the order of the day, now. Their network of contacts is growing, allowing them to glean the routes of ships they'd like to avoid and also to catch, as well as sell goods.

Abeni nods, one hand ghosting over his shoulder as she goes, leading the men on the boarding party down. The remaining pirates on the *Misericorde* watch from their place by the rail, some of the sailors on the *Spica* studying them. Visible surprise passes across Captain Baker's face when they take the mentioned crates of wine, and not his other cargo.

"You're not taking everything?"

Danso gives a half-smile. "Just what we need. That's our thanks to you for your cooperation and the decent treatment of your men. As far as it's in my power, other pirates will know of your reputation and leave you be. We've no interest in scaring and stealing from the good men on the sea."

Captain Baker smiles at that, shaking his head in shock. "A merciful pirate. Color me surprised, sir. I suppose I should be careful whose stories I listen to, shouldn't I?"

Danso bows before stepping away, the edges of his green coat blowing in the wind.

"The best possible outcome," Abeni says as they both return to the deck of the *Misericorde*. She grins, and Danso finds her glee contagious. "Some of those sailors on board were calling you *Robin Hood the Merciful*. Perhaps that second part will make it onto the wanted flyers, and then people won't know what to do with themselves."

Danso chuckles, a lightness in his step. He looks out at the assembled crew as they get ready to set sail. Some are former merchant sailors or naval hands. Some are escaped slaves and some are runaway indentured servants. Some are log cutters and convicts. Some are Black and some are white. Some are English and some are Spanish and some are French. It's a group of people you can't find anywhere but on a pirate ship, and he is proud at the thought. Jahni's there with his arm tossed around Flora's shoulders as soon as Danso steps back aboard, both of them looking up at him with so much admiration that Danso thinks he might cry.

"Robin Hood the Merciful," Jahni says in awe, because it sounds like a gallant adventurer's name, a knight from some age long past. In this part of the world, so few people like them are ever turned into legends. Into heroes.

Abeni picks up a giggling Flora, not so easy anymore now that Flora's twelve and not hopelessly skinny.

"And Maid Marian!" Flora crows.

They all laugh, like a family. Danso never thought he would have a family again, and he can scarcely believe this is real. He turns back around, and Captain Baker and his crew are still watching, still wondering, and for the first time, Danso revels in it all.

Maybe those sailors will tell this story, instead of some false tale about bloodthirsty villains.

Maybe they'll tell the truth.

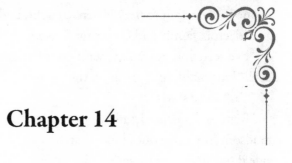

Chapter 14

Kingston, Jamaica. The Delacroix Home. May 1702.

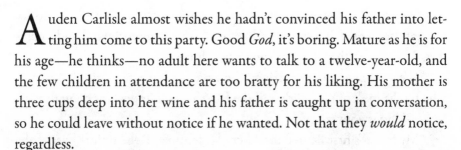

A uden Carlisle almost wishes he hadn't convinced his father into letting him come to this party. Good *God*, it's boring. Mature as he is for
his age—he thinks—no adult here wants to talk to a twelve-year-old, and
the few children in attendance are too bratty for his liking. His mother is
three cups deep into her wine and his father is caught up in conversation,
so he could leave without notice if he wanted. Not that they *would* notice,
regardless.

He takes in the scene around him. A shade of light blue paint coats the
walls, and a magnificent gold and crystal chandelier hangs from the ceiling.
Conversation buzzes through the room. Auden catches the scent of rasp-
berry wine. Perhaps he can nick some, later.

Just as he's considering sneaking out, he spots the host family near the
center of the ballroom, and they, unlike most people in Kingston aside
from interesting sailors coming in and out, are *not* boring. The Delacroix
boy is there too. Auden hadn't noticed him before.

The Delacroix family stands in a semi-circle across from a small group
of people Auden doesn't know, engaged in conversation a short distance
away from the dancing. The smile plastered on René Delacroix's face
doesn't reach his eyes, his posture straight as an arrow. René's between his
parents, Governor Travers on the other side of Captain Delacroix. Auden
walks up slowly, perusing the table of sweets while he listens in, and trying
to decide between the plum cake and the orange pudding. Anyone who is

anyone in Kingston society is here tonight, and everyone wants to talk to the Delacroix family and Governor Travers.

"I've seen you out sailing with your father," one of the women says to René. "Do you like going out on the ocean?"

"Yes," René starts. "I—"

"René is a talented sailor," Governor Travers says, speaking over his grandson. "It runs in our blood, that. It's best to know about ships and their trade if one invests in them."

René's plaster smile cracks. Captain Delacroix puts an arm around his son's shoulders, and at first, Auden thinks he's keeping René in line. The captain squeezes his son's shoulder very gently, shooting a concerned glance at the governor as if worried the older man might explode should he notice his grandson's faltering smile. Perhaps it is a mix of a reprimand and a comfort. A reminder that the governor is watching.

"We've seen you out sparring," the woman's husband adds. A ship captain, by the look of his hands and the fact that he's important enough to be here. "Who is your tutor?"

"My father's first lieutenant, Nicholas Jerome." René points over at the man in question, who stands with a half-full glass of white wine in his hands while he talks to a man in naval uniform. The naval officer is doing more of the talking, and Jerome nods as he listens, his black hair tied back without a strand out of place.

"Nicholas is quite the talent with a sword," Captain Delacroix says. "He became René's tutor quite by accident after René convinced him into playing sword games on my ship years ago."

"I'm sure he'll teach you to be quite a hand at it then," the man replies. "Maybe it will be helpful if pirates grow plentiful in the West Indies again, and it seems like they will. Someone to defend Kingston from the scoundrels like that Robin Hood the Merciful fellow we keep hearing about, or Henry Avery, if he ever shows himself again. Imagine calling a pirate merciful." The man scoffs. "Someone ought to change the name."

Captain Delacroix laughs, saying something like *indeed they should, John*, before looking over at his wife, who offers only the tiniest fraction of a smile in return. If that's any indication, they must be fighting. Auden's seen his parents do it enough to know the signs, though Mrs. Delacroix is a sight better about maintaining herself in public.

"Well, Astra," one of the women says. Alexandra Taylor, Auden thinks is her name. "René will have no trouble finding a wife when the time comes, I'm sure, with all his talents. Your boy will be quite a catch."

Mrs. Delacroix's smile widens when she looks at her son, and she seems fond of Mrs. Taylor, but there's a pain in her eyes Auden doesn't have a name for when she speaks. "I'm sure, but we've quite a while until then."

René gives his mother a real smile, but he twitches uncomfortably at the words.

"We shall secure the best possible marriage when the time comes." Governor Travers pats his grandson's cheek like he's playing at fondness, and Auden notices René doing his best not to pull back from the touch.

The group breaks up a few minutes later, and René ducks out from beneath his father's arm. He whispers something in his mother's ear before locating a chair near the edge of the room, swiping at the sweat beading on his hairline. Auden puts a piece of the plum cake into his pocket, straightens his coat, and walks over to René. The other boy's eyes trace the floor, one foot swinging back and forth.

"They all talked about you as if you weren't even there," Auden says. "I'm sorry you had to stand through that. Dreadful."

René jumps in a strangely graceful way before staring at Auden, his eyebrows meeting in the middle.

"Auden Carlisle." Auden sticks his hand out for the other boy to shake. "I know who you are, of course. René Delacroix."

René accepts Auden's hand warily, his grip firm. "I know who you are, too. I've seen you playing those card games with other boys down by the docks. Gambling. Your father is the most successful new privateer around."

So successful at capturing French ships for the war he almost forgets I exist, Auden almost says, worrying his lip before slapping a smile back on his face. "Happy to see my reputation precedes me," he says instead. "Where is your friend? The one—"

"Don't." René cuts him off, his shyness turning sharp.

"I was going to say the one with the spectacles," Auden answers, slow. "I don't know his first name. Just that he's a Seymour, and his father died. My father did business with the Seymours in London before we came here."

"I'm sorry." René turns sheepish. "It just wouldn't be the first time someone insulted Frantz or called him names. I won't stand for it. But it's Frantz. His name, I mean."

"Understood entirely," Auden replies. "In any case, where is he?"

René frowns. "He's not allowed at the party. My grandfather didn't deem it appropriate. My father didn't argue."

Auden doesn't need to ask why Frantz isn't allowed, because he already knows. "Let's go find him then."

"Your father won't look for you?"

"Guaranteed he won't, and my mother's had too much wine to notice. They'd rather talk to people here than keep up with where I am."

"Mine *will* notice."

"I think the trouble is worth it, don't you?" Auden puts a hand on René's forearm. He's startled when the other boy winces and pulls away. "Did I hurt you? What's wrong with your arm?"

René hesitates. "I hurt it, recently. There's a bruise there."

An over-loud laugh resounds through the room, ringing hollow and false. René's gaze shifts to the floor, and for a moment Auden doesn't understand why. He hears the laugh again, looking up to find Governor Travers nearby. His eyes flit to René's forearm.

Oh.

"We should go," Auden says, unable to keep the anger out of his voice. "My father beats his sailors, so at least it doesn't leave him any room to beat me. I'm sorry if that's what's happening to you."

René considers Auden, a full smile breaking out and lighting up his entire face. It's a contagious sort of thing, and Auden smiles too.

"You're going to get me in trouble, aren't you?" René whispers.

"*Oh.*" Auden swipes a brown curl behind his ear, that smile turning to a grin. "Without a doubt. Come on, while your father and grandfather are distracted."

Auden looks at René for permission before taking the uninjured arm and pulling him through the crowd until they're out of the room. René directs him through the house and up the stairs, the chatter from the ballroom fading away behind them.

"I've seen you giving some of that money you won gambling to people in the street," René says, and Auden looks up, seeing a gleam of approval in the eyes of this potential friend. "Is that why you'll only play cards with the wealthier boys? I thought maybe it was because you didn't want to associate with the poor boys, but then I saw you doing that."

Despite himself, Auden blushes. "I certainly won't gamble with people who can't afford to lose. Most of the brats I play against just steal it from their fathers."

René smiles again. "Isn't that what you do?"

"Part of it is my allowance," Auden insists. "But yes. The difference between them and me is that I'm not a brat."

René stops in front of a door near the end of the hallway. "Here." He knocks softly as though he fears someone will hear him all the way upstairs. "Frantz? It's René. And I've brought someone. Can we come in?"

Frantz calls out his assent, and the two of them step inside, far from the prying eyes of the party. A stack of maps sits on Frantz's nightstand, an old spyglass resting on top. A naval sailing instruction book meant for young midshipmen lays open next to the maps, *R. Delacroix* written inside the cover.

"I wasn't expecting you until later." Frantz marks his place in his book and closes it. *The Assayer*, by Galileo. "Shouldn't you still be at the party?"

"Yes," René admits. "We snuck out."

"Can't blame you," Frantz says, but he looks worried. He glances down at René's injured arm, still covered by the eye-searing, mustard-colored coat. Auden's sure René didn't select *that* atrocious thing for himself—it most certainly was the governor's choice, given his own was the same color.

"They were all talking over him and about him like he wasn't even there," Auden offers, drawing Frantz's attention back to him. "It seemed appropriate to sneak out while we could."

Frantz quirks an eyebrow, a half-smile sliding onto his face as he gets up from the bed and puts his hand out for Auden to shake. "Frantz Seymour."

"Auden Carlisle."

"Oh, the boy who gambles at the docks!" Frantz exclaims. "Yes, I've seen you before. You'll have to teach me how to play. Faro's not a game I know."

Auden smirks. "Didn't expect the two of you to be such rebels."

"Yes you did," René argues. "Otherwise you wouldn't have come over to me."

"I'm caught!" Auden laughs, then grows more solemn. "To be fair, I was worried. Your grandfather seems dreadful, even from a distance."

René gives Auden a tight, weary smile, shrugging off his coat and rolling up his sleeves in deference to the hot weather outside. The bruise is nasty, long purple streaks spread out in the shape of fingertips as though the governor's hand still won't let go of René.

"I'm still so angry they wouldn't let you come to the ball, Frantz," René continues, fire in his eyes. "It's ridiculous. Bloody bastards."

"You really have started cursing like a sailor, René." Frantz flicks his friend affectionately in the other arm. "In any case, it doesn't sound like I missed very much. But I'm glad you're here. And with a new friend!"

Auden winks at him, a surge of joy bubbling up in his chest. His family barely pays him any attention anymore and he doesn't have any *real* friends, but these two seem promising. He scans Frantz's bed and spots a newspaper headline peeking out from under the bedclothes, easily covered up if someone comes inside unexpectedly.

Robin Hood and Maid Marian Commit More Sea Robberies!

"An admirer of that Robin Hood pirate, are you?" Auden asks Frantz. "He and his quartermaster are brilliant thieves. I like them because my father hates them, and I do my best to do the opposite of my father, these days."

Frantz grins. "René and I admire him and his quartermaster. That's not something we'd share with many people, obviously, but René's got a whole collection of newspaper stories about them hidden away. We just heard an interesting story from some sailors, where they only stole wine from a ship and left the rest, because the captain was good to his men. I'd wager that some people would like to say that one isn't true."

"Jerome would die if he knew I had them." René glances sidelong at Auden. "My father's first lieutenant. He ended up on my father's crew because

Robin Hood and Maid Marian were a convict and a slave who escaped on his watch and his old captain had him transferred."

"I'll be damned!" Auden exclaims. "That's something, isn't it?"

René gazes at him, a bright gleam of an idea in his eyes. "Say, Auden?"

"Yes, René?"

René shares a quick glance with Frantz, and they seem to understand each other without speaking. "Would you mind teaching us that game you play? Faro? We don't know it."

Auden puts a hand on his hip. "Not that I mind, but what does the grandson of the governor want to do with a gambling game? Money isn't exactly a problem for you, is it?"

René grins, he *really* grins, and Auden sees the mischief in it, now, when it's not so forced.

Interesting.

"In case I need money of my own," René answers. "Gambling with you might be a way for Frantz and me to get it. We're both good at cards."

Auden meets René's eyes, intrigued. "Money of your own for *what*, pray tell?"

"That's for me to know and you to find out." René's grin grows, and Frantz looks between them with eagerness. "Teach us?"

Auden reaches down into his pocket, pulling out a deck of cards and the cake from earlier. "All right, lads. Let's see what I can teach you before they come up here looking for us."

His two new friends nod enthusiastically in return, and Auden knows that here, hiding away in this room from the adults and the party below them, that this is the beginning of a beautiful friendship.

Chapter 15

Kingston, Jamaica. June 1703.

Jerome finds René still asleep at half-past eight.

The bedclothes almost cover René's head entirely, Michel's copy of William Dampier's *A New Voyage Round the World* lying face down and open next to his right hand. Dampier is a famous buccaneer turned explorer, and the worn edges of the pages indicate this isn't the first time René's read the book.

"Up, René."

René cracks his eyes open, pausing for a moment in what Jerome can only assume is bewilderment at being awake. "Why are *you* here?"

"Because you're late for your lesson with me, that's why. We were meant to start fifteen minutes ago," Jerome says, disliking the irritated way in which René said *you*. "Your father said your mother was supposed to wake you up to come and meet me since he had to leave early this morning."

"She did." René closes his eyes again, turning over and away from Jerome. "But I fell back asleep. Mrs. Hudson knocked on my door, too, so don't blame her."

"Well, you're getting up now. I have better things to do than coax a thirteen-year-old boy out of bed."

"*Well*, then go *away*," René protests, pulling the bedclothes over his head, which muffles his voice. "I'm on holiday for two weeks since Mr. Edwards and Mr. Daniels are both away," he continues, referencing the two tutors he shares with Frantz. "Let me sleep and go do those better things you just mentioned."

"No. Your father and I are sailing out in two days. We're having this lesson."

Jerome tugs on the bedcovers from the bottom. René is forced to sit up, trying and failing to yank them back.

"You're ridiculous," Jerome grumbles.

"*You're* ridiculous," René echoes, swinging his legs over the side of the bed and rubbing his eyes.

Jerome heaves a sigh. Time for another tactic. He retrieves the mug of coffee he's brought up as an enticement. René loves the beverage as much as his father does, almost to the point of sacrilege, and much to his grandfather's displeasure. Good Englishmen drink tea, after all.

"I brought this." Steam curls up from the cup as Jerome hands it over, a rich, chocolate-tinged scent perfuming the air. "Drink it, and then get dressed." He pauses, an amused smirk tugging at the corner of his mouth. "You look like an irritated cherub with your hair all mussed like that."

René takes a long swig of his coffee and shoves at Jerome's leg with his bare foot, though he's fighting a smile. Jerome loves René and Michel in equal measure, one as a brother and one as nearly a father, but lately, things have been complicated.

Twenty minutes later René comes downstairs hastily dressed, thanking a flustered Peter, and assuring him that he doesn't need any more help. He's wearing his favorite navy-blue coat, and the red ribbon Jerome gave him long ago. His shirt is untucked from his breeches and one button isn't done on his waistcoat, but it will have to do. They walk through town largely in silence, René carrying one sword and Jerome the other. Jerome finds he misses René peppering him with questions like he did in earlier years.

René stops in his tracks outside a tavern, his gaze catching on a flyer tacked to the door.

Wanted: Robin Hood the Merciful and his quartermaster, Maid Marian.

Jerome scowls. He hates that ridiculous moniker. He glances at the drawing of Danso's face, thinking that for once, it's fairly accurate. The long locs. The broad shoulders. The anger. He remembers that bubbling, brewing rage in the convict's eyes.

He's tried to forget the other things he saw. The kinder things.

Memory sweeps Jerome up in its grasp, the night Danso and the slave escaped overtaking him. Why did they let him go? It doesn't make sense. All these years later, it *still* doesn't make sense. He's kept a notebook for a while now, full of scraps of information he gleans from sailors and newspapers and anyone who might talk about the infamous Robin Hood and his quartermaster. Desperation claws at him whenever he hears their names, desperation to hunt them down and bring them in, but they haven't been asked to chase pirates since the voyage when Arthur died, so Jerome is hesitant to raise the subject despite Michel's earlier promises to keep at the Navy for that opportunity. His own feelings of failure are not more important than Michel's grief, but as more stories about pirates spill into lore, as he sees the brother he chose looking with interest at these flyers, he's determined to bring it up again.

He studies Danso's visage, remembering a moment on the *Agincourt* when the other convict laborer aboard—before he died from scurvy, anyway—asked Danso where he was from as they scrubbed the quarterdeck.

I'm just a nothing from Bristol, the man said, and Jerome thought about his father, who hailed from the same port town. Their family lived there, for a few years, and his own accent indicates such. *Came here looking for work. Got in trouble for thieving. What about you?*

My father's family was from Senegambia. He escaped from a sugar plantation, Danso said, looking unsure. *My mother was from here. Carib.*

We're both thieves in the end, aren't we? the other convict asked. *Ended up in the same place.*

Jerome shakes his head, pulling himself away from the vivid recollection. He's disturbed by the admiration in René's eyes, a smile slipping onto the boy's face at the sight of a wanted pirate.

"René." He puts a hand on René's shoulder, noticing him flinch slightly. "Come now, we have a lesson to attend to."

René pulls away. "How did they get away from you?" he asks once they start walking again. "Robin Hood and Maid Marian? You've never told me the details."

There's a challenge in the boy's voice, and Jerome's angry, too much so for the situation at hand.

"They aren't good people." Jerome doesn't answer the question, and René frowns. "Believe me, they don't deserve a moment of your attention. Tuck in your shirt, please."

They run into Frantz and Auden as they reach their usual spot on the shore, the other two boys eager to watch the lesson.

"Why must I use the court sword *still*?" René asks a few minutes later, examining the weapon. "What about a cutlass? That's what you and my father use."

"The court sword is best for practice right now," Jerome answers, unsheathing his own. "We'll try the cutlass when you're sixteen. It's a more dangerous weapon."

"But if you use cutlasses most often in a fight at sea then what's the point?" Auden questions, twirling a stray piece of his wavy brown hair around his finger, and Jerome feels an automatic spike of aggravation. Auden Carlisle has annoyed him since the beginning, and he's a bad influence on René and Frantz.

Jerome turns around. "Because. You must master one thing at a time and then move forward. Governor Travers and Captain Delacroix might drop by, and I would prefer to show them the progress René has made so far rather than fumble through something to suit your fancy. Besides, René is far more likely to use a court sword, in his position. A cutlass is meant for close combat." He looks over at René, whose eyes darken at the mention of his position. "Why did you insist on bringing him along?"

"Because he wanted to come?" René answers, tilting his head.

Jerome's eyes flit over to Frantz, who has his nose buried in a pile of pamphlets. "What are you reading, Frantz?"

Frantz doesn't hear, squinting in thought as he reads down the page.

"Frantz?" Jerome clears his throat, speaking louder.

Frantz jumps at the sound of his name, his spectacles sliding down his nose. "Yes?"

"I asked what you were reading."

"Oh." He folds the pamphlet closed, marking his place. "Some old pamphlets by Edmond Halley that belonged to my father. Uncle Michel found them and gave them to me a few days ago."

"The astronomer?" Auden asks, a spark of interest in his green eyes.

Jerome raises his eyebrows. "You know who Edmond Halley is?"

"My father makes his living sailing," Auden says, and it irritates Jerome that his response still sounds so good-natured despite the insult. "And as I too want to make my career in that fashion, I do occasionally read. Usually what Frantz or René recommend."

Jerome's self-conscious with the three boys watching him. "Come on then, René. Let's start."

René unsheathes the court sword with natural ease. Jerome moves behind him, adjusting his grip on the hilt with one hand, his other resting on René's forearm. The boy jerks, his eyes going down toward Jerome's hand instead of paying attention to the altered grip, his body tensing as he sucks in a breath.

"Does your arm hurt?" Jerome asks, quiet enough so that only René hears him.

"I'm fine."

Then, Jerome realizes, memories of the day the governor bruised René's arm tumbling into his mind. The fingertip bruise remained for several weeks after. There have been incidents since then, but that one still sticks out. The situation upsets Michel, and Jerome's never certain what advice to give. He does wish René would behave.

Although, a small voice whispers in the back of his mind, *even if he was perfect, would it be enough for the governor?*

He shakes it off, focusing back on the lesson.

"My apologies." Jerome carefully removes his hand from René's forearm. René looks at him, surprise flaring in his eyes among the anxiety. "Tighten your fingers on the hilt a little now. Palm up. Good."

They begin, fifteen minutes passing before Astra approaches them.

"Mama." René's eyes light up when he sees his mother, lowering his sword.

A knot of anger forms in Jerome's stomach, and he's frustrated that René only listens to his mother now, and barely ever to Michel. René pays rapt attention to Jerome during their sword lessons, but otherwise? Jerome can't pinpoint the exact moment things changed. He just knows they have. Arthur's death sent a crack running through the foundation of their life here. That, he knows for certain.

"I came to see you practice." Astra smiles over at Auden and Frantz, who visibly relax in her presence. "If that's all right, Lieutenant Jerome?"

Jerome inclines his head. "Of course. You are very welcome." He turns back toward René now, the sun beating down on them. "Hold the sword higher, René,"

Jerome advances, making a stance for an attack. "Now deflect."

René does, and the court swords make what Jerome is sure René would call a 'satisfying' clang.

"Good show, René!" Auden calls out, and René grins in response, his eyes catching on his friend.

"Now fade," Jerome continues, his gaze falling briefly to René's feet to watch his footwork. René goes backward, his feet in the same position, then immediately jumps forward again, and Jerome's caught off guard.

Dammit. The empty fade. He should have known better than to teach him that.

With the advantage, René presses down on Jerome's sword. His much smaller size doesn't allow him to hold for long, but he does so longer than Jerome expects. Jerome's height permits him to pull his own sword out from under René's, and in the split second of surprise Jerome advances again and René retreats in the same moment. They go back and forth, Jerome moving into some faster footwork and René almost matching the speed. Jerome attacks, and René does a perfect circular parry before his own riposte. Jerome blocks it, their swords crossing perfectly in the middle above them.

René's smile reaches his eyes, his face glowing with exhilaration. Jerome smiles in turn. Whatever his annoyance at René's behavior, he misses seeing him look happy.

"Sheath." Jerome says. He inclines his head toward his student. "That was very impressive. Remember not to depend on strength too much unless you must, because it will only tire you out. Speed is more important, and strategy most of all. Think. Outsmart. You did that nicely at the end. That parry was especially well done."

Auden whoops in approval, and René laughs.

"You're a good teacher," René says, sounding like his old self as he dabs sweat from his forehead and catches his breath.

"You are very fearsome, darling," Astra adds, drawing laughter from Frantz and a blush from René. "I really—"

Shouting from further down the harbor interrupts her words, and Jerome swings around, searching for the source of the ruckus. It's coming from the direction of the *Navigator*, and a small group of the crew is on deck, Michel and Governor Travers himself coming up from the hold. He can't read their expressions from this distance, but they seem harried. Michel gives orders to the men aboard before stalking off the ship with Governor Travers walking beside him. Frantz tenses as the pair approach their spot on the beach, Auden slipping an arm around his waist. Astra steps up next to René, perhaps unconsciously, focused on her father rather than her oddly irate husband.

"There are thieves all around this island, and I've heard word of some bands of gypsies in the Bahamas who might make their way here," Governor Travers says as he walks up with Michel. "Not to mention the Maroons, who just got into a skirmish with some of the militia in Spanish Town last week. I'm not surprised this happened. I'll put a better patrol on the harbor, immediately. The night watch is lacking."

Jerome's hand twitches on his court sword. The grip loosens so much that René notices, surveying Jerome before turning back toward Michel, who looks uncharacteristically livid.

"What's going on?" Jerome puts away his sword, the metal catching the sunlight as it slides into the sheath.

"We've been robbed," Michel replies, his voice low with frustration. "The *Navigator*, that is."

"What?" Jerome asks. "Who? How much?"

"Only a few smaller things, based on the inventory we took a few days ago while doing the loading," Michel explains. "I imagine the crates of sugar were too large to steal without notice. But the silks that were transferred to us were missing, which were the most expensive. I cannot imagine how endless my report will have to be, or what the insurers will say. They also ripped a page from my log, the one about the ship's new name. It's odd."

"We will need to question your men, Michel." Governor Travers crosses his arms over his chest, saltwater spilled on his embroidered waistcoat.

"It could have been some of them working together, thinking that you wouldn't notice a few crates missing."

"Father's men wouldn't steal from the ship like that," René protests, defensive of the men around whom he has grown up. Michel's shoulders tighten at the word *Father*, which René now uses more than *Papa*.

Governor Travers' eyes snap sharply over René, and Astra wraps an arm around her son's shoulders.

"You don't understand the depths of depravity to which a common sailor might sink, René. Besides that, you are not always the best judge of character." Governor Travers looks at Frantz, his lip curling in disdain.

As soon as the governor glances away Frantz narrows his eyes, Auden's grip around his waist growing tighter.

"I think we should let the boys be on their way." Astra kisses her son's temple when she lets him go, her gaze flickering over to Frantz and Auden with concern. "They don't need to be a part of this conversation."

"How did René do with his lesson?" Governor Travers asks, grasping onto the boys' presence for a moment longer.

Jerome nods. "Excellently, sir. Frankly, he very nearly had me with an empty fade."

"Well *done* René," Michel says, coming over and clasping his son's shoulder.

René doesn't pull away, but he does stiffen. That never happened, in the early years. Before Arthur's death. Before that bruise on René's arm. Before ... everything.

Jerome longs for those days. It frightens him, sometimes, being a part of this family, because you can lose your family, and he's been through that already. This new one could opt to cut him out if he doesn't fit, because while they chose him, he is not their blood. Despite those fears, he cannot let them go. This is home, whatever comes.

"You've taught him well," Governor Travers adds, almost smiling, and smiling is no common thing for him.

Jerome bows. "Thank you, Governor Travers. Your grandson is a talented swordsman for his age, but I appreciate your kind words."

"Credit is given where it is due, lad," Governor Travers replies. "I can only hope that one day my grandson will be as disciplined as you are, instead of wasting his time on less worthy pursuits."

The governor looks at Frantz again, his glance lingering briefly on Auden with a touch more approval. Auden keeps hold of Frantz, raising his eyebrows in challenge.

Daring, for a thirteen-year-old. For anyone.

René clenches and unclenches his right fist several times in rapid succession, taking a deep breath.

"Are you quite all right, René?" Governor Travers asks, the movement drawing his attention back over. "And fix your waistcoat. It's out of sorts."

René grits his teeth, his tone polite and full of held-back fire. "Yes, sir."

"You should be grateful to Jerome," Governor Travers continues, "for being such a patient teacher. Especially with your behavior lately."

"I am grateful, Grandfather," René replies, forced civility in every syllable.

"You have quite a natural talent." Governor Travers says. "No doubt passed on from both sides of your lineage. A great deal to live up to."

René smiles again but it doesn't reach his eyes, the expression more strained than Jerome's yet seen as the exhilarated light from earlier recedes. "May we go as Mama suggested?"

Governor Travers gestures him away with one hand, and René whispers something in his mother's ear before dashing off without uttering another word to Michel, Jerome, or his grandfather, slipping one hand into Frantz's and one into Auden's. They have a secret hideaway somewhere, Jerome suspects, he's just not sure where. Possibly the palm tree grove near the beach, but he hasn't caught them there yet. He also suspects René and Frantz are gambling as Auden does, but he doesn't have proof of that, either. Only suspicions. That might be why René was so tired this morning. He's been caught out late at night more than once.

Children are oddly talented at subterfuge.

"I think I may have an idea of who might have stolen from us, sir," Jerome says, avoiding the use of Michel's first name around Governor Travers, who prefers formality.

Michel tilts his head, looking as if he's grasping onto the idea of who Jerome might mean, but doesn't voice it. "Who?"

Jerome swallows, aware that what he wants to say might sound absurd for the usual pattern of piracy. "I think it might have been Danso. Or Robin Hood the Merciful and Maid Marian, as the papers call them." He rolls his eyes. "There have been sightings of them in this area, according to those same papers, and even more dependable, sailors coming into port here."

"I heard they'd been spotted near here as well. They got into a skirmish with a naval patrol ship, but why would he and his crew simply steal our shipment?" Michel asks. "There's no glory in that for them. It would be odd."

"We heard those rumors about them dropping off money in poorer areas of the islands," Jerome argues, even if he never usually disagrees with Michel. "Maybe this is where they're getting that money from. It's a smaller amount than they'd steal from chasing down a ship at sea."

Governor Travers furrows his eyebrows, tapping one finger against his lips. "I had a letter from the governor of Barbados, and he did say they've had a few in-harbor robberies lately. Small-time thefts. They assumed it was regular thieves, but Lieutenant Jerome may be right."

Michel doesn't answer immediately. He doesn't think Jerome is responsible for Danso's escape, or that Danso's continued exploits will impact Jerome's career. But Jerome knows better, and he worries. Jerome knows that Michel's affection clouds his judgement. Jerome will *never* stop blaming himself. Perhaps if Danso and Abeni hadn't become pirates, he could let it go. But they are, and he can't.

"It is not out of the question," Michel concedes. "Nicholas has excellent instincts. I only thought we might need a bit more investigation before we set on a suspect. We don't want to waste our time."

Astra raises her eyebrows, brushing one hand against her deep green gown. "It seems the Robin Hood of pirates can do anything. Perhaps he and his quartermaster are immortal, like I hear some of the men at the docks saying." There's amusement in her voice, and a strange, sarcastic challenge, too, similar to the one in René's when he asked Jerome about Danso and the woman escaping.

Jerome meets her eyes, thinking she looks downright angry at him. Not for the first time, he feels suspicious of her. He just can't pinpoint a concrete reason as to why. She reminds him of his mother, sometimes, with her sharpness. Her secrets. He'd like to know what those secrets are.

"I assure you, madam," he says, biting his tongue against disrespect toward his commanding officer's wife and the governor's daughter, "they are *not*."

She smiles at him. Smirks? He's not certain he's seen a woman like her smirk before.

"No, I suppose not. But I do love a good story." Astra looks at her husband, and Michel looks back, smoothing his already perfect hair. "I must take my leave, I'm afraid. I'll see you at home, Michel."

She walks away and Michel stares after her, irritation rippling across his face, his countenance more severe than usual. "I don't know what's gotten into her lately."

"Astra has always had a strange affinity for ... rogues." Governor Travers lands on the word with an odd tone, as if *rogues* wasn't the word he was looking for. "In any case, we should go speak to the customs officers and find out what they know. The governors of other islands in the Indies have worried over the pirate sympathizers in port and the network the thieves are creating. Makes them harder to catch if they know what routes to avoid. I won't have pirates stealing from us in the dark of night. Not in *my* colony."

Michel agrees, and Jerome falls into step with him as Governor Travers walks ahead of them.

"Perhaps it wasn't Danso," Michel whispers, an attempt at reassurance as he presses Jerome's shoulder. "We don't know that it was. Come with me to the house for a bit when we're done with this business, won't you? I found a copy of *The Odyssey* in the bookshop the other day I wanted to give you. I know it's your favorite."

Jerome nods, not wanting to argue over the matter. "Thank you, Michel. It's kind of you to pick that up for me."

Only, he's certain Danso and his woman quartermaster *are* the thieves they're looking for. Call it a sailor's hunch, but he knows. He remembers Orion's light spilling down onto the deck of the *Agincourt* when the two escaped from him, the memory as sharp and vivid as ever.

Orion, the hunter.

He swears he'll hunt them down one day. And he won't let René fall under their spell, either. Whatever it takes.

Interlude IX: Of the Progress of Outlaws

Kingston, Jamaica. June 1703.

———❦———

"I cannot believe we are here," Abeni grumbles in Danso's ear from their position crouched in a familiar grove of trees near the harbor. "I cannot believe that this is where we chose to go, of every port town in the West Indies. I cannot believe you allowed it."

"I lead according to the will of the crew," Danso protests. "The men voted to come here."

"Kingston is the lion's den for pirates." Abeni speaks in a loud, irritated whisper. "You know that as well as I do. Sometimes the men like a challenge too much."

"We agreed it was time to start pushing back against the East India presence in the Caribbean," Danso argues. "But in a way that's less dangerous than confronting them at sea, with their guns. They've got less of a grip here than in the East, but we'll see how long that lasts. They expect us to come in firing. They don't expect this." He looks over, trying out a smile. She glares back at him, unmoved. "You say the men like a challenge, but you aren't exactly challenge-averse, you know. If my quartermaster disagrees with me—"

"Don't tease me." Abeni shoves him. He makes a great fuss of pretending to fall, earning a second glare, albeit a fond one.

"These smaller targets are important," he says. "They give us the money to leave on people's doorsteps. You agreed with me before, and you have no trouble saying when you disagree."

Abeni huffs, a smirk sliding across her face. "Are you certain you're not just doing something daring so that you might add to your growing reputation in the papers? I can just see it now." She waves her hand in a curve out in front of her. "Robin Hood the Merciful Strikes Again in the Heart of English Territory Without Firing a Shot!

"I admit it crossed my mind." Danso gives the wry response, receiving a swat for his trouble. "You're forgetting your own nickname, aren't you? *Maid Marian?*"

She swats at him again. "I love you like a brother, Danso, so don't expect me to start kissing you. There won't be any swooning. I do like the Maid Marian stories the men have told me, otherwise."

Danso laughs, the sound rumbling up from deep in his chest. "All right, my friend. No kissing or swooning."

They lay in wait with six of their crew, biding their time until the paltry four guards from the English Navy make their way further down the harbor and leave the East India ship they've got their eyes on unmanned. Kingston Harbor in daylight is armed to the teeth. In darkness, less so. For now. With Andrew Travers in charge that is likely to change, at least as soon as he gets word of this.

"I wonder how Astra is." Abeni looks off into the distance where they can just see the Delacroix house on the horizon, about a mile from the docks at the top of the hill.

"I hope she's well." Danso remembers her face when she left them on the *Carina*. He remembers the promise he made her. The first promise he'd made in years.

"I think of her often," Abeni says. "I wonder what she's doing now."

Danso nods in agreement. "It's odd. That perhaps Astra's son might be one of the very men in charge of stomping out people like us. His grandfather cleared out the last of the old buccaneers from Port Royal, and he has strict rules for any new privateers so he can be sure they don't fall into real piracy. His father is an East India captain. Good to his men, I hear, but no rule-breaker like his wife."

"Or the boy could be like his mother," Abeni argues. "Governor Travers is the nasty sort, but Astra obviously isn't much like him if she helped us. Maybe it will be the same with the lad."

"What was his name again?" Danso eyes the guards, watching them move away.

"René." Abeni speaks the name as if part of her feels like she knows him. "He'd be about Flora's age now, I think. A touch younger than Jahni."

Danso opens his mouth to respond, but then the guards move out of sight, and he's drawn to the task at hand.

"Our first objective is the goods on board," Danso whispers. "East India ships like this one often carry cotton and silks, which we can make use of." Most of their plunder must go to the crew and the common fund for the ship's upkeep, but he likes having this extra money to do good. "If you see any money lying about, take advantage."

They walk toward the *Navigator*, sneaking aboard without issue. Danso keeps watch on deck while Abeni and the others race below searching for goods. The *Misericorde* sits anchored a short distance away from the harbor proper, flying English colors to hide in plain sight, though putting the lanterns out largely cloaks the ship in darkness. Danso isn't foolish enough to stay in port overnight in a place like Kingston, but the disguise works for now, and they will not have this chance again. Not here. After a few minutes, the other crew members return with a small crate each and one for him—the larger ones are far too heavy and require the block and tackle. They make toward the longboats they tied up nearby, but Abeni doesn't come back above. She emerges five minutes after the others, carrying one smaller crate and a piece of paper in her hands.

"Danso." She holds out the page, clearly ripped from the ship's log. "This is Michel Delacroix's ship."

"No. His ship is the *Steorra*. We made sure."

"It's been renamed, according to this log. This page was bookmarked. This was why we couldn't sort out who the captain of this ship was."

"I believe you." Danso takes the paper. "But we have to go."

They make their way through the darkness and back to the *Misericorde* without incident. Once the crates are stowed away, Danso pulls the piece of paper out of his pocket. He runs his fingers over the lines of writing, an old habit learned when Jahni's father taught him to read, because he only knew a little, as a child.

This ship has been renamed The Navigator in honor of our fallen sailing master, Arthur Seymour, who fell in defense of our captain, Michel Delacroix, during a storm on December 15th, 1701.

"Signed *Captain M. Delacroix,*" Danso breathes.

It *is* his ship.

"Not only that," Abeni urges. "Read the signature below."

Danso complies, his eyes widening when they land on the signature just below the captain's.

N. Jerome, first lieutenant.

Danso thinks of the young East India sailor now and again. He thinks of the secrets and the vulnerability and the fear buried not so deep beneath the surface. He thinks of the rage in Jerome's eyes and Orion's light dripping *down down down* the night sky.

They need to get out of here. Now.

They have business elsewhere in Jamaica, on the other side of the island in Saint James Parish, which boasts little activity other than lard exports, the sparseness making it safer to dock there. Ebele cultivated a contact that Abeni keeps in touch with whenever they come nearby—not often, given the danger here. The customs officer gives them the latest information coming out of Spanish Town and Kingston, for some coin, and it helps them keep ahead of the Navy and the East India Company.

"Jerome's moved up in the world," Danso mutters. "I know how powerful Michel Delacroix is, but I hadn't realized Jerome was on his crew now. And apparently of great importance. East India was known for hunting pirates in the Indian Ocean with zeal just a few years ago. There are rumblings they want to crack down on piracy in the West Indies before it can take real hold again. Before there's more of us." He stops, the name *Seymour* caught on the tip of his tongue. Seymour, the sailing master.

"This must be the man we helped in Saint-Domingue. He worked for East India, didn't he?" Abeni says, without Danso needing to say anything, running her finger over the word *Arthur*. "It happened so fast I'd almost forgotten. I wonder what happened to his wife and son. Wasn't he the one who told Astra about Barlow? That was why you recognized his name that day."

"Yes, he was," Danso whispers, a pang of grief for a man he knew for only a moment twinging in his chest as he looks up at the vast and glittering sky. If Seymour hadn't told Astra about Barlow, they might never have made it to Ebele, let alone out of Kingston, in one piece. He glances in the direction of the Delacroix house, making out Gemini just above. "He seemed very kind."

Castor and Pollux, Ebele says in his memory. *Gemini's brightest stars. Greek mythology says they protect sailors, you know.*

Abeni's eyes trace the same set of stars. "I know we've been trying to maneuver around Captain Delacroix as much as we could for thinking of Astra and because he's good to his men, but if Jerome has it out to catch us .... You said that he suspected your plan to run that night. That he had a knack for details."

"Yes," Danso says softly, something like fate clutching at him. "I did say that."

Danso breathes a sigh of relief when the men pull the anchor up so they can set off. A sense of foreboding fills him up. Images tumble into his head, hazy and smeared and oddly familiar as if they're his own memories, but he doesn't recognize the players. A shiver runs down his spine.

He won't come back to Kingston again.

Chapter 16

Kingston, Jamaica. May 1704.

———⟨∾⟩———

"René, you will explain yourself. Now."

René flinches at the anger in his father's voice, at the cold, flat tone. He does this instead of shouting, making René feel like a burden with every disappointed word. It's not frightening like his grandfather's harsh, loud yelling, but it hurts because René cares about what his father thinks. He hasn't cared what his grandfather thought since he was small, and the memories of wishing for the governor's love are almost faded away. Now he only wishes he didn't have to fight the old man's voice in his head.

His father caught him gambling.

Or, about to gamble. No money had been put out yet, thankfully. He'd been out alone with Auden since Frantz was in bed with the same head cold René's mother has.

René sticks his thumbs into the space where his breeches meet his shirt, keeping a good distance between himself and his father. They ended up in the library once they came inside— René's choice. Michel's near one set of bookshelves and René near the worn reading chair in the corner.

"Explain what?" René stares his father down. "That I was playing cards with friends? You play cards at parties all the time."

Michel strides across the room with pointed, echoing footsteps, a strand of neatly brushed hair falling into his eye. He stops short, smacking René's cards down on the table next to the reading chair.

"Do not play coy with me, son. Jerome said he suspected that you and Frantz both had been gambling with Auden recently, and he was right."

"We weren't gambling," René insists. "You didn't see any money, did you?"

Michel frowns, suspicion flaring in his eyes. "Not *yet*."

René swallows back a retort. There *is* money hidden, and he can't let his father find it. Fortunately, most of it is with Auden because Captain Carlisle pays less attention, but some is also hidden under the loose floorboard beneath René's bed, and yet more in Frantz's room, tucked away in a chest of Uncle Arthur's old things.

Money they might need to run away, if they have to.

Michel sighs. "René, you cannot keep this up. Sneaking down to the docks at all hours and talking to God knows who when I've told you no a thousand times. Those sailors might spin a good yarn, but you don't know who they are. And now you're gambling."

The words *spin a good yarn* make René glance with old affection around the library, his eyes running over the different spines facing outward toward him, a story living on the pages of each and every one. He spies the much-loved copy of *Don Quixote* resting on the small writing desk in the corner, a particular memory appearing like a watercolor painting in his mind, the sounds sharper than the images. He and Frantz had been sharing the large, cozy reading chair with *Don Quixote* spread across their laps, when Michel came in.

Let me read aloud to you a while, Michel said. *Would you like that?* His finger ran down the page, his voice falling to a whisper. *The truth may be stretched thin, but it never breaks, and it always surfaces above lies, as oil floats on water.*

Your father's favorite passage in this book, Michel told Frantz absent-mindedly. *Your mother read this to him first, I think. When you were just born.* He stopped abruptly then, bidding them goodnight and leaving the library behind, Arthur's ghost trailing at his heels.

René doesn't tell his father that he and Frantz read the stories and newspaper articles about pirates until they know them by heart. He doesn't tell him that he reads the stories about Robin Hood the Merciful and his woman quartermaster to help himself fall asleep at night. He and Frantz added the pirate stories to the old book of sea legends Prescott gave René years before, writing down the tales sailors tell them at the docks, tales about Ebele and Danso and the woman quartermaster whose real name no one seems to know yet. About all sorts of pirates. Hope breathes within the pages, making him believe the world can change. That *his* world can change. The stories are in his blood by now, but reading them makes him feel safe. They make him remember that what he and Frantz dream about is real. They can sail together. They *can*. It is not so wild a thing to imagine.

René doesn't answer.

Michel shakes his head. "This will stop right now. Do you hear me? All of it. People are going to talk if they aren't already. No matter our wealth and status, no family of means will consider a future betrothal to their daughter if you're set on behaving this way. You may not be thinking of it now, but those matters are less than a decade away. You have to think, René. The future will come faster than you realize, and what you do now matters. You are the blood of French and English nobility. You are the grandson of the governor of Jamaica. An heir to a title. Eyes are on you. Constantly."

Those words are a swift kick to René's stomach, the air knocked out of him. He's been hoping to avoid this conversation for a while longer, to avoid talking about this topic with his father, who will probably never understand what he's about to say, or won't believe him, or won't take him seriously. René doesn't have a word or a phrase for the surety that's been building within him for the last year or so, but he feels certain about it even still.

"I don't"—René struggles, his cheeks burning with embarrassment—"I don't want to marry a woman when I'm older. Auden likes to talk about the girls he likes but I don't ...." He trails off, because he doesn't know what to say. He doesn't know if others feel how he does, but they must, surely? He can't be alone.

His father looks back at him, a strange, sharp glint in his eyes as he opens his mouth and then closes it again.

"What do you mean, son?"

René swallows, a lump growing in his throat. "I mean I don't want to be married. Ever."

Auden's known as a flirt with girls their age around Kingston, though he's only kissed one that René knows of. Frantz confided to René a few weeks ago that he isn't sure how he feels on the matter—kissing girls that is, or other boys, or if he feels like René does—but René knows he isn't interested in kissing anyone at all. He knows he's expected to be thinking about girls, now, but he isn't. He has seen sailors kissing each other in the shadows of Kingston harbor at night, but he hasn't felt that way, either.

Silence pours into the room, the absence of sound overwhelming until the grandfather clock downstairs finally chimes the hour, the noise ringing in René's ears. A familiar panic starts creeping up from the pit of his stomach with nauseating swiftness. He grasps the edge of the reading chair he's spent so much time in, his hand shaking.

Maybe he shouldn't have said anything. Maybe he ....

That sharp look remains in his father's eyes, but René can't tell if it's fear or disapproval or anger. He can't tell if it's all three at once or something entirely different. Michel sucks in a breath through his teeth, hesitating before he speaks again, and René realizes what his father is going to say.

Oh.

"Father, please don't—"

"Now, René." Michel clears his throat, awkwardness humming in the air between them. "If you're having *feelings* for Frantz, then I—"

"What?" René raises his voice, cutting his father off. "That's not what I said."

He loves Frantz. The person he confides in and trusts more than anyone is Frantz. He doesn't like to imagine living *without* Frantz. But he's not interested in kissing Frantz. He's not interested in kissing anyone. His friendships mean everything to him, and he doesn't want something else. Maybe that will change one day, but maybe it won't.

Michel shakes his head, confusion passing across his face as he opens his mouth and closes it a second time, whatever admonition he's searching for apparently eluding him.

"Me saying that I don't want to get married doesn't mean that I'm feeling romantic things for other boys." René is determined to be brave, even if he's afraid, and there's something new in his father's expression, something like alarm, or shame perhaps, red creeping into his cheeks. "I know that happens because people whisper about it instead of just minding their own business and letting people be happy, but I don't want to kiss anyone. I don't want to be married. Ever. That's it."

Frustration replaces the momentary gentleness in Michel's tone, and he turns away from René, placing his palms flat on the nearby writing desk. The old piece of furniture is scratched, partly from René's childish attempts to write directly on it with a quill as a little boy.

"René, son, you're fourteen. You don't know what you want. But I'm sure you'll understand, eventually. I wasn't always thinking of these things when I was your age, either, but it came. Marriage will be required of you, when you're older. Children. An heir."

René clenches his fist, a familiar throbbing in his temple. He's been getting headaches for a few months now. Sometimes, he's forced to lie in the dark for an afternoon to ease the pain.

"I'm trying to tell you something," René insists, resisting an urge to cry, and he thinks his father is refusing to tell *him* something, he just doesn't know what, exactly. "I'm trying to be honest like you want, and you won't listen."

René's heart shudders in his chest. He shouldn't have said anything. He shouldn't have *said* anything. The earlier panic spreads faster and faster and faster, a thin sheen of sweat breaking out across his body, and for a moment he thinks he might retch, nausea bubbling up until he's forced to swallow it back. This feeling is unfortunately familiar—he feels it every time he sees his grandfather. The thread connecting him with his father unravels until it nearly rips entirely, one final, tiny, ragged piece hanging on because René still can't let go.

Then, his own voice explodes across the room. Around his grandfather, it is always *control control control* because otherwise he ends up bruised, but with Michel his temper gives way more easily.

"You don't listen. Jerome doesn't listen. Grandfather hates me. Mama is the only one who listens to me or to Frantz now that Uncle Arthur is gone, and you don't listen to her. I'm trying to tell you something I was afraid to say and all you can do is say *no, René, you're wrong*? I know my own mind!"

Michel whips around, his light blue coat and breeches drawing out his eyes, his features even sharper than usual. It's strange, sometimes, for René to see his own eyes reflected back at him when he looks at his father, when so much else between them is broken.

"I will listen when you stop behaving like this. I will listen when you stop gambling and arguing and not doing as you're told. You will stop going to the docks. You will stop *playing cards* with boys in the street. And you will accept the plans we have laid out for you. Taking up your grandfather's title and estate. Marriage when you're older. Appropriate behavior for a young man of your standing. Some young men of our class might see fit to behave like rascals in their youth, but that will not be the case with you. I know you want to be a captain, René, but that's not what's in your future, and you will learn to embrace the damn good life that awaits you, and its responsibilities. Am I understood? I want an answer."

The day his grandfather bruised his arm comes rushing back into René's mind.

Say yes, sir, I will obey you.

Yes, sir.

Yes, sir, what?

Yes, sir, I will obey you.

The memory lands hard on René's head, and he shuts his eyes for a moment, the past and the present colliding together with an ear-shattering screech. His father isn't his grandfather, but those words, that tone, it's as if the old wretch has come in and twisted Michel up until René can't see the man he knew anymore. He puts his trembling hands in his pockets, and he can't bear for his father to see. He has to get out of here. Now.

He gazes at an older painting done just after his family's arrival in Jamaica, depicting him with both his parents when he was five, just before he met Jerome for the first time. It used to be in the parlor, but they moved it up here a few years ago, replacing the one downstairs with a portrait also containing his grandfather.

"I understand that you sound like Grandfather." René knows the impact the words will have, but he throws them like knives, anyway. "And you *swore* that would never happen. I miss you, and you're standing right here."

"René." His father softens, his posture still perfectly straight, but for the first time, he looks truly small. "I am trying to help you"

"No, you aren't." René seizes his coat from the reading chair and pulls it on, walking swiftly toward the door.

"We are not done, René," Michel says, the candlelight making the pale gold embroidery on his coat shine. "You do not leave in the middle of a conversation." He strides over, taking René's wrist in hand to prevent him from leaving. Not to the point of pain, but firmly enough that René flinches. "René," he repeats, and René's so very tempted to just embrace his father and ask him *why*. "I'm not going to hurt you."

"You are hurting me." René pulls his coat tighter about him. "Whether you hit me or not. Please just let me go."

"René, my boy." Michel softens, but the way he says *my boy* makes René feel like a burden.

"Let me go!" René shouts, with a strangled, tattered sob.

His father jumps, his eyes widening, but he does let go.

René rubs at his temples as he steps toward the door, the sharp pain growing stronger.

"Does your head hurt again?" Michel asks, his frustration morphing temporarily into concern. "I thought those herbal treatments the doctor gave you were helping."

René wipes away the tears tracing a pattern down his cheek, the tears he didn't mean to allow. "You don't care about that. If you cared you'd find a way to stop Grandfather from hitting me. You'd stop him from saying nasty things about Frantz. You would have listened to me tonight."

"You cannot go, René," Michel says. "We need to discuss this because I do care. Very much."

"I imagine I can do whatever I like," René retorts. "Whenever you're willing to listen, I'm willing to talk. I suppose you'd rather I not talk at all, if it would keep Grandfather happy."

"René, I'm *sorry*."

René ignores his father, walking out and breaking into a run once he's halfway down the stairs, dashing out the front door towards the shore. He looks back toward the house once more. A fresh candle glows in the library window. He doesn't expect his father to follow him, but he looks behind a few times anyway, keeping an ear out for footsteps before slowing to a brisk walk. He must calm down. He must breathe, and then he can quell that sick, overwhelming feeling in the pit of his stomach, the one that appears almost every time he sees his grandfather coming, and sometimes when he's nowhere near. He always feels so out of control when this happens, and he wishes he could make it stop.

The ghosts of old Jamaica come with him as he walks toward the shore. He has hazy memories of its earlier wildness from when he first moved here, the island dotted with smaller farms and serving as a spot for new beginnings. There were whispers about Henry Morgan and the buccaneers, then—he remembers sailors weaving tales about them over fires near the harbor. Jamaica, and the rest of the West Indies for that matter, are still wild, but in a different way. There are fewer rules here in practice even if the rules still exist. It takes a long time to report anything back to England or France or Spain, the local governors and magistrates full of corruption and self-interest. The wildness is tamed and controlled by the rich sugar plantation owners now, a cruel savagery rather than the free-spirited feeling of days past. Wealthy white aristocrats like his own family hold sway, making money off the backs of slaves and poor sailors and wiping out the people who lived here first, according to Frantz. René feels terrible guilt over it, wishing he could do something. Wishing he could be the opposite of his grandfather. Anger is in the air, that much René can tell. Anger that will have to go somewhere.

He walks the familiar path until he finds a spot on the cliff above the water, sitting and catching his breath. He pulls his knees closer to his chest and rests his head between them, willing his heart to slow down and letting the panic recede, the residue leaving him with a lingering stomachache and sore, burning muscles.

Things are getting worse here. Every day, they're getting worse. Except if he tries to get out and then gets caught, there will be hell to pay. He can only imagine his grandfather's wrath, and what might happen as a result. That's what scares him most. That, and the idea of leaving his mother behind. Going out on the sea doesn't scare him at all. He can do that. They can do that, him and Frantz and Auden.

If you go, I'm coming with you, Auden said a few weeks ago, carving their names into one of the palm trees in the grove tucked away from the harbor—their secret hiding spot. *What's stopping you, if I can ask?*

I can't have my inheritance from my father until I'm of age, Frantz replied. *And that's several years away. Hence the gambling money, in case of emergency. If we wait till we're older, we could leave with my father's money. It's easier to get that than anything on René's end, even if René's would be more. His grandfather has to die, for him to inherit.*

I hate the idea of leaving my mother, too, René added. *I can barely stand to think about it, and it makes me hesitate every time I really consider leaving. But if we do go, we've wondered if we might be able to find Frantz's mother.*

I would know if she were dead, Frantz said, nodding in agreement with René. *She must be out there. She must be.*

Someone comes up behind him with a heavy tread. Heavier than his father's. René looks up at the dark, star-studded sky, a few wisps of cloud smearing the moonlight, and he thinks he should have known Jerome would find him here. The ocean rumbles beneath them as waves crash onto the sand. The sound is muted from this height and soothing in its constancy, some of the tension sliding from his shoulders. The light casts Jerome's black hair silver when he sits down, and it softens his imposing figure. He sets his sketchpad on his knees, the moon illuminating the drawing of a half-finished *Navigator* beneath Orion's belt.

"Seems we share a similar favorite spot." Jerome points upward. "Gemini's a bit faded tonight, but you can still see it."

A half-smile slips onto René's face, loss and nostalgia weighing it down as he looks up at the constellation. It's been his favorite since he was five years old and met the man beside him, learning that the stars Castor and Pollux were named after two mythical brothers.

"Why are you out here?" Jerome asks, prodding into René's silence.

"I had an argument with my father."

"Where is Frantz?"

"Asleep." René looks Jerome in the eyes. "He was having nightmares about Uncle Arthur and Chantal the other day, and was finally sleeping peacefully. He has the same head cold my mother does. I didn't want to bother him."

Jerome's fingers brush against René's shoulder in comfort before he pulls back, clearing his throat. For a moment René thinks Jerome might force him home, but a shared feeling rests in the air, both of them reaching for the old easiness between them.

"I never see you draw people." René gestures at the drawing. "That's a good likeness of the *Navigator*, though."

"I never really considered drawing people. Perhaps because I wouldn't want someone drawing me, either. Why were you arguing with your father?"

"Just about my future, and marriage, things like that," René replies. He knows Jerome will talk to his father about it anyway, and he doesn't mention the gambling because he doesn't want that lecture right now. "I don't want to be married." He opts not to elaborate.

René wraps his arms around his knees, staring out at the ocean as a breeze ruffles through his hair. Several strands of his own come loose, while Jerome's stay almost perfectly in place. He's so tired of other people telling him how he feels and who he is and what he'll do with the rest of his life.

"It cannot be so bad, the life awaiting you," Jerome says, and though there's the usual terseness in his tone, René hasn't heard him sound so soft in a long time.

"I feel trapped," René whispers, his throat constricting. "My life is set for me. A marriage will be set for me. Eventually, I'll have to go to a place I left when I was three years old and take up a house and a title I don't want, and I won't be allowed to be with Frantz all the time like I am now. I have no choice. I never have the freedom to be myself. Frantz certainly doesn't. I feel badly for even feeling this way, sometimes, because there are people here on this island who are literally trapped, and I know I have so much that others don't. But I still wish I could choose the way forward."

"On the contrary, you have more freedom than you realize." Jerome's voice hardens again with a lecture. "You only refuse to see it."

"I don't refuse," René snaps. "I *do* see, and even if I didn't, my grandfather would knock it back into me rather literally, wouldn't he? He wants to break me, Jerome." René takes a deep, shuddering breath. "To make me be ... someone else. He makes me feel worthless. Bad at the core. All the time."

"I have no control over your grandfather—" Jerome tries, but René cuts him off.

"You don't stop him. My father doesn't stop him, and he won't listen to my mother." René pauses, glancing over at Jerome and controlling his temper. "I know you can't personally say something to him without risking your job. I understand that now. But you could encourage my father to try harder. He listens to you."

Jerome looks sad, something glistening in his gray eyes and making them look a little silver. "Your father cares desperately for your future."

"He doesn't—" René struggles with the words because he hasn't said them aloud yet, even to Frantz and Auden. "He loves what I am. Not who I am." The fresh pain from the earlier conversation with his father throbs anew, an open, festering wound in his heart. "It's the same with Frantz, just for different reasons."

"Your father took Frantz in," Jerome argues. "Loves him like another son."

"He thinks he does," René says, "but when he looks at him all he sees is Uncle Arthur. He limits Frantz like so many others do *because that's the way the world is*, which is a stupid reason if I ever heard one. Frantz is the smartest person I've ever met, and he should be allowed to do whatever he wants. It's not fair." Anger at Jerome's stubbornness fills René's chest, but he wants to know something. He has to know. "Please tell me you don't think I'm bad, Jerome. Sometimes I think my father does, and it scares me."

Silence wedges between them, and René wishes he could take the confession back.

Jerome *does* think he's bad, doesn't he?

Jerome stays silent, reaching in his pocket for something, but when he pulls his hand away, he isn't holding anything.

"I don't think you're bad, René. Not in some inherent, unfixable way. If I thought that, I wouldn't consider you a brother."

A youthful half-smile slides onto Jerome's face, but he's not done speaking. René can tell.

"I care about you and your father, and I dislike seeing you fight and feeling as if I have to choose between you. I want you to understand that he has your best interests in mind. I do think you need to amend some of your more recent behavior. He's right about that."

René huffs, resting his chin on his knees. "Of course you side with him instead of me."

Jerome opens his mouth, but René doesn't even let him start.

"I know what you want to say. *René, you're a child, and the adults know best.* Well, they don't. Go away, Jerome, if you're just going to lecture me."

Jerome sighs, sounding more long-suffering than René thinks he should. "You don't know what it's like to have to work for the respect of others. You belong to a respectable family. It is extremely frustrating to me to watch you treat that as if it's nothing. To watch you mingle with riffraff when you go down to the docks. You do not belong with those people. I want to protect you, René. But you have to let me."

René wants to shout at him, he wants to show him every place his grandfather ever left a bruise, but there's a strange vulnerability in Jerome's expression like he might divulge something, so he remains quiet.

"I'm going to tell you something, but it must remain a secret. Do I have your word?"

René nods. "Yes. I promise."

What secrets does *Jerome* have?

Jerome takes a deep breath, his fingers clenching tight over his sketchpad. "My father was an Englishman, but my mother was Romani. Manouche, as the French say. Or a"—he tenses before he says the next word—"a gypsy, as most others refer to her people. Or is. I don't know if she's dead or alive. What I told you before about being separated from her was true." Jerome stares out at the stars and shuts his eyes for a long moment, like he might be praying. "Both my parents dabbled in piracy, my father especially. Your father is generous enough to forgive all of that."

Your grandfather would not forgive it, is what Jerome doesn't say aloud, and a great many things fall into place in René's mind. There was a sword lesson a while back, and he remembers Jerome flinching when the governor said the word *gypsies* with disdain. Jerome has darker hair and more olive skin than most other English sailors, but René's never really thought twice about it. He has seen some higher-born people's gazes linger on Jerome, and now he realizes why.

They suspected something.

"I did not have the sort of education you and Frantz have received," Jerome continues before René can speak. "My mother was one of the few in her family who knew how to read and write in English, so she taught me. My father never learned at all. I have what I have because I moved beyond the lives my parents led and the associations being Romani carries with it, just or not. And your father, he saw the potential in me, even when he found out the truth. No one else ever did."

"Oh," René replies softly, knowing he needs to say something, but he wants to let Jerome finish.

"My mother's family was forced out of countless places for generations before they arrived in France, and they weren't accepted there, either." Jerome studies the stars again, as if seeking solace in their dimmer light. "They didn't belong anywhere. When my mother left them for my father, *we* didn't belong anywhere. I never did, until I joined your father's crew. It was the first place I truly felt at home."

René knows that it's men like his grandfather, men who hold power in places like this, who make Jerome feel this way, and he doesn't know how to fix that. How many other people in René's own class make people like Jerome feel so terrible about where they come from? He thinks of Jerome's mother, wondering if she's still alive and what happened to her. He can't help but think of Chantal, and how the violence of the West Indies swallows people up like the ocean, leaving no trace until they pop up again. If they do.

René meets Jerome's gaze, touched at being trusted with the secret, but it sits heavy in his hands because it shouldn't have to be one. "People say all sorts of bad things about gypsies. Doesn't that make you sad?"

A deep, undeniable pain gleams in Jerome's eyes, but it's gone when he blinks, replaced with determination. "People think what they think, and I must react accordingly. That's not going to change, and I can usually pass mostly unnoticed, which my mother couldn't do. Which Frantz can't do."

René knows it isn't his place to speak toward the loathing he hears in Jerome's voice, a loathing toward a part of himself. *Romani*, René repeats in his head, noticing the way *gypsy* makes Jerome flinch. He won't use that word again.

"Jerome," René says, "you are so smart, and one of the best sailors I've ever seen, and an incredible swordsman, and it's not fair that you had to wait for someone like my father to give you a chance. I know I'm not the right one to talk to you about this, but—"

"I don't want to talk to anyone. This is to stay between us." Jerome hesitates before reaching over and taking one of René's hands tightly in his own—a vulnerable thing, for him. "Obedience breeds peace. I know matters are difficult right now, but they will improve if you just do as you're told. That's the choice you have to make."

René bites his lip and swallows back an urge to cry. Panic threatens him again. "I don't want to be like my grandfather." The words come out in a high, cracked squeak from the effort of keeping back tears. "I'm so scared of that."

"René." Jerome's almost gentle, but that *almost* is the important part. "Obeying him doesn't mean you have to be exactly like him. It will just make things easier for you."

A sharp comment burns its way up René's throat, and he can't stop it from spilling out.

"No it won't!" His shout echoes against the night sky as he rips his hand out of Jerome's, wondering if his grief might shatter the stars. He has lost his old friend, hasn't he? No. No. The Jerome he knew is still in there. He must be. But if he is, why won't he help? "It won't when nothing I do is ever right."

Jerome's scowl washes away any softness that might have remained, his voice going cold. "You haven't listened to a word I've said, have you?"

"I am listening, but I—"

"You have to stop this, René," Jerome interrupts, an ire in his eyes René's not sure he's seen before. "You have a family. A home. A life waiting for you. Fighting with your grandfather and gambling and listening to sailors tell nonsense tales about pirates is not appropriate."

"You sound like my father."

"Good!" Jerome exclaims, throwing his hands up in the air. "One of us ought to. Let's go, I'm taking you home. You shouldn't be out this late."

René jumps. Jerome didn't slap him, but he might as well have. "Why are you suddenly angry that I'm out here?"

Jerome stands up, gesturing at René to follow. "Let's go."

There's truly no point in arguing, so René follows Jerome, neither of them speaking for most of the walk home.

"You're just angry because you shared something with me," René says when he can no longer bear the quiet. "Because I won't just do as you say."

Jerome's continued silence echoes into the night.

Chapter 17

Kingston, Jamaica. November 1704.

Astra's relieved when the boys fall asleep early.

Expecting to return from tea with Mrs. Taylor to a calm evening in her garden, she came home to a disaster instead.

Her father with a cane in hand. A bent-over René, grasping his calves with Frantz by his side. Rips in her son's breeches. Rivulets of blood running down his legs. Her boy, her sweet, darling boy swallowing sobs and cries of pain back down, the force of it sounding as if it might tear his throat open. Crying in front of her father is against the rules, of course. She learned that as a young girl, though she earned a raised voice and an afternoon locked in her room rather than physical violence.

It should be you doing this, Michel, her father shouted, barely even acknowledging her entrance.

No, sir. Michel was firm in his response, tugging her father away from René. *That's enough now.*

Why don't you love me anymore? René asked Michel in an odd, flat tone once her father was gone, and it broke Astra's heart. Her bright, vibrant boy never sounded like that. *What did I do?*

René, mon étoile. Michel used the old term of endearment, resting a hand on René's shoulder. *Son, I love you more than my own life.*

Don't call me that. René shoved Michel's hand away, and there were no questions, this time, from him or from Frantz about whether they could go on the next voyage with Michel, because he would only say no. Astra means to find out why, when they used to go with him several times a year, on shorter trips. Michel helped her clean up the cuts on René's legs and then disappeared off somewhere, leaving her to comfort the boys.

He still hasn't come back.

She throws her bedchamber door open, retreating here after having tried and failed at playing her harpsichord as a distraction from her rage. How dare Michel leave like this, with some nonsense excuse about needing time alone when he could have easily had it here? Good God, what it must be like to be so selfish. She could happily slap him. The chair in front of her vanity squeaks when she tosses herself into it, and she begins taking some of the pins out of her hair until one catches painfully on a strand. This tiny thing makes her fury overflow. A scream builds in her throat. She pulls the pillow from behind her back and screams into that, the high-pitched sound muffled by the fabric. She's never wanted to be a man, but sometimes, especially right now, having their power would be something. She could scream until the windows shattered, and even that would not make a man listen to her, at least not any of the grown ones in this household. Her breath comes in short gasps as she wills herself calm, opting to take her jewelry off instead—Molly can tend to her hair once Michel gets back, whenever that will be. She feels terrible for keeping her sweet ladies' maid up late.

Her hand stills over the gold bracelet she wears on her left arm. It's a trinket from Imogen in London, given as a gift just before the wedding to Michel. Astra holds that moment close to her chest, that fleeting, secret moment, and the ghost of Imogen's fingers trail across her wrist as she unclasps the bracelet, like it might have only been yesterday.

The front door flying open and banging back against the wall interrupts her remembering. She turns around at the sound of two sets of footsteps on the stairs.

"I've already told you I don't agree about caning children!" Michel shouts. Her father must have found him on his walk home. "The bruises you've left have been bad enough, and now you've made him bleed."

"My grandson grows less disciplined by the day," her father replies, a note of possession in his voice. "Corporal punishment never hurt a sailor or a child besides, and the boy is not so young, anymore. He ought to be able to take it, and you ought to have a firmer hand with your son *and* your sailors, Michel. If René lived with me, I wouldn't stand for this behavior."

Those words send chills down Astra's spine, and she steps out into the hallway when the two men reach the landing. "Do be quiet, both of you," she hisses, drawing their attention. "Let's go into Michel's study."

No protest comes—a miracle, given her father's presence—and Michel gestures them inside. He sits down in the chair behind his desk, all his papers arranged in perfect order, and a full decanter of brandy resting in the corner. Her father takes a seat, shoving Michel's small stack of novels out of the way with a roll of his eyes. Cyrano de Bergerac's *The Other World: Comical History of the States and Empires of the Moon* sits on top—a book Astra knows Michel and Arthur read together on their first journey to the West Indies. The one when Arthur met Chantal. A volume of Honoré d'Urfé's novel *l'Astrée* lays beneath, one of Michel's secret favorites as a young man and something Astra bonded with him over when they first met. She sits down next to her father, one hand grasping the arm of the chair.

Michel grits his teeth. "Beating René is not the answer to anything. Has his behavior concerned me recently? Yes. But you are constantly berating him and insulting his closest friend. What did you expect him to do?"

That, Astra thinks, is one of the truest things Michel's said recently. The trouble is, whenever he takes a stand, he always backs down, eventually. She's about to add her own comment, but her father speaks before she can. Shocking.

"*Obey* me."

Her father is merciless, and the anxiety in Michel's eyes morphs into barely quelled panic.

"The Seymour boy is a bad influence!" her father continues. "I have always said so. He encourages René's behavior. Before you practically adopted the brat, did René gamble? Did he spend all his leisure hours with ruffians at the docks? Did he have this idiotic fantasy of sailing around the world instead of taking up his proper station in life? Christ, Michel, I can't claim to know what you were thinking, taking him in, unless you were deliberately trying to ruin your son's life."

"Father, this is our son you're talking about—" Astra begins, but oddly, it's Michel who cuts her off, and not her father. A first, she thinks.

"I was *thinking*"—Michel grasps onto the edge of his desk, his voice turned to ice—"that he is the son of my dearest friend, the friend who died saving my life. This is his home. Taking Frantz in was in Arthur's will."

"He has forgotten his place. What will he do when René inherits, hmm?"

"Frantz will inherit his own money," Astra interrupts. "And frankly, Father, I don't care if you don't like him. Frantz is our family and René's best friend. That isn't going to change."

Her father swings around in his seat, and she tightens her grip on the arm of her chair, willing herself not to jolt. She'll be damned if he thinks her afraid of him.

"He may have money, but he doesn't belong in high society," he says. "You know that, Astra." He huffs, turning his attention back to Michel. "You can't be weak, Michel. You have to have a firmer hand with René, or you'll ruin him. You don't want that, do you?"

"No, sir." Michel's quieter now, his temporary show of open defiance fading away. "None of us want that, but you are beating him, and I won't stand for it anymore."

"Kindly do not make me regret bringing you into this family." Governor Travers drums his fingers on the desk, unimpressed with the near ultimatum and clearly believing that Michel *will* stand for it. "You put enough fantasies about being a captain into René's head when he was younger even though you knew it would never be because he is to inherit my title. You need to make up for that foolishness now. You will find a way to amend his behavior, or we'll be discussing him coming to Spanish Town to live with me. Am I understood?"

"Yes, sir." Michel answers quickly, a quaver in his voice, and he doesn't argue again.

Governor Travers gets up, pushing the chair back with a loud scraping sound. "I'm going back to Spanish Town."

A dark laugh slips past Astra's lips. "Do you honestly think I'll let you take my son?"

Her father turns on his heel, those familiar half-moon spectacles sliding down his nose. "I don't recall asking for your opinion. Good night." He slams the door to the study shut behind him, the lavender scent from his powdered wig remaining even as his footsteps recede down the hallway.

Finally, Astra is alone with her husband.

"I know what it's like." Her tone is gentle even as anger pulses in her veins. "He could make me doubt my own memory, sometimes, and make me feel worthless with a few words. You aren't weak, Michel. Don't listen to him."

"I have every reason to fear him," Michel says, not really speaking to her point. "We both do, Astra. You heard that threat about taking René."

"He can't."

"He can and you know it."

Part of her does know it, but she can't go there. She can't *think* that. Her father is king in this place, far away from anyone who will tell him no. What are a few legalities, to Governor Andrew Travers?

"He has every magistrate in Jamaica in his pocket." Michel runs a hand over his face, heaving a sigh. "None of them will fight him over it. And what good will complaining to someone in London do? It will take too long. No," he mutters, half to himself. "We have to sort this out." He reaches across the expanse of his desk, trying to take her hand, but she pulls away.

"I miss feeling like your husband," he says.

He means it. She knows he does. But what good does that do, really, what he means? He doesn't act on anything, even as their lives, their family, are being ripped apart by her father's merciless hands. He's abandoned her in every way that matters. Old, scratched-up memories of laughing with Michel on the stairs and curling up in bed to read to their son swirl around Astra's head. She opens her mouth to respond, but Michel seems to realize what she wants to say.

"I don't just mean sharing your bed," he continues, "though I do miss it. I respect your ability to refuse me when it comes to that, and you've made yourself clear these past few months. I mean feeling like we're partners."

She glares, the words cold, sharp, and aiming to injure him. "Treat me like a partner, then. And until you make some better effort at helping me with this mess, kindly do not bring up again how much you miss bedding me. You disappeared earlier at the exact moment I needed you, so forgive me if I'm not receptive to your charms."

Michel furrows his eyebrows, visibly swallowing back a retort. "You don't have to put it so bluntly." He pauses, something making him soften, but she doesn't know what. "I do love you, Astra. Please know that."

I do love you, Astra. The proclamation echoes in Astra's memory. It was the last thing Imogen ever said to her.

Her hands clench over the edge of Michel's desk, her knuckles popping white as the blood rushes toward her fingertips. Her mind flashes back to London and the sound of a door flying open. It flashes back to her father's shouts when he found her with Imogen in her bedroom, the pair of them stark naked. Her hands in Imogen's gorgeous chestnut hair. Imogen kissing her senseless as they laughed against each other's lips. Both of them swiftly on their way to *more,* and decidedly not for the first time. Rumors of her 'flirtations' with Imogen, as her father called them—the fact that she was in love fell on deaf ears—spread through London, though no one knew the relationship went on for years before they were discovered. Her father married her off to the child of a business contact in Paris, hoping he could hide his shame. A country away, Michel and his family knew nothing of the incident in London. Michel still doesn't. She exchanges letters with Imogen twice a year and no more, because more is too dangerous. For a long while, Michel was kind, even if they disagreed sometimes. And unlike most of her friends' husbands, he was actually considerate of her when they were intimate. Given she's only ever been interested in other women, having a husband who didn't ignore her in bed made that part of things easier.

"Making a proclamation like that isn't going to change anything! Prove it to me." She raises her voice against her better judgment, knowing it might wake the boys. "My son, *our* son, goes to bed most nights afraid of his grandfather, and Frantz is made to feel lesser in his own home, and you won't do anything permanent about it because what? You're afraid? Or does part of you think René deserves it?"

Michel pulls back in his chair, hurt flashing in his eyes. "I do not think that. I do wish he would behave. It would be easier if he would just *behave.* He's going to ruin his prospects. For marriage. For social standing at all, despite the money and title and land he'll have, if this keeps up. You know as well as I do, Astra, that in our circles, behavior matters above all. Rules exist for a reason. To flout them is to earn social shame. I don't want that for our boy."

Vulnerability seeps into Michel's tone, vulnerability of a particular kind, but she's not certain he knows it's there. She recalls one evening when she was sick with a head cold, and she awoke to shouts. Anger. René saying *I'm trying to tell you something*, but he was gone by the time she got herself out of bed. Michel was strange, that night, muttering something about René insisting he never wanted to be married, and staring with a sharp look out the widow like he might have been arguing with himself rather than worrying about René. Astra's always wondered if their son was different on that spectrum of things. Like she is, though perhaps not quite. Just different, somehow. She's wondered it about Michel, too. Michel and Arthur both. Arthur was deeply in love with Chantal, but there was a time, she's fairly sure, that he was in love with Michel. She will not, however, bring this up with her husband. She knows the power of shame as a social tool. As a way of keeping people in line. People talked about her, after Imogen, but the difference between her and Michel is that she simply didn't care—she only wanted Imogen back.

Astra shakes her head, softening and taking a different tack. "I do love you, Michel." And it's true. She can't love him in the way she's supposed to love a husband, but she does love him. "You used to be my friend. You are the father of my son. You are written all over him just as I am. We used to laugh together. Don't you remember? You used to be a good man. Ever since Arthur died, you've been different. Are you scared to leave here because he died? Like you're leaving him behind?"

"I don't want to talk about Arthur." Michel's voice cracks in half, every word throbbing with grief. "Please, Astra."

"Michel." Astra covers his hand with her own even as fury still sits in the pit of her stomach. "I know you miss him."

Michel presses her fingers for only a moment before taking his hand back. "I can't talk about him, Astra."

"You need to," she insists. "Frantz needs you to. He needs to hear you talk about his father. He's grieving, Michel. Just like you. Just like all of us."

"I *can't*!" Michel's words ring through the room, the sound sharp-edged and broken in the quiet of the slumbering house. He turns his head and stares off into the distance, guilt shadowing his eyes as he reaches down into his pocket for the watch Arthur gave him long ago.

Astra leans forward in her chair, pressing the matter. "If we had to, we could leave this place. We could escape my father. We absolutely have that choice. Your family would have us, in France. Your brother would be delighted. We would just have to be smart about it."

Michel sighs, but Astra knows him well enough to see it's only covering something else. "Arthur said something similar before he died." Tears shine in his eyes when he looks at her, and he wipes them away as they run down his cheek. "He was too much like the boys, seeing things that could never be. He died a hero. He died saving my life. I can't live up to that. I know Remy would have us, but if I sneak away in the dead of night from your father, I've failed. Besides, our lives are here now. My career. René is still your father's heir, whatever else happens. We cannot simply be rid of him."

Arthur was smart, Astra wants to say, but she keeps it to herself. She misses Arthur, too. She misses the flowers he brought her from his housekeeper's garden. She misses the way he made the boys laugh. If not for Arthur, she never would have known about Captain Barlow.

She leans back against her chair. "What are we going to do? I saw that fire in you tonight, Michel, before you let it fade. We need that fire right now."

"What do you *want*, Astra?" He softens, looking young again somehow.

"I want you to step in for our René. For Frantz." Her words tremble, she trembles, and she lets him see because then maybe he'll understand. "In a way that will actually change things. You either have to set rules about the time my father spends with René and when he's allowed around Frantz, or we have to go. I don't have the power you do to influence him. I've *tried*. A woman's arguments are nothing to him. I'm an ornament, just like my mother."

Michel retreats behind his mask, his expression hardening. "René must behave. He and Frantz both must. None of this gambling or going down to the docks. None of this dream they have of sailing together. It can't be."

"Michel."

"It is not *possible*." Michel cuts her off for the second time in one night. "René must take up the life he was born to. It's what's best for him, and he acts as if it's something horrible, as if he won't have wealth and position and some connection to the sea. And Frantz is safer with me than he would be anywhere else. You know how much I dislike the way your father treats René, but one day it will pass, I'm certain, and if we argue too much he will try and take René from us flat out. God knows what sort of leverage he would use to do it, even if a magistrate argued the point. He could remove me from my captaincy if I didn't agree, and then make it impossible for me to find another. I can't have that happen."

"Oh please." Astra shakes her head. "Unlike English second sons, you were able to inherit money from your father, even if not his title and land. Between that, my dowry, and the money you've earned and invested, we would be fine. You could find another post in France, where my father has no influence, and your brother does. What you mean is you like the posting you have and don't want to give it up."

Michel stares at her, his mouth hanging open. "This job is who I am. Sailing is who I am. The black mark of losing this post would be no small matter, and French ship owners might distrust my loyalty, after working for East India. You don't understand."

"Oh, of course." Sarcasm laces tight around her words. "I'm a simple woman, after all."

"Astra."

She raises a hand. "Enough, Michel."

He clears his throat, sitting up even straighter in his chair. "In the meantime, until we can sort this out, I'll do my best to minimize René's pain."

Minimize his pain. Hot, potent anger rushes through Astra, and she narrows her eyes as she stares her husband down. *Minimize his pain*, how dare he even think such a thing, let alone speak it aloud? She will not soften, now. She will not be distracted by how much Michel's eyes look like their son's. She will not, ever, let her father take René away.

"We don't have to *minimize* our son's pain. We can prevent it," she says. "Besides that, you don't seem to grasp the danger my father presents to

Frantz. It's real, and the older Frantz gets, the more imminent it becomes. You say you love those boys but ....."

"Of course I love them." Michel smacks his hand down on the desk, genuinely affronted. "Don't you dare question that, Astra."

She leans closer. The grandfather clock downstairs chimes the hour. She locks eyes with her husband, refusing to let go. "Prove it. Prove that you love them more than your career. More than whatever peace you think you're keeping."

After that, there's nothing else to say.

She pauses in the doorway on her way out, and as Michel looks at her again, the man she thought she knew fades into someone else. The man whose face lit up the first time he saw his son is gone. She doesn't have the feeling she did then, that despite everything, despite aching for Imogen, despite leaving London and memories of the mother she lost at fifteen behind, despite the fact that she could never love Michel in exactly the way he wanted, that maybe they could be a family. Her father's on the verge of ruining that, and Michel's letting him.

She leaves the study without another word, padding down the hall to René's room. Both boys are there, their gangly bodies sprawled across the bed. She puts a soft kiss on Frantz's curls, wishing she could give him his own mother back and wondering if Chantal's alive. God, she hopes so. She met Chantal a few times. A sweet, clever woman. Far shyer than Arthur, but deeply, radically kind in the same way. Michel put out some inquiries into her whereabouts to no avail. He gave up shortly after, believing her lost. Astra won't give up, even if there's not much she herself can do.

She settles into the rocking chair on René's side of the bed, running the back of her hand down his cheek. "I'm sorry, darling," she whispers, putting her free hand on his cut-up leg. "I'm so sorry."

She's wondered before if she might have to send them away from here, and with her father's threat, what he said about René living with him ....

Can she do it? Can she send her son and the one who is as good as out into the wilds of the world alone? She wishes she could run and take them with her, run to France, to Michel's brother Remy. She could ask him to take them in and convince Michel away from Jamaica, but her chances of not being found out in the process are small. She's conspicuous, the boys on their own less so. They can work as sailors. She can't. Even in disguise she couldn't pass as a man, and she doesn't have the skills, besides.

Her heart hurts. She hates this godforsaken island.

René shifts, his eyes cracking open. "Mama?" His voice has grown deeper over the past few months, and she's still adjusting. She knows he's not a small child anymore, but fourteen still seems so painfully young to her.

"I just wanted to sit with you a while," she tells him, his hand searching sleepily for hers, grasping it tight.

"I thought I heard you and Father shouting."

"Just sleep, my love." She squeezes his hand. "I'll be right here."

"I love you," he replies, barely audible. "Sometimes I think you and Frantz and Auden are the only ones who love me, anymore."

Tears prick Astra's eyes, resolve settling in her chest. "I love you, too. I always will. I promise."

He nods into the pillow, sleep claiming him again. She keeps a hold of his hand as the tears flow down her face unabated. She has to do something. She has to do *something*. Maybe she won't have to send them away, but if she does ... well if she does she needs to start sorting how she'll get them out. She'll put money away, slowly, to start with. If things don't change in a year—maybe even less—she'll have to do more than that. And maybe she won't have to do it alone.

Her way out of this, her way to protect the boys, might be connected to the biggest secret of all. Bigger than Imogen. Bigger than anything she's ever kept tucked away, as far as consequences go. She didn't know then, in that fleeting impulse of a moment when she ushered Danso and Abeni inside her house, that she was playing host to the future Robin Hood and Maid Marian of the high seas. She smiles, just a little. She thinks of standing in Captain Barlow's cabin and that promise Danso made, that earnest, heart-wrenching vow made by a man who'd been through so much pain, and she felt something healing in the weak, early morning light.

One day, if you find yourself needing help, we will do whatever we can in return for what you've done for us today. I promise that now.

Can she take him up on it? Can she send René and Frantz to them? To pirates?

She doesn't know much about the ins and outs of piracy, but she trusts that love she saw in Abeni's eyes, that vow Danso made. She can't trust her father, and right now, her husband is slipping away. Arthur is dead. The only trouble is, she doesn't know how to find the people she's looking for. She doesn't know the best way to get the boys out, except perhaps Barlow himself, though she would have to wait for him to make port here. There have been some rumblings about sailors flocking toward the turmoil in New Providence Island, but she doesn't know if Danso and Abeni are. She supposes she'll have to wait and see.

There's a choice on the horizon.

She falls asleep with her secrets in a chair next to her son, wondering there in the dark, if soon, she'll have to take on even more.

Interlude X: On the Beginnings of the Pirate Republic in Nassau Town

The Atlantic Ocean off the Coast of Florida. October 1704.

⸻ ❧ ⸻

"N"assau is on New Providence Island, isn't it?" Flora asks from her perch on Papa Danso's bed. She folds the newspaper in her hands, relishing the feel of it beneath her fingers. "In the Bahamas?"

"Yes," Jahni says, sitting in his hammock that's slung near his uncle's bed in the captain's cabin. "The French and Spanish fleets burned it a couple of years ago. Parts of it, anyway."

"Because of the war?" Flora keeps her eyes on the paper even as she waits for Jahni's answer.

Jahni enjoys keeping up with the goings-on of the world, even if she never understands what Spain and England and France have to fight about. Much less that's worth people dying for. She understands the concept of war. They're fighting one of their own when it comes down to it, if on a smaller scale. But she's never quite clear on why European countries *always* manage to be fighting with one another over one thing or the other, including over islands thousands of miles away that weren't theirs in the first place.

"Because of the war," Jahni echoes, looking over at the paper. "What're they saying, there?"

"That the English government in Nassau may crumble in a few months if things don't improve."

She runs her hand across the headline. The Merciers never taught her to read, so her mother did so with Papa Danso's help after they rescued her, along with some of the other crew members on the *Misericorde*. She took to it with eagerness, but the process was slow because she spent the first few months aboard Ebele's ship fearing the Merciers would snatch her away again, as well as growing used to life at sea. Now the rocking of the ship lulls her to sleep. Then, it only made her nightmares worse.

There are good people in this world, my darling, Abeni said one night when Flora awoke crying from dark dreams. *They're not all like the Merciers, I promise you. Just look at the people we've met. Captain Ebele and his crew. Papa Danso. I know it won't change what the Merciers did to you. But I hope it will help you through.*

Flora clung to her mother that night, the present mixing in with the shreds of the past she remembered before cruelty separated them. Her mother's voice was gentle, easing her back into sleep. Flora's always admired her mother's resilience and her determination to hold onto joy, even when the world threw tragedy at her feet.

Tragedy is not all they are.

"It's a great deal of fighting for one small island." Jahni draws her out of the reverie. He puts his hand out for the paper and Flora passes it over, watching him scan the first few lines of the article. It's a month outdated, but she doubts much has changed. "I heard Abeni and Uncle Ajani talking about—"

"Making port there," Flora finishes. "They thought if there was no government it might be another place we could sell our goods, and we could even stay there. Make port for more than a day."

"Robins was telling me there's precedent for islands like that." Jahni folds the *Boston News-Letter* in half, reading down further. "Pirate islands, that is. There was Tortuga that belonged to the buccaneers. And St. Mary's in the Indian Ocean, near Madagascar, I think? A Jewish pirate once escaped to an island near Brazil, and they never caught him. Moses Cohen Henriques was his name. He formed another pirate settlement there. And Port Royal was once a gathering place for pirates, even if not a pirate island officially. There's precedent, is what I mean."

"Really?" Flora asks, enthused. "That's something, isn't it? What if we had an island all our own?"

"Let's not get ahead of ourselves." Jahni taps the brim of Flora's tricorn, and she swats at him, laughing. "The English may yet hold it. But it would be something."

Flora gazes at Papa Danso's desk as she thinks, looking at some of the wanted flyers with his face on them that her mother tore down when they were briefly in Boston one night. She remembers one of the white men on the crew pretending to be the captain so they could sneak past the customs officer to meet with a contact, because Papa Danso isn't allowed to be a captain except on a pirate ship, and calling himself one would elicit suspicion.

"It would be nice to have a place we could go. A place we could call home." Flora looks down at the floor, swinging her feet back and forth. The *Misericorde's* really the only home she's ever known. She loves this ship. She loves the sea. But she does wonder what a home on land might feel like. A proper house. They never spend more than a day or two in harbor, and only in particular places. Places where they have contacts. Places where they use their wiles and hide in plain sight.

Home. She says the word inside her head, trying it out.

Jahni clasps her hand. "It would be nice," he agrees, with a smile that reaches his eyes, eyes that look like Papa Danso's, dark brown and warm with tiny flecks of gold. "Let's hope for it, shall we?"

Flora nods, flopping back down onto Papa Danso's bed and crossing her arms behind her head. Jahni shifts his loose locs away from his face and picks up the book he'd been reading, something by John Locke they bought last time they were in port. Books are a treasure: expensive and difficult to acquire when you're a pirate never lingering in port too long. Perhaps next time they should raid the library of a captain, she muses, and see what sorts of books they might come across.

Nassau. She likes the sound of it.

Chapter 18

Kingston, Jamaica. March 1705.

Auden suspects that if it's possible to die of boredom, he might expire before supper ends, a life snuffed out at a fresh fifteen years of age—as of last week.

"Auden," his mother whispers from her place next to him. One hand rests on her growing belly. In a few months, his new sibling will arrive. "Sit up, dear. You're slouching."

"Yes, Mama," he grumbles, straightening his back and sitting up in the ornate, uncomfortable wooden chair.

His mother pats his shoulder, the ruffle on the sleeve of her gown brushing against his coat before she starts a conversation with Astra on her other side, forgetting him entirely. Jerome sits next to Captain Delacroix, studying his wine and largely speaking when spoken to, while René sits across from Auden, his expression marble as he studies his food, doing whatever he can to avoid his grandfather's attention. Flames flicker in the golden candelabras, lending the room a glimmer, while the fine white china with pale red floral designs sits stark against the mahogany table. The room seems like it was decorated by Astra, and that, at least, makes Auden smile, even as he picks with disinterest at the chicken on his plate.

Frantz, at Governor Travers' insistence, is not in attendance.

Auden perks up when his father's voice cuts through the cloud of monotonous conversation, starting to ask Captain Delacroix something about East India. Interesting. He nudges René's foot under the table, drawing his attention.

"More slaves are pouring into the Indies, to the sugar plantations," Captain Carlisle says. "And some to the tobacco. I know East India has a hand in that trade?"

Captain Delacroix looks at his son out of the corner of his eye, shifting in his chair and clearing his throat, folding the fingers of his left hand toward his palm.

"Some East India ships do transport slaves, in the East." He's vague as to whether or not his own is one of them here in the West. "There are plans to grow the fleet here in Jamaica and some of the other English colonies. Soon, I expect. Some individual merchant ships are agreeing to sail under our colors. Gets them better access to the busiest ports."

Auden's heart pumps stinging fury through him. He remembers sitting on the deck of the *Nightingale* when his father was a simple but well-off merchant captain, listening to him talk about the honor of his profession and his love of the open ocean. The years passed and his father made even more money, earning a name for himself until he was offered the privateer's commission on behalf of England, when it was clear a war over the Spanish succession was coming. The details of that still confuse him, truth be told. Why England needs to fight France and also a few Spaniards over a Spanish monarch he only half understands.

If he can say anything for Captain Delacroix, at least the sailors on the *Navigator* look content enough. He can't say the same for the sailors on the *Nightingale*. Bruises mark the skin of disobedient men, human error an unforgivable sin punished by the lash and the fist. They always look hungry, too, their clothes ripped and ragged.

"I suspect the economy here will boom even more," Auden's father answers. "I don't think this area has ever been better off."

"Decidedly not." Governor Travers sips claret from his crystal glass. "It was savagery before, with the natives and then the chaotic days of Henry Morgan and the buccaneers. I had to do a considerable amount of work driving pirates out of Port Royal when I took the governorship. It was still a hive, even when we arrived in Jamaica after the earthquake. Not to mention those damned Maroons in the mountains. I'm sure they'll get it into their heads to revolt sooner or later."

René's utensils clatter against his plate. Thankfully his grandfather doesn't seem to notice the small noise, and René shoots a small, tight smile at Auden. After an agonizing three-quarters of an hour, the men go to drink brandy in the drawing room and the women have tea in the parlor, allowing Auden and René to escape. No one notices as they slip up to Frantz's bedchamber. No one except Jerome, who sees them but says nothing, narrowing his eyes as they dash up the stairs.

"Are you done early?" Frantz asks when they come in. He sits up from where he's laying against the pillows, a book resting closed beside him.

"Escaped." Auden falls onto the foot of the bed without ceremony. "They scarcely noticed, though I don't know how long that will last."

"How was it?"

"Frightful," René replies, fiddling with his cravat. "They went on for ages."

René sits down on Frantz's other side, nudging him with his elbow and smiling softly. Auden wants to bring up Captain Delacroix's odd behavior when the slave trade was mentioned at the supper table, except there's no delicate way to do it. He supposes he'll just have to do it indelicately.

"I don't really know how to say this." Auden bites his lip as René and Frantz's eyes dart over to him. "But I think your father's transporting slaves, René."

"What?" René's voice goes higher, but he doesn't sound entirely surprised at the notion. "What makes you say so?"

"He acted strangely at supper when my father mentioned the slave trade and East India's hand in it," Auden says.

Frantz's hand clenches over the bedclothes. There's been no word from his mother, and Auden knows his friend fears she's been captured by slave runners. Besides that, he obviously would have the most to be upset over if this is true.

"He hesitated before he spoke. He looked out of the corner of his eye at you," Auden continues, "like he didn't want you suspecting. He shifted in his seat. When does he sail out again?"

"Tomorrow at the afternoon tide," René answers, looking as if he's piecing something together, though he doesn't say more.

"We should go—" Frantz begins, cut off by the sound of a knock.

"Boys?" Captain Delacroix asks as he opens the door, a plate with a piece of Banbury cake balanced on his left hand. Pauline the cook claims that only those from Oxfordshire—like her—can make a proper Banbury cake, and Auden can't disagree when this is the result. It's one of his and Frantz's favorites. "There you are. You need to come back downstairs for dessert. We didn't know where you'd gotten to, but Jerome said he saw you come upstairs." The captain smooths the bronze embroidery on his red coat, then adjusts his already perfect cravat.

Auden bites his lip against a sharp remark. It won't do any good for him to shout at Captain Delacroix, but God, he wants to.

René narrows his eyes. "What's the cake for?"

"For Frantz, of course. Wouldn't want him missing out."

"Of course not," Frantz mutters, his words sharp with sarcasm.

"What's that, Frantz?" Captain Delacroix smiles tight as plaster.

"Nothing." Frantz takes the plate, sitting it on the bedside table. He catches Captain Delacroix's eye before turning away, his arms crossed over his chest.

"Come along, boys." Captain Delacroix ushers René and Auden out the door. "Jerome said he might take you out to spar for a little while, René, if we're done early enough, so you should go eat."

Auden takes René's wrist in his own sweaty hand as they listen from down the hall. Captain Delacroix disappears into the room again, leaving the door ajar.

"Frantz," Captain Delacroix says, "I'm sorry, my lad, but—"

"My father would have never even *entertained* the idea of me not sharing the table with the household when there were guests." Frantz's voice is steely, and René's pulse speeds up beneath Auden's fingers. "You say I belong here, but I obviously don't. I suppose what Governor Travers wants is more important than how I feel. I'm used to it by now, so just leave me alone, if you please."

"Your father ...." Captain Delacroix doesn't say what Arthur was or would have done. They hear him pat the bed twice with his hand. "Enjoy the cake."

There's a pause, the sound of a shoe heel turning around on the wooden floor, and Captain Delacroix speaks again instead of leaving.

"You haven't called me Uncle Michel lately. Why is that?"

"I made the mistake of calling you that in front of Governor Travers," Frantz says with uncharacteristic bitterness. "He thought it too familiar. I imagined if he didn't like it then you would say I shouldn't do it."

"Frantz, you don't have to listen to him about that."

"Don't I? I don't want to talk anymore. You should go back to your party."

Auden pulls René away, and they run down the stairs so Captain Delacroix doesn't know they listened in.

When they reach the landing René tugs Auden close, whispering in his ear. "I think you were right. And I think before he was cut off Frantz was suggesting we go see for ourselves. Tomorrow morning we'll go and see if my father is transporting slaves."

Chapter 19

Kingston. The Next Morning.

They meet in the garden. René listens for the sound of footsteps before he closes the door as gently as he can, the house laying quiet behind him.

Auden gives a pronounced yawn, stretching both arms up into the air. "When you said morning, I didn't know you meant before dawn."

"They'll be at the ship early to finish preparations and load the supply," René says. "I just wanted to make sure we weren't caught."

"I'm mostly teasing you," Auden replies. "Adding some lightheartedness to this unfortunate errand."

Frantz stuffs his hands into his pockets, a sure sign of his nerves, and René hopes Auden's suspicions are unfounded. Otherwise, his father has betrayed Frantz utterly, and René doesn't know how he can make up for that. He can't. He can only be there if things fall to pieces.

"No matter what we find"—Auden loops one arm through Frantz's, tugging him closer—"we're in this together. You were right to say we should go and look. We need to know what's happening. *You* need to know, most of all."

"Yes." Frantz stares in the direction they'll take to reach the harbor, a flash of rage in his kind eyes. "I do."

"We're here," René adds, his hand on Frantz's shoulder. "I promise you."

For the first time this morning, Frantz gives an inch of a smile. "I know. That's one thing I don't have to doubt."

René leads them out, his gaze trailing over the garden as they go. It's his mother's special place, and he often finds her out here tending to her flowers, the lignum vitae and hibiscus blooming more beautifully than any others nearby. Sometimes he sits with her while she plants new seeds, taking joy in the way she smiles. He knows the path to the harbor by heart, despite the darkness. The sun peeks over the edge of the horizon, casting an eerie glow over the ground as they walk and breaking into the blue-black sky. Even if he didn't know the way by sight, the smell of saltwater in the air would spur him onward. They pause when they reach the ocean, waiting for the naval patrol to move out of sight. René's heart smashes against his chest as he stops short of the gangway leading to the *Navigator*. The ship he loves looms against the sky, a single ray of orange-red sunlight striking the foremast and bleeding down the wood. Fear creeps through his veins like poison. His hands tremble, but he cannot lose his head. He cannot.

He doesn't know how he's certain, but something awful awaits them on this ship. This ship that was once the place he was happiest. This ship that holds some of his most cherished memories. The mast that broke and killed Uncle Arthur looks like new as the dregs of early sunlight throw it into relief, but his blood is long gone. Maybe Arthur could have saved them from everything that's happened since his death. Maybe not. René supposes they'll never know. He's been aboard since they lost Uncle Arthur, but the collection of scratches and the splintered wood seem more prominent now, as if the *Navigator* keeps track of the sins committed by her captain. Frantz and Auden each take one of René's hands, and they press together for a moment before walking onward, the sea and salt-worn wood creaking under their feet.

"We have to go down below," Frantz says once they're aboard. "There won't be any sign up here."

Frantz leads the way. They go *down down down* beneath the lower deck until they reach the hatch to the hold, a stench hitting their noses instantly. There's a lock on the hold door, so Frantz breaks it with the hammer he brought along for that purpose, the sound smashing into the eerie silence.

"That smell is like the sleeping quarters of my father's ship on the last day of sail in the summer." Auden's voice rips at the seams as they climb down the ladder, because it's almost inevitable now that their suspicions are correct. What else could it be? "What the—"

The sight before their eyes makes vomit crawl up René's throat, burning and foul before he swallows it back. Rows of men and women sit in the hold, all hunched together and crowded in the small space. There are thirty of them, at least. Most aren't in irons, but one or two are, likely having caused trouble. Wet, humid heat rests like a fog in the air, sending sweat pouring down René's face even more than the usual Jamaican weather does.

Then, he remembers. A wealthy planter somewhere on the island died in debt, his slaves sold off to another plantation in Barbados. He heard some people talking about it in the center of town. These people must be the slaves.

Some of them look up, but others sleep in the manner of those who aren't truly getting any rest. Frantz breathes sharp and ragged beside René, but René can't be panicked. He has to be clear-headed. He *has* to be, for his friend. They can't free them—that might get the slaves killed outright. Tears fill Frantz's eyes, his entire body shaking. René's mind rights itself, and he wraps an arm around his friend's waist.

"We have to go," René says to Auden, because Frantz scarcely appears to hear him. "We have to go. Now."

Auden leads the way, René's hand on Frantz's back as all three of them go up. Frantz moves from René's grasp once they reach the deck. He leans on the rail and gasps for air, his eyes wide and staring at the ocean beneath. The sun bursts over the horizon, piercing the darkness with light and setting the sky aflame, a golden glow rushing over the three of them. René doesn't touch Frantz at first, suspecting he needs his space. Auden grabs René's hand, his fingers clenching tight. There's fear in his green eyes, fear like René's never seen in them before. That same fear takes root in his own soul, burying itself deep, and he wants to vomit over the side of the ship.

Frantz turns around, running a shaking hand through his hair. "I should have ... I can't ... how *could* he ...."

Frantz takes René's other hand, letting Auden slip an arm around his shoulders.

"I'm so sorry, Frantz," René says softly, a sharp pain stabbing at the spaces between his ribs whenever he breathes in deep. He swears from this moment that he'll do whatever he can to help end this cruelty. Maybe that means running away. Maybe that means piracy. He doesn't know. He doesn't know, but he *has* to do something. He has seen enslaved people all his life, and that was bad enough, but his *father* did this. "I'm so sorry my father's done this. I love you. I promise. You don't deserve this. We'll figure this out together. All three of us."

"I love you, too." Frantz's voice is hoarse as he presses René's hand tighter, his eyes wet and filled with broken-up rage. René remembers that look in Uncle Arthur's eyes, the look of someone pushed too far yet determined to right the wrong anyway, no matter what it took.

"We should—" René begins, his eyes flitting up back toward town as a figure in a dark coat becomes visible in the distance, long strands of black hair blown about in the morning breeze. Panic flutters in René's chest.

Jerome. Of course it's Jerome.

"We have to go," he says, repeating the same words from just minutes ago. "We have to go now."

One of the naval sailors on patrol runs up to Jerome, who points at the *Navigator*, shouting something René can't quite hear. The naval officer sprints toward the ship, clearly worrying the slaves might run for it with the broken lock. Auden and René seize Frantz's hands, all three of them breaking into a run down the dock and making toward their secret grove of trees, but René knows Jerome sees them. If they can just get out of sight and dash somewhere and lose him ....

Before he can finish the thought, Jerome's footsteps grow closer and closer, and then there's a hand seizing the collar of René's coat and yanking him backward, pulling his feet directly off the ground for a moment as his hand slips out of Frantz's. Frantz and Auden swing around immediately, still holding tight to one another. Jerome drags René back a few paces, breathing hard.

"René!" Frantz shouts, his voice sharp with worry, but Auden won't let go of him, preventing him from running forward. "Let go of him, Jerome."

"Go!" René calls out, knowing he can't escape Jerome's grip, and there's not much point in trying.

"Boys," Jerome growls, "let's go back to the house."

Both Frantz and Auden hesitate, looking from René to Jerome. René directs his attention to Frantz, communicating without speaking like they have since they were small. If he can make Jerome focus on him, at least Frantz might have a moment before he has to face Michel. Right now, it's all he can give him.

Frantz doesn't move.

"Frantz," Jerome starts, almost looking sorry, still keeping hold of René's collar. "There's nothing to be afraid of."

"You're a *liar*." Frantz's words pierce the air as he stares Jerome down, and he doesn't need to shout for them to make an impact.

"Go," René repeats. "Please go!"

Auden and Frantz disappear behind the palm trees, and some of René's initial panic ebbs, though the sense of danger remains—danger from a man he once trusted with his whole heart.

"Let go of me," René snaps, pulling against Jerome's hold.

"Walk," Jerome commands.

René obeys. He has to obey when Jerome sounds like that. Like stone. Jerome keeps a firm hold of René's collar, walking him in the direction of home.

"How *could* you?" René spits, fury and dread rushing through his veins, thick and heavy. "How could you treat those people that way? How could my father do this to Frantz?"

"You had no business poking around down there, boy," Jerome responds, cold. "What were you thinking, telling Frantz and Auden to run? Frantz will have to come home, and Auden will have to go back to his parents. Running from me as if I intended on harming you. Ridiculous."

The trouble is, right now René wonders if Jerome *will* harm him. He's not certain he's ever truly feared that before. Not protecting him is one thing. This is something else.

"You know what my grandfather will do to me if he finds out about this." The stream of words spills out of René's mouth, Frantz's horrified expression seared into his mind. "Do you even care about that?"

Jerome stops hard in his tracks, and what he says next burns René's heart, his mind, his soul, *everything*.

"You will deserve *whatever* punishment you receive."

Jerome looks him dead in the face with those granite gray eyes, and when René looks back, there's no trace of softness there. No mercy. Nothing. René searches for that man he met on the deck of the *Navigator*. The man who looked at the stars with a hint of wonder. The man who played with him, the sound of the clattering wooden toys lighting up his world. The man who taught him to wield a sword and the man who called René's family his own, even if it scared him. But that man isn't here, and René wonders if the brother he chose is lost to the sea beyond. He wonders if he can ever get him back.

I care about you and your father, and I dislike seeing you fight. I do not like feeling as if I have to choose between you.

René supposes Jerome's made his choice.

Tears fill René's eyes, obscuring his vision and breaking free despite his efforts. He swipes at them with his sleeve, pain thudding against his chest. Jerome tightens his grip once they reach the house, hauling René inside toward the drawing room. René's father stands at the window with his hands behind his back, looking even taller than usual, half in the shadows and half in the light. Michel turns, a frown etched into his face and a glint of ire in his blue eyes. For the first time in his life, René fears his father. Jerome lets go of René's collar, half shoving him forward.

"Thank you, Nicholas."

"Sir, Frantz and Auden ran away from me, I'm afraid. We'll have to go searching for them."

René wipes his eyes once more before glaring up at his father, wishing he wasn't crying. "How did you know where we were?"

"I believe I will be the one asking the questions, René," Michel says, his tone like a smack to the face.

"How did you *know*?" René's shout is more a strangled cry than anything else, panic roaring to life in his chest as he loses control of himself. Losing control in front of first his grandfather, and now his father, breaks his own rule, but this is too much. It's too *much*.

Nothing feels safe, nothing feels right, even here in this room with two men he once trusted without question. He remembers his old dreams of Frantz in the slave trade after the auction they saw, the day burned into his memory forever because he couldn't avoid seeing an auction again. Not in

Kingston, where ships so often drop people brought directly from Africa's western coast. His father transported sugar from the plantations, but he never thought his father could .... His thoughts break off. René disagrees with his father all the time. He can't trust him, anymore. But Michel was kind once. Still, sometimes. Was that ever real? Did he imagine it? Surely not. Not for this long. Why did his father do this? The dark cloud that's been hanging over the house for years breaks, a storm pouring forth.

He chose the wrong heroes, didn't he?

When he was young, his father and Jerome and Uncle Arthur all seemed larger than life. Brave. Everything he wanted to be. But only one of them lived up to that, and he died saving the father who hasn't. That's something like a story, isn't it? A tragedy of the highest order. He doesn't want his father dead, of course, but right now, part of René feels like the father he knew is just *gone*.

René thinks of his storybook upstairs, of the pirate tales in the newspapers, and how reading those lull him to sleep. Maybe he's been finding new heroes, all on his own. He just doesn't know if they're real enough to put his trust in.

"You three are not as clever as you think," Michel replies, giving in. "I noticed Auden's eyes on me last night, and you were jumpy when I came upstairs. When you and Frantz were missing from your beds this morning, I put the pieces together and sent Jerome after you."

"Couldn't deign to come yourself?" René spits. "Always sending Jerome to run the errands you don't like, especially when it comes to me."

"*Hush*." His father's voice cracks through the air, even if he doesn't raise it. "I'd hoped you would *listen* to him because you clearly won't listen to me any longer, but apparently that is also a lost cause."

René ignores the reprimand, flinching at his father's odd vehemence. "How could you do this?"

"Son, you need to—" Michel tries, softening again, and René can't bear it.

"Those people were locked in *your* hold!" René shouts. "And even if you don't care about them, don't you care about Frantz?"

His father reaches out like he might brush René's shoulder before thinking better of the idea, his hand hanging awkwardly in midair. "Of course I care about Frantz. I will speak to him. I would have been speaking to him now if the three of you hadn't run off as if you thought you were in some kind of mortal danger from me. Frantz is not a slave, and he never will be."

"Those people looked just like him." René's voice breaks. "I won't let you talk to him. I won't. He *trusted* you. *I* trusted you not to do this. Not *this*, not ...."

René trails off, and his father grasps his shoulder. Too tight. Too hard. Jerome's close behind. René hears him breathing.

Something in him *explodes*.

For the first time in his life, he shoves his father.

Once.

Twice.

Three times.

Michel loses his grip on René's shoulder, but the shoving doesn't do much else.

"René." Michel sounds upset now. "That's enough, mon fils."

Jerome pulls René away, taking a fistful of his coat, Michel's fingertips resting on René's chest.

"You had no business being on the ship without my permission." His father echoes Jerome's earlier words, both his and Jerome's hands lingering in their places and trapping René between them. "You are not required to know every detail of what my job entails."

"You didn't want me to know," René argues, batting his father's hand away. "You didn't want Frantz to know, which means this isn't the first time. You've been transporting slaves sold in Jamaica for a while, haven't you? That's why you've been letting us sail with you less often."

Michel sighs, a small crack in his demeanor, and he nods at Jerome, who lets go of René's coat.

"I do not take pleasure in transporting slaves," he says, but that only makes René angrier because he knows his father is trying to absolve himself when he doesn't deserve it. "But sometimes I must. It isn't often, but it's come up recently. I am kinder than a Royal African Company slaver captain. I'm better for those slaves than someone like that."

"Stop doing the job!" René shouts. "You can't be kind to them when you're taking them to their new *owner*. What is *wrong* with you?"

A marked pall falls over the room, thick and unrelenting. Michel steps forward, leaning down so he's almost nose to nose with his son, and René can't tear his eyes away.

"You are not the one giving orders here, my boy," his father whispers. "I am."

"What if the circumstance was different?" René lowers his voice, matching his father's. "And Frantz was on that ship and you didn't know him? You would just ship him off like you do the others because it's your *job*. What if Chantal was there? Would you even notice her, or just count her among the rest of your *cargo*?"

"That is *enough*." Michel turns away, his eyes glistening with tears, but the remorse doesn't change what he's done. "Nicholas, please take René upstairs and put him in his room, then go and speak to Captain Rogers. He's on standby to go to Barbados in our place. I am going out to look for Frantz and Auden. René, do not leave your room. Do you understand me?"

"I understand that you have utterly betrayed Frantz." René knows he should tamp down his rage, but he can't. He won't. "And I understand you don't love either of us enough to disobey your orders or my grandfather."

"Mon etoile," Michel says, some of the anger flooding out of him. "I do love you. Both of you. This isn't about that. It's just the way of things."

"Don't call me that." René steps away from his father, the old endearment wounding him. "Don't call me that ever again."

Michel doesn't press, storming across the entrance hall and out the door. It closes with a thud behind him, and Jerome gestures René up the stairs.

"Where is your secret hideaway you think no one knows about?" Jerome asks as they reach René's room.

René doesn't even glance at Jerome, too furious to meet his eyes. "That's none of your business. Nothing about me is your business anymore."

"Oh really?" Jerome sneers. "So you think you're just going to find another sword master, then?"

"You don't care about me!" René whips around and Jerome jolts, clearly surprised at the fervor. "Why would I want you teaching me anything? I'm fourteen, almost fifteen. I'll take it from here myself."

"René," Jerome says, a shred of kindness in his voice.

"You said I'll deserve what I get." René's emotions are overpowering, debilitating, because he still loves Jerome and wishes he didn't. "Well, you deserve what you get, too. For transporting human beings. For lying to me and to Frantz. For not standing up for me. And part of what you deserve is the loss of my trust. Get out."

"You weren't supposed to be on the ship without permission." Jerome sounds hollow now, taken aback by the reaction. "You know that. Your father has his own feelings about the trade, but he must do as ordered. We all must. That's how it works, René."

Wrath sparks like fire in René's chest, a searing sin of a thing he cannot control, and he shouldn't shout again—he has learned better than to shout with his grandfather—but now, he roars. Louder than he meant to. Deeper.

"I said get *out*, Jerome!"

Jerome freezes, almost looking frightened. He smooths his expression, huffing and slamming the door closed. René goes over to the window seat, sitting down and resting his head in his hands, the memory of the slaves in the hold and Frantz's expression burned across his brain, the putrid stench still in his nose. He's only in his room for a half-hour before there's a knock on the door. It's softer than his father's or Jerome's, so it can only be his mother. She opens the door, stepping inside and closing it firmly behind her, latching the lock.

She comes over, taking one of his hands. "My darling." She swipes a loose hair back, her usually immaculate appearance out of sorts. "I heard what happened, somewhat. Are you all right?"

He shakes his head and admits the truth to the only adult he can trust. "No."

He tells her everything.

The grief wells in his chest when he's done, and words come pouring out of his mouth, utterly out of his control.

"I couldn't help them." Tears fill his eyes, and he sobs a few times, easier about crying in front of his mother. "I couldn't *help* them. I couldn't help Frantz."

His mother wraps her arms around him and brings him close, his head resting against her chest.

"You couldn't have, darling." She puts a hand on the back of his neck. "I know you wanted to help them. But you couldn't have."

"I want to," René whispers. "Frantz was so upset, and he doesn't deserve that."

"Frantz and Auden are outside in my garden." Astra pulls back, offering him a watery smile. "I was out early on a walk this morning and came back that way to look at my flowers. They told me what happened and said you'd been brought home to your father by Jerome. They were worried about you, so I suspect we shouldn't keep them waiting."

"Father told me to stay here."

"I don't care what he said."

René nods, following her out quietly through the hallway in case anyone comes in. They reach the side door out to the garden, and his mother squeezes his hand.

"I'll keep watch here, but don't be too long," she says. "Then you and Frantz will have to come inside and send Auden home. I know Frantz might not want to come back here, but I'll do everything I can to make him feel safe. I promise you both. I won't be going anywhere."

"Mama?" René asks, looking at her. "Did you know what he was doing?"

"I figured it out about three weeks ago when I saw one of his logs," Astra admits, twisting a stray strand of hair around her finger. "I confronted him about it, but I hadn't sorted out a way to tell you or Frantz yet. I'm sorry, darling. Truly. It's reprehensible, and he knows it. I should have found a way to tell you earlier, I just wasn't sure how."

"It's not your fault. I know you do everything you can. I love you."

"And I you."

She puts a kiss to his forehead before he steps out into the garden, the trees and flowers shielding it completely from the front path to the house.

As soon as he steps out, Frantz and Auden fling their arms around him, all three of them pressing together.

Frantz speaks first. "Are you all right?"

"Am *I* all right? I'm the one who should be asking if *you're* all right."

Auden shakes his head, exasperated.

"What happened?" Frantz answers, none of them letting go of each other's hands after they break the embrace.

"It doesn't really matter. There were excuses and explanations and shouting. My father went out looking for you and Auden. Transferred the voyage over to another crew."

They should run. He knows they should run, and he wants to say so, but he holds off, for now, saving those thoughts for later when they can all think clearly and talk it through. When they can plan.

"Your father transferred the slaves over to another crew?" Frantz's question holds the ring of an idea, and René suspects he knows where this is going.

"Yes. But he said they won't be able to leave for another day or two."

"I want to help them," Frantz says, and René thinks he's never heard him sound more determined, which is saying something.

"Free them?" Auden asks.

"No." Frantz frowns, adjusting his spectacles. "That won't help them because we don't have anywhere to send them except a Maroon camp we don't know the exact location of. It would endanger them. But if we could simply give them decent food or clean water or anything at all to make them more comfortable. The risk is worth it, if you'll both join me."

"We will." A sense of foreboding comes alive in René's chest, but he defies it. "We'll do it together. Tonight."

Chapter 20

Kingston, Jamaica. Later that Night.

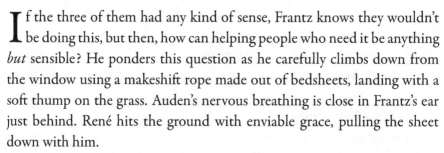

If the three of them had any kind of sense, Frantz knows they wouldn't be doing this, but then, how can helping people who need it be anything *but* sensible? He ponders this question as he carefully climbs down from the window using a makeshift rope made out of bedsheets, landing with a soft thump on the grass. Auden's nervous breathing is close in Frantz's ear just behind. René hits the ground with enviable grace, pulling the sheet down with him.

"All right," René whispers, as if fearing his father will hear from inside. Michel didn't go to sleep for hours, checking on them multiple times until it was past midnight, which is why they couldn't risk going down the stairs. "Auden, you have what we need?"

"All accounted for." Auden lifts a knapsack with a jug of fresh water and some fruit. It isn't much, but it's the best they can do.

"Ready, Frantz?" René asks, even if both of them know that being ready for something like this is impossible.

"Ready. As I'll ever be, anyway."

They walk slowly toward the docks, looking behind them every few steps, though Frantz isn't under any impression they won't get caught. He can't scrub his mind clean of the image of those men and women locked in that hot, putrid cargo hold. Those people who look like him. Those people who could *be* him, his mother, so many others he once knew on Saint-Domingue. He thinks of his mother and her smile, aching for her, desperate to know what *happened* to her. The absence of answers torments him.

If he finds out she's working on a plantation somewhere, he will find her and he will get her out, making good on the promise his father didn't get to see done. Arthur's full laugh resounds in his head, and something about it drives Frantz onward. They approach the docks, moonlight guiding their steps.

"Naval sailors," René breathes. "And some East India men, too. Right in front of the *Navigator*. That's more than the usual night patrol, which is double what it was before that theft in the harbor a bit back." He squints, looking closer. "I see Williams and Allen, my father's men. They must not have moved the slaves to Captain Rogers' ship yet."

Anger pulses in Frantz's veins, mixed with the remaining love he still holds for Michel Delacroix. "I'm not surprised. Come on," he mutters, thinking of ways to create a distraction. "Leave. *Leave.*"

A shout pierces the night air a solid ten minutes later, breaking their watch. One naval officer says something inaudible to one of the East India men, all ten of them running down the shore and just out of sight.

"Now?" Frantz asks.

René nods, and they walk as quickly and quietly as possible toward the ship, not hesitating at the gangway as they did before. There's no time for that, and they know what they'll find besides. Frantz halts just before the opening to the cargo hold, a hot, sick swoop of anxiety in his stomach. He doesn't want to see this again, but his desire to help pushes him onward, and the feeling of René and Auden squeezing his fingers gives him the courage he needs. He pulls the hatch open as Auden strikes a match for the lantern he brought, the flame a solitary pool of violent light in the dark space. One of the women looks at Frantz.

"You were here earlier."

"Yes." Frantz swallows. He has to be brave like his father. He has to be grown up.

"Why are you here again? You're nothing but boys."

Auden stands back, careful with the lantern, but both he and René follow Frantz's lead.

Frantz steps closer. "I don't really know how to explain the situation, but my friends and I, we've come to give you some water, and some food. It was the best we could manage."

"These are your friends?" The woman's eyes flit between René and Auden with distrust.

"Yes," Frantz answers again. "They wanted to help. I trust them with everything I am."

The woman smiles. It's tired, it's sadder than Frantz can bear, but a sudden trust emerges within it, and she reaches out her hand. He reaches back, and she briefly enfolds his hand in hers. The touch reminds him of his mother, the woman's skin the same shade as Chantal's and darker than his own. The memory of his mother's voice sings an old lullaby in his ear, the same one she sang when he was a child and the storms kept him awake. She grew up on Saint-Domingue with her newly freed parents in an ever-shifting world, watching the island change hands between Spain and France. Wherever she is now, the memory of her lullaby gives him the strength to face the atrocity in front of him. He touches the necklace she gave him long ago, and takes a breath.

"What's your name?" he asks.

"Amaka. And you?"

"Frantz. This is René and Auden."

"Thank you," she says. "To all of you."

Frantz hands the water jug to Amaka, who takes a large gulp. The jug gets passed around to all of the slaves in turn, the ones who are awake shaking the shoulders of the ones who aren't. Frantz recognizes some Twi, thinking Amaka must be Akan, but she's clearly been in the English-speaking world a long while. The smell down here seeps into Frantz's pores, and it breaks him that he cannot save these people. It breaks him that he cannot set them free. He tells himself that one day he will find a way to overturn ships like these and give the people aboard a safe place to go. He knows just how easily he could have been one of them. His grandparents were stolen from the shores of the Gold Coast, only set free by sheer luck a decade later.

All of René's words about pirates, all of the stories they've read to each other about Robin Hood the Merciful and Maid Marian, come rushing back. There have been whispers about the return of pirates to the Caribbean, articles in colonial and European newspapers discussing old pirate legends, as well as new ones emerging in the hustle and bustle of the West Indies and the American colonies. A larger part of him than he even realized longs to be a part of a crew like Danso's, where people like him aren't just free, they're also fighting back. They're making something new.

They're about to take out the fruit they've brought when the hatch opens again, slamming back against the wood. Auden blows out the light, but they're found out, nevertheless. Michel stands above them with a lantern of his own, fury etched into every feature, his breathing erratic and his normally smooth hair all out of order.

"René, Frantz, Auden, come up here this *instant*."

It unnerves Frantz how enraged he sounds without shouting.

The dark obscures René and Auden's expressions from him, but Frantz knows there's no choice. He looks once more at Amaka, who sends him a small, melancholy smile back, but he doesn't miss the undercurrent of anger in her eyes directed at the sound of Michel's voice. Frantz goes up first, René in the middle and Auden behind. Michel steps back, allowing them out of the hold and leading them back above, his expression no more forgiving in the moonlight.

Michel looks them up and down, a hard glint in his eyes. He's half-dressed in breeches, a shirt, and tossed on boots, his coat wrinkled and his waistcoat missing. "René, I specifically told you never to come aboard this ship without my permission. I told you this very morning. Now not only are you interfering with my work, but you are also interfering with another captain's work. And you've led Frantz and Auden here with your foolishness."

"It was my idea," Frantz says before anyone else speaks. "I was the one who wanted to come down here and give proper food and water to those people. Someone should." He steps forward in challenge, anxiety buzzing in his chest and his stomach and up and down his arms. He clenches his fists, keeping it at bay. Because no matter what Michel has done for him, no matter the claims of love, this is not right, and it hasn't been right for a very long time. He remembers how he felt this morning, vomiting once they reached the palm tree grove, Auden's hand resting on his back. He remembers Michel's *Frantz please let's speak about this* from the other side of his bedchamber door once he returned home, and his own resounding *no* in response. He remembers the feelings of shame and confusion when Michel encouraged him and limited him in the same breath.

Michel shakes his head, running a hand over his face. "Frantz, I understand you are trying to take the burden from René."

"No," Frantz presses, "I'm not saying they didn't want to come with me, and I know they'd admit the same. But both times it was initially my idea."

"Frantz," Michel replies, with such condescension that Frantz wants to shove him overboard and into the sea. "I'm sure you don't—"

"Mean what I said? Yes, I did." He almost says *I am my father's son*, but he's afraid Michel will simply say *no you are not*, so he says something else, instead. "I'm tired of you blaming René as if I cannot summon a disobedient thought of my own accord."

Silence rings in Frantz's ears. Michel's expression softens, but he still stands angry, straight-backed, and resolute before them.

"I never said that."

"You didn't need to say it." René steps forward, speaking up. Frantz doesn't like the way his voice shakes, as if he's holding onto the last shred of hope he possesses. "I understand you think I'm a troublemaker, Father, but I'm pleased to be one, and was happy to follow Frantz's lead today."

"We were just giving those men and women water and food." Auden steps up evenly with the other two. "They look as if they've barely had enough to survive."

"That's because their previous master mistreated them badly," Michel snaps. "They were underfed when they boarded and I'm doing my best to make sure that's corrected and that their needs are met while they are under my care."

"Their needs are met while they're locked in a cargo hold?" René retorts, fire flashing in his eyes. He shakes out the trembling in his voice, and it grows solid again.

Michel sets his jaw. "You should be glad it's me, and not someone else. Someone cruel."

Something inside Frantz explodes, and for the first time he can truly recall, his temper burns down to the wick.

"I should be *glad*?" Frantz's shout echoes into the night, his belief in Michel Delacroix shattering on the deck around them. His father died under the shadow of the mast they stand beneath, sacrificing his own life for the man who has cut Frantz down to the bone, promises turned to absolute, utter ash. "Dammit, Uncle Michel. Damn *you*."

Michel stares at him, shaken out of his condescending lecture. He should be on their side, and it hurts that he isn't. Frantz wonders where they might be if his father wasn't dead. He wonders if Michel would have done this. But Arthur *is* dead, and Michel *has* done this.

"Frantz—" Michel's about to lecture them again, no doubt, but two of the naval officers from earlier dash up to them, interrupting whatever he might have said.

"Everything all right, Captain Delacroix?" one asks, eyeing the four of them.

"I added some of my men to your usual patrol, tonight," Michel says, and René's eyes meet Frantz's own. They were right about that. "Is there a reason I'm not seeing them?"

"There was a situation down at the other end of the docks," the officer answers, "a fight between several drunken men that was getting bloody, so we had to leave our post. Our apologies, sir. Your men Williams and Allen and the rest of ours were containing some of the offenders, but I'm sure they'll be back."

"It's all right, lads." Michel nods at the two young officers, though he still sounds disgruntled. "As you were."

"Goodnight, Captain Delacroix," the sailors reply, but when Frantz looks back, they're whispering to each other.

"Now you've caused a scene." Michel's words cut the air once the sailors are an earshot away. His eyes fall on René, and there's real grief, real fear in them, that Frantz doesn't understand. "I had no intention of telling your grandfather about this. But now he'll certainly find out from someone else, and God knows we don't need people gossiping about us more than they already do, with how you've been behaving."

René twitches but says nothing, clenching and unclenching his right fist. After a few minutes they reach Auden's home, a large house not far from the harbor. Late as it is, there's still candlelight visible through one of the downstairs windows. Before Michel can knock on the door, Captain Carlisle opens it.

"Michel." He frowns when he sees his son by Michel's elbow. "What's going on?

"Aldridge," Michel replies. "I'll leave Auden to explain the details, but I'm afraid I found the boys on the *Navigator* without permission and I'm here to deliver Auden back to you. I'd stay to explain, but I need to take René and Frantz home. If you need to speak with me, I'll be in my office in the morning."

"Yes." Captain Carlisle eyes Frantz in a way that makes him uncomfortable. "I understand. Thank you for bringing Auden home."

"You're welcome," Michel says. "Goodnight."

Captain Carlisle grasps Auden's collar, shoving him into the house and muttering angrily under his breath. Auden's face falls, the merry light in his green eyes going out, and Frantz hates leaving him here. He hates it.

They walk alone with Michel for a few minutes in utter silence, the sound of the waves off in the distance the only noise breaking through. Frantz wants to run toward the water and breathe in the fresh, salty air. Maybe he'll be free of this place one day, but he won't ever forget, because even the sea can't wash away what he just saw. It can't wash away the betrayal, and he's angry at himself for not seeing it coming. His father couldn't trust Michel, in the end, not really, not like before, so why did he think he could? He should have *seen* this. His father saw the best in Michel, but he's not sure he can, and sometimes he's angry about who the storm stole away, and who it didn't. His grief has never been his guardian's priority, trapped as he is in his own.

"The two of you have dabbled in behavior I never expected of either of you." Michel finally speaks, his voice thick with frustration. "Disobeying me. Going to the docks without a chaperone and talking to God knows who after I expressly forbade it. Gambling. You will not spend time with such people any longer, do you hear me? Auden seems a bad influence on you, which is unfortunate given my working relationship with his father, so there is little I can do about it even if he's the source of the latter problem."

"Don't bring Auden into this." René crosses his arms over his chest as they walk up the drive. "Don't blame him for things that are your fault."

Michel spins on his heel and René flinches, preparing for a hit out of reflex.

"I am not going to hit you, René," Michel says, gentler. "I never have."

René doesn't answer, refusing to look at his father. A too bright, dangerous gleam flashes in his eyes, a gleam Frantz has seen more often, lately. There have always been two sides to René: the sweet, precocious boy Frantz met, and the young man full of righteous, resilient rage. Uncle Michel, he thinks, does not give that second part enough credence.

"Don't the two of you realize that I'm trying to protect you?" Michel's voice grows strained as he ushers them inside, closing the door behind him. "That I'm trying to make certain you lead happy lives? There are consequences for breaking the rules, as unjust as some of them may be. You embarrassed me tonight."

René opens his mouth, but Michel holds up a hand, silencing him, his straight blond hair hanging loose and tousled from sleep.

"If something doesn't change"—Michel speaks slowly, not looking either of them in the face, and that only makes Frantz's heart beat harder—"I'm going to have to separate you."

"*Separate* us?" René asks, his eyes wide with disbelief. "What ...." He stumbles, uncharacteristically inarticulate, shock and pain crushing down on every syllable. "You can't send Frantz away!"

"I wouldn't," Michel says, and Frantz can't think, he can't breathe, but logically, he must be. "I would send you to boarding school in England. For a year, perhaps two, depending on how you behaved. Frantz would remain here."

Frantz has never been shot, but those words pierce him like bullets might, lodging beneath his skin and burning with agony. He can't think his way out of this. Losing René is his worst fear, because he's lost so much already that he always wondered if God or the universe or whatever power would take his friend, too. He thought Governor Travers might do it. He never, not once, thought that his father's dearest friend, his godfather, would do the job himself.

"You can't." A few tears slip from René's eyes. "You can't make me leave Frantz. You swore you would never do this. Since I was eight years old, you swore it. I should have known you were lying to me. I should have known it that first day Grandfather hit me, and you said my friendship with Frantz would never be a sacrifice to his vanity."

"I never predicted you would behave this badly," Michel replies, almost pleading with them. There's regret in his eyes, but he doesn't retract his threat. "This is not for your grandfather." There's a lie in there somewhere, Frantz hears it, but he doesn't know *how* it's a lie, exactly. "I won't let you ruin your lives. Besides that, you are putting my reputation at risk. How do you suppose it looks when my own children constantly disobey me?"

Tears well in Frantz's eyes, and he searches for what he wants to say. "You promised my father. You *promised* him. You promised *me* ... you ...." His words jumble up in his throat, tangled and knotted and stuck, and the next ones come out before he thinks, but the feeling is born of truth regardless. "And I'm not your child."

"Promises cannot always remain unbroken, my lad. But you are a son to me." Michel's voice goes hoarse. "I know what your father would have wanted. You have to trust me on that point." He reaches out for Frantz's shoulder, but Frantz steps away from the touch.

"Don't," Frantz snaps. He grasps René's hand, and it shakes as he takes hold. "He was *my* father, and you don't get to say that. You're transporting people who look like me, you're threatening to separate me from René, and you say I should trust you?" He swallows, steeling himself, fleeting memories of this same man comforting him after a nightmare rushing through his mind.

It's all right, my boy, Michel said one late night when Frantz woke up screaming. Michel tucked him under his arm, wiping some of the anxious sweat from his forehead. *I miss your father too. So much. He'll always be with us. You're safe here with us, I promise. I'll try again with inquiries about your mother.*

"How could you do this to us?" Frantz shouts, brushing the memory away. "How could you do this to those people?"

"You don't understand." Michel swipes his hand through the air, an odd fear crackling around him as if he's trying to convince himself as much as them. "I'm looking out for your best interests. Things are not simple and Governor Travers—"

"Stand up to him," René interrupts, intensity coming off him in sparks. "That's how you'll protect us like you say you want to. And stop transporting slaves."

A dark jolt of laughter bursts out of Michel, and Frantz isn't sure he's ever heard anything like that from him before. "A list of demands. Son, you do not tell me what to do. I am your father and Frantz's guardian. I have the final say. Period."

René glares at Michel, and that gleam from earlier is back, the gleam Frantz first saw at the slave auction years ago. "You just don't want to risk your job or your reputation or Grandfather's wrath. I suppose you don't care anymore if Mama is angry at you."

"Listen to me, René. Right now." Michel's words are sharp, harsh, desperate, and they make René jump. "You have three options. Behave, and stay here. Go to boarding school. Or end up living with your grandfather."

René stares at Michel, and Frantz does too.

There's that lie of omission he heard earlier.

"What?" René asks, his voice cracking. "You want me to live with him?"

"No." Michel steps forward and grasps René's fingers, a touch gentler. "I absolutely do not, but it's something he's brought up when discussing your behavior."

Father and son stare at each other, rage and pain simmering in the air between them.

"You're being a coward," René finally says, tearing his hand out of his father's, though Frantz notes that he says *being* and not *are*. "I know grandfather frightens you. He frightens me too. But I believe you can stand up to him. I've seen you try. Papa, *please,* I'm so scared of being left with him."

René falters, and Michel shuts his eyes before visibly steadying himself.

"You can't let him take me." René continues. "You can't separate me from Frantz just because of him. We could go. We could leave."

"Fix your behavior," Michel says, and he turns cold like he thinks that's what's called for, "and we won't have to worry about any of this."

René takes in a deep, shaky breath. "Papa—"

Papa, and not *Father,* for the second time in a row.

"Bed," Michel interrupts. "Both of you. Do not, under any circumstance, leave this house. We will talk more in the morning." He pauses, looking back at his son. "And René, if you ever call me a coward again, I promise you will not see the outside of this house for a month, and you'll be packing your bags for London before you can even start to argue."

Michel sees them into their rooms, and Frantz listens for the fade of his footsteps, knowing René will come as soon as he suspects his father won't hear, or perhaps not caring if he does. A few minutes later Frantz is proven right, and René's coming into his room, climbing up on the bed and throwing his arms open wide. Frantz doesn't hesitate, and René holds him tight like he's afraid Michel might come rip him away right now. Frantz lets himself cry as they cling to each other, old grief and new grief and grief that *could* happen, grief that he fears, crashing down on his head with all the roaring of a waterfall.

"We'll make a plan." René's crying too, just more quietly, because now every adult except Astra demands that his feelings should never make a sound. "A plan to run away. We'll get out of here. We will."

"Yes." Frantz pulls away, his hands sliding into René's. There can be no argument. Not now. "I agree." He sniffs, wiping his eyes. "We have saved some money, so it's something. How do we get word to Auden if we're stuck in here?"

A fond half-smile slides onto René's face even if his eyes are still wet, and Frantz shares it despite the circumstance.

"I suspect he'll figure out a way to come to us," René says. "His father might be angry, but he's not attentive enough to keep Auden in the house. We should probably listen for the sound of rocks at our window."

"We could toss notes down to him," Frantz suggests. "Your father and Jerome will have to go out soon enough, even if they've transferred this voyage over to the other captain. Perhaps we can try and wait until then. We'll have to be on our best behavior."

"I won't let him separate us," René whispers, with that familiar, affectionate warmth. Frantz doesn't trust easily, but with René it's been natural since the day they met, built upon by everything that came after.

"I won't let your grandfather take you to live with him," Frantz answers. "I swear, René."

"I think we can survive out there," René says, holding Frantz's hands tighter as a visible shudder passes through him. "We can find work on ships. It won't be easy, but I think we can do it. Do you?"

Faith lights up René's eyes. Faith, and fear. Faith in *them*. Nerves prick at Frantz's stomach and tie it in knots, but something in his spirit that has attached itself to René and to Auden and to the sea beyond, tells him they can do this. He presses René's hands, and he doesn't let go.

"I think we have to. Because we can't stay here."

Chapter 21

Kingston, Jamaica. The Next Evening.

René and Frantz are sitting on René's bed the next evening when a small rock goes *tink* against the window. Despite everything, René grins—as usual, Auden is right on time.

His father left the house early this morning, but not before informing them once more that they were not to leave unless accompanied, their lessons canceled for the day. They nodded and obeyed, putting on the façade of expected behavior, his mother's insistence the only reason they've been allowed to sit together. He pushes the window open, finding exactly who he expected.

"Are you two all right?" Auden asks in a loud whisper. "Will I get you in more trouble?"

"The only one home is my mother," René answers, keeping his voice low in case his father, Jerome, or his grandfather approach the drive. "We're all right but a lot has happened. We're stuck here unless accompanied. Are *you* all right?"

Auden shrugs, noncommittal. "My father upbraided me for about an hour, loudly enough that it woke my mother up. I'll have to be careful around the docks for a week or so, but he's too preoccupied to keep me housebound, what with the new, and I assume more important, baby on the way who will be less disappointing than myself. What happened with the captain?"

"Too much of a risk to say aloud," René says, folding up the letter they wrote to Auden this morning explaining the events of last night and their plans to run away, including their need for passage out. If anyone can find a ship to carry the three of them away, it's Auden.

Frantz drops the letter down and Auden catches it. "Read that," he instructs, and the pair of them wait as Auden complies, his eyebrows knitted together in concentration.

Auden looks up, a gleam of nervous excitement in his eyes. "All noted. The plan is in motion. I'll find a way for us, never you fear." He turns, the wheels of a carriage crunching against the gravel of the drive. "I'd better go. I'll be back in a couple of hours." He hesitates for a moment, taking in a sharp breath, his gaze flicking toward the drive and then back to them. "Just be careful, all right?"

The front door opens, so René and Frantz only smile in return, turning from the window and leaving it open for fear of drawing any attention. They move to the doorway of René's room just as someone steps into the entrance hall, and René knows who that someone is just from the sound of his footsteps.

"Father," his mother says, her voice higher than normal. He and Frantz go quietly from his room and toward the top of the stairs, listening. "I wasn't expecting you."

"I heard word of what occurred on the *Navigator* yesterday, and that Michel transferred his cargo to another captain," Governor Travers says. "He did not see fit to send word about the transfer or René and the Seymour brat's behavior, which could have reached me in a few hours if he was prompt on the matter. One of my naval contacts alerted me instead."

"It's been a busy twenty-four hours," Astra replies, an attempt at placating him. The fact that his father kept this from his grandfather doesn't reduce René's anger, but it does speak to some better part of him, the part René knew when he was small. He wishes his father would choose a side. He wishes he would choose their side.

"Where is René?"

"Father, let's not, all right?"

René and Frantz inch forward until they're on the top stair.

"I have a right to speak to my own grandson, Astra," Governor Travers snaps. "I have a right to discipline him for what he's done."

"Oh, you have a right, you say?" Astra throws the words like daggers. "Do you have a right to hit him?"

René goes down a few more steps with Frantz at his side, the entrance hall coming into view. His grandfather's normally pristine coat is rumpled from travel, his shoes lacking their usual shine.

"You may be a fully grown woman, but I am your father, and you will not speak to me that way."

"Then respect me as a parent and stop hitting my child."

Governor Travers leans forward, all but snarling. "Do not dictate to me."

"You've been out of control since the day Mother died."

René tenses as his mother bites out the insult, holding her ground while his grandfather moves nearer. "She tried to make the best out of her marriage to you. She was the only thing that kept your behavior in line, because she wouldn't come to your bed otherwise. Isn't that right? I won't let you do this to my son anymore, Father. You've done enough to try and make me feel worthless. I won't see that continue on with René or with Frantz."

"That is *quite* enough, Astra," Governor Travers seethes, though his confidence falters just enough to notice. "You are out of order."

"I'm not even certain you cared when she died." Astra steps forward now. "I think all you cared about was losing your newborn son at the same time."

His grandfather seizes his mother's arm, something René's never seen before, and Frantz sucks in a breath of surprise.

"Don't you dare tell me how I felt about my own wife," Governor Travers growls. "You are too soft on René. I plan to stop that now." He squeezes her wrist tighter when she pulls away. "You should know better than anyone that I will not be disobeyed."

"You took someone I loved from me once." Astra winces at the tight grip. "You broke my heart and then stomped on the pieces. But I won't let you hurt René anymore."

Something in René snaps at the pain in his mother's voice, at the sight of his grandfather touching her like this, and he bolts down the stairs with Frantz just behind.

"Let her go!"

His grandfather spins around on his heel and drops Astra's wrist as his eyes narrow beneath the gold spectacles, his face flushing red. "Don't you take that tone with me. I've had enough of this."

"Maybe I've had enough," René retorts, the mere thought of running away from here making all of his rage bubble to the surface. All his rules to keep himself safe, all his discretion, vanish.

"You dare speak to me this way?" His grandfather steps closer. "You interfered in a business venture and tampered with cargo. You have blatantly disobeyed your father. You have allowed this wretched boy"—he points a finger at Frantz, lips curled in contempt—"to corrupt you nearly beyond repair, and I tell you I will forgive it no longer."

"You are a cruel, tyrannical old man." René knows he'll pay immediately, but he doesn't care anymore. "Frantz is worth a hundred of you."

A terrible, treacherous pause hangs in the air, and the governor's next words slither out from between clenched teeth.

"*What* did you say to me, boy?"

Memories tumble into René's head. Harsh, hateful memories. His grandfather has been endlessly cruel to him since he was very small. Sometimes—often—René wonders if he *is* bad, if he was born that way, somehow, but the little boy he was didn't deserve what happened to him. And maybe, just maybe, the young man he is now doesn't either.

"You heard me, sir." René starts shaking, but he doesn't back down. He moves from between his mother and Frantz, stepping closer to his grandfather. "I know you're going to hit me, so you might as well just do it, but no matter what you say, I know now that I don't deserve it." He stops, breathless, his palms cold and clammy. "Don't you touch my mother again."

For so long, he wondered if he did deserve it. Sometimes those nasty voices in his head still say he does. He tries his best not to believe them, but that, he suspects, will be a long journey.

His grandfather advances, eyes dark with ire.

"Father, *no!*" Astra's shout pierces the air, but Governor Travers slides away before she can grab his coat.

René doesn't have time to move before his grandfather's fist comes flying toward him. The governor's knuckles make a hard impact with René's nose, the signet ring adding a sharp edge. Pain explodes in his face. This is worse than a slap. This is worse, even, than when his grandfather bruised his arm. It might be worse than the caning. It *hurts*. A shout bursts from his lips, the skin throbbing like fire, and a bone snaps. He swears it does. Blood drips from his nose, a bright red smear coming away on his hand. There's not a moment for any thought other than *pain* before he's being swept back, his mother's familiar floral scent enveloping him. Frantz is there too soon after, his breath close in René's ear.

Silence falls. Pointed footsteps echo into it, the heels of his grandfather's expensive shoes clicking against the hardwood. He stops inches from them. René's heart shudders as his mother puts one arm in front of him, putting him close at her side. It doesn't matter, to her, that he is as tall as she is, almost.

"Astra." Governor Travers speaks his daughter's name slowly. With scorn. The cold in it terrifies René, and while he never wishes for his father anymore because it doesn't do any good, he does right now. His father would never let anyone treat his wife in such a way. "Give me the boy."

"No."

"I said give me the boy. Now."

Fire burns through ice, drip drip *dripping* down onto every word.

"I said *now*, Astra!"

The governor's voice rises, virulent violence threaded through and tied around tight. Bile crawls up René's throat.

"And I said no, you absolute bastard!" Astra shouts. "You wretched, wicked—"

A slap rings through the room, and for once, René isn't the target.

His mother is.

Never, *ever*, has his grandfather laid a hand on her like this. Not in René's entire life. Snide comments? Yes. Verbal lashings? Not uncommon. But not this, and from the momentarily shocked look on his face, the governor is surprised at himself too, apparently above, until this moment, hitting women, despite all the emotional cruelty he inflicts on them. The combination of surprise and the force of the blow makes Astra stumble backward, giving Governor Travers the chance to seize René by his collar before Frantz can even move to stop him. He shoves René up against the wall, hard, and René swears he will not break his own rule. He will not cry. Crying is useless to him.

"How dare you hit her!" His voice rests on the edge of a scream, and his control is gone as he thrashes, desperate to slide out of his grandfather's grip. "Hit me all you want but not her, not—"

A slap cuts him off, a squeak of pain escaping him. His nose *hurts*.

"How would you like to come live with me?" his grandfather snarls. "I think you'd dance to another tune then. You are *my* heir, René. You were born for that purpose, and you will behave as such or suffer the consequences."

"Father, stop it!" Astra's voice pierces the air, and she *is* screaming. "Stop it right now!"

"I'll knock the boy's head into the wall if you don't shut *up*, Astra!" Governor Travers shouts before focusing on René. "What do you have to say to me, René?"

He looks ready to raise his fist again when René doesn't answer. Except, a familiar hand shoots out, catching his wrist.

"Stop hurting him!" Frantz yells. "Damn you."

Governor Travers yanks his wrist out of Frantz's grasp, releasing his hold on René. "You do not touch me. Michel has protected you all these years, but you are one step away from learning what a real punishment is. You don't belong here."

"I don't care what you think of me," Frantz says, his temper finally giving way, and René does fear the look in his grandfather's eyes now, because while he might pay in pain, Frantz could pay in jail time. Worse. "But I won't watch you hurt René any longer."

Before René can move, his grandfather grabs both of Frantz's wrists, holding them tight until Frantz gasps in pain, still staring the older man down. Astra calls out a protest. She screams *Father you will let him go now*, but René can tell from the glimmer of fear in her eyes—a glimmer he's never seen before, not like this—that she fears stepping in again will only end in more violence.

"Your impudent father's not here to protect you from me anymore, and I've been patient enough." Governor Travers grins when Frantz winces.

"How would you like to see the inside of a jail cell for touching the royal governor?"

René's good sense shuts off, and he moves toward his grandfather with a running start. Something bursts inside him, some new part of himself buried *deep deep* down and born of righteous rage. He wants to hit his grandfather. He wants to hurt him. Before, he just wanted to make him stop.

He still believes in stories. The world has told him a thousand times in his fourteen years that his heart is too soft. But he is no longer that little boy desperate to be good enough for his grandfather to love him. Now he knows he will never be good enough for that. No one could be.

"René darling, *no*," Astra warns, and her screams from earlier are sobs, and René's heart breaks, but for once, he doesn't listen to his mother. He can't.

Before he can shove his grandfather, before he can even make contact, the old man releases Frantz and takes a tight hold of René's shirt instead, jerking him painfully close.

"On your knees, you devilish boy."

"No," René spits, and for the first time, his grandfather's name-calling is right. He would drop the bastard into a lake of eternal fire if he could, and he would smile while he did it. "I won't."

"This instant!" His grandfather's voice thunders through the room, and René's nose throbs and his ears ring and Frantz breathes hard and his mother is biting back sobs, so he does it. He does it, and he hates the man in front of him more than he will ever hate anyone else. He's certain of it.

Governor Travers leans close, grasping René's collar tighter and half-cutting off his airflow, the next declaration nothing less than an outright threat. "If we were in England, I would throw you in Bedlam and see how you liked it, you monstrous, worthless child. You will obey me, René."

"You can't make me." René coughs, sucking in a breath. He knows what Bedlam is. Technically a hospital, it's not much more than a prison for those deemed mentally unwell.

"Oh, can't I?" his grandfather asks. "I think we'll just see what I can make you do."

"Let him go!" Frantz shouts.

"Father, for God's sake, stop." Astra scoops Frantz toward her, holding him close, René sees it when he glances over, but he's yanked back to attention by his grandfather slapping him a second time.

"Touch the boy," Governor Travers warns her, "and see what it gets him." He turns back toward René, a slick smirk sliding across his face when he grasps René's chin hard in one hand. René shakes madly as his grandfather runs a thumb up and down his burning cheek in a mockery of gentleness, and he cannot stop. "I can do worse than a broken nose, my boy. But I promise, if you're a good lad, I'll never hurt you again."

"Liar," René growls, deeper than he knew was possible. "You hurt me before you ever hit me."

This earns him a knee to the stomach that makes him crumple, his palms slamming against the floor as he catches himself even if he cannot catch his breath. Then his mother is saying something to Frantz, something like *stay back, love*, and she's running over, she's grabbing at his grandfather's coat and he's shoving her, though she stays on her feet. The front door opens at the same time, and his mother screams something, she screams his father's name, and René's vision goes blurry for one terrifying moment, blood still dripping from his nose.

Footsteps. A voice coming closer. His father? Yes. There's a French accent. His nose throbs as his vision rights itself, a metallic taste in his mouth. He thinks of his father's expression as he stood by the window after they found the slaves, looking irate and cold and resolute. Even if his father stops this, René doesn't feel protected.

"Andrew that is *enough*." Michel pulls on the back of Governor Travers' coat, tugging him away. "You will not shove Astra again, do you hear me? What have you done to René?"

Governor Travers clears his throat without deigning to answer, dusting himself off. Astra dashes over to René with Frantz in tow, helping him up with a whispered *oh my darling* on her lips. Red creeps into her face from the earlier slap as she shields both himself and Frantz with her own body. His grandfather is horrible to her, but he has never hit her. He did it because she stood in the way, and René can't have that. He can't have his mother hurting like he hurts—she hurts enough as it is. She'll never stop trying to protect him, and it's just another reason that he has to *go*. There is no home here. Not anymore. He'll come back for her when he's older. He swears he will.

"Let's go to the parlor and speak," Michel says, casting a glance at Astra like he's not sure if her cheek is red from anger or something else. The governor follows with a huff, but the door only falls partway shut.

"Oh René, your nose," his mother whispers, and René winces at her touch, pain radiating through his face.

"I think it's actually broken." Frantz looks closer, his eyebrows furrowed. "Good-for-nothing blackguard."

"Are you all right?" René asks, putting his sleeve up against the bleeding. "Your wrists?"

"I'm all right," Frantz echoes, fond and exasperated all at once. "We've got more to be concerned with right now."

Astra turns toward a very concerned-looking Molly, who's come from the direction of the kitchen, and with only a shared word or two the kindhearted maid is off for the doctor. What explanation they'll give this time, René doesn't know.

Jerome approaches, awkwardly holding out a handkerchief. "Better for stopping the bleeding than your sleeve," he says, his voice dull and flat with shock.

René nods, accepting the gesture. He steps away from Jerome once he takes the handkerchief, uncomfortable after their altercation yesterday.

"You should have encouraged Michel to stop my father before this." Astra rounds on Jerome. "Now look. You'll teach my son to fight but you won't defend him."

"I'm sorry, madam." Jerome looks surprised but keeps his tone respectful. "I was only doing as—"

"Oh, as Michel said, I'm sure," Astra turns away from him, throwing her hands up in the air. "I've had enough."

The sound of rising voices from the other side of the door cuts off the conversation, and they all turn to listen.

"You have failed to contain any of this," Governor Travers snaps. "The Seymour boy is a disgrace, and taking him in was a mistake. Your choice is whether or not you will allow that brat to stain your reputation as he did Arthur Seymour's."

Frantz breathes in sharply, and René slips an arm through his friend's, pulling him closer. Real, sickening fear pulsates in his veins.

"I made a promise"—Michel wavers, sounding like he might be shaking—"a promise to my dearest friend on his deathbed. A friend whose sacrifice saved my life and who I would be dead without. I am not one to break such things."

René knows from the experience of just last night what a lie that is. Guilt lays heavy on his father's words, but René doesn't know if it's enough to make him change his ways. Something tells him no, but there's a tinge of hope at the edges of his spirit as he hears his father take this small stand. Even if they leave, he doesn't think he can ever truly give up on his father or Jerome. He just can't wait on them anymore. If he goes and they change, they'll have to find a way to let him know.

"Michel, my lad." René doesn't miss the sinister condescension in his grandfather's tone, the sound sending chills up his spine. "How can you break a promise to a man who is no longer alive to know the difference?"

"Sir—"

Michel falls silent abruptly, and René pictures his grandfather raising his hand.

"Hear me now, Michel. I'm leaving for a brief trip to Barbados in two days to discuss the growing piracy problem with the governor there. Upon my return, I'll be bringing René to live with me. Make sure his bags are packed."

A long, deep silence echoes through the room. Bile crawls up René's throat again and he spins away from everyone in the room before dry heaving, but nothing comes up. Frantz's hand goes to his back, then his mother turns him gently around, tucking him close against her side again.

Finally, his father speaks.

"Andrew, no. He's my son. I'll handle it. We can discuss things when you are in less of a temper."

The words tremble with fear, and Michel's not shouting, this time.

He's begging.

"You aren't handling it," Governor Travers says, and René practically hears him rolling his eyes. "You are a good captain but a disappointing father, I'm afraid."

"You can't do this, Andrew."

The use of his grandfather's Christian name a second time, René notes. A show of power. Even rebellion. Or it would be, if terror wasn't laced through every word.

"I can. You know I can." Governor Travers pauses, his voice softening, but it's poison, still. "No magistrate on this island would stop me, and even if you found one nearby who might, I can think of a few ways to secure your agreement. I could ...." He lingers here, and René pictures him waggling his fingers in the air, pretending as if an idea is just occurring to him rather than something he's held close to his chest, just waiting for the moment to strike. "Recommend to the Court of Directors that you be removed from your post, for instance. You do love it so, I know, but you should take care to remember that you wouldn't have it if not for me."

"I was extremely qualified for this captaincy," Michel snaps, and René thinks that he sounds more furious about this than anything that's happened. He loves sailing too, very much, but he doesn't love it more than, well, the people he loves.

"Of course," his grandfather continues, insidiously indulgent. "But it was not easy to convince the powers that be in the Company that a Frenchman would protect English interests. I did that for you."

"Andrew—"

"Or," Governor Travers interrupts, "if that does not convince you, I could throw the Seymour brat in jail if you did not agree to give René to me. It would be as simple as telling the magistrate he attacked me, and then who's to say what might happen? Remember, Michel, you don't need an heir. Your brother has those. René has always been as much mine as he is yours, and I will do with the boy as I see fit."

The governor stalks out of the parlor without another word, scoffing in disgust when he sees René under his mother's arm before storming out and slamming the front door behind him. Michel steps out of the parlor and toward René, the entire group's eyes on him.

"Let me see your nose," he says, gentler than René expects.

"It's fine." René can't bear the idea of his father touching him. He can't bear any of this and he *has* to. He has to get out of here. He has to get *out*.

"René, son, please, just let me see. It's still bleeding."

Michel shifts the handkerchief aside, touching the tender spot, and he is, for a fleeting moment, the father René knew when he was younger. The father who swung him up unto his hip as they laughed beneath the stars on the deck of the *Navigator*. The father who helped him, Frantz, Arthur, and Jerome build a sandcastle on the beach one day, playfully flicking sand at Uncle Arthur.

"Don't touch me," René says, a plea rather than a demand. "Please don't touch me again. He struck me and broke my nose. That's all you need to know."

His father steps back as if struck himself, his eyes half-wild. He turns toward Frantz instead, sweat beading at his hairline.

"Frantz, what were you thinking? Don't ever touch Governor Travers like that again, I don't care what's happening."

"Are you seriously blaming them?" Astra asks, a glint of fury in her eyes.

"Do not, Astra," Michel snaps, his eyes flitting to her cheek again. "I don't want to hear it."

Astra stares at him. René's never heard his father speak to his mother like that.

"I was thinking he already broke René's nose and was on his way to breaking something else," Frantz interjects, balling his hands into fists. "I can't stand by and just let that happen."

Michel grows pale, his nostrils flared. "If you don't start behaving, I will separate the two of you until you do." He sniffs, his voice cracking as he speaks again. "I will not let you ruin your lives. Neither of you understands how dangerous breaking the rules is, but I am going to make you understand."

Pain pounds just above René's temple. He looks at the Delacroix and Travers coats of arms hanging in the entrance hall with a pair of crossed swords beneath, but this place isn't home anymore. It can't be.

"Michel," Astra breathes, "what has gotten into you?"

"I will no longer allow you to coddle them, Astra. You heard those threats your father just made, and it will take everything in my power to stop him from taking René. If I can even do it without endangering Frantz. This is the end of it. René must take up his position and Frantz must learn his place."

A long silence permeates the room again, somehow thunderous in René's ears, and he thinks of the one thing that might hurt his father most. The next words come out freshly sharpened, cutting into his throat just as surely as they will his father's heart. Tears fall from his eyes when he speaks, and he knows he shouldn't use what he's about to say as a weapon, but he can't help it.

"Arthur Seymour would be *ashamed* of you."

Grief and rage and love drench the words. René won't take them back.

"*René*," Jerome whispers harshly, shocked out of his silence.

But René only has eyes for his father.

His father stares at him, and René swears he hears something break, something echoing in his own soul, more painful than his throbbing nose, but with it comes an odd relief, a sense of rebirth. This old life is fading, and he knows now for certain it cannot be mended. Not until his father changes. For now, the only saving grace is to leave it behind entirely. Michel tears his eyes away from René and looks at Frantz as if searching for a protest. As if he sees father rather than son. That, at least, is nothing new.

"He's right," Frantz agrees, and he is not gentle, because Michel does not deserve his gentleness.

This last judgment shatters Michel entirely, tears breaking loose from his eyes before he wipes them away

"You will go upstairs and wait for the doctor," he tells them in a hard, unforgiving tone, a far cry from the father of a few moments ago asking to look at his nose. "In your rooms. Separately. Nicholas, please make sure they do, if you would."

"Yes, sir." Jerome nods, something of his younger self in his eyes. René remembers the twenty-one-year-old man he crossed swords with that night on the *Navigator*, and it seems like a scene from another life. The stories he loves seem more real to him than that night does right now, and what's true and what isn't he's not sure he could say.

"You're going to let him take me, aren't you?" René tears his eyes from Jerome, focusing back on his father. "You're just going to do it."

"Do not question me, René!" Michel shouts, a sob escaping him. "After the doctor sees to your nose, we will discuss how you will behave from now on, and there will not be any more arguments. Now go upstairs."

René falls silent, the world growing fuzzy and unreal around him.

"Come along, boys," Jerome says, firm and cutting off any further dialogue.

"Astra, I need to speak with you." Michel gestures toward the parlor he just exited with the governor.

Astra presses kisses onto both René and Frantz's foreheads before she goes. As soon as the parlor door closes, as soon as Michel asks *did he hit you*, she explodes, her *that doesn't matter*! echoing in René's ears as he enters the kitchen with Frantz and Jerome. Frantz offers to clean up René's nose himself, but Jerome insists on doing it, his eyes flicking to the red rings around Frantz's wrists. The sharp pain in René's nose grows at least somewhat duller, but he suspects the ache won't dissipate for some time. He doesn't really want Jerome touching him, but there isn't a choice.

"Don't fuss too much with your nose until the doctor arrives." Jerome stands up, gesturing them forward. "Frantz, we'll need to keep an eye out for any swelling around your wrists. Both of you need to take these cold cloths with you. Keep one on your nose, René, and leave the packing I put in there—it's stemming the bleeding. Let's go upstairs."

With no choice but to do as told, René and Frantz look at each other once more before following Jerome, still hearing Michel and Astra's voices, the sounds fading as they walk further away.

"Into your rooms," Jerome says. "And no sneaking out, or I'll hear it."

"Yes, *sir*," René says.

"Enough, René. Do not mock me."

"So, you believe I got what was coming to me?" René asks. "You believe I got what I *deserved*, do you? I hope you're pleased."

"I am not pleased." Jerome grows irritated. "But it still does not mean you should have disobeyed your father as you have."

"This was too far, but it was fine up until now?" Rage wraps around René's every syllable. "Some *mercy* from first Lieutenant Nicholas Jerome of the East India Company. Who knew it was possible? Some captain you'll make one day, when all your sailors run when they hear you coming."

"Bed!" Jerome exclaims, his eyes flashing with repressed anger. "Now."

René catches Frantz's eye before they close each of their doors. He listens for Jerome's footfalls going down the stairs, though they stop there, and René suspects he's sitting at the bottom, both listening out for their disobedience and waiting for Michel. It's too risky to try sneaking into Frantz's room, so René opens his window, hoping the creak and his glance at Frantz a few moments ago will signal his friend. He hears Frantz's window open, and while they cannot see each other, they can hear enough to talk. They're quiet, the enormity of the evening sinking in before Frantz speaks.

"We cannot wait for your father and Jerome to go on their next voyage," Frantz whispers. "Unless Auden cannot find us passage until later, I think we should go as soon as possible."

"Yes," René agrees, "I was about to say the same. Auden said he would be back tonight if he could. We should tell him we need to get out quickly. Before my grandfather returns from Barbados."

"It's a danger," Frantz says, "with your father and Jerome still here. But—"

"We have nothing to lose," René finishes, the image of his grandfather carting Frantz off to jail haunting him. "I cannot imagine staying here for any longer than necessary with my grandfather's threat against you."

"Or the one about you," Frantz presses. "No. We have to go. If we don't, you might have more broken bones next, living under his roof. And I might be in jail."

"We'll find a way out." René takes a deep breath, and he believes in them like he believes in his favorite stories. "I know it. I trust Auden. I trust the three of us."

"Yes," Frantz says, a smile clear in his voice. "So do I."

René looks up at the stars spread out across the canvass of the sky, spotting Orion and Gemini off in the distance, bright in late winter, or whatever counts as winter in Jamaica. He looks down at the shoreline, the music of the sea calling out to him.

I'm waiting for you, the water says. *Come home.*

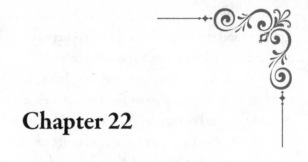

Chapter 22

Kingston, Jamaica. Four Days Later.

René's not surprised when Auden finds them passage, because Auden can talk anyone into anything.

He can also get out of his house.

Tomorrow night with the tide. Auden kept his voice as low as possible as he stood outside René's window yesterday. *We'll get passage on the Carina with Captain Barlow. We have to be on board by 9 o'clock.*

The old buccaneer, René said, reaching into his running mental catalog of the ships and captains in Kingston. *I stumbled upon my mother and your father talking about him one day, Frantz.*

The one people whisper about. Frantz nodded. *They say he helps escaped slaves sometimes, and even that Ebele pirate who trained Danso and his quartermaster. But no one can prove it.*

"Do we have everything?" René asks, rifling through his knapsack, which is filled to the brim with two extra sets of clothes, some bread, some chocolates, and a cask of water. The money they got gambling is tucked safely into its own separate, smaller bag inside, the other half of their funds with Frantz.

René's traded his usual buckle shoes for the boots he wears sailing. There's no room for a second coat, so he selects his favorite navy blue one, hoping it will do the job for long enough. He rummages through his wardrobe, stumbling upon the old red ribbon Jerome gave him for his seventh birthday. The old, tattered red silk slides through his fingers, and he places it in the bag on a whim. Next, he opens the book of pirate stories and sea myths Prescott made him years ago—the newspaper clippings about Robin Hood the Merciful still tucked between the pages. He adds it to his bag, and there isn't room for much more.

"I think so," Frantz says, contemplating his own bag, which includes two books he was able to stuff inside, as well as some of his father's navigational tools, and of course, Arthur's final letter to Chantal.

"I know you never forget, but your freedom papers?"

Frantz pats his inside coat pocket. "I don't know how well they'll serve me if the people who ask me to present them know we're being searched for. Because they will be looking for us. All over."

"Yes," René says, knowing what a low profile they'll be required to keep. "We'll have to find a way to get you new ones. Forged ones."

He touches his still tender nose. The doctor pronounced it too swollen to set back in place the night his grandfather broke it, returning the next morning to do so. A small plaster rests over the bridge, covering the wound left by the governor's ring and holding the reset fracture in place. It smells of wine vinegar, and he hates his grandfather for this added irritation.

Frantz nods. "Now I suppose we just have to wait. Are you going to write that letter to your mother?"

"Yes." René gestures to the writing utensils on his desk, tension tying knots up his spine. If there's one thing he dislikes most about this entire ordeal, the thing that makes nausea burn in the pit of his stomach, it's leaving his mother behind. He thought about telling her initially but didn't want to give her that burden, didn't want her in any sort of trouble if the secret came spilling out. He can't think about leaving her too much, or he fears his heart will break. "But there's something else we need to do before we go to the ship."

"What's that?" Frantz questions, arching one eyebrow.

"My sword. Jerome has it in his rooms. He ended up taking mine home last time."

Frantz pauses, huffing in disbelief. "Don't mistake me, I'm not opposed to you stealing the swords, but from *Jerome*? If he finds us—"

"He won't. I heard him talking to my father this morning. They have a meeting with another captain tonight, so if we time it correctly then we

should be fine. We can't go out there without something to defend ourselves."

"All right." Frantz sighs, clearly taking the point but still sounding only
half-convinced. "We'll have to be careful."

A half-hour later, René seals up the letter for his mother. His father left
for the aforementioned meeting earlier, telling Mrs. Hudson and the other servants that René and Frantz shouldn't leave the house, but that Astra
would be home. Except, his mother left on an errand too, over an hour ago,
and part of him wonders if she left to murder his grandfather. Thinking of
his mother hurts. It hurts it hurts it *hurts*. He hopes she'll understand, and
he hopes that one day, he'll come back for her. He swears he will.

They shut their bags, listening closely for the sounds of anyone nearby
and finding only quiet. He breathes in deep, settling his nerves. The sun
sets beyond the windows, casting an orange glow through his bedchamber,
and he gazes around one last time, his eyes falling on the old wooden toy
sword sitting atop a chest in the corner. The old book on sailing his father
gave him for his eleventh birthday lays next to it, the pages worn-out and
the content memorized. Something makes him pick it up, sliding it in near
the top of his bag. So many memories happened in this room. Staying up
too late reading by the candlelight. Helping Frantz through nightmares after Uncle Arthur died. Crying after his grandfather hit him too hard, again,
Frantz's hand running up and down his back in comfort. Jerome pulling the
covers off his bed, waking him up for a sword lesson. He will miss it, but he
cannot stay.

They're doing this. They're *really* doing this.

Grief settles into his chest as they tread the familiar hallway toward his
mother's bedchamber. He was happy here, once. The floor creaks, and they
duck into Astra's room just as Molly and Peter walk by.

"I don't know what to make of it," Peter says. "It's not my place to disagree with Captain Delacroix openly, but I'm worried for those boys, and
he doesn't seem himself. He snapped at me for the first time I can recall yesterday. I knew things had gotten worse, but I saw René's face the next morning and I could scarcely believe it. Mrs. Hudson is worried too. She heard
the captain and the madam up shouting again last night over what they're

going to do to keep the governor from taking René that doesn't put Frantz in danger."

"Mistress Delacroix started crying last night when I was helping her undress," Molly whispers. "She's terribly upset about everything."

Their voices fade away, but Frantz and René remain there for a few minutes after placing the letter under a perfume bottle, waiting for the two servants to clear the area and head toward their quarters on the other end of the house. René thinks of Mrs. Hudson and Pauline and James and how much he'll miss them, touched at Molly and Peter's concern. They've been kind to him since he was small, and he'll never forget that. They wait another minute or so, the footsteps fading away.

Except then there are more footsteps. Different footsteps.

His mother comes around the corner and into the room, jumping when she sees them, a tiny sound of alarm escaping her lips.

"René?" Her eyes land on their bags and the letter, and she looks between the two of them. "Frantz? What are you doing?"

"You said you were running an errand." René's pulse quickens, because he's not certain if she'll stop them. "Father's not home early too, is he?"

"No," his mother says, kind when she notices him tense. She grasps at the skirts of her light green, floral-patterned brocade gown, gazing at them with an intensity he recognizes in himself. "You're running away, aren't you? I can't think why else you'd be carrying bags and leaving me letters."

There's a silence as René locks eyes with his mother, unable to read her. He searches for an argument, but he's not sure anything could make a mother let go of her child and send him out into the wilds of the world, which is why he didn't want to lay this at her feet. The eye contact only breaks because she steps back toward the door, shutting it closed behind her. René's stomach doesn't sink like it usually would, because he's always trusted her.

"Mama?" he asks, and the next question comes out of a gut feeling rather than something rational. "Where were you?"

Astra doesn't respond immediately, gesturing them both closer to her before speaking in a low voice. "I was down at the harbor talking to a certain Captain Barlow. Except, it seems our Auden beat me to it."

René stares at her, and Frantz does too.

"I ..." René tries. "You ...."

Astra puts a shaking hand on his cheek, tears glistening in her eyes. "I've been wondering for months if I might have to make this choice, and after what happened a few days ago, the threats to both of you, I wanted to find you a way out. But it seems you were ahead of me. Captain Barlow said he wouldn't take any of Auden's money, but I gave him a little, to pay for what you would need."

"Mama," René whispers, and he's struck by the enormity of her love, her willingness to lose him to protect him and Frantz both. He's been betrayed by his father and Jerome. But never by her.

A small, restrained sob pierces the quiet, and Astra wraps her arms around them in an embrace, holding them tight against her. René closes his eyes, grasping at the sleeve of her gown, knowing how much he'll miss her, and swearing to the deepest parts of himself that he'll come back for her one day. She lets go, her fingers lingering on his arm for a moment before she turns toward her armoire, digging around in the back of one of the drawers and pulling out a small pouch.

"Take this." She hands it to René. "It's money. I've been putting it away."

"You won't get in trouble with Father?"

She waves her hand nonchalantly. "No. I'm allowed to spend money as I see fit, for the most part. The household finances are my domain. He'll never know it's missing, and on the off chance he does, I'll tell him I spent it on new gardening tools or a gown. You'll need it."

"Thank you," René breathes, gratitude rushing through him, because this will get them further than the small amount they've tucked away from gambling. "I'm sorry, Mama. I'm so sorry we have to go."

"Oh, my dear." She puts a hand on his face. "You're not the ones who should be sorry. I would go with you if I didn't think it would get you caught."

She moves over to Frantz, pressing a kiss to his hair. "Your father would be proud of you, sweetheart. You are so smart and kind, and another son to me. Truly. I love you, and I only wish I could have fixed this. But you deserve better. I hope you find your mother out there."

"I love you too." Frantz blinks back tears behind his spectacles. "And thank you. For everything. For this."

She ruffles his curls. "You're welcome, my sweet boy."

Questions spin through René's mind. How will she keep this lie from his father? How does she know Captain Barlow, and why did she go to him? He wants to ask, but he's not sure there's time.

His mother glances out the window as the sun starts its slow descent in the sky. "We'd best get you out before your father returns."

There's something strange in her voice. A story churning beneath the surface, begging to be told.

"What if Father suspects you helped us?"

"He won't. Even if he did, I would risk that for you, darling. I have a plan in mind. That letter of yours will help."

She puts both hands on his face, such love in her eyes that it steals his breath away. Not for the first time, he feels something kindred in their spirits. Something stronger than the blood they share. Something telling him she understands what it is to be different, to want something else than what was given to her. Tears slip from his eyes. He doesn't want to add to her burden, not when this is already so difficult, but he buries his head against her chest anyway, vowing that he will never forget how she always smells like flowers.

"My darling boy," she whispers, toying with his curls. "It will be all right. I promise you."

When she pulls away, she looks at them as if deciding something. "I know you both are aware of the man and woman who escaped from Jerome before he joined the *Navigator's* crew?" she asks, confusing René. "The pirates the papers like to call Robin Hood the Merciful and Maid Marian?"

"Yes," René answers, tilting his head and drawing out the word. He reaches back for a hazy memory, remembering his grandfather saying something about someone in Kingston helping them escape.

"There was always talk that someone in Kingston hid them and helped them get out," Astra says, connecting with René's thoughts. She takes a deep breath, a secret on the tip of her tongue, that story René heard a moment ago. "That person was me."

Silence sits between them as René parses what he just heard. He always suspected she carried secrets, but this is beyond anything he expected.

Yet somehow it makes sense.

"What?" René recovers himself, Frantz gasping in surprise beside him.

"We don't have time for the details," his mother says, "but I helped them. Ajani Danso and Abeni. They promised if I ever needed help that they would gladly consent in return for getting them out of Kingston. I think if you need somewhere to turn, you should search for them. And tell them who you are."

René stares at her again, his mind buzzing. He realizes it's the first time he's heard the woman quartermaster's real name.

"Are you telling me to go look for pirates?" he asks, exhilaration rushing through his veins.

Astra raises her eyebrows. "I know about those newspapers you read. The ones you keep under your bed."

"But you never said anything!" René protests, almost laughing.

His mother smiles. "You had the right to your secrets, my love. I never thought I'd see Danso and Abeni again, never thought I'd need their help, but now ...."

"You trust them?" Frantz asks, hope brimming in his voice. "They helped my parents once, the last time we saw my mother, but Papa told me I could only tell René."

Astra's eyes brighten even as she sounds far away and caught in the past. "I knew them for so little time, but yes. I trust them. I think they're doing good even if they're breaking the law, and I think they'll honor their promise to me if you need help. Captain Barlow helped me get them out, which is why I went to him tonight. He got them to Ebele. I think your father suspected me, Frantz, but kept my secret. He was the one who told me about Barlow's efforts, and hinted to me once that he might have encountered Danso himself."

Frantz's entire face lights up, and he reaches for Arthur's old pocketwatch.

A wide, reckless grin spreads across René's lips. "If we decide to look for them, where should we go?"

"There's been talk in the papers about sailors starting to flock to Nassau Town on New Providence Island." Astra lowers her voice again, clearly fearing someone might hear them talking. "Given it's largely without a government now. But I wouldn't start there. Your father will pursue you all over the islands and up and down the coast of the mainland colonies, I should think, and you'll need to throw him off the scent. Make him think you've left the Indies. Look for some work and then search them out. Find out if they're there first, because I don't know what else is going on in Nassau."

Astra squeezes her eyes shut, a guilty, pained expression on her face. She rests a hand on the white coverlet embroidered with burgundy flowers, gathering the material in her fingers before releasing it, her eyes roving over her favorite book sitting on the nightstand: *The Blazing World*, by Margaret Cavendish.

"I know neither of us wants to hurt Father, angry as we are." René's so, *so* angry at Michel, but he's sad for him, still. He doesn't cherish the idea of hurting him, but there's no choice. "But this has to be more important. He isn't just hurting us." He swallows at the memory of the slaves. "He's hurting other people, too."

"I know," Astra says. "I know."

"I'm sorry you have to keep this secret."

His mother keeps more secrets than he even knows, he suspects, and now he's giving her yet another. She touches the gold bracelet on her arm just like she did that night long ago when his grandfather knocked Prescott's book to the floor. He was so young then, but he sensed a secret in her that night.

Imogen. That was the name on the old letter that fell out of his mother's armoire when she searched for thread to repair his beloved book.

Who was she?

"Be careful." She kisses René's forehead, her hair that is the same shade as his own brushing against his cheek, and she's careful to avoid the black eye he now sports from his grandfather's blow. "Promise me you will."

"I promise. Thank you." René's voice cracks. "I love you. So much, Mama."

"And I you." Astra runs a thumb across his cheek, and it's so different from the mocking way his grandfather did so the other evening. "Both of you. And that's why I know I have to let you go. Don't ever let anyone out there crush you, René. And don't let the memories of this place do it, either. You are my heart. Never forget that."

He embraces her again and holds tight, his fingers clinging to the back of her gown before he lets go. She walks them to the side door near her garden, searching around to make sure no one approaches and looking at them one last time as if painting a picture in her mind. She pulls them both to her once more, murmuring *I love you* three times in succession before releasing them, writing the words in perfect script across René's memory. He knows he'll never forget this moment.

I love you.

I love you.

I love you.

"Go," she whispers, still clasping René's hand, tears pouring down her cheeks. "Take care of each other. I'll see you again one day. I swear it."

Astra's fingers slide against René's palm, and he knows he'll always remember the ghost of his mother's last touch on his fingertips, holding on for just a second to the edge of his navy-blue coat when she lets go of his hand.

They run and they run and they run, René's sides screaming for relief. He wants to cry. He wants to scream. He wants to take his mother's hand and shout *please come with me*. They run until they're nearly out of breath just to make sure they're away from the house, stopping near Jerome's to snatch a rest.

"I can't believe it's happening," Frantz says, bending over with his hands on his knees as he sucks in air.

"I know." René starts walking again even if he wants to break down—his true grief will have to wait until they're away. "This way to Jerome's. Shouldn't take more than a few minutes to get the swords."

They run a bit more, finding themselves in front of Jerome's small house not far from the shore. He rents it from the widow of a merchant captain, and he's lived here ever since he took over the position of second lieutenant on the *Navigator*. Before that, he kept a room at the boarding house like some of the other men without wives or children.

"How will we get in?" Frantz asks. "Jerome certainly wouldn't leave without locking the door."

"No." René thinks, trying to figure out a way in. "You're right. I'm going to try the window. But stay here. I'll go in."

"René." Frantz releases a breath through his nose. "I told you. We're in this together."

"I know we are." René grasps his hand. "But on the chance that someone other than Jerome catches us, it would be far worse if you were caught stealing from an East India officer's house. Besides, I'm in need of a lookout."

"All right." Frantz sounds disgruntled, but he relents. "Try the window so we can get out of here. I don't like this."

René nods, turning to try the bedroom window on the side of the house.

"Damn. It's locked."

"Here." Frantz hands him a nearby rock, large enough to do the job. "Bust the glass."

"Thought you didn't like this?" René smirks.

"Oh, don't smirk." Frantz rolls his eyes. "Auden's rubbing off on you. I don't like it, but it doesn't mean I don't think you're right about the necessity. Just throw it."

René does, and the glass breaks, making a louder sound than he likes. He reaches carefully through, avoiding the broken pieces and undoing the latch.

"Quickly," Frantz reminds him. "He might come back early."

René searches around once he climbs through the window, spotting the two court swords and taking the one with his initials etched into the sheath, attaching it to the shoulder belt lying next to it and slinging it across his chest. He gazes at the room, his eyes landing on a box resting atop a chest in the corner, the only other piece of furniture in the sparse room aside from the bed, a small mirror, and the modest wardrobe. There's no indication of Jerome's personality here, no paintings, no colors, nothing but a few sketchpads and a copy of Homer's *The Odyssey*, a gift from Michel. Grief strikes him. An ache. He misses Jerome already, but really, he's been missing him for a long time, hasn't he? He opens the box, finding a pistol, the one usually strapped to Jerome's belt when he's at sea, but he must have not needed it this evening. He busies himself with the process of loading it as Uncle Arthur taught him, though Frantz is the better shot. He certainly won't aim for anyone, but if someone tries to stop them it might serve as a distraction if fired into the air.

He's about to reach into the under layer of the box when Frantz calls to him through the open window.

"René, someone's coming around. I don't know if it's Jerome, but we need to go."

Something tells him to take the box. He makes certain the gun isn't in a firing position before shoving the entire thing in his bag and climbing out just as the front door opens. A voice rings through the small house like thunder.

"René! That better not be you in my house!"

René seizes Frantz's hand, and they take off running even faster than before, not stopping until they reach the beach, though they're a good distance from where the *Carina* is docked. Footsteps thud close behind them, boots hitting hard, packed sand.

Jerome's chasing them.

The clouds overhead release a drizzle of rain. There's no real sign of a storm approaching, just a misting to slice through the heat and humidity. No lightning, no thunder, just rain rain *rain*. The sun set a short while ago, the ships set like ghosts against the sky. Kingston Harbor is massive but largely deserted at night, the patrol much less during these hours. There are, however, more men than there used to be. René's grandfather made it so.

"We have to keep going," Frantz says, straining for breath. "We have to go."

They start running again, but the footsteps grow alarmingly close, and Jerome seizes Frantz by the back of his coat, René's hand aching with emptiness without his friend's held within it.

"What on *earth* are the two of you doing?" Jerome shouts, his black hair damp against his face as he holds tightly to Frantz's collar.

"Let him go, Jerome." Every fiber of René's being aches with desperation, heavy pain making his entire body throb. He has never wanted something so badly in his entire life.

Jerome stares at him, understanding dawning on his face, and René's stomach sinks. If they're caught now, they might never have this chance again. Not for a long time. Not until after his father sends him to boarding school or his grandfather takes him to Spanish Town. By then, there's no telling what fiction his grandfather might invent to lock Frantz away. He can't bear it. He *can't*.

"You're running away. You think I wouldn't figure that out after what you just did? Breaking my window and stealing from me? Foolish boy."

"Just let him go," René pleads, drawing on Jerome's remaining affection. "Just ... please, Jerome. Please do this for me. Let us go. Let *me* go."

"You can't do this," Jerome insists. "Running away is not the answer."

"I can do whatever I like!" René all but screams, his throat raw from the effort. Pleas will get him nowhere, it seems, and he shouldn't have expected anything else. Not from the man Jerome is now. Deep, righteous rage makes his blood boil in his veins, just like it did that night his grandfather broke his nose. That part of him fully lives now, as much a piece of his soul as the bright little boy who has always believed in stories. This side of him has always been there, hasn't it? Perhaps it was born the first time his grandfather hit him, or simply grew up alongside the violence sewn inextricably into life in the West Indies. Slavery. Hangings. Beatings, whether his own or the ones sailors are subjected to if they aren't lucky enough to have a decent captain. Death. Death wrought by men like his grandfather. And now his father, too, even if Michel doesn't want to admit it. He would rather risk the ocean swallowing him whole than staying here. "Get out of our way, Jerome. I'm warning you."

Jerome laughs, and the sound sends chills shooting down René's spine.

"A warning. You insolent little brat," Jerome growls, tightening his grip on Frantz's collar. "I'd like to see what you think you can do to me."

"Let me go, dammit!" Frantz exclaims, pulling away with all his might, but Jerome is too tall and too strong.

Jerome ignores him.

"What, your little privateer friend got you passage somewhere?" he asks, the words nothing less than a snarl, and slick with scorn. "I knew Auden was trouble when I first laid eyes on him."

René holds back a dark laugh of his own. If only Jerome knew that Astra helped this process along. Auden is brilliant, of course, but there's no point in bickering over that.

"It's none of your business." René's voice whips into the air with a crack of rage, echoing what he said after they found the slaves on the *Navigator*. "I don't have to answer to a coward, and that's what you are."

"How dare you!" Jerome shouts, his eyes darkening with fury.

René reaches inside his bag for the gun he stole, distracting Jerome from his tirade. He pulls it out and cocks it, pointing it far out to the side and up so it doesn't accidentally hit either Jerome or Frantz.

"René, what are you doing?" Jerome asks. "Do not—"

The shot goes off, exploding in René's ears. The bullet lodges in a nearby palm tree, the bark breaking and splattering across the sand. Jerome's surprise at the sound alone makes him let go of Frantz, who scrambles back over to René, his glare sharp as the point of a knife.

"You do not shoot at people, boy."

Boy, not René. That always means trouble.

"I wasn't shooting at you." René grips the gun, his hand shaking from what he just did. "I was shooting at the tree to make you let go. I'm not as good a shot as Frantz, but I think I can aim well enough so as not to hit you."

"Drop the gun *immediately*."

The air around Jerome crackles with danger, and René should stop, he knows he should, but he won't. Not now.

"No." The pistol only held one shot, but René's certain more ammunition and powder are inside the box, so he won't give up so easily, even if it's empty now. Not when they might need it for future danger.

"René. Let go."

"No."

Jerome stalks forward, grabbing René's arm and attempting to wrestle him to the ground. They both slip on the damp sand until they fall, and Jerome reaches for the gun, but René keeps hold. He kicks at Jerome, but despite his own new height Jerome is a fully grown man, and he pins René's legs to the ground with his knees, taking the gun and throwing it a good distance away. René swings, catching Jerome's face, the attempt so wild that Jerome grabs hold of one wrist and then the other.

"Calm down." Jerome's voice grows thick with frustration. "You are going to hurt yourself more than me."

You must maintain control, René hears Jerome say, a memory from their sparring lessons. *You must have balance and precision.*

"You don't have power over me." René twists in an attempt to get away. "You aren't my father." He pushes at Jerome, but nothing happens. "You aren't *anything.*"

A lie. Jerome is his family. His brother.

Brothers don't do this.

Hurt passes through Jerome's eyes, and he bites his lip like he might be holding something back. "So, this is the game you're going to play now? That you care nothing for me?"

For a moment René deflates, but he keeps steady even as grief rushes through every crevice, every nook and cranny of his body, until it might be all he is. Just a sad boy clinging to stories. Just a boy who could never be good enough. He holds his mother's earlier words warm against his chest, and they ease the pain, somewhat.

"I care about Frantz more." René's angry tears mix in with the light rain running down his cheeks, and the one last piece of him that can't give up on his chosen brother emerges, temporarily muting his rage. "He isn't safe here. I'm not safe. My father chose my grandfather, he chose his career, his peace, over us, and you chose to side with him instead of taking a stand. I love you and you just don't *care*. Why don't you care?"

"I do." The words slip from Jerome's mouth, and there might be tears glistening in his eyes at this declaration. "I'm trying to *help*, you selfish, senseless boy. It's all I've ever tried to do. This will break your father's heart. Do you want to live with that?"

René thrashes in answer, and Jerome has trouble keeping hold. His wrist comes free first. Then a leg. A target presents itself, and René slams his knee into Jerome's stomach. Pain is the punishment for his attack as Jerome backhands him, the East India ring Michel gave him for his last birthday swiping hard across René's right eyebrow. Blood trickles down from the small wound, a dull pain mixing in with the remaining ache and bruising from his grandfather's blows, a sharp jolt going through his broken nose.

Jerome stops dead, still pinning one of René's arms to the sand, but no apology passes his lips. The same memory playing in Jerome's eyes swirls in

René's own mind. The memory of his grandfather bruising his arm when he was twelve.

I am not going to strike you, René. I have never done so.

This particular broken promise breaks his heart.

"Let him *go*!"

Jerome's eyes go wide and he loses his grip, falling flat to the sand with a grunt of pain. And then Frantz is there, breathing hard and holding a tree branch in his hands. It takes René a moment to understand what just happened, but he lets Frantz pull him up from the ground.

"Thank you," René says, half-smiling despite the situation. "You're a genius."

"You shot a tree and got tackled for me." Frantz finishes the smile René started. "Let's go."

René looks over at Jerome, who remains unmoving on the sand.

"Is he all right?" René looks back once more at the man who used to be his hero and who will always be his brother.

"Just dazed." Frantz points at Jerome's chest rising and falling. "He won't be out for long. We have to go."

They hear one last muttered *René, stop,* before Jerome passes out, and it makes René's chest twinge.

It doesn't change his mind.

They race off toward the ship, Auden, and their freedom ahead, some of the misting rain letting up as they reach the other end of the harbor. They find the *Carina* at 8:59 exactly according to Frantz's pocket watch, leaping from the gangway and onto the deck. Auden meets them with a worried grin.

"I thought I told you to tell your friends not to be late," the man René recognizes as Captain Barlow says.

"They made it," Auden says. "So, technically they weren't."

"Why are you bleeding, boy?" Captain Barlow asks without introduction, looking at René. "Your mother said you had a broken nose and a black eye, but this looks new."

"We encountered some trouble on our way here," René admits.

"Mhmm." Captain Barlow raises his eyebrows, fighting a smile. "I told your mother I'd take care of you and here you are bleeding. Go below deck and find a hammock. I don't want anyone seeing you." He turns to his crew. "Anchors aweigh, lads! Let's get going. I don't want anyone following us. We need to go with the tide and the wind while it's ours."

There's a thrill in René's chest when he meets Frantz's and Auden's eyes, their smiles matching his own. They head to the general sleeping quarters near the bow, finding three hammocks side-by-side. René reaches into his bag, pulling out the box that formerly held the gun he lost in the tussle.

"What's that?" Auden asks. "And where'd you get the sword?"

"Jerome," René says, matter-of-fact. "We broke into his house to get mine back. He was the reason we almost didn't make it, so I suppose that was rash on my part, but I wanted the sword. Also, my mother apparently had the same idea as you did about Captain Barlow. She helped us get out."

"You stole from Jerome?" Auden raises his eyebrows. "Impressive. Also, I'm not surprised—your mother is a genius. I've always said so. What was that shot I heard go off?"

"René shot a tree to make Jerome let go of me," Frantz replies, checking through his own bag.

"Then Frantz hit him with a tree branch to make him let go of me." René opens the box, lifting off the top. "I lost the gun, unfortunately."

"Extremely impressive. I would expect no less," Auden declares. "You two, having all the fun without me. Don't feel too badly about the gun. I stole one from my father for Frantz to have. And one of his daggers, for me. What's in the box?"

"The gun was in here," René mutters. "And there are bullets and ...." He stops, his hand landing on the other remaining item in the box, something he certainly hadn't meant to steal: a bracelet. He examines it, *Romani* etched on the inside. A gift from Jerome's mother, he supposes. Why had Jerome kept it?

"What's that?" Frantz asks, eyeing it with curiosity.

René can't think of a single thing aside from this that he has never told Frantz and Auden, but he promised Jerome that night he wouldn't tell anyone, so he kept the secret, even from the two people closest to him, and he keeps it now, too. He puts the bracelet back in the box, latching it shut before placing it in the bottom of his bag with everything else on top. "It's nothing. Just something of Jerome's I didn't intend to take."

Auden hands him a handkerchief to wipe the blood off his face while Frantz imparts the story about Astra's connection with Robin Hood and Maid Marian, as well as Captain Barlow. They hear the sound of the anchor going up, and the *Carina* starts sailing away. With wordless agreement they slip up to the top of the stairs, peeking out onto the deck. The night stands before them, stars bleeding into the dark sky as the moon rises. Frantz and Auden each take one of René's hands and he squeezes theirs, his heart too full to speak just now. The wind ruffles his hair, and he knows Jerome won't have time to alert his father and ready a ship in time to catch up with them. Gemini shines bright above them through the dissipating rain, Castor and Pollux twinkling most of all, the pair of stars deriving their names from two brothers in Greek myth long considered the protectors of sailors. René breathes in the salty air, and no matter the ache in his face, joy springs up in his soul, mixed with utter relief.

They are *free*.

Chapter 23

Kingston.

J erome awakes to the sound of voices murmuring around him, his back aching and a dull pain throbbing in his forehead.

What happened?

"Lieutenant Jerome?" someone asks, and Jerome squints, his vision a touch blurry before clearing.

Admiral Adams, the commander of the Jamaican naval fleet and Michel's main contact in the Royal Navy, stands nearby. They've worked with him a great deal lately to protect English ships and interests against the backdrop of the war over the Spanish succession.

"I ... yes, sir." Jerome sits up, brushing sand off his coat.

"Are you quite all right?" the admiral inquires, helping him to his feet. "What happened?"

Then, Jerome remembers. In a flash of over bright, sickening color, he remembers.

René and Frantz are gone.

Let me go.

The pain in René's voice stays with him, and he cannot banish it. Frantz hit him in the head with a branch. That's right. Things hadn't gone black immediately, but he must have passed out briefly.

"I have to see Mich ... I have to see Captain Delacroix immediately," he says, correcting himself. "I must go now. His son has run away, along with his ward, Arthur Seymour's boy."

"What?" Admiral Adams asks, looking at the two officers standing by his side.

"They must have gotten away on a ship," Jerome continues. "I don't know which one. And I don't know if they made a deal with someone or stowed away. I believe Aldridge Carlisle's son accompanied them."

"I'll have the logs checked this instant, and interview the dock workers," Admiral Adams responds. "Though there's far less activity at this time of day, so I don't know if anyone would have seen them board. None of my fleet left the harbor tonight. I know for certain. Do ask the captain if he'd like me to send out a ship to patrol in the morning. Would you like me to accompany you to see him?"

"No." Jerome presses a hand to the back of his head—no blood, but it aches. "I think I may need privacy to impart this news."

"Understood. Are you quite sure you're all right? I could send word to Governor Travers, but I understood that he's traveling at present."

"I'll be fine, thank you, sir." Jerome looks at René's blood smeared across his knuckles, feeling disturbed and anxious. "And yes, he just left for Barbados. But right now, I need to get to Captain Delacroix."

"Of course." Admiral Adams nods his head, the moonlight illuminating the silver strands in his dark brown hair, and Jerome thinks it's the first time he's seen him without his powdered wig. "I'll let you know about the log information, and do let me know if we should send out a patrol. Anything I can do to assist, I will. Should I send a man to alert Captain Carlisle?"

"Thank you, sir," Jerome answers, "but I think Captain Delacroix might like to speak to Captain Carlisle himself. I appreciate the offer. I have no doubt I will see you in the morning, as we will likely take you up on the offer of assistance."

Jerome thanks the admiral again, starting off at a slow run down the familiar path toward the Delacroix home, his ankle twinging from his awkward fall.

What will he say?

How will he say it?

How does he tell a father his son has run away?

How does he tell Michel he let the boys slip through his fingers just like Danso and Abeni? He's come so far, and yet now it feels not so far at all. He stops when he steps on something where the sand meets the grass, picking up a soggy pamphlet from the ground.

Pirates are Hostis Humanis Generis!

The enemy of all mankind.

A piece of literature written by a Cotton Mather-inspired minister, no doubt. He spares a glance at the heavens as he runs, Orion bright above him, the constellation at its most powerful in the early March sky. Something breaks inside him. Something has *changed*.

"I will find you, René," he whispers, to nothing and no one but the stars above, his eyes scanning Orion's belt. "I will hunt you down, however long it takes."

His home is broken. René broke it.

What if René tells his secret to someone? Anyone? If he's truly gone, Jerome has no control over the matter anymore.

Why did he divulge that secret when he didn't have to?

Because René has always been a brother.

The one Jerome chose for himself.

Was, a voice whispers somewhere deep within him. A dark voice.

Is, he counters, though the anger does not vanish.

His mind won't allow him any more coherent thoughts after that, all his speculation and his worry and his anger and his loss jumbled together in a tangled knot. He arrives at the Delacroix house, met by Mrs. Hudson's surprised face at the door.

Jerome removes his hat. "I apologize for the hour, but I have urgent news for the captain. May I come in?"

"Yes, of course, Lieutenant," Mrs. Hudson says, allowing him inside and glancing over at Peter, who stands near the staircase. "Peter, is the captain in his study?"

"He went upstairs to see the boys." Peter eyes Jerome, biting his lip. "He just arrived home barely before you knocked, Lieutenant Jerome. The madam just awoke from a rest and hasn't seen them. She's with Molly in the parlor. But I haven't seen René or Frantz. We thought they were napping or reading, but when we went up to retrieve them for supper they weren't there. Then we thought perhaps Mistress or Captain Delacroix took them out, but that doesn't seem to be the case. Have you seen them?"

Michel's shouts come ringing down from the second floor, calling the boys' names, his voice echoing into the empty hallway. He comes thundering down the stairs without his usual grace, stopping short when he sees Jerome in the entrance hall. His clothes look more ruffled than usual, his hair untidy.

"Nicholas, have you seen the boys?" Michel asks, looking irritated and ready for a lecture. He grips a glass of brandy, still full. He must have poured some in his study after searching for the boys upstairs. "I swear, if they've snuck out of this house again I'm going to station some of the men by the front door."

"Sir." Jerome keeps his tone even, panic threatening him. "I think perhaps you should sit down."

"What's happened?" Michel looks closer at Jerome, eyeing the bloody knuckles and the messy hair.

"Sir, I really think you should sit."

"I appreciate you trying to be gentle with whatever news you're bearing." Michel's knuckles pop white around his glass. "But kindly tell me whatever is on your mind."

"Sir," Jerome repeats for the third time, keenly aware of the servants' eyes on him. "René and Frantz have run away."

Michel stares at him, no comprehension passing across his face. "I'm sorry," he responds, flat. "I think I misheard you."

You failure, that voice from earlier inside Jerome's head says, ringing loud and unforgiving.

"René and Frantz are gone, sir. They've left Kingston."

The brandy glass slips from Michel's hand, falling to the floor and shattering everywhere, amber liquid running over the jagged, broken pieces and onto the hardwood. Jerome lunges forward, catching Michel by the upper arms before he falls. Michel's fingers wrap around Jerome's elbows, using him as an anchor.

"Steady there," Jerome whispers. "Steady."

If Arthur were here he would pull Michel into an embrace, but Jerome isn't sure that's proper, caught as he is somewhere between protégé and first officer and friend.

Michel meets Jerome's eyes then drops his gaze, sucking in a breath and mastering himself. "Where did they go? How did they go?"

"I'm not certain yet," Jerome answers. "Admiral Adams is having the logs checked to see which ships sailed out tonight."

"I will have that captain *hung*." Michel's voice grows deep, rumbling like thunder with the threat. "Mark my words."

"I don't know if they made a deal or if they stowed away," Jerome says, placating, though he doesn't disagree, if the captain did this on purpose. "I don't know if we can ever know that, so it may be difficult to bring charges if we do discover whose ship took them. I suspect they went with Auden as well, so we'll need to talk to Captain Carlisle. Admiral Adams has also offered to send out a patrol in the morning."

"We should go now." Michel looks half-mad, grasping Jerome's elbows tighter, his eyes bloodshot. "We have to go *now*."

"My advice would be to wait," Jerome tells him. "If we can get log information, if we can get any information at all, it will help us narrow the search."

Michel gulps in some air, eyes running over Jerome's bloodied knuckles again, but he doesn't comment.

"Astra!" Michel calls out, letting go of Jerome. "Astra!"

In a minute or two there's the rustling of skirts and footsteps growing closer, Astra and Molly's faces appearing around the corner. Red stains Astra's eyes even if she looks otherwise composed. She's been upset for days, so the tears are not surprising, but there's a tightness in her face, something in the way she holds herself too straight, that strikes Jerome.

Surely she can't have helped them?

He chases the thought away, reprimanding himself for thinking such a thing of the wife of his commanding officer.

Yet it doesn't quite leave him.

"Michel, why are you shouting?" Astra asks. "If the boys have snuck out of the house again I couldn't blame them, no matter how angry you are."

Jerome bites his lip, uncomfortable at her aggression in front of the servants and himself.

"Astra, they have run away." Michel's more openly angry at his wife than Jerome's seen before. "This is no time to argue with me."

"What are you talking about?" The color runs out of Astra's cheeks. "What do you mean they've run away? Their absence for supper doesn't mean they've left the island entirely. They're fourteen, for heaven's sake."

"Astra," Michel repeats, gentler. "Nicholas says they've run away." Michel turns toward Jerome, a question in his eyes. "Jerome, can you tell us—"

Astra picks up her skirts, dashing toward the stairs and running up, stopping her husband's words in their tracks.

"Astra they aren't up there," Michel calls out, baffled, but she ignores him. "Didn't you hear Peter say that?"

They receive a response by the way of doors opening and closing as Astra searches the upstairs, silence falling after she goes into her own bedchamber.

"Madam?" Molly calls up.

"Astra?" Michel adds on, taking a step toward the stairs.

Astra appears at the top again, a single sheet of paper in her hand. She walks down slowly, reading what Jerome assumes is a letter.

"What is that?" Michel asks, sounding afraid. "What are you reading?"

"René left a letter on my vanity. I didn't see it when I woke from my rest." Astra looks up, the paper fluttering in her shaking hand. "They did run away."

She reaches the bottom, and whatever Jerome's earlier thoughts, the tears in her eyes now are real, and there's no faking her distress. Still, the hitch in her voice nags at him. She hands Michel the letter, and he holds out it so Jerome can read too.

Dear Mama,

I couldn't leave without telling you goodbye. Frantz and I are leaving Jamaica with Auden. Things can't change here, much as I wish they could. Ever since I found out Father was transporting slaves, I knew I would have to leave someday, but when Grandfather broke my nose and threatened to put Frantz in jail, I knew I had to leave as soon as possible. I can't stand to be separat-

ed from Frantz any more than I can stand another beating from Grandfather. I can't bear the idea of being sent to live with a man who hates me, and I don't think Father can stop it from happening. I love Father and Jerome, but I can't trust them anymore. I wish I could. Father lied about transporting slaves. Jerome said I deserved what Grandfather did to me. I know I'm not perfect, but I also know I didn't deserve a broken nose. You did everything you could to help us, and then Grandfather ended up hurting you, too, and I don't want that. You deserve better, and if going keeps you a little safer, I'll do that in exchange for all the things you've done for me.

I'm so sorry we have to leave you behind, but know that one day I'll come back for you. I promise. You are one of the bravest people I know. Just like Uncle Arthur was.

I love you. I love you so, so much.

René

"Oh my God," Michel whispers, clutching the letter. "Oh my *God.*"

He reaches out with his free hand, clasping Astra's. A cloud of quiet hangs over the room, everyone looking for answers from the man who usually has them, but now possesses none.

"Captain?" Mrs. Hudson says, having retrieved a broom from the kitchen to sweep up the broken glass. "What can we do?"

"Peter," Michel says, partially recovering himself, "please go tell Admiral Adams I will gladly accept his offer of a patrol in the morning. I will speak with him then, as early as possible. Then please go tell James to fetch Aldridge Carlisle," he continues, referencing the Delacroix's carriage driver. "I don't want him finding out from anyone but me."

"Yes, sir, right away," Peter replies, and he's gone out the door without another word.

"Molly." Michel turns toward the maid. "Kindly take a note to the printers' house. I believe you know where it is? Tell him, or whoever answers his door, that I will have a description drawn up for printing by midday at the latest so we can get the flyers distributed, and that I will need at least enough for us when we set sail, tomorrow evening or the next morning."

"Yes, Captain Delacroix," Molly says, pressing Astra's free hand before she goes.

"Mrs. Hudson, please go to Mrs. Riley's boarding house and find second lieutenant Rollins. He and several of the other men keep rooms there, and he'll be able to alert most of the crew quickly with their help," Michel continues. "Ask him to get Prescott first, so he can begin making preparations for sail."

"Sir," Jerome adds, "my home is near the boarding house. If Mrs. Hudson picks up my sketchpad and pencils, I could work on sketches of the boys."

"I'll be glad to do both," Mrs. Hudson replies. "I'll go right now. Ma'am," she says, turning to Astra, "anything?"

"No." Astra shakes her head. "I will send notes to my friends in the morning. I am not ready to have anyone call, yet. If you could ask Pauline to make some tea for when the Carlisles arrive, that would be enough."

Soon Mrs. Hudson goes too, leaving Astra, Michel, and Jerome alone. Michel takes them quietly toward the drawing room, asking the most important question once they're all seated.

"What happened? How did you find them?"

"They broke into my house. I found them after I left you with Captain Taylor," Jerome says without ceremony. "My bedchamber window was broken. They took René's court sword and the box with my best pistol in it." He does not add that the box also contained the bracelet his mother gave him. He doubts René meant to steal that, and even if Michel knows about his past, he doesn't like bringing it up. "I ran to the harbor and saw them there. I seized Frantz, and then René and I got into a tussle. I was doing my best to stop them from getting away. Frantz struck me with a tree branch and I passed out. Admiral Adams brought me around."

"Are your knuckles bleeding?" Michel pulls the spare handkerchief out of his pocket, handing it over to Jerome. "Are you concussed?"

"No." Jerome doesn't really wish to tell this part of the story. "I'm afraid René kneed me in the stomach, and I struck him out of instinct. My knuckles swept just above his eyebrow and the ring drew blood. It was not my intention. As to being concussed, possibly. I will see the doctor before we go. My vision was only blurry for a moment, though my head aches a bit. It's nothing, most likely. I am sorry about hitting René."

He promised René he would never do such a thing, but the boy doesn't deserve his sympathy. Not anymore.

"It's understandable," Michel replies. "It seems like he was out of control. I know you wouldn't do that normally."

"I do apologize, sir," Jerome says. "I was trying to contain him, but it doesn't surprise me that his agility with a sword translates to physical agility generally. He's young, but I shouldn't have underestimated him. Or Frantz, for that matter."

Astra glares, getting up abruptly from her precarious perch on the settee. "I need to go upstairs."

"Astra, please wait," Michel begs her, tears welling in his eyes.

"I desperately need a moment alone, Michel," she says, one hand ghosting across his shoulder. "Please."

Michel doesn't argue further, and Astra's bedchamber door slams shut upstairs a few moments later. There's one stifled sob, and then pure, utter silence. Michel winces at the single noise, tears flooding down his own cheeks unabated. Jerome hasn't seen Michel cry like this since Arthur died, and he doesn't know what to do. At least in those dark days, Michel and Astra could focus on what Frantz needed after losing his father, and Jerome could help take care of René, the crew serving as a support in a shared loss.

Now, Jerome isn't sure where to begin at all.

"This is my fault." Michel covers his face with his hands before sliding them back, his fingers tangling in his hair.

"No, sir." Jerome's face grows hotter as the minutes pass. Damn those boys for doing this. "I respectfully disagree."

I care about Frantz more, he hears René say, selfishly disregarding the father who loved him so much.

"It is not your fault," Jerome continues, fueled more by his anger at René than his comfort with the emotional situation. If he is the only one who will stand by Michel's side, then he must do his best. "You gave those boys the world, and this is their answer."

"The slaves." Michel's voice cracks. "I—"

"You were following your orders, even if your personal feelings were conflicted. It's what we all must do, sometimes."

"Yes," Michel answers. "But allowing my father-in-law such license was not something I had to do. Although God knows what I could really do to stop him other than running away. He was going to take René and he was threatening Frantz and I thought I could just tighten my grip to make them behave rather than looking for a solution. But I missed this."

"They should not have run away," Jerome says, adamant. "You were trying to give those boys their best chance."

Michel makes no response, a sob breaking through whatever he might have said next. Jerome waits, then puts a hand on Michel's back, heartily wishing Arthur was here. Arthur was talented at this, and he is not. If Arthur were here, this might not have happened. But Arthur Seymour isn't here. He is.

"I'm sorry I couldn't stop them." A rush of sympathy gushes into Jerome's voice, and he wills himself not to cry, because crying is useless to him.

He has failed the man who brought him up from the life of an ordinary sailor. The man who turned him into an officer. The man who opened the door to his home and his family. The man who is almost like a father, and certainly a friend. A hero, to him, even if he still worries it might make him weak. Perhaps he's failed René, too, by not being strict enough, by not warning Michel enough about his behavior. He ignores the melancholy bubbling up in the pit of his stomach. He refuses to miss René, not when he's morphed into this ungrateful, stubborn brat. Besides, missing him, grieving him, will only distract from the process of finding him and Frantz both.

Michel studies the floor, eyes catching on a scratch in the wood. "You did everything you could. René and Frantz are capable of a great deal when determined, and I underestimated them, and Auden Carlisle. I didn't see it coming, and I should have. I should have locked them in their rooms, but I worried that was too harsh. Foolish boys," he continues, the first hint of anger spilling over. "God, I can only begin to imagine what my father-in-law will say about this. I'm glad he's not here tonight. I'm not certain I could handle him."

The sound of a knock on the door impedes their conversation, and Michel greets Captain Carlisle and his wife. Astra reappears downstairs, drawing the other mother into the kitchen for tea while the men discuss the next step, and Jerome sits down to begin the sketches right after Mrs. Hudson's return.

When they're gone in another hour—two? Jerome scarcely notices the passing of time, tonight—he goes into the study to pour Michel another glass of brandy. He waits at the top of the stairs, disinclined to intrude upon whatever conversation Michel and Astra are having.

"I don't have anything else to say tonight, Michel," Astra says, hoarse from crying.

"Don't be angry at me."

"Why didn't you *listen* to me? I begged you to listen to me, to let us leave this place and go back to Europe. Being harder on them when my father was already trying to crush them wasn't the damn answer."

"I'm sorry, Astra. I am."

"I wish I could believe you." Astra pauses, her voice going lower than usual. "You have no idea how much. You threatened to separate them, Michel. My father was going to take René. You are shipping slaves, and Frantz had every right to his devastation. We both should have seen this coming." She pauses again, sighing. "If you were to find them, things would have to change here, and you don't seem to know that."

"The world they want doesn't exist." Michel grows exasperated. "They have to live in the one that does. There is no other option."

"Except to find the courage to forge a new one," Astra says. "I'm going to bed. Don't disturb me unless it's important."

Jerome freezes at the top of the stairs. He's heard Astra argue with Michel, but this feels like resignation more than a fight. This feels like the end of something. Anger shoots through him—Michel is *not* the one to blame here. Jerome starts down as Astra comes up, the two of them meeting in the middle. Astra's eyes run over Jerome's still bloody knuckles.

"I'm sorry, madam." Jerome's lost for anything else to say, unsure, exactly, what part of tonight he's apologizing for. "Truly."

"I'm certain." Astra's words are sharp, sarcastic, and they hold no mercy. "Go to my husband, Lieutenant Jerome. I'm sure he has more to say to you than I do." She goes without another word, closing her bedchamber door behind her.

Irritation pricks at him. Back to Lieutenant Jerome then, is it? Astra, it seems, will be no ally to their search, even if she should be the most stead-fast. Does she not want to find her son? With every moment, he only grows more suspicious.

Jerome goes back toward the drawing room, stopping short when he hears Michel whisper into the emptiness.

"I'm sorry, Arthur. I'm afraid I may have failed you, my friend."

Jerome waits for a beat then clears his throat, announcing his presence. He hands Michel the new glass of brandy, sitting down on the settee with his own. Michel runs a thumb over the inscription on his beloved pocket watch before setting it back in his coat.

"Thank you, lad." Michel takes a sip of the brandy. "Are you all right? I've barely asked. Come here in the morning, and I'll summon Doctor Williams."

"I'll be fine." Jerome drinks his own brandy, remembering an evening when he was younger and unused to the strength of Michel's preferred liquor. He kept accepting refills as he sat with Michel and Arthur in the former's study, unsure if he should say no. Much to the other two men's amusement, he became rather unintentionally drunk. He slept in one of the Delacroix guestrooms that night, embarrassed and with the sensation of rocks in his head the next morning. This only increased Michel's affec-tion toward him, much to Jerome's bafflement. "I was just surprised. Frantz swung harder than I expected, and I was too focused on René to see him coming. I'm sorry I let them slip through my fingers."

Just like Danso and his damned quartermaster, right down to the gun-shot fired through the air. Just like them.

"It isn't your fault, Nicholas. They were determined to get away. And I didn't even consider that they'd try."

Michel fiddles with a worn crucifix beneath his collar. Born into a Catholic tradition in France, he's converted and attended Protestant ser-vices since marrying into an English family, but Jerome's seen him toy with this piece of jewelry before.

"Do you ever pray, Jerome?" Michel asks, glancing over at him.

Jerome hesitates. He remembers the night he let Danso and the woman slip through his grasp. He remembers praying—pleading—for the first time in years. Maybe God heard him that night when he spoke to the stars instead. Some people might say so, because look where he is now.

Except now ....

Now everything is broken again.

The only difference is he isn't alone. That might change if Michel blames him for this one day, and he finds the idea terrifies him. Two more people have escaped him, but this night is different than that fateful one so many years ago. Tonight, he swore on the stars. On Orion himself. He didn't beg. He didn't pray.

He's a different man.

"Not often, sir. But I did the night Danso escaped from me."

Jerome wants to say more, but his gratitude toward Michel is too much to voice, tonight, so he hopes his mentor takes his meaning. Michel smiles at him despite his grief, grasping Jerome's shoulder warmly.

"We'll find them." Jerome meets Michel's eyes. "I swear it. I'll do anything I can to help you."

"I know you will, lad." Michel stares down at his drink, swirling the brandy around in the glass. "I only hope we can find them quickly. If it's too long, I have no idea who they'll be."

Jerome looks out the window at the stars, finding he cannot argue.

Chapter 24

Boston, Massachusetts. August 1706.

"Get off my ship!"

René hits the dock hard as the captain shoves him off the edge of the gangway, the wood cutting into his arm and leaving a long, thin scratch. Another scar, no doubt, but at least he got this one on his own terms. Mostly.

"Some bastards on your ship stole our money!" Auden shouts, drawing the attention of some other sailors in Boston harbor. "And you're kicking *us* off?"

René takes Frantz's offered hand and gets up from the ground, both of them watching Auden closely. Dusk falls around them, the orange-red light glinting off the burnished auburn tips of Frantz's black curls, and René holds his hand tighter, keeping his other free to pull Auden away.

The merchant captain narrows his eyes. "They say they didn't, and there isn't any evidence, you hear? I've known them longer than I've known you brats. I can find sailors who make less trouble than you three."

"Your thieving sailors are trouble," Auden growls.

"William," René warns, pulling his friend away by the back of his too-small coat, the made-up name as odd on his tongue as ever.

"Michael," Auden protests, glancing down at René's bleeding arm.

The use of his false name still sounds so strange to René, even after all this time. He picked it on a whim, not thinking, until later, that it was merely the English version of his father's name. Even in the back of his mind, he can't quite escape Kingston.

"I know," René whispers, glaring back at the captain. "But it's over. Let's go." He looks at the captain, unable to stop himself from speaking once more, though more calmly than Auden. "They *did* steal our money."

The captain takes a step forward in warning. "If you lads don't get, you might find yourself in trouble with the magistrate, and I doubt you'd like the life of a convict. You certainly aren't too young to get a flogging or be sent to the noose, if I can prove it's you who's been stealing."

Auden opens his mouth to argue then closes it again, all three of them knowing too well the truth of that threat. René's seen more convict laborers since he ran away than he saw even in Jamaica, which is saying something. He's seen floggings, on shipboard. This very captain ordered one a few weeks ago on another sailor, and René remembers the blood running down the man's back in streams of red, his cries of pain echoing into the air. The sailor walked around with crisscrossed scars afterward, but stayed aboard because that's how he survives. And needless to say, they've all seen a hanging.

Frantz tugs on René's coat sleeve, handing him his knapsack. The merchant captain stalks off and back onto his ship the *Sparrow*, not giving them a second thought.

Deckhands are replaceable, and that's all they are.

"He didn't even give us our last month's wages," Auden grumbles, his green eyes gleaming with uncharacteristic angst as he focuses on René. "Not that we were planning to stay much longer now that we're back in this part of the world, if we want to stick to your mother's advice to us, but it was good solid work and kept us safe from your father. Especially after what happened in Nevis."

"I know." A wave of desperate anger floods René's veins as he presses Auden's hand, his friend's pulse racing beneath the skin. They needed that money. "But hopefully our time on the *Sparrow* has my father thinking we've left the Indies."

They'll figure this out.

They *have* to figure this out.

He didn't run from Kingston, he hasn't spent months dodging his father's chase, to fail now. He's sixteen. He can sort this. Frantz digs into his own bag, pulling out the pouch of money. Or the money that's left, anyway. René supposes the men only stole most of it to make it look less suspicious.

"We have a shilling left." Frantz puts his hand down into the pouch as if willing more to appear by magic. "And the two pence you have in your pocket, René. That won't get us far, so we will have to resort to uh. Other measures. And save this."

René nods. They ran out of the money they brought with them—their own from gambling, and the money his mother gave them—and they were shorted on their bare wages from the *Sparrow* more than once. All that said, this won't be the first time they've stolen.

"We need to get away from the harbor," René says. "Find a place to think."

Frantz and Auden agree, the three of them walking away from the ocean and toward a bustling Boston, one of the few New World ports they haven't seen. René looks toward the city, and for a moment he's swept up in the sheer magnitude of it all. Kingston is busy, too, but this is something different. Something older. Boston is loud and crowded and full of more people than René might have imagined before. More than New York. More than Charles Town. More than St. Michael's Town in Barbados. Certainly more than Kingston, which is still growing. He was born in London, but he barely remembers it for how small he was when they left, and it's the same with Paris. He only has fleeting, blurry memories of those cities, ancient in comparison to this one, which was founded in 1630, if he remembers correctly.

More ships than he can count line the harbor, people milling about in every direction. Captains with the sun gleaming off the shiny buttons on their coats. Deckhands with tattered trousers unloading cargo brought from Europe and the East and West Indies and all over. Customs officers taking notes and collecting dock fees. Ships of all sizes stand against the dusky horizon, frigates and brigantines and sloops, coming here from near and far to trade. Buildings dot the skyline as far as the eye can see, some squat and some taller, a mismatched chaos that somehow makes sense. The smell of the sea wafts toward them from one direction and cooking from the other, with perhaps a hint of something less pleasant from a third. He notes a certain kind of awe in Frantz's face as they walk past a pair of well-dressed men pouring over a new, leatherbound book on celestial navigation, and he wishes he could steal it. The reverie breaks when Auden speaks as they reach a tavern not far distant from the docks.

"René." Auden pulls down an old, faded flyer from the door, handing it over.

René takes it, his blood running cold as his pulse picks up.

Of course.

He's seen this before. They've all seen this before.

Missing: René Delacroix, Frantz Seymour, Auden Carlisle. Any sightings or information should be sent to Captain Michel Delacroix of the East India ship Navigator in Kingston, Jamaica, or to Governor Andrew Travers, Royal Governor of Jamaica, in Spanish Town.

More information, including a large reward sum, is beneath, along with sketches of their faces. The paper is so worn out they're barely recognizable.

"These things again," Frantz mutters. "You'd think they'd have given up by now. Jerome's drawing skills put to use against us."

"The drawings are definitely his." René speaks half-unconsciously as he grasps the flyer tighter. "Sharp lines." He rips the paper before crumpling it and sending it flying through the air, where it meets its fate seconds later by falling into a muddy puddle.

Auden pats René on the shoulder. "And you say I'm the rash one."

René smiles and Auden winks at him, lightening the heavy feeling in his chest a little.

They can do this. They can *do* this.

They make their way toward an alley between two buildings, all the better not to be seen if a sailor in harbor recognizes them. René sits on the ground as exhaustion takes over, his stomach burning from hunger. He crosses his legs, noting the torn breeches, which at least aren't as obviously too small as his coat and shirt. They've long outgrown the clothes they brought with them, and the quality of these spares is what they could afford at the time, which wasn't much. Frantz hands them each a hunk of bread from inside his bag, and René raises his eyebrows, another smile slipping onto his face.

"Where did you get these?"

Frantz peers at René over the rims of his spectacles. "Stole them this morning shortly before we were ah ... ejected. You two aren't the only ones with light fingers."

Auden tears off a piece of bread in enthusiasm, tipping his head toward Frantz. "Never let anyone say you're only smart with book learning, my friend. You're a genius in more ways than one."

Frantz tips his head back toward Auden in silent reply, a smirk playing at his lips even as his hands shake slightly from hunger. René rubs at a streak of dirt before digging into his bread.

They're in trouble. That much is painfully clear. They are almost out of money, they've been kicked off a ship without their wages, and their circumstances are starting to take a toll. He looks over at Frantz and Auden, both of whom have lost weight rather than gained it, just like he has. Food on merchant ships isn't exactly known for keeping anyone's belly full. But the good news, the *only* good news, is that they've lost his father's trail. At least he thinks so. Flyers of their faces cover the West Indies and the mainland colonies, but they haven't been close to being dragged back to Kingston since that terrifying night in Nevis, where Captain Barlow dropped them a month after they ran, looking hesitant to leave them even though he had to in order to cover his tracks and theirs. A crew René's father must have hired knocked on the door of the inn where they were hiding.

We're looking for three young men. Fifteen, or thereabout. Have you seen them? We caught word that they might have been on a ship that made port here recently. Captain Delacroix is on St. Kitts searching there, so if you lie and we find out, I can promise there will be hell to pay. He'll bring it to you personally.

Then, the innkeeper's voice. *I've seen them.*

A shiver runs down René's spine when he remembers the three of them climbing a bedsheet out the window, running into the dark and away from the shouts and the pounding footsteps. They got work on the *Sparrow* a little over a month later. The ship was headed to London, then Bristol, and then back to the American colonies, which they hoped would both confuse Michel's search and also get them back closer to where they wanted to be—listening for word of Danso and Abeni on Nassau. Going to Nassau without that word was no small thing, given how difficult it is to get there, these days. They couldn't risk it for nothing.

When they arrived in Boston Harbor, they got just that. Word, that is. A story that a sailor from another ship was telling their boatswain as they unloaded, a story about Danso, Abeni, and Nassau. They heard whispers in Bristol too, but this is more dependable and closer to the source.

He looks up, finding Frantz watching him.

"You think it's time to try and get to Nassau, don't you?" Frantz asks, running his hands together so the remaining breadcrumbs fall to the ground.

René smiles, warmed by just how well Frantz knows him. "I do. What about the two of you?"

"If we can get someone to take us there, I'm for it," Auden agrees. "It's just the matter of how."

Frantz nods, pushing his spectacles up his nose. "Those sailors in Bristol were telling stories about Nassau, and then the one we heard while unloading today. Seems as much evidence as we'll get to take the risk of going there, and even more reason to make good on what your mother said, René."

René stands up, surprising the other two. "I saw another tavern down the way, I'm going to see if I can get any information from people in there. I'll come find you here when I'm done, if that's all right?"

Auden raises a finger, opening his mouth in protest. "Hang on. Don't you think I should go? You're always saying I'm so charming."

René bites his lip, laughing. "You are. But I'm afraid I'm the better actor. They'll know you're up to something."

"And they'll be suspicious of me," Frantz adds. "What'll you tell them?"

René taps his finger on his chin, pondering. "I'll tell them that my uncle fled to the interior of New Providence Island, and he's the only family I have, only no one will go there because of the pirates. Should work well enough. I got good at lying to my father and pretending in front of my grandfather. This shouldn't be any different."

Auden stands up too, pinching René's cheeks. "And you have such a cherubic face! No one would ever suspect you have the lightest fingers of the three of us."

You look like an irritated cherub with your hair all mussed like that.
Jerome's words from long ago ring in René's head, digging into the open
wound somewhere deep in the part of his heart that belongs to the little
boy he once was. The little boy whose spirit he still trusts in.

Frantz laughs, tapping Auden's hand. "More like an angry archangel if
you don't stop teasing him. We'll be here René, but if you're gone more than
an hour, we're coming in. That tavern we passed before the one with the flyer? With the red door?"

"You with your eye for detail!" Auden exclaims, shoving Frantz with
fondness as he sits back down. "Is it that one, René?"

"It is." René smooths his long, dirty hair out of his face, tying it back
with the red ribbon Jerome gave him years ago. "Stay here, all right? I need
to be able to find you, and if I'm not back in the time Frantz said, come get
me."

"Don't get arrested!" Frantz calls out with some worry as René goes.

René turns back around, giving them both a grin. "I'm not Auden, so
don't worry."

Auden calls out a good-natured insult René can't quite hear. He sticks
his hands in his raggedy pockets as he goes, his fingers poking out through
the other side.

"I have an uncle on New Providence Island," he repeats to himself. "And
I just need to get there, is all. Me and my two friends. Do you know anyone
who goes there? I'm Michael Brown," he continues, repeating the name he's
used since they ran away, easier to remember now than at first.

He finds the tavern with the red door again, this one devoid of the
missing flyers bearing his image. The weathered sign out front reads *Harbor's Delight*, and in smaller lettering below, *Boston's Oldest Tavern*. He slips
inside, feeling for the spare pence pieces in his pocket that might buy him a
drink. He finds the tavern half-full, all the better for him to take a stool by
the bar where a middle-aged woman stands, pouring drinks for the sailors
inside. He claims one at the end of the row without much notice, rubbing again at the streak of dirt on his face before folding his hands. The
woman spots him after a few minutes, extracting herself from a knot of men
who won't stop asking for more. Their voices are louder than necessary, no
doubt spurred by too much liquor. She's well-dressed enough to be the tav-

ern owner's wife, he thinks, and she looks about his mother's age, but with dark brown hair.

"Haven't seen you in here before." She tilts her head as if thinking she might recognize him, and René's stomach drops.

Does she recognize him from the flyers?

He smiles, hoping it works. "I'm new to Boston," he tells her. "Me and my two friends, that is. Just came in on the *Sparrow* from Bristol, by way of New York."

She returns the smile, studying his dirty clothes with a motherly air as if she wants to send him upstairs to the inn to have a bath.

Truth be told, he would love a proper bath.

"A young sailor. I see. What can I get you, lad?"

"What will"—he unfolds his hands, looking at the coins—"one pence get me?"

"A mug of coffee or the beer men like to drink when they don't care how it tastes. Preference?"

"The coffee, please." He puts the coin down, though she doesn't take it immediately.

She nods at him with a fond smile playing at her lips, rolling her eyes as the group of men she was serving earlier grow rowdier. René watches her pour the coffee, the familiar, chocolate-tinged aroma wafting toward him and reminding him of his father. The memory makes his chest hurt.

Michael Brown, he tells himself. *Not René Delacroix. Not here.*

"Hey!" one of the men from the rowdy group calls out, slurring his words. "More ale!"

She spins on her heel, giving the man a tight smile. "In a minute, Davies. You've got half a mug left as it is. I'm busy here."

The smile turns real as she places the mug down in front of René, steam curling up into the air. She still doesn't take the coin he laid down on the counter.

"Thank you." He takes a sip, noticing the gleam of concern in her eyes.

He supposes he does look a bit pitiful, all ripped clothes and dirty hair and just ... everything, but he can't be the only bedraggled young sailor who comes into the tavern, which speaks to a kindness in her that he appreciates.

"You must know a lot about the ships coming in and out of Boston, with the tavern being right here," he says, with the air of making conversation.

"I'm familiar with a lot of the crews." She pulls out a rag and cleans the counter around her. "Lots of ships come in and out of Boston. Is there somewhere you're trying to go?"

René takes another sip of his coffee, the slightly burnt liquid a little bitter on his tongue. "There wasn't room for my friends and me on the *Sparrow* anymore." He swallows the lie. "But it wasn't going where we wanted to go anyway."

She stops cleaning, looking up at him again. "And where might that be?"

"I have an uncle on New Providence Island." René taps the edge of his mug. "Matthew Brown. He's all the family I've got left, and I can't get passage there because of the"—he leans forward, and she leans forward too, listening—"the pirates. In Nassau."

She nods, pushing a strand of hair behind her ear. "We've seen a fair few pirate hangings in Boston. They arrested that Captain Kidd fellow here. You said you have an uncle?"

"Yes. He's a blacksmith, but he had to run to the interior when the pirates took over Nassau Town. You don't happen to know anyone who still trades there, do you? It would be a great help."

"And you aren't aiming to join the pirates, are you?" she asks, and he can't truly tell whether she approves or disapproves of the idea. He thinks it might be the former.

René shakes his head. "No, ma'am. I'm just trying to get to my uncle and take my two friends with me. Orphans, all of us. Them a long time back, me more recently."

She studies him again, his heart *thud thud thudding* in his chest.

"I know of a couple," she admits, lowering her voice as another table calls her over. "Captain Jones of the *Blackbird* and Captain Lee of the *Elizabeth*. If you find them in the harbor they might be willing to talk. Both are in port." She pauses, patting his hand. "Be careful, lad."

"Thank you, ma'am," René breathes, the grin on his face a real one. "I appreciate it."

She slides the coin back to him. "Keep it. I think you'll be needing this more than I do for a mug of burnt coffee."

He thanks her again before downing the last of his drink and racing out the door toward the harbor. He still has some time before he's supposed to meet Frantz and Auden, and if he can bring back this news ....

He finds Captain Jones first, a grizzled old merchant who reminds him a bit of Captain Barlow.

"If you and your friends are willing to work on the way, I'll take you," Captain Jones says at hearing René's request. "Don't ask for anything other than food and drink, you hear? I don't have it. And keep my comings and goings to Nassau to yourself. We leave next Thursday, a week from now, and we'll be stopping in Charles Town on the way. So it'll be a few weeks 'till you're there."

"I'll take it," René replies, relief rushing through him. "Thank you, sir."

If things go right, they might be in Nassau, and soon.

He walks back through the market on his way to Frantz and Auden, pilfering some fruit from a stand as he walks past, the owner busy flirting with a nearby young woman. Both of his friends jump as he approaches.

"I talked to a woman in a tavern," René tells them, almost forgetting to breathe, "and she gave me the name of a man who sails to New Providence. And then I found him in the harbor, and he said he'd take us if we worked and didn't ask for anything but food, and that he isn't leaving until next week, and that he's stopping in Charles Town first. I agreed. Is that all right?"

Auden crows, and Frantz flicks him in the arm as his voice echoes through the alley.

"Is that all right?" Auden exclaims in a whisper. "My good man, it's *magnificent*. We'll have to make do sleeping on the streets 'till we leave, not that we haven't done that before." He pulls out two pieces of eight. "We did get this. Enough to eat on, maybe."

René puts a hand on his hip, raising his eyebrows. "I thought I told you to stay here."

"Now see here, René Delacroix." Auden pokes René in the chest. "You aren't my captain just yet, so don't be so bossy. You should be pleased."

René laughs. "How did you get it, dare I ask?"

"I bumped a rich-looking fellow as he walked past, and Frantz picked it up so fast the man didn't even notice coins were missing. Too busy reading his paper."

René pulls out the fruit. "I suppose this is a meager contribution in comparison to that. Thank you."

Frantz puts an arm around René's shoulders, shaking his head. "Meager. You got us passage to Nassau! We'll have to keep a better eye on our things, this time. I'm surprised they didn't steal my father's backstaff or your sword or anything else. But if we can make it there, we'll look for Danso and his quartermaster." Frantz looks up at the stars, a thousand memories glimmering in his eyes when they land on Polaris. "I think my father would be proud of us for this. Perhaps he's been guiding us. I like to think so."

"So do I," René whispers, pulling both his friends in for an embrace. "So do I."

It's cooler outside now that the sun's down, but there's nowhere for them to go, so they curl up on the ground together, covered by their small, raggedy coats.

René takes one look at the sky, his gaze landing on Scorpius. A hazy memory enters his mind, Jerome's deep voice echoing faintly in his head.

Several legends say that Scorpius killed Orion, and afterward, Artemis asked Zeus to put Orion up in the sky. But Orion runs every summer, when the Scorpion arrives.

His eyes move toward Frantz's favorite constellation next. Ophiuchus, it's called, sitting opposite Orion and brightening in summer as the hunter fades. An odd shiver runs down René's spine, and he shuts his eyes, letting all of it wash away, hope sitting in the center of his chest.

Nassau, he thinks, just before sleep claims him. The word sounds like a promise. Like a story.

Nassau.

Chapter 25

Nassau, New Providence Island, The Bahamas. October 1706.

René wakes abruptly, pulled from the claws of a nightmare.

He opens his eyes, surveying his surroundings as the sun comes up, red-gold streaks dripping like paint down the horizon. He looks out at the shallow harbor, several ships anchored a short distance off.

Right.

Nassau.

He's on the beach in Nassau with Frantz and Auden. With no other options left, they slept here last night upon their arrival, hidden by a few palm trees.

Auden lays on his left and Frantz on his right, both sleeping restlessly, their jaws clenched tight. Frantz's hand holds his knapsack even in slumber, Auden's eyes scrunched against a bad dream. René sits up, shaking sand from his hair. His stomach growls, staging a protest against the lack of food, his limbs heavy and his temper short. They'll have to find something soon. He looks down at his bag, filled with nothing much now but the few mementos from his childhood and some things picked up along the way, his sword and shoulder belt laying on top, discarded before sleep. He studies his old boots, which now scrape against his heels with almost every step. Frantz's are worn down in the soles. Auden's peel at the toe. All of them have blisters on their feet. Needless to say, it won't do. Not for much longer.

The sun peeks further over the horizon, casting a bright glow over the water, and René thinks of watching the sunrise from the deck of the *Navigator*. He hasn't allowed himself to miss his father and Jerome because then he has to think of how they betrayed him, how they hurt him, and he's been too busy surviving to do that, but he misses his mother like a dull ache every day. He fingers the edge of the red neckerchief he purchased when they were forced to buy new clothes. Sun and saltwater have faded the material, but the memory of buying it warms him.

Why red? René asked as Auden handed it to him with a smile.

It suits you, Auden said, pushing it into his hands with a touch of Uncle Arthur in his voice, even if the two never met.

A cough presses against his chest and bursts out, still lingering after several weeks—the remnants of a nasty head cold he got during their last days in Boston. Frantz rustles beside him, sitting up and putting on his spectacles.

"Morning," Frantz says, looking around and readjusting to the new environment. "Everything all right? I heard you coughing."

René rubs his sore chest. "I think so. It hurts a bit, but I'm sure it'll ease up eventually. You don't need to worry."

Frantz puts his arm around René's shoulders. "Don't tell me not to worry. I'm your best friend. It's my job to find a way to get you some medicine."

René smiles, leaning against Frantz. He dares not think of their old dream of being captain and navigator. His father told him once that he would be a good captain, but maybe that was a lie too. So much else was. Maybe he's not strong enough, talented enough, for a captaincy. But if he can sail, if he can be free with Frantz and Auden, if he can play a small part in making the world a better place, in undoing his grandfather and his father's legacy, that will be enough. For now, he wants to help focus on an even more important dream: finding Chantal.

She's alive, Frantz said in Boston. *I just feel it.*

Auden shifts on the sand, rubbing his eyes and shaking the sand from his brown curls.

"You two having a moment without me, are you?" he asks, sliding up to join them and sitting on René's other side.

Frantz arches an eyebrow. "We were just waiting for you."

Auden's stomach growls. "Ah. I suppose we haven't eaten properly since the evening before last, have we?"

"No," Frantz says. "Just that bit of bread yesterday afternoon on the ship. And we're flat out of money."

"The market we saw might be less crowded in the morning," Auden points out. "More carts left unattended and such. Now might be the time. I'd say we could try fishing, but no tools for that, either."

"Good idea," René replies. "Let's go. The market wasn't far from here, was it?"

"Just a few minutes' walk." Frantz stands up, dusting himself off before lifting his knapsack onto his shoulders.

"Lead the way," Auden says. "I scarcely remember anything from last night. It was too dark."

They follow Frantz in the direction of the market. Some of the buildings they pass look dilapidated, and René isn't surprised. The island has been in flux since the late 1690s, when Henry Avery successfully bribed the governor, Nicholas Trott, to let pirates do business in Nassau— René remembers his father talking about it when he was younger. Several years after that the French and Spanish attacked in tandem, settlers fled, and England hasn't sent a governor since. It seems some newer inhabitants are trying to build the town back up if the market is any indication. Most of the normal townsfolk fled to the interior when it became clear England wasn't coming back, nor Spain, at least according to the papers. This is not like the harbor in Kingston, where officers and dock workers patrol every inch in the daylight.

"There." René points at a stand filled with mangoes. "The owner isn't there, and it's at the end of the row for an easy escape. And there's no one across from him right now. Agreed?"

Auden and Frantz nod. René leads the way, gesturing for the other two to stand behind him as a cover.

A shout echoes through the air as soon as René's finger touches a single mango.

"You there!" a man shouts, storming up from the direction they planned for their escape. "Just what do you think you're doing, stealing from my cart?"

"Stealing?" Auden slides up next to René, putting on his best charming grin. A woman at a stand nearby observes them, pushing her curtain of long, straight black hair behind her ear. "We were just examining the product."

"I'm sure," the man says with disbelief. "Where's your money?"

"We weren't sure we were going to buy from you just yet," Auden says, sounding less convincing this time.

"No one steals from my cart." The man raises a hand as if to strike them, and it takes everything in René's self-control not to jump. Before the merchant can make good on his threat, the woman who was observing them runs over.

"Let them go, Abney," she says.

René notices that her clothing is different than the intricate gowns his mother wore. Her ankle-length dark blue skirt is tied at the waist, and she wears a loose tan shirt and something like a waistcoat. Her long black hair falls loose down her back, where his mother's was always pinned up unless it was late at night or early in the morning. Instead of delicate bracelets, this woman wears gold bangles that flash against her sun-bronzed skin.

"And just why would I do that?" the man called Abney asks, drawing René back to the scene.

"Because they're boys who are obviously hungry," the woman answers, irritation in her eyes. "And I'm sure you've got something better to do than make a show of dominance. Have some pity."

Abney huffs. "Don't try and steal from me again, brats. Or I won't be so merciful next time."

The woman rolls her eyes, but Abney relents, going back to his cart.

"You chose the wrong person to steal from, lads." Her gaze lingers on René's face as if she recognizes him. "Abney is grumpy, especially in the morning."

"Isn't this supposed to be some sort of lawless place?" Frantz crosses his arms over his chest. "With pirates, and the lot?"

"We have our own little society here," the woman tells them, "outlaws or no. The pirates steal from merchant ships, not each other, or the other people who call this place home. Usually."

"Thank you for helping us," René adds. The woman stops, contemplating him again, and something about her looks familiar.

"You look familiar." She echoes his own thoughts, narrowing her eyes in interest. "Have I seen you around here before?"

"Probably," René lies. "The three of us have been here a while."

A bad lie, he realizes. The community here is still small enough for people to notice newcomers.

"Right," she answers, not convinced. "Tell me, when was the last time you ate, if you were so desperate as to steal mangoes?"

"Yesterday," René says. "But we'll be going. Thank you again."

"To steal from someone else?" she asks, and there *is* something familiar in the way she raises her eyebrows at him.

She sighs at their silence, her lips quirking upward. "Come on then. I'll get you something." She looks them up and down, concern flickering in her eyes. "You look like you could use a place to rest."

René mirrors Frantz, crossing his arms over his chest and tensing up. Trusting anyone is difficult. "We're fine."

She eyes the sand on their clothing. "Fine sleeping on a beach?"

"We'd rather sleep on a beach than go back where we came from," Frantz says.

"I can't just let you go hungry," she replies. "So come on, follow me. I live just down the way."

Without any more reason for an argument they go along with her, walking silently for a few minutes until they reach a small one-room home not far from the market. She ushers them inside, indicating they should sit down at the little round table in the corner of the room as she goes about looking through cabinets, pulling down some fruit, bread, and cheese.

She brushes a piece of her loose black hair behind her ear. "I'm Tiena. And you three are?"

"I'm Auden," Auden answers. "The one with the spectacles is Frantz, and the one with blond hair is René."

René winces at the sound of his real name, but here on Nassau he supposes it's all right. He hopes, anyway. They planned to give Danso and Abeni their real names, at least. Perhaps not just anyone.

"Charmed, I'm sure, as they say." She puts three wooden plates down in front of them. "Start with this."

"We're very grateful." René's stomach leaps at the sight of food, growling again in anticipation. "But why are you helping us?"

"I'm not the sort to let three young boys go hungry." She smiles, the ends clipped so it doesn't reach her eyes. "Which is fortunate for the three of you. I had a boy, once. Ate everything he could get his hands on. Which wasn't much, sometimes. I wasn't doing as well in those days."

"What do you sell in the market?" Frantz asks, taking a bite of the cheese and wrapping it in bread, nearly swallowing it down whole.

"Clothing, mostly. We're starting to get more pirates around since the English abandoned the place, and I buy material from them. People here need clothes, too, and the lads take some out and sell them for me on black markets that are around."

René looks around the tiny house, which is even smaller than Jerome's in Kingston. They sit in the area serving as a kitchen and dining space, the bed on the far side of the room. The rest of the house is taken up by two chairs and a worktable, a small garden in view outside the window. He smiles, reminded of his mother.

"Are you sure it's only been a day since you ate?" Tiena pulls her hair over to one side, shifting it over her shoulder.

"Technically we only had a bit of bread yesterday." Auden speaks between mouthfuls. "We haven't eaten properly since two days ago."

"Well, eat up," she says, a hint of sadness in her tone as she turns away, taking a plate for herself. "I can't send you out back into the world hungry, or you might try and steal from the wrong person again."

She joins them at the table, her long sleeves sliding back as she reaches forward, taking some of the fruit. René's eyes catch on a brown leather bracelet she's wearing, jumping at the familiarity. The same designs decorating Jerome's bracelet that he accidentally stole are etched into hers, and at first, he can't tear his eyes away. He breaks his gaze, but she's too quick-witted to miss it.

"Something the matter?" There's an edge in her voice. A familiar edge.

"No." He looks down again, feeling Frantz and Auden's eyes on him. "Nothing."

"You were looking at my bracelet. Why?"

"I—" René finds himself unable to answer her, because how can he even explain? He makes a decision, turning and rifling through his bag until he finds the bracelet at the bottom.

He pulls it out, Frantz and Auden eyeing it with curiosity. They saw the outside of it the night they ran away, but René hasn't elaborated on it since. Something in his heart couldn't tell Jerome's secret, even to the people closest to him, because Jerome had so desperately asked him not to. He hands the bracelet over, and there's surprise in Tiena's eyes as she seems to recognize it, taking it from him and looking for the etching on the inside.

"This belonged to my son," she says, and the surprise in her eyes morphs into worry, obviously thinking Jerome might be dead. "I'd recognize it anywhere because I made it for him when he was a boy."

René touches the small scar cutting across his right eyebrow. "Is your son Nicholas Jerome?" He speaks the words in barely more than a whisper, the name causing a searing pain in the center of his chest.

Jerome's mother. He knows it before she even answers. Some part of him knew as soon as she raised her eyebrows at him.

"Yes." Tiena's voice cracks, a thousand questions flooding into the single word. René finds he scarcely knows how to respond, and it doesn't help when he imagines his own mother missing him, with no news of his safety or whereabouts. "You know him? Please tell me if he's all right."

"He's alive," René says, watching Auden shake his head in disbelief before looking back at Tiena. "Or he was a little over a year ago when the three of us ran away. From the news I've been able to get, I don't believe that's changed."

She leans forward toward him, searching his face for answers. "How do you know him? Why do you have his bracelet?"

"He works for my father, Captain Michel Delacroix of the East India Company," René says, mentioning his father's name to a stranger for the first time since running away. He hopes he hasn't made a mistake, but he has little room to lie. "And I didn't mean to steal it."

"You didn't *mean* to steal it?" She clasps the bracelet tighter, taking a deep breath. "Let's start from the beginning. You said he works for your father?"

"Since I was five."

"You're the boys from the missing posters I saw. I knew I recognized you."

"Please don't tell anyone." René hates pleading with people because it reminds him of pleading with his grandfather, but he has to plead with her. "We cannot go back where we came from."

"I won't." She softens, looking at them with grief. "I've kept my share of secrets."

"Thank you," René whispers. "We appreciate that."

"Did Nicholas give you that?" She gestures toward the scar. "You were touching it."

René finds he cannot quite make himself answer.

"We were running away," Frantz supplies. "Nicholas caught us. There was a bit of a tussle."

"You were close?"

"We were," René says, wistful. "When Frantz and I were small he would play with us. He was my sword instructor. I learned a lot from him."

Tiena tilts her head, looking unbearably sad and yet relieved, all at once. "He was a part of your family."

"Yes." René nods. "He was."

"I spent years looking for him." Tiena's melancholy voice fills the silence. "But I could never find him. I looked all over but you know how it is, I'm sure. The sea makes people disappear. Did he mention me?"

René curls his fingers tight against his right palm. "He mentioned his past to me once. That he was partly of Romani descent. Though he mentioned you to me before that, about you losing each other one day and that he hadn't seen you since."

Tiena sounds very close to tears now. "I'm sure he thinks I abandoned him, but it couldn't be further from the truth. We got separated in a marketplace, and I was arrested by some magistrate's men who thought I was stealing. When they released me from jail two days later, I couldn't find my son anywhere. Nicholas was twelve, then, and his father had left us over a year before, never coming back when he escaped jail. I'm going to step outside for a moment. But you eat, I'll be back."

"How do we tell her that her son's turned into ... himself?" Auden asks when the door closes. "I feel terrible for her."

"I think we answer the questions she has," Frantz replies, his eyes on René as he coughs again. "She should have the truth."

"She seems to just want to know about him," René adds. "We are the best people to answer to that. I'm sorry I didn't tell you the truth about him, but I couldn't. He begged me not to tell anyone."

"No, that's all right." Frantz reaches across the table, squeezing René's hand. "We understand. Though a great deal makes sense now. About him."

The door opens after a few minutes and the three of them fall silent, watching Tiena. Her eyes are red, but she clearly can't stand for anyone to actually see her cry. Now that René thinks about it, Jerome had been much the same.

Did he ever see Jerome truly cry? When Uncle Arthur died, maybe.

She sits down again, tapping her hand on the table. "I'm sorry. When I couldn't find him for all those years I feared he had died, and I never expected just hearing about him at random like this. I suppose I didn't consider that he'd end up working for East India or anything similar. Perhaps that I should have."

"Why?" René asks.

"He was always nervous as a child," she says, and René isn't surprised. "We left my family in France when he was very small, and after three years or so in Bristol we came to the West Indies, going around from island to island while his father found work on ships. Nicholas didn't like the looks people gave me, and by extension, him. He has my dark hair but lighter skin, so people suspect less when he's not with me, I imagine. Skin tone alone is not a tell for my people, because some of us are darker and some of us appear nearly white, but lightness helps him pass, especially in the Indies. His father said my being Romani brought bad luck. I think Nicholas picked that up along the way, because the world kept repeating Thomas' words." She brushes her thumb absentmindedly across her palm. "Is he happy?"

"I ..." René tries, and he cannot remember another moment where he had such trouble articulating himself. He's not certain Jerome knows how to be happy in the way she means. "He likes his job. And he's close with my father, a bit like a younger brother or second son to him. He does well for himself. I know he worked hard to get where he is. He worked on different merchant ships for a long time, until East India hired him. He has had happy moments, if that helps."

Tiena looks at him, but he cannot read her expression. He often had that problem where her son was concerned.

"I'm sorry he hurt you," she says, and he knows she's talking about more than just his scar. "I won't make you tell me why you ran away, because I suspect it's painful to talk about and you wouldn't have done so without a reason. But might I ask how you ended up with the bracelet?"

"Nicholas tutored me in swordsmanship for years." The first name sounds odd on René's tongue, because he'd picked up the habit of calling Jerome by his last name when he was a boy, and never changed it even when his father called Jerome *Nicholas* more frequently. "So, I went to steal my sword from his rooms, but I saw a box with a gun in it. Then the door opened, and I just took the whole box and got out. I didn't realize the bracelet was inside. I know it must have been all he had left of you."

Tiena pats his hand. "It's all right. I'm shocked he kept it, but perhaps it speaks to some affection he still holds. I can hope that, at least."

"Will you look for him?" Frantz asks, no doubt missing his own mother. "In Jamaica?"

"I think I have to, though I'm not sure he'll be pleased to see me. But I don't truly know if I could do anything else. I've missed him terribly."

"You're his mother." Empathy brims in Auden's voice. "Surely he would want to see you."

René remembers how absent Auden's own parents were, treating Auden as a decoration rather than a son. Auden's mother was with child when they left, and René can only imagine it will be much the same with the new son or daughter.

"He's always been uncomfortable with a side of himself, and he sounds ashamed of me. It is not simple, I think."

"He shouldn't be ashamed," Frantz says with a bite of frustration. René knows it isn't directed at Tiena, but at Jerome himself. Jerome, who takes part in the slave trade despite the fact that Romani people have been enslaved. Jerome, who knows what it is to be endangered because of what he looks like.

"No, he shouldn't be. But the world taught him to be, and that is a hard lesson to unlearn." She looks at them fondly. "I sense the three of you are, ah, troublemakers?"

Auden grins. "Oh, we are. The two of them will tell you I make the most trouble, but don't let them fool you."

Tiena laughs, lightening the mood, and it sounds far fuller and more natural than her son's ever did. René remembers the first time Jerome did anything other than wryly chuckle in front of him—at a joke of Uncle Arthur's, though he can't remember what. Jerome seemed almost surprised at himself. Tiena's laugh is quiet but genuine, her smile wider and less restrained.

"I'm afraid I must get to the market," she says, getting up from the table. "But if you promise not to steal from me, I might agree to let you take a rest here."

"We won't steal anything," René promises. "Thank you. We could not be more grateful."

"I know what it is to be desperate. Wait for me here and I'll send you on your way with some food, all right? I'll just be gone a few hours."

"Thank you," René repeats. "We came here looking for someone, and I was wondering if you might know them?"

Tiena rests a hand on her hip. "Someone?"

"They call him Robin Hood the Merciful? And his crew? His last name is Danso."

Tiena nods. "I know him, and his quartermaster, Abeni. They started making port here when people stopped asking questions about eight months ago or so, and I believe they're here now. Do you know them?"

René bites his lip. "It's complicated."

"I'm certain," Tiena says, amused. "They took over an abandoned house not too far from the tavern. I might look for them there, first. The tavern, I mean. After you rest."

They agree, and after a few minutes she's gone again, still holding her son's bracelet in her hands. The three of them pile into her bed, sinking into the mattress.

René closes his eyes, and with Frantz and Auden warm on either side of him, for the first time in ages, he falls into a deep, unbroken sleep.

Chapter 26

Nassau. Later that Evening.

They leave Tiena at dusk, promising to visit if they stay on the island and giving her the information she needs to find Jerome. René has to trust she won't tell on him, and his instincts say she won't. Not when she's made this place her home. They wave at her, and she waves back. René turns toward Frantz and Auden, slipping an arm through each of theirs. They're headed toward a tavern full of pirates. A tavern with people inside who might hold the key to their future.

Said tavern is more raucous than René expects.

No one notices when they step inside, so René peers around, taking in the scene. There's an odd mix of people, some clearly pirates and some merchants who consort with them, the rest somewhere in-between. The more he sees of Nassau, the more he realizes the town doesn't really possess an identity anymore. It doesn't belong to anything or anyone.

Not yet.

But something builds in the air. Something rebellious. Something forbidden. Something powerful.

Here, the seeds have been planted for the return of widespread piracy to the West Indies. A piracy built upon the legacy of Avery and Morgan and the old Brethren of the Coast. Something new. Something different.

Something *better*.

"I could learn to like it here," Auden whispers, eying the people with various drinks in their hands, laughter flooding into the cozy room. He points at a man standing near the bar. "Say, is that him? Danso?"

René looks at the man in question, and time stops. It stops like he's reached the best part of a story. The man resembles the sketches they've seen on the wanted posters and in the paper: tall and broad with warm, dark brown skin, his long locs tied back with a simple black ribbon, and his coat a shade of Lincoln green with silver buttons.

"It looks like him," Frantz says. "From what I remember, anyway, and from looking at all the drawings. And there's a woman next to him there. Abeni, I assume."

René eyes the woman. She's small-built with muscular arms, her dark brown skin a shade lighter than Danso's and her black curls kept short. She wears a deep, chocolate brown coat with golden embroidery on the edges of the sleeves, tan breeches, and a yellow kerchief around her neck. Two younger people stand next to them, a boy and a girl somewhere around their age, René thinks.

"They look friendly." Nerves line the anticipation in Auden's voice. "Don't they?"

René releases a breath, because he doesn't know what to say to the people who were his heroes in the dark of night, but he has to say something. "I say we go speak to them. Agreed?"

The other two nod, all three of them stepping forward. Intense awe rushes through René's veins. Stories of these two people spanned his childhood. Stories brought to life in his imagination as he fell asleep at night. Stories of the first real pirates in the West Indies in years other than a scattered few like Avery, a resurgence in rebellion that's only growing. He remembers the tales about the Jewish pirates near Madagascar—the first known thieves to overturn slave ships—wondering if Danso and Abeni read them too. Abeni draws René's attention when she laughs, raising her arm to reveal a tattoo partially covering a brand on her skin.

They nudge their way through the crowd, and they've nearly reached Danso when a man crosses their path, drunk. René steps on his foot and the man whips around, his sunburnt skin mottled red in rage.

"Trying to steal from me, boy?"

"No," René says. "You stepped in our path, is all."

"A likely story." The man seizes René's forearm. René winces but controls himself, staring the man down as a nauseating, sour stench wafts toward him.

"Hey!" Frantz shouts. "Let him go!"

"Brats trying to steal from me," the man mutters, holding tighter to René's arm. Frantz and Auden make to shove him away when a voice cuts through the room, the man who might be Danso stepping forward.

"Ackland," he says, commanding the attention of the entire tavern as the ruckus quiets, a hush descending over the crowd. "These boys have done nothing to wrong you. Let go of him, please."

"*Robin Hood the Merciful*," Ackland spits. "That's what they call you now, isn't it? Come to save the day again?"

Danso. It *is* Danso.

"I promise you"—grave anger slices into Danso's tone—"if you do not let these boys go, I will be rather less merciful."

"Your threats don't frighten me." Ackland nearly loses his balance. "At all."

"Perhaps not." Danso remains unimpressed, irritation flickering in his eyes. "But regardless, you have no quarrel with these young men."

"They tried to steal from me. What are you going to do about that, Danso?"

"No, we didn't," Auden replies, exasperated. "René just stepped on your toes because *you* got in our way."

"Exactly," Frantz chimes in. "So I suggest you let him go."

"What are you brats, sixteen at best?" Ackland laughs derisively. "I think I can take you."

René tries pulling away again, and when Ackland won't let go, Danso seizes his chance. He pushes at Ackland's chest, knocking him away from René with a force that looks effortless. Ackland makes toward Danso, but at the look in Danso's eyes he backs away again, more bluster than actual bravery.

"Watch your back, Danso." Ackland pushes his hat further down on his head and stomps out the door, leaving René, Frantz, and Auden stunned behind him.

"I'm sorry about that," Danso says, his voice gentle, something within it making René feel safe. "Ackland was discharged from the navy for unsuitable behavior, and I'm afraid he's been drowning in rum ever since he arrived in Nassau. We don't agree on very much, he and I, but he hasn't the power to do anything about it here. Nor anywhere else to go," he continues, with a hint of pity. "Are you three new to Nassau?"

René searches for what to say. "Yes. But in the interest of honesty, we came here looking for you, sir."

"Me?" Danso tilts his head, smiling at being called *sir*. "Were you looking to join my crew?"

"You know my mother," René says, plowing forward. "She said she helped you when you and your quartermaster escaped from Kingston?"

Danso's eyes go round, his breath audibly hitching. "Abeni." He crooks one finger, beckoning his famed quartermaster over, and René has a fleeting sense of injustice that of all the tales he's heard about the pair of them, he never heard Abeni's name until his mother spoke it— only that she was a Maroon, and a woman. "We need to take these boys outside. Bring Jahni and Flora with you."

"What's the matter?" Abeni comes over, her eyes locking on René like she's seen him before.

"These boys know Astra Delacroix." Danso leans in close to her ear, keeping his voice low. Abeni looks back at him, sharing his shock, one hand going to a locket around her neck. "This is her son." He gestures at René.

"Oh my goodness," Abeni says. "I ... oh my goodness. Yes, let's go outside, I'll get Jahni and Flora."

"We aren't in trouble, are we?" Frantz asks, suspicious at the lack of explanation, one hand closing over René's wrist and the other grasping Auden's coat.

"No no." Danso ushers them outside. "This place just isn't entirely devoid of people who would report you back to Kingston, yet. Those missing flyers were all over."

None of them answer, following Danso and Abeni outside, the boy and girl close behind them. They must be their children, or otherwise some sort of family members. The boy might be two years or so older than himself, René thinks, and the girl around sixteen, like him. They step outside into the warm night air, the sounds of the tavern following them out until the door closes, leaving them alone with the stars.

"This is my nephew, Jahni," Danso says, noticing René's questioning look. "And this is Abeni's daughter, Flora, who I also call my own."

René looks at Jahni more closely, realizing just how much he resembles Danso. Flora has the same eyes as her mother, and she smiles curiously at them, her thick black curls tumbling loose down her back. Jahni gives them a nod, his expression intrigued, but he keeps quiet while Flora waves with an enthusiasm René didn't expect. Both Frantz and Auden return the smile she offers, and René can't help but do the same.

"You're René?" Abeni asks. "And these are your friends?"

"Yes." Relief sweeps over him until his limbs might melt. "I'm René."

Abeni smiles at him like her daughter did—except she seems on the verge of tears. Danso puts a hand on Abeni's back, his eyes vastly kinder than any drawing René's ever seen on a wanted poster.

"And this is Auden Carlisle and Frantz Seymour." René indicates Frantz. "And I think you've met Frantz before. At least we believe so."

"At the harbor in Saint-Domingue," Frantz adds, wonder glimmering in his eyes. "I was ten or so and you helped—"

"Your father," Danso finishes, and the gentleness in his words makes some of the tension flood out of René's shoulders. "Yes, I remember. We'd heard he died. I'm so sorry." He pauses, looking at them for a long moment. "What brings you lads here to Nassau?"

"Frantz became my parents' ward," René continues, "after his father died and his mother went missing. We all ran away from Jamaica last year after we found my father shipping slaves and after some trouble with my grandfather. There was danger and ... threats." He lands awkwardly on the word because he doesn't know how to give a quick summation of it all. "We'd read about you in the papers already. Kept track of all the stories. My mother helped us get out and said that once we lost my father's trail, once we made him believe we must have left the Indies, that we should try to figure out if you were in Nassau. She told us that you promised you would help her if she asked, because she helped you get out of Kingston. And I suppose helping us is what she's asking, by way of me."

Danso gazes at René, a real, wide smile spreading across his face. Abeni shares it, and there's love in the way they look at each other. That was one thing that drew René to collect the stories about the two of them in the first place—the way they built a family together. The way they chose each other and everyone on their crew, no matter their race or creed. Seeing Danso and Abeni in the flesh makes him realize how right he was to put his trust in their story.

"She did help us," Danso says.

This moment matters, René knows it does, just like the night he asked Jerome to play, or the evening Auden came up to him at that party, or the morning when he met Frantz, the sunlight striking Nassau Town on the map they poured over.

"And I did promise that," Danso continues. "I just never knew how it might come to fruition. When I saw those flyers, I did wonder."

Danso takes a deep breath, and René swears this is fate.

Something powerful lives in the night surrounding them. Something like magic. The air shimmers silver, and he's sure the stars themselves are listening, too.

He's about to hear a story.

Stories saved his life. Stories kept him going. Every night. Every day. Every hour, as things crumbled to pieces around him. He read book after book after book, but he always loved the handwritten one Prescott gave him so long ago the best. They were stories you couldn't find in a bookshop, passed down from sailor to sailor and changed just a little bit every time they were told on the deck of a ship late at night. So many tales became a part of that book as time passed. Stories about Grace O'Malley in his mother's flowing cursive. Stories about the ghosts and spirits of the sea in Uncle Arthur's script, legible only because René was used to reading it. Stories from the *Navigator's* crew. Stories from Frantz about Olokun and other sea deities from the lore of the West African coast, passed down to him from his mother.

There are two written down in the back of the book, the last ones to be added.

One about Orion in Jerome's neat writing, and another about Castor and Pollux in his father's cramped lines, the small, loopy letters crowded together from years of trying to save space in his ship's log.

René carries all those stories with him. The stories of the people he never wanted to leave behind, the stories of the people he ran from, and the stories of people who might just be looking down on them from the untold number of stars stitched into heaven's canvas.

But there's always been one story that meant more to him than anything.

The story of the man and woman standing right in front of him.

The story that told him, that *promised* him, that he and Frantz could sail together one day. The story that told him he could have something different than his grandfather's life or his father's legacy.

The words on those pages said *you are full of light.* They said *you can banish the darkness.* They whispered *you are not what your grandfather says you are, and you never will be.*

Now, the story is about to become real.

There's no newspaper to distort it. He isn't sewing together the whispered shreds of stories he gathered in Kingston harbor, collected from sailors kind enough to tell him a tale. He can know the truth his mother possessed all along, the promise she preserved until she used it to set him free. He remembers the touch of her hand as he ran from the house, her fingers brushing his palm.

He won't ever forget it.

Piracy means freedom. Piracy means sailing with Frantz, like he's dreamt since he was eight years old. Piracy means he doesn't have to be like his father, who lived in such fear of shame that he lost himself.

It means he will never, ever, become Governor Andrew Travers.

"Let's sit." Danso gestures at all of them, and René sits between Frantz and Auden on the sand as the ocean rushes up just inches away. "We'll tell you how your mother helped us, and where we've been since, which is more than the papers want to say. And even more than sailors in port know."

"But we'll start from the beginning," Abeni adds, meeting René's eyes, "because you know Nicholas Jerome, don't you?"

"Yes." René thinks back to that fateful first night and the light in Jerome's eyes reflecting the stars. That light shone brighter until everything that happened extinguished the glow. He runs a thumb over the scar across his eyebrow. "I do."

"We came to Nassau after word spread that the English had lost their power here." Danso's voice cuts into the hubbub of Nassau around them, his story coming to an end. "We are often out at sea, of course, but we thought this might be like—"

"Home." The word slips from Frantz's mouth, floating tremulous and unsure through the air.

Frantz has been in Nassau for a day, and yet there's a sense of safety here, or as much a sense of safety as a life of piracy might grant. His soul feels safe. Empowered. *Alive.* These people aren't just pirates. They're a family. As Frantz looks at René, his friend might be that eight-year-old boy he met so long ago, brimming with joy and eagerness. Zeal glimmers in René's eyes from the stories they just heard. The stories about Ebele. The stories about finding Flora and Jahni. The stories about learning piracy as whispered rumors of Robin Hood and Maid Marian spread across the West Indies.

All of them bear scars from Kingston. Scars that changed them. But in Nassau they might find the brightness within themselves again, the brightness they held onto for so long with trembling fingers. Frantz remembers looking at those maps with René that first day, the sunlight filtering through the window and striking the spot marked *Nassau Town, New Providence Island.* He looks at Danso and Abeni and then at Jahni and Flora, in awe of these people who look like him fighting a war against those who might chain them, and helping people along the way. Poor sailors. Enslaved people. Pressganged men. People who love differently. They're forging an entirely new way of life. Frantz knows that both of his parents would love this place, and their quiet rebellion, their courage, their kindness, sparks the air here. He misses them both with a deep, pounding ache. His father sleeps in the stars, but his mother ... maybe he can find her now.

He turns sixteen next month, six months after René and eight after Auden, and he can't think of a better way to start anew.

Danso meets Frantz's gaze, his brown eyes like dark, liquid gold in the firelight of the nearby tavern. "Yes. Like home."

"How did you get here?" Jahni speaks, studying Frantz, René, and Auden. "A lot of ships won't come near."

"I persuaded a woman in a tavern to tell us which ships in Boston might be willing to drop us here," René says, looking a little sly. "Then we talked to a captain."

Auden laughs, the sound fuller and more musical than it was in Kingston. "René is terribly charming when he wants to be."

Jahni grins, looking a bit shy, and Frantz feels something kindred in his spirit. "Impressive."

"We got passage away from Kingston on the *Carina,*" Auden tells them, and Abeni and Danso's faces light up. "Captain Barlow. He wouldn't tell us the truth, but René's mother did. He smuggled you out of Kingston?"

"He did." Abeni rests her chin in one hand, looking delighted despite herself. "And how did you convince him?"

Auden grins. "I'm charming too, you see. But apparently, René's mother came to talk to him not long after I did, so I think that helped my case."

"Papa." Flora grasps Abeni's hand as she looks at Danso. "They should stay here with us."

Danso pauses, looking at the three of them with a fatherly air even as his face tightens with unease. Frantz isn't exactly sure that's the right word. René must see it too, because he tenses, reaching out for both Frantz and Auden's hands.

"I ... we ...." René stumbles over the words, a marked difference from his usual eloquence. "We don't want to be any trouble to you, Captain Danso. I promise we don't."

Danso waves his hand, ending René's anxious ramble. "I didn't pause because I want to send the three of you away, lad." He glances at Abeni, and they communicate something without speaking. "I *do* think you should all stay. Join our crew."

René's grip tightens, and Frantz's own heart pounds and pounds and pounds.

"You do?" René asks.

There's a twinkle in Danso's eyes. "I do. Just know that we will need to be cautious, as I know both your father, René, and Jerome, as well, are no doubt still looking for the three of you."

"I don't want to put another target on your back, sir," René whispers. "I hadn't really thought of that when we came here. We just needed somewhere to go."

Danso puts a hand on René's knee, and Frantz notices that René doesn't flinch as sharply as he normally might when someone new touches him.

"I've had a target on my back for a long time. I'm not going to leave the three of you alone to fend for yourselves just because it might cause that target to be a little larger. I want to honor the promise I made to your mother. Would you like to join our crew? We have room, still."

Flora bounces up and down from her seat in the sand as she keeps hold of her mother's hand and seizes Jahni's arm, pulling him close. Jahni shakes his head with the fondness of a brother, twirling one of his locs with a finger, and Frantz wants to be friends with them both, already.

René looks at Auden and then at Frantz for final approval. Auden nods, and Frantz does too.

"Yes." René's voice bursts into the night, full of feeling and danger and certainty. "We would like that very much. We're good sailors, all of us. We'll do the work, I promise. And we know how to fight."

Danso shakes his head, biting his lip against a smile. "I have no doubt. We might save the fighting part until you're a little older, or at least have been with us for a bit."

There's another pause, a question burgeoning on Frantz's lips. *The* question, really.

"Captain Danso? Could I ask you something?"

Abeni must catch something in his voice, because she's looking at him as Danso responds.

"Of course, Frantz. What is it?"

Frantz lets go of René's hand, folding his fingers together and looking at Danso and Abeni directly. "René mentioned it, but my mother's been missing for several years, since before my father died, and he feared she might have been picked up by illegal runners. I thought maybe you could help me find her. If she's out there."

"Oh," Abeni breathes, speaking before Danso has a chance, surprising Frantz when she reaches across for his hand, her touch warm. "Yes. We'll help you find her."

Frantz finds himself pressing her hand back, unsure. "Just like that?"

"Flora and I both know what slavery is like," Abeni whispers. "If your mother has been captured, we'll try our best to find her. It's what we do." She smiles at him, and there's a glimmer in her eyes that reminds him of his mother, though with more mischief. "So yes. Just like that."

"Thank you," Frantz whispers. "Thank you so much. I have some leads that will hopefully help."

Danso gets up from the ground, dusting the sand from his breeches. "What do you say we take you back into the tavern for some supper and to meet some of the crew? Then we can talk some more. We've an extra bedroom in our house here, too, where you can stay. The house used to belong to a merchant when the English held the island, and we've taken it for our own."

Abeni pulls Frantz up from the sand as Jahni does the same with René and Flora with Auden, the seven of them walking back toward the tavern.

René falls into step with Frantz, starlight threading through his hair. "We did it," he says, pressing Frantz's fingers, excitement pulsing through his voice. "We're going to find your mother. We're going to be pirates."

Frantz wonders if maybe one day they might be captain and navigator, too, or if that dream is lost. For now, he'll gladly take this one.

"Yes." Frantz wraps his arm around René's waist, too emotional to say very much. "Yes we are."

Chapter 27

Kingston, Jamaica. November 1706.

J erome stands outside Michel's office near the docks, wishing he could shut his ears. Chop them off. Something.

They're arguing.

Again.

"It has been over a year now, Michel!" Governor Travers shouts. "We need to try something new. Circling back around to the two captains whose ships left late that night is useless, and even I can't make up proof solid enough to bring Wilson or Barlow in, especially when Barlow is known for odd hours and barely makes port here anymore. Barlow wasn't even in the logs, someone just thought they saw him, and you can't prove the boys didn't just stow away. You've found nothing concrete since St. Kitts and Nevis."

"We will find them, sir. We have to keep looking. We—"

"People disappear all the time, and we have no idea where they are." Governor Travers cuts Michel off. "We don't even know if René is alive."

"I'm *trying*, Andrew," Michel responds. "We looked everywhere. I hired an entire ship of men to help. I have contacts in New York, Boston, Charles Town, Paris, and London with their ears to the ground. I even wrote the governors in Barbados and Antigua, but I doubt the boys are still in the islands."

There's a pause, and Jerome pictures the governor leaning over Michel's desk, looking at him over the rim of his gold spectacles.

"That misbehaving boy was my only heir," Governor Travers says, and Jerome detects the slightest hint of grief in the older man's voice, though it's more grief over the loss of an heir than his grandson in particular. "I should have insisted he come live with me sooner. If we find him, we must circulate the story I told the papers that he was kidnapped by pirates. Even then people will talk."

"I want my son back. I want Arthur's son back." Michel bites out the words, clearly fighting for control. "That's what matters to me. I don't care about anything else."

"Calm down, Michel," Governor Travers says. "I am simply saying that René not only ran away, but he ran away in the company of that Seymour boy, and people will—"

"Sir, *please.*"

"That boy was always a terrible influence, just like his father. You became a better captain once Arthur Seymour was gone," Governor Travers continues, ignoring him. Jerome winces when Michel smacks his hand on the desk in response, but the governor keeps talking. "It's not as if Astra has proven particularly fertile, or you would have more than one child as it is, so she's not likely to fall pregnant at her age. And if she did, she might end up like her mother, dead just past forty. That damned fool doctor ...." He trails off, clearing his throat. "If we don't find René, my family name will die out. You don't understand that pain. Your brother has two boys of his own."

There's the beginning of the conversation Jerome didn't hear before walking up, and now he feels even more awkward standing here. There's a long pause, and Jerome prays for the conversation to end.

"I gathered Astra wasn't sharing your bed lately," Governor Travers finally says, in response to Michel's silence. "I take it that's more recent, so perhaps you should have made sure she wasn't doing anything to end pregnancies previously, or we might not be in this situation. Women do, you know, without telling their husbands. There's still a chance for a child, however small. But it's a narrow window before it will be impossible."

Jerome shuts his eyes. Good God he does not want to hear this, but he was due to meet Michel five minutes ago, and therefore cannot go.

"Sir," Michel protests, "I would really rather not discuss these matters with anyone other than my wife."

"Well," Governor Travers lingers on the word, the threat silky smooth and unspoken, though it sounds something like *your business is my business*. With East India's success in the West, his pull in Parliament and among the upper nobility, not to mention his mercantile connections, he's only becoming more powerful, not less. "Why don't you try wooing her? Persuade her. You're French, you're supposed to be good at that, aren't you? You always wanted another child, besides."

"Andrew, please stop."

You're a smart man," Governor Travers says, softening just a touch. "Kindly do not disappoint me."

The governor steps outside a moment later, spotting Jerome and offering his usual stiff smile.

"Jerome." He nods, seemingly unconcerned that they've likely been overheard. "I hope you're well?"

"Yes, Governor Travers, I am, thank you." Jerome clears his throat, keeping his eyes trained on the governor as Michel emerges. "And yourself?"

"I'm quite fine, thank you, Lieutenant."

"I heard from Michel you might be retiring from the governorship soon?"

"In a year or so, when they find a sufficient replacement for me, but they'd like me to continue advisement even when they find someone new. The Company wants to form an outpost of directors here in the West Indies so we can make some decisions without constantly waiting for word from London, and I am to be in charge of that. It will be a better use of time, at my age. It gives me more control over East India concerns, and I can still exert influence over the goings on here on the island. I'm sure you understand."

"I do, sir," Jerome says. "Congratulations."

"Thank you." Governor Travers tips his hat. "Good day to you both, gentlemen. I have to get back to Spanish Town."

Michel and Jerome both respond in kind, watching as the governor walks away. Jerome tries pretending he didn't hear any part of their conversation, but Michel immediately speaks to the point when they go inside his office.

"I apologize that you had to hear some of that." Michel holds his hands behind his back, gazing out the window toward the sea. "I hadn't expected it to take so long. Or for it to get quite so personal."

"It's fine, sir." Discomfort tightens the lines in Michel's face, and Jerome pauses before pressing forward. "Are you all right?"

Michel keeps looking out the window, only half present. "I am not quite myself. Things are tumultuous and there is ... pressure." He reaches into his pocket, pulling out the flyer Jerome knows he keeps there. René's face sits in the center with Frantz's and Auden's below, all three names at the bottom and *missing* emblazoned across the top, the contact and reward information on the back. "I had thought we'd have found them by now."

"I know. We'll find them. We will, Michel."

Jerome still can't believe he let them slip through his fingers. People are always slipping through his fingers and turning his life upside down.

Michel traces the sketch of René with the tip of his finger before clearing his throat and putting the flyer back in his pocket, grief and anger making the frown lines around his mouth more apparent. Those lines are deeper than they used to be, and Jerome remembers thinking how young Michel looked at five and thirty when they first met a decade ago.

"Yes, well. That isn't what I asked you here for. I have news."

"News?"

Michel smiles, pulling a much cleaner piece of paper out of his inside coat pocket, bearing the seal of the English Royal Navy. Jerome takes it, looking up and meeting Michel's eye in surprise. He breaks the seal, his heart racing as he reads every last word on the page, hardly able to believe what he's holding.

"A naval commission?" he asks, flabbergasted. "Is this—"

"Yes indeed, my good sir," Michel responds. "There are no buying commissions in the English Navy, but I have several close contacts in their ranks—"

"Sir," Jerome interrupts. "I couldn't possibly—"

"And they have heard of your talents." Michel raises a hand, stopping Jerome in his protests. "And all the skills that recommend you. I told them of your discipline and your courage, that you're one of the finest men I've ever worked with. They are short of officers in the colonies because of the war and are in need of good men. Queen Anne is concerned with protecting England's interests here. You'll have to sit a lieutenant's test as a formality, but it won't be a trouble for you."

"Sir, I—" Jerome says, the ability to complete a sentence eluding him. He counts all the things Michel Delacroix has done for him in his life. More than anyone else ever has. More than his own mother, even, and certainly more than his father. Both his parents abandoned him, but Michel never has. Michel gave him a home. A family, really.

"It's a special commission, actually"—Michel grins at Jerome's loss of poise, and Jerome finds it reminds him strikingly of Arthur—"doing work to curb piracy around the islands and up the coast of the mainland colonies, too. Admiral Adams spoke to me about an alliance between East India and the Navy to do something like that, and he's tapped Captain Bennet to sail in tandem with me, and you will serve with him. He's an older man, so I suspect in a few years' time this could lead to your own ship. So, although I'm letting them snap you up, I couldn't let go of working with you. If we accept, we're set to start the task in six months' time."

Jerome glances at the smattering of pirate wanted flyers on Michel's desk. They appeared there a few weeks ago, and now he realizes why. Danso's is partially visible, half hidden beneath another rogue's face. Finally, Jerome has a chance to catch Danso and his quartermaster. Finally, he has a chance to clear this mark off his record and right his failure from so many years ago. The failure that haunts him every time the words *Robin Hood the Merciful* and *Maid Marian* shout at him from the newspapers, or when their names brim on the tip of a sailor's tongue.

But it's not your only error, is it? a voice whispers in the back of his head, but he pushes that away, for now.

It's a start.

"*Thank you*, Michel." Jerome clears his throat, willing himself steady. "I hope you know my gratitude for everything you have done for me. Since the beginning. The chance you took on me. I'm relieved we'll still be working together, or I'm not sure I'd go."

Michel clasps his shoulder with warmth, a familiar gesture Jerome's gotten used to over the years, but there's something in Michel's eyes. Something sad and desperate.

"I know. But you are the worthiest protégé I could have hoped for. You have also been a friend when I was in great need of one. I cannot thank you enough for that." Michel's voice quivers, and Jerome pats his arm.

"Of course," Jerome says. "I'm glad to help you wherever I can, Michel."

"Admiral Adams pressed hard for this from the Admiralty," Michel says. "They didn't take the spike in piracy a few years ago seriously enough. Henry Avery and the like, not to mention Danso and others. There are plenty at large, and he and most in the merchant community anticipate another spike. We are to serve as the test case, to show what we can do to prevent the Caribbean and the Atlantic from being overrun while most resources are being diverted toward the war. Especially with Nassau in play." Michel looks over at Jerome, a fond smile playing at his lips that makes Jerome smile softly back. "Too many naval captains aren't willing to take the job yet because they want the credit for the war with Spain."

Jerome tilts his head. "But you knew I would—"

"Rise to the occasion," Michel finishes. "It's why I suggested your name to them. Some fresh eyes in the Navy with sympathy for the position of merchant sailors, who are most harmed by pirates, after all. Perfect fit. Besides, I told you years ago I'd help you chase pirates if it would set your mind at ease about Danso. Then this chance arose, and it gave me the opportunity to give someone I care about what they wish for. Perhaps we may find the famous Robin Hood in our efforts. I can't say I'd mind something new to divert me."

Michel considers him, and Jerome cannot help but recall its similarity with how he used to look at René.

"I cannot express my appreciation enough," Jerome whispers, all the memories and their years together resting between them. "For everything."

Michel presses his shoulder again with a smile. "Would you mind accompanying me back to the house for a few minutes? I'm afraid I need to retrieve my log. I left it after our last voyage so I could do the report in my study."

Jerome nods in assent, following Michel's lead back toward the house.

"I have news as well," Michel tells him while they walk, the unrelenting Jamaican sun beating down upon them. "Another ship is to come under my command, sometimes to sail along with us, and sometimes to take over any business I might not have time for while I'm busy assisting the Navy. I will do some merchant work, still, but this new ship will help with that when I cannot. I received the news from London this morning, which is why my father-in-law was in my office. I suppose I shall be Commodore Delacroix. I admit I quite like the sound of it. The ship is the *Polaris*, with the captain still to be named. They've a few men they're deciding between."

"Congratulations, sir," Jerome says, his interest piqued. "You've certainly earned it."

"We both have, I think. I shall have to have a new sword commissioned in honor of your joining the Royal Navy, to mark the occasion."

"Michel, you don't—"

"I know I don't have to." Michel turns to him as they reach the drive leading to the Delacroix house. "But allow me my indulgences, won't you?"

"Of course," Jerome nods, a sense of pride filling him up. Sometimes he still isn't sure what to make of being a part of something, of having someone who is like a father and a friend all at once, of being respected. Things are different now. He was forced to choose between a chosen father and a chosen brother, watching as their relationship shattered into a thousand unrecognizable pieces.

He knows he made the right choice.

The home he found is broken now, but it's home even still, and he swears he'll put it back together again.

They go inside, finding Astra emerging from her harpsichord room.

"Hello, my dear." Michel leans down, kissing Astra's cheek. She allows it, her posture stiff and too perfect.

"I wasn't expecting you," she says. "Hello, Lieutenant Jerome."

"I'm just here for my log," Michel tells her. "I left it in my study."

Astra reaches out and adjusts Michel's windblown cravat, though there's no romance in the gesture, just habit and affection that's only an echo of the fondness Jerome once witnessed between them. Nearly every time he came into this house in those terrible months after the boys first went missing, Michel and Astra were fighting. Yelling. Crying. He and

Michel were barely home in those days, busy as they were searching. Now, at least when he's here, the fights have ceased, and he's not sure if that's better or worse. Perhaps the two of them have only come to realize that despite their differences, they've both lost their child. Losing a child is not rare, of course, but death might be easier, in some regards, rather than this endless mystery without closure. He is determined to give Michel that closure, because he knows those boys aren't dead. He *knows* it.

"Thank you." Michel smiles back at Astra, the exhaustion Jerome's become familiar with clear in his eyes, a far cry from the bright-eyed young captain from years ago.

A memory haunts him, a memory of one of the endless days spent searching for the boys when Michel almost fell asleep standing at the wheel.

Sleep, Jerome told him, gentle as he'd ever been. *You have to sleep, Michel.*

Michel draws him back into the present. "I thought Nicholas might like to take a look at the work we've done upstairs in the library. He hasn't seen it yet."

"Certainly." Astra looks at Jerome warmly, but said warmth is gone in a flash. Perhaps he only imagined it. She is not fond of him, these days, keeping to politeness and nothing else.

Jerome nods, sensing they need time alone, and heads toward the stairs. Their voices float toward him as he goes.

"What did my father want?" Astra grows cold. Angry.

"He ..." Michel begins, uneasy, and Jerome quickens his step, having heard enough of Michel and Astra's extremely private business for one day.

He walks up the stairs, his footsteps echoing in the absence of laughter flowing forth from René and Frantz's rooms. He stands in front of Frantz's bedchamber, the covers neater than Frantz would have kept them, rumpled as they usually were from him curling up and reading in bed. There's a stack of maps still on the bedside table, one of his coats laying across the chair in the corner.

He finds himself in front of René's room next, but cannot make himself enter. He hasn't had any cause to come upstairs since the boys ran away other than visits to Michel's study, so it's the first time he's looked at the room in over a year. For all the time that's passed, it looks exactly the same, not even covered in a layer of dust. Both rooms have been kept clean by the servants at Astra's request, no doubt. The seascapes still hang on the wall, the sunlight hitting them just so. A book lays open on the window seat, a pair of abandoned shoes resting next to it as if René had just slid them off to read. Jerome regards the bed next, his eyes catching on a familiar object.

René's wooden toy sword.

That definitely wasn't originally on the bed, probably placed there for sentimental reasons. René was hardly without it for years, always going about with it practically attached to his hand. Jerome remembers the warmth in his chest the night he tucked René into bed after their sword game on the *Navigator,* and how he'd thought of him then as the younger brother he always wished for. There's an echo of that feeling now, but he pushes it down deep until he can't feel it anymore. The boy doesn't deserve any of his emotion, and it's useless besides.

Footsteps resound behind him, firm but still gentler than Michel's, and Astra appears beside him, her arms crossed over her chest as she leans against the doorframe.

"You should have it," she says, more kindness in her tone than he has come to expect in the past months.

"Pardon?" Jerome asks, holding his hands tightly together behind his back.

Shadows darken her eyes, leaving him with a feeling of guilt he doesn't want. He's never understood Astra Delacroix, and now is no exception. He senses her secrets—he just can't name them.

Yet.

"The sword," Astra repeats, softer. "You should take it."

"I couldn't, madam."

"It obviously means something to you, or you wouldn't be standing here."

Silence wedges between them, thick and suffocating. She blames him too, for losing the boys. For what she sees as his complicity in their treatment.

Jerome steps away. "I didn't intend to upset you. I'll be going."

"Nicholas." Astra removes some of the harshness from her voice, the lack of trust remaining apparent in the flatness. "Wait."

He turns around with his hands still behind his back, twisting his fingers. "Yes?"

"I really think you should have the sword." A pinch of worn-out warmth slips in when she speaks again, a remnant of days past. "There's no need to pretend like what happened didn't happen. I have my mementos. So does Michel. So should you."

"Forgive me, madam." He keeps his tone even, indicating that he means no disrespect. "But I didn't think you'd want me to have something like that. I know you were not—"

"Pleased with the way you treated René and Frantz in those last months?" Astra interrupts. "No, I wasn't." There's a challenge in her eyes that reminds Jerome abruptly of her son. "That has not changed. But I know what those sword lessons meant to you because I know what they meant to my son."

For a moment, all Jerome can see in his mind's eye is a little boy. A bright smile. Fair hair blowing in the warm evening breeze.

He clears his throat. "I will take it, then."

She nods, watching him walk into the room and retrieve the toy off the bed. He takes one look around, the ghost of a small hand tugging on his coat.

Will you teach me about swords?

He shakes his head, chasing away the memory and the shadowy images of René, Frantz, and later Auden sitting on the window seat. The sword sits heavier in his hand than he remembers, and he feels foolish carrying a toy.

"Thank you," he says.

"Nicholas?" Astra asks again. "I'm sure you're wondering why I'm so insistent on this."

He looks at her, indicating that he's listening, but he is quickly tiring of this conversation and her judgment.

"I wanted you to have it because I remember the young man who first joined my husband's crew and played pretend with my little boy." Astra blinks back tears, giving her eyes the sheen of a porcelain doll's. "I remember the young man who made a lonely child happy. I wanted you to remember that young man. And learn something from him."

Jerome stares at her, his breath catching in his chest. "Good day," he says without further elaboration, tipping his hat to her before going back down the stairs and to the front door to wait for Michel. Astra doesn't follow him.

He looks at the sword again, huffing. He certainly can't do anything about Astra Delacroix's determination to erase any of René's fault in this. The past is the past, and the fact is that René ran away, taking Frantz and Auden with him and spitting in the face of a good life. Jerome has no doubt that when they find him—and they *will* find him—that pulling him out of whatever delinquency he's discovered will be no small task.

If it can even be done at all.

Later that night, Jerome finds himself walking along the shore after dark, his habit when he can't sleep. He carries the small wooden sword with him, stopping when he reaches the line where the water meets the sand, the ocean running up over his boots and greeting him like an old friend. This night is the opposite of the one when René first asked him to play. The stars are faded, and the constellations are hidden by clouds, the crescent moon the only splash of light showing him the way. It drips down onto the waves and glints off the edges, the sky a painting of darkness.

Those fateful words ring in his head again.

Will you play swords with me, sir?

Jerome stares at the chipped, worn wooden sword. He remembers René pressing the second of the pair into his hands years ago, his touch warm.

You keep this one, eight-year-old René said, that shy but bright smile on his face. The smile yet untouched by his grandfather's slap. There was something of the world in it, as if he knew of the oncoming storm that would shatter his family, but hope outshone the darkness.

They're safer with you.

I want you to keep it. Please, Jerome?

All right. If you're so insistent.

He kept the other sword in the corner of his bedroom for years, stowing it away until they played again. He gave it back to Michel one day once they moved onto real training swords, useless as it was for how advanced his lessons with René had become, but the boy apparently kept his as the years passed. A slice of moonlight catches on some writing toward the edge, a childish scrawl written in faded black ink.

R. Delacroix.

Rage erupts in Jerome when he lays eyes on the name. He tightens his grip around the handle and the bottom, breaking the middle over his knee in one swift movement. The sword splits in half, and he nicks his finger on one of the sharp edges. Blood trickles down his skin—a payment in absentia for the blood he drew when he struck René. His temper got the better of him then, but he's not sorry. The look in René's eyes, glimmering with the pain of a broken promise, haunts him still.

He shakes his head, tossing the first piece of the sword out into the ocean on impulse, his eyes lingering on the handwriting on the other half before he throws it into the water too, a wave swallowing up both pieces. He sniffs, wiping his eyes.

Crying about this is useless to him.

"I will find you, boy," he whispers, remembering with startling clarity the exhaustion on Michel's face after weeks of searching, hoarse as he asked Jerome to go over what they knew with him, just one more time. René has abandoned his father, but Jerome won't do the same.

If René had just *behaved*, if he simply did *as he was told*, then none of this would have happened. There would be no trail of broken people left in his wake. He knows Governor Travers was harsh, but if René had just obeyed and waited a bit longer, things would have worked out. He's sure of that. Michel could have protected Frantz.

It would have been *fine*.

His entire body trembles with rage, but something floating back up in the water catches his eye. Barely visible in the darkness, a piece of the shattered sword breaks through the ocean's surface before sinking once more beneath the overwhelming current.

What if you're wrong? a small voice asks in the back of his head, and he realizes that it sounds like Frantz's, seeing the boy's sharp, intelligent eyes in his mind, eyes that resemble his father's, dark brown and kind and flecked with amber. Arthur Seymour always confused Jerome. Arthur was a good man, but he broke the rules, too.

Arthur died in the middle of everything, and everything happened after they lost him.

Here on this beach, there are only ghosts.

"I am not wrong," Jerome says aloud to himself, standing up straighter.

He walks off with a sure, determined stride, ignoring his shaking hands. But something in the night whispers his name. Something that sounds like the voice of a five-year-old boy. He spins around just in time to see one-half of the wooden sword wash back up on shore. The piece lodges in the wet sand, the handwriting on the bottom visible once more. He watches as the water bubbles over *R. Delacroix* before pulling back again, leaving the broken toy behind on the shores of Kingston harbor.

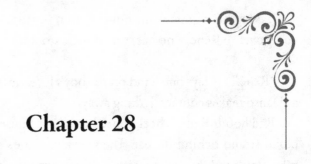

Chapter 28

The Caribbean Sea. November 1706.

The sun glints off the handle of Danso's cutlass and into his eyes, partially obscuring his vision as he spars with Jahni on deck. It's a perfect sailing day, the wind just right and the sea cooperative, the smell of salt caught in the air.

"You picked the better position," Danso says, their cutlasses clanging together. "The sun's right in my line of sight. Smart lad."

"Or just lucky." Jahni smiles, and he always looks so much like his mother when he does. There's something about the life in it, Danso decides. The sincerity. Abeni always says Jahni looks like him, but there's so much of Joliette in his nephew.

Jahni's discerning gaze drifts over to René, who leans against the railing watching some of the others. Abeni is teaching Flora and Auden techniques with her dirk. Asante, the *Misericorde's* longtime sailing master, examines the ship's chip log with Frantz before tossing it over the stern to measure how fast they're going, an hourglass also in hand.

"You know"—Jahni lowers his voice—"René was saying he hasn't had as much practice with a cutlass as he'd like."

"Oh?" Danso parries Jahni's attack. "I saw him sparring with Auden just the other day. Seemed a natural."

"He's used small swords and had just started with the cutlass when he ran away, so he told me. He did lose his old tutor, but I think he might be amenable to a new one."

Taking his nephew's meaning, Danso squeezes Jahni's shoulder before going over to René, who has turned back around toward the deep turquoise sea.

"René." He lays one hand on the boy's forearm, but René jumps as soon as Danso makes contact, jerking away.

Red floods René's cheeks once he realizes himself, and he pushes a stray blond strand behind his ear. The sleeve of René's coat slides up, a freshly inked tattoo of an anchor with a ribbon around the middle visible on his forearm. A tattoo like that is a traditional sign that a sailor has crossed the Atlantic, and Danso can't help but notice the name the ribbon bears.

Astra.

"Sorry, sir. I was just surprised." He glances down at the tattoo when he notices Danso looking. "One of your crew heard that Frantz, Auden, and I had been to England and back, and said we ought to follow the tradition. So we all got one."

Danso nods. "I agree. And you can just call me Danso, you know. No need for the sir." He offers a small smile, hoping it might reassure the lad. "And it's all right. No harm done."

René nods, not saying anything else. Danso doesn't want to push the boy, but he seems upset. A group of men drink near the forecastle, and René looks over at them with intrigue.

"That drink I tried earlier today was interesting. I never had it before. What's in it?"

"It was fermented corn, sweet potatoes, cassava, and pineapple, mixed with a little rum," Danso tells him. "A drink native to my mother's side of the family. She was Carib, or Kalinago, of which there is only a smattering left. She passed the recipe down to me and to my sister. It seems to help prevent scurvy and it's not too strong, so it's good for the men, when we can get what we need for it."

René nods, smiling in a distant sort of way. "I know that there aren't many of the native people that used to live here left. There's even less of the Taino than of the Caribs, aren't there?"

"The Spanish killed most of the Taino. Only a few remain," Danso replies, a sadness swelling up in his chest. "My mother's people were a touch more fortunate."

René smiles at him again, looking melancholy. "I'm sorry. That's terrible. And your father, he was enslaved, you said? If you don't mind my asking."

"He was. He escaped when he was about your age. He was from Senegambia. Or, well, my grandparents were. They were the ones brought over, though they died before he was even two, so he took the name *Danso* from another Gambian man he knew and used it as a surname." Danso studies René, looking down at the forearm he touched a moment ago. "Do you have an old injury on that arm? The one with the tattoo?"

"Oh." René clearly didn't expect the inquiry, but while his tone is guarded, he seems happy Danso is talking with him. "My grandfather almost broke it, once."

"Once?"

The boys told him about finding the slaves on Michel Delacroix's ship, of his threats to separate them, and of Governor Travers' anger toward Frantz, but this, they did not mention.

"I'm not sure how to talk about it," René says softly. "But no. It wasn't just once."

René touches his nose, the light receding from his eyes, and when Danso looks closer he sees that it is indeed just a touch out of place. A sign it was once broken, no doubt. A small scar shoots through the corner of one of René's eyebrow as well, both marks subtle but startling on such a young face.

"Do you mind talking about it with me?" Danso asks.

René hesitates before his gaze moves first to Flora, then to Jahni, and back to Danso. He breathes in, clenching and unclenching his right hand.

"No. I don't mind."

Danso studies René. The splash of faint freckles across his nose from the sun. The intense blue of his eyes. The delicate facial features passed down from Astra. It was a fleeting moment, that night in the Delacroix house, but Danso will never forget her, or the way she looked at him as the fateful promise tumbled out of his mouth.

Danso treads carefully. "Did your father hit you?"

"No." René shakes his head. "But he couldn't stop my grandfather. Couldn't, at first, then wouldn't." He looks down, moving his foot back and forth across the deck in a semi-circle. "Why do you want to know about this? Has my work suffered?"

"My lad, no," Danso says, and René's eyes go round at the endearment. "In fact, you have a very admirable focus, if the past few weeks are any indication. You're a natural sailor. I simply would like to know you."

René meets Danso's gaze. "You like to know the people you sail with."

"I do," Danso replies, anger bubbling up at the sort of ill-treatment that would cause René to jump like that, wondering just how often Governor Travers hit his grandson. "We become a family, in such close quarters."

Something in Danso's heart draws him to René, Frantz, and Auden as it did to Flora and Abeni, and obviously to Jahni. Their determination. Their resourcefulness. Their need of a place and people to call home.

"My father, he felt the same, and the men liked him." René's tone is disdainful, but he said *my father* with love. "Though he didn't treat the crew as equals like you do. They didn't vote for anything. He listened, but he had the final word. He did take interest in them. Cared about them. Especially about Jerome, actually." He pauses, a shy smile flickering on his lips. "I'm afraid I don't know how to talk about this, either. I know Jerome took part in treating both you and Abeni terribly."

"It seems he did some harm to you also," Danso answers, and he notices René's hand lingering over the hilt of the cutlass strapped to his shoulder belt.

"It's not the same," René protests, looking away. "What Jerome did to me was painful and it wasn't right, but it's not the same as what he did to you and Abeni, or what he did to those slaves. My father took part in something he once said he didn't agree with, and he betrayed Frantz by doing it, and Jerome didn't argue. Even my grandfather hitting me is ...." He glances up at Danso, his eyes a little wet even as rage flickers within them. "My grandfather threatened to throw Frantz in jail. That's worse."

"It's not the same, no, but it is its own kind of horror." Danso pauses, thinking he might be getting to something. "It doesn't mean you weren't badly hurt. By your grandfather. By your father. By Jerome. That kind of treatment is no small thing. None of them had a right to hurt you, let alone to do the things they did. You didn't deserve that, René. You didn't deserve to have people you should have been able to trust abuse you. No child does."

René falls silent, his attention drifting out to sea again as if gaining his confidence from the water, and fury bubbles in the pit of Danso's stomach at the idea that Michel Delacroix did not protect the children under his care. He and Abeni fought so hard for the children they almost lost forever, and the idea that someone wouldn't do enough to stop the abuse of not just one, but two young boys? He cannot fathom such a thing. It is no surprise, given what he just heard, that Astra made the painful decision to send the boys away, and he is touched by the idea that she sent them looking for him.

"The night we made the decision to run"—René's voice is so soft Danso scarcely hears it over the breeze—"my grandfather found out we'd snuck on board my father's ship to help the slaves we told you about. My mother tried to stop him, but things got out of control, and he struck me until I was bruised and bleeding. Broke my nose. Hit my mother. Frantz got in the way and got hurt for his trouble, and that was when my grandfather threatened charges against him. He said he was going to take me from my parents and make me live with him so he could sort me out. A devil, he called me." That rage Danso noticed earlier grows brighter in René's eyes. "And my father ... I thought he would step in, then. I'd known it for a long time, but that was when I realized, when *we* realized, that he wasn't going to save us. That Jerome wasn't going to save us. Jerome hit me too. Just before we got away." René struggles for words here. "He told me I deserved whatever punishment I might get from my grandfather. So, thank you. For saying I didn't."

Danso wants to cry, but he keeps himself under control. "You're very welcome, René."

René's face lights up again, washing some of the melancholy and the anger away. "I so admired you and Abeni. Those stories about you both. They kept me going, and Frantz too. I kept old newspaper clippings about you under my bed, and they got me through so much. Not that I would tell Jerome, of course."

Danso laughs, but he's overcome at the image of this young man falling asleep at night thinking of stories about *him*. Him, and Abeni. "Certainly not."

"I wasn't sure how to bring it up," René says, and there's a trust in his voice that Danso thinks is natural to his character, chipped at from circumstance, "but we ran into Jerome's mother on Nassau."

Danso's jaw drops. "I ... really? Who is she?"

"A Romani woman called Tiena. She works—"

"In the marketplace," Danso finishes. "We all know her, but she never says her last name." Danso remembers Abeni telling him she thought that Jerome might be at least partly Romani, the pieces falling together. She was right. "There are some Romani people on the island, from various places. Some have escaped slavery, and others persecution in Europe. Did Jerome tell you about his background?"

René nods.

Silence falls, and Danso watches René smile as he gazes at the various groups scattered across the deck again. Flora holds Abeni's dagger as her mother adjusts her grip, Auden watching intently.

"I know most sailors are strange about women aboard ships," René says, "but I think it's wonderful, women being able to sail and fight. I think my mother would be intrigued. She used to tell me stories about Grace O'Malley, the Irish pirate. Abeni's amazing with that dagger."

Danso grins. He'll have to get René to tell Abeni and Flora about Grace O'Malley. "She is. And she insisted on that new clothing for you, which is a sure sign of her affection. Speaking of, are those new boots working out? Breaking them in? And is your cough better?"

"They're wonderful, thank you." René's tone sounds lighter now, and happy. "We couldn't be more grateful. And yes. The herbal tea Mullins gave me helped a great deal." He pauses, considering Danso with a serious look before he pulls something out of his coat pocket.

A journal.

"I wanted to tell you that I started writing down some of those stories you told us a few weeks ago in Nassau, when we arrived," René says, his cheeks flushing a little red again. "I had this homemade storybook as a child that one of my father's sailors made for me, and it actually had a story about Captain Ebele in it, and I just thought I might start writing down some more about you, and Abeni, and the things I see while I'm on your crew.

And I was hoping maybe you all could add to it and fill more in, Abeni and Flora and Jahni and everyone. Is that all right?"

He hands it to Danso, who reads the title of the story written on the first page.

Escaping the Hunter—A Tale of Orion, A Promise, and Things Revealed by the Stars.

Beneath are some lines about the night he and Abeni escaped from Kingston, and Astra's name, too.

"I was especially hoping you would maybe write something here, at the start," René adds. "I wrote a little of what my mother told me, and Jerome, and you and Abeni, but I think that part ought to come from the people who were there. Again, if it's all right."

"It's more than all right. If I may ask, what prompted this?" Danso asks.

"The papers tell lies about you," René says, and there's an intensity about him that resonates with Danso, like he might be standing where lightning just struck. "If I hadn't heard the better stories from sailors, I might never have known how to read between the lines of what the papers or my father or Jerome said. I just think we should make sure the truth is kept safe. Hearing about you and Abeni changed my life."

Danso, very near to crying now, reaches out for René's shoulder, receiving a nod of permission before putting his hand there and squeezing gently. This young man has barely joined them, and already he wants to protect the crew's legacy. The idea that stories about him, Abeni, and their ragtag group of thieves got a hurting child through the darkness means more to him than he can say.

"I'm sure the men would love it, too, and can add their own," he says, finally managing words. "The ones who can't write can tell their stories and you can get them down, and if you lend the book to me a while, I can definitely put a few in. Perhaps one day those tales will move beyond just the confines of this ship."

René grins, fully, entirely, bright as the sun above their heads, and Danso loves the boy, like he's been meant to since that promise he whispered to Astra Delacroix a decade ago.

"May I ask you one more thing, Danso?"

"Of course, lad. Anything."

René chews on his lip. "I noticed that you and Abeni are very good friends, and not ... something else."

Danso chuckles, glancing over at Abeni briefly. "Abeni is my dear friend and partner. I've always been content with my friends and my family. It's been that way since I can remember. I'm not sure you'll ever find me looking for a wife, or for something of that kind with another man, like Robins and Collins have."

The boy's eyes light up, and Danso isn't entirely sure what he's said, but it's clear it means something.

"Me too," René answers. "Apologies for prying."

Danso gives René's shoulder one more squeeze. "Jahni says you're a rather knowledgeable swordsman but that you hadn't gotten to do much cutlass training yet."

"Jerome was very precise in his staging." René rolls his eyes, but there's wounded affection in his words. "He wasn't fond of using the cutlass too much until I was sixteen, and even then, he said it wasn't right for someone of my station, and that a small sword was more appropriate."

"Correct me if I'm wrong, but are you not sixteen now?" Danso quirks one eyebrow.

René laughs, the sound lifting Danso's heart. "I am."

"We won't be breaking any of Jerome's rules, then."

"I'd prefer if we did," René quips. "But I'm sure we're covering enough of that already. He'd faint if he knew where I was."

"I would say so." Danso pulls his cutlass from its sheath, René's face aglow as he does the same, the draw quick and fluid. "Prepare for battle, my good young sir."

Another memory flickers in René's eyes. Something from long ago. Something important. It fades to watercolor when their swords cross, the present spinning around them in bright shades of oil paint.

Here on the deck of this ship, a new chapter begins.

And Danso is ready.

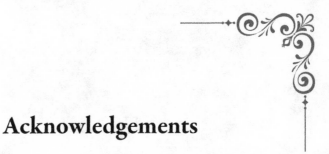

Acknowledgements

I have an endless list of people to thank, and probably can't list them all, but I will do my best!

First, to my partner Barbara, who has been here for me through this years-long process and who has never wavered in her support. She always helped me brainstorm, listened to me read aloud, and cheered me up during bad moods. These books would not be the same without you. Secondly to Spencer, the best cat to ever exist. I miss you so much, but you kept me company through so many late nights drafting and revising. You are in these pages.

Thirdly, to Abby Gavit, for the truly incredible cover art. You are so talented!

Fourth, to the Les Mis fandom (special shoutout to Anne Marie and Alex M!), and every friend I've made in it. This book and its sequels were born in that fandom years ago, and without your encouragement, your enthusiasm, and your love, they simply wouldn't exist. Thank you.

Next up are Janna, Rose, and Isa, my Twitter group chat girls who gave me a place to land on that chaotic website. You encouraged me in my decision to self-publish, you're always there for publishing rants, and you're all amazing.

To Elyse, Maggie, Alex V. and Isaac, for being epic friends and also helping me edit and/or brainstorm this beast of a book at various stages. You're wonderful!

Also to Hannah, Erika, Sarah, and Katy, who have been there for me in my writing life and out. Thank you for literally everything.

Lastly, to my parents. You may not be here, but you always told me to follow my dreams. So here I go!

Up Next

Sailing by Carina's Star (The Constellation Trilogy, #2)
Coming 2023

About the Author

Katie is a librarian and activist by day, a writer of historical fiction by night, and a lover of musicals always. You can usually find her talking about Les Mis, pirates, Paris, and anything to do with The Phantom of the Opera. Her work focuses on queerness, challenging historical narratives, what makes up a family, and the space between grief and resilience.

Read more at https://kcrabbauthor.pubsitepro.com/.

CPSIA information can be obtained
at www.ICGtesting.com
Printed in the USA
LVHW032248200522
719346LV00011B/961